By L.H. Cosway

I haven't been everywhere, but it's on my list.

\-   Susan Sontag.

For this world of readers and writers. There's nowhere else I'd rather be than here with you. May we all have an adventure just like Lille's, in the pages and in our minds.

One

Jack and Lille met on a hill

I had a list.

I was trying to tick one thing off it, but I was having trouble convincing Shay to assist me. In the small Wexford town where I lived, there was only one tattoo parlour, and Shay Cosgrove owned and ran the place. He was several years older than I was, and I had a tiny crush on him, but that was another matter entirely.

Right then, I was trying to convince him to give me a tattoo, and he was having none of it.

"I'm sorry, Lille," he said while crossing his tatted-up, muscular arms across his chest and giving me a placid look, "but if I put ink on you, your mother will have my guts for garters, and going up against Miranda Baker is not on my bucket list."

"But getting a tattoo is on *my* bucket list, and I adore your work, and I don't want to have to drive all the way into the city to get it done, and…."

He cut me off when he placed two fingers on my lips to shut me up. I swallowed and blinked, momentarily forgetting everything I was about to say because, as I mentioned earlier, I had a crush on him and his fingers were on my lips.

Gulp.

My eyes got all big and round, and my breathing accelerated. Shay smirked knowingly as he withdrew his hand from my mouth. Smug bastard. The sad thing was, he was well aware of my crush, but he found me about as attractive as a flat, lifeless piece of cardboard. All of the girls in this town fancied Shay, but he only went for the sexy, sassy hot chicks who were no doubt wild in the sack.

I was not sexy or sassy, and my clothing was as plain Jane as you could get (thank you, Mother) — ergo, not hot.

I was the arty girl with her head in the clouds, and it was not considered cool to be seen with me. In fact, it was considered the complete opposite of cool.

But I was an artist, just like he was, so I thought we could bond over our shared loved of canvas and paint. That never happened. At best, Shay tolerated me. At worst, he wished I'd bugger off and quit pestering him with questions about tattoos.

How does the gun work?

What kind of ink do you use?

How often does the skin get infected?

Can I have a go of the gun?

What's the weirdest thing you've ever tattooed on someone?

So yeah, I was a question-asker. Most evenings I'd find a reason to stop by the parlour and admire his drawings, which were hung up all over the walls. I'd try to show him my own stuff, but he was uninterested.

Shay was into dark art, like Giger and Kalmakov.

I was into Pop art, like Warhol and Lichtenstein. I was all about colour.

Anyway, back to my list. It only contained ten items so far, and getting a tattoo was one of them. I'd designed it myself. It was a multi-coloured, paint-splashed hot air balloon. I'd wanted to get the tattoo first, because most of the other items on my list were about having an adventure and breaking free. For me, nothing symbolised an adventure more than a hot air balloon.

Where would it take you?

What would you do when you got there?

Who would you meet?

And since hot air balloon rides also had a chance of ending in disaster, I thought it was all the more appropriate. After all, there's no point to an adventure if safety is guaranteed. The whole purpose is the unknown, the danger.

I craved it more than anything.

Shay had gone back to his sketching table, his back turned to me, when he said, "I'm not doing the tattoo, Lille, so you might as well get going."

I swallowed the lump in my throat and headed for the door. Just before I stepped outside, I turned around and said, "If you're afraid of someone as ridiculous as my mother, then you must work so hard on all those muscles to hide the fact that you're a massive wimp, Shay Cosgrove."

I sounded like a petulant child. Plus, I was being hypocritical, because if anyone was afraid of my mother, it was me. Still, I felt the need to put Shay in his place. He thought he was so hip and cool, but really he was just a pretentious small-town arsehole.

Wow, I think my crush just disappeared. Cowardice was a surprisingly big turn-off.

"Lille," he began in an annoyed tone, but I left before he could get the last word in. I had to get to work anyway. I muttered my annoyance to myself as I struggled up the hill to the restaurant. Everywhere in this town you were either going up a hill or down a hill. It was like whoever built it was having a good old joke on behalf of all its future inhabitants.

While I was on my summer break from college, where I was studying for a degree in business (at my mother's behest), I was working part-time at a small restaurant in town. I was scheduled for the Sunday afternoon shift, and the place would be packed with families having dinner. I liked this shift best because my boss, Nelly, let me do face painting for the kids while the parents enjoyed their meals.

On a normal day I was a waitress, but on Sundays I got to be an artist. Well, as much as turning little boys into Spiderman and little girls into fairies counted as being an artist. I especially liked it when the girls wanted to be Spiderman and the boys wanted to be fairies.

I was all for breaking the mould.

And I loved kids. In fact, I felt far more comfortable talking to five-year-olds than I did talking to adults. Kids told you exactly what they were thinking. Adults said one thing when they really meant another entirely. It was confusing.

I had a hard time connecting with most people. My curiosity and endless questions tended to turn them off. Mum said I came across too eager, and that I had to work on being more aloof and unattainable, whatever that means. I thought on this as I went inside the restaurant and began to set up my face paints at an empty table by the door. I smiled as I heard several little girls squeal in delight when they saw me. I was known as the face-painting lady around these parts and elicited much excitement in children.

I waved hello to Nelly, who was standing by the service counter, and then let my eyes drift over the patrons. I recognised all of the regulars, but two tables down sat an old woman and a young man I'd noticed a couple of days ago. They'd been in every day since, and caught my interest mainly because the woman must have been in her sixties, and her hair was as red as a Coca-Cola can. She also wore about a hundred necklaces all tangled around her neck.

The man had long, wavy dark brown hair and brown eyes. His skin was tanned, and he wore a battered old T-shirt. His equally battered brown fedora hat sat on the table in front of him. He reminded me a little of a sexy gypsy, though less of a *My Big Fat Gypsy Wedding* gypsy, and more of a Johnny Depp in *Chocolat* gypsy. He was tall, and his muscles made Shay's look like puppy fat in comparison. Plus, there was the man bun his hair was messily tied up in. I was a swooning mess for a man bun. Always had been.

In other words, he was hot...and I was staring. I'd found myself staring at him a lot this past week, but never caught him staring back (much to my disappointment.) The woman he was sitting with caught my eye and gave me a mischievous wink. I smiled to myself and looked away. There was a queue of kids lining up to have their faces painted, so I tried to focus on my job rather than the odd couple sitting two tables down.

A little while later as I went to grab a glass of water, Nelly took me aside and asked, "See those two in there?"

I nodded.

"They're from the circus, the one set up just outside of town. I think the woman is the owner. She's a strange-looking character altogether."

I absorbed this information with another nod. I was well aware of the circus. In fact, tonight was its last show before it moved on, and I'd been saving up a little cash to go see it. My mind was awash with possibilities. I wanted to see clowns, elephants, lions, and acrobats. I wanted to see it all. I'd asked my sometimes friend Delia if she wanted to come, but she'd given me the brush-off. I say "sometimes friend" because sometimes she ignores me, especially if her other friends are around. I think she really only tolerates me because my mum runs this big important tech company, and she wants to get in good with the local high-flying businesswoman. Really, I should be offended, but when you live in a small town in the southeast of Ireland, you kind of have to take what you can get in terms of friends.

As the evening wore on, most of the diners trickled out, and the odd couple, as I'd started to refer to them in my head, were the only ones left in the restaurant. I was passing through the kitchen when John the cook had to run to the bathroom and asked me to keep an eye on some eggs. I nodded, and he hurried off. It was my own fault that I wasn't paying proper attention, because I went to grab the handle and instead burned my hand on the side of the pan.

"Ouch!" I screeched, loud enough to wake the dead. I held my hand to my chest, wincing at the pain. Half the inside of my palm was burned raw. A moment later, both Nelly and the odd couple came rushing into the kitchen to see what the racket was about.

"What happened?" Nelly asked breathlessly.

I bit my lip. "Burned my hand. Sorry about, uh, the screaming."

"I thought an axe murderer had broken into the place," Nelly said. "Come here and let me see."

Taking a step toward her, I glanced at the dark-haired man. His deep, almost black eyes were fixed on my hand. His face was unreadable.

"It's okay, I'll take care of this," Nelly said, waving them both back outside. Now the man was staring into my eyes, and I got a little shiver down my spine, though it wasn't unpleasant. They both went back to their table, and Nelly put some burn cream on my hand and wrapped it up.

A few minutes later, the restaurant door opened, and a mother and daughter walked in. The little girl was eager to know if the face-painting lady was still around. I mustered a smile and went to ask her what she wanted to be. Since it wasn't my dominant hand that had been burned, I could just about manage painting.

"I want to be a pirate," she declared as she pulled herself up onto a seat in front of me.

"Oh, good choice!" I replied. Now I was thinking about Johnny Depp in *Pirates of the Caribbean*. I had old Johnny on the brain today.

I drew a fake goatee onto the little girl, complete with an eye patch and a red bandana. Then I took things a step further when I did a skull and crossbones on her cheek. When her mother came to get her, she didn't look too pleased that I'd transformed her child into a hairy-faced marauder, but I just shrugged. It *was* what she'd asked for.

"She looks like she wants to make you walk the plank," a voice said just behind me. I turned to see the Coca-Cola-haired lady standing there. Her accent was London cockney at its finest, and when she smiled, she had a million wrinkles around her eyes. They weren't ugly. In fact, they were beautiful, full of character and experience. I wanted to colour them in with every shade of the rainbow.

"Hmm, well, I am in the mood for a swim," I replied humorously, and her smile widened. A shadow fell behind her as she rummaged in her bag and pulled out a flyer for the circus. The shadow belonged to Mr Tall, Dark, and Exotic. He stood there, unfathomable eyes on me, causing me to blush. All at once I felt sweaty, hot, and strangely self-conscious. It was like his eyes were taking the sum total of my parts, but I had no clue as to the result he'd settled on.

The woman continued, "You should come see the show tonight, girly. It's our last one."

"I'd already planned to. I can't wait," I exclaimed, picking up the flyer and folding it into a neat square.

"I'll wait for you outside, Marina," said the man gruffly, his eyes meeting mine once more before he moved by us and walked outside. I watched him as he stopped, pulled a pack of cigarettes from his pocket, and lit up. His grey T-shirt showed the muscles in his arms and his tanned skin. Quite like Marina, I would have liked to paint him, too, but for *very* different reasons.

I'd been surprised to hear his deep Dublin accent. I was expecting something…I don't know, foreign. I heard Marina laughing and brought my attention back to her.

"If I were from the American south, I'd say he was a mighty ornery bastard," she chuckled. "Never did manage to learn any social niceties, that one."

I swallowed and couldn't help but ask, "Is he a part of the circus?"

"Oh, yes, Jack's a fire-eater. He's a big attraction with the ladies, as you might guess. A pity he never mastered the art of charming them."

Her words made me imagine Jack sitting at a dinner table, knife and fork in hand, ready to dig into a plate of fire.

"Oh, well, I suppose when you look like that, you don't really need charm." The words were out of my mouth before I had the chance to censor them, and Marina let out a loud guffaw of a laugh.

"I like you. You say what you think. I hope your hand heals up fast," she said, and patted me on the shoulder before following Jack out the door. I twisted in my seat and watched them say a few words to one another before walking down the hill away from the restaurant.

When I arrived home after my shift, I wanted to run straight upstairs, take a shower, put on something nice, and head out to the circus. Unfortunately, Mum was waiting for me when I got there, her arms crossed over her chest, face stern and an opened letter in her hand.

I narrowed my gaze when I saw the letter had my name on it. "Did you open my mail?" I asked indignantly. I should have been more surprised, but I was used to her control-freak behaviour by this stage.

"Yes, and I'm glad I did. These are your end-of-year exam results, and I have to say they leave a lot to be desired."

She walked towards me and shoved the letter into my hand, her designer heels clicking on the hardwood floor. I unfolded it and took a look. I'd gotten mostly Cs, a D, and a couple of Bs. They certainly weren't the worst results in the world, but Mum expected perfection.

"Considering I never wanted to do this degree, I think these results are pretty good," I said bravely. Abruptly she turned, walked back to me, and slapped me hard across the face. I gasped and clutched my cheek in my hand in shock. Mum wasn't often physically violent — words were her weapon of choice — but every now and again she'd strike me. It usually meant something hadn't gone right for her at work, so she was taking that frustration out on me.

"You're an ungrateful little bitch!" she shouted. "After all the money I've spent on your education, you go and say something like that."

I stood there, speechless, as she grabbed my hip, pinching her fingers into the fleshy part. "And look at this.

You're putting on weight. I'm going to have to start controlling your calorie intake again."

Tears stung my eyes, but I refused to let them fall. I wouldn't give her that victory. And the fact of the matter was, there was nothing wrong with my weight. My mother simply possessed a talent for seeing flaws where there weren't any. She was so miserable that she couldn't see any of the beauty in the world. She wanted straight boring lines, and if anyone dared to veer away from them, she would make their lives hell.

All my life I felt like I'd been living in quiet desperation. Following my mother's rules and biding my time, waiting for the moment when I could finally break free. The thing was, I was twenty-one now, and my time still hadn't come. I had a disturbing image of me still living under my mother's roof at thirty, still keeping to her straight lines, never walking on the cracks, and it made me feel like screaming.

But I didn't. Instead, I turned calmly away from her and walked quietly up the stairs to my bedroom. I felt like my refusal to respond to her actions showed more strength than weakness. I would not sink to her petty level. Once there, I sat down at my dressing table, stared into the mirror, and took a calming breath. Then I opened a drawer and pulled out the folded piece of paper where I'd written my list, letting my eyes trail down the numbered items.

1. Dump Henry Jackson.
2. Get a tattoo.
3. Have sex with a stranger.
4. Do something dangerous.
5. Visit a place I've never been before.
6. Fall in love.
7. Make a new friend.

8. Quit my degree.
9. Become a real artist.
10. Move out of my mother's house.

I felt a small stirring of pride that I'd already completed number one several weeks ago before college let out for the summer. Henry was the son of one of my mother's business associates and had been enrolled in the same course as me. Mum set us up on a date during my second year of studying, and we'd been conducting a dull, chemistry-free relationship for the last two years. Quite like the subject we were studying, the sex was all business. So I'd decided it was finally time to put an end to it. Mum was furious when she found out, and I could tell she was already plotting a way in which to get Henry and me back together.

It wasn't going to happen.

As I went to change out of my work clothes, the flyer for the circus slipped from my pocket. I picked it up and read the little section at the back that gave a snippet of its history. Apparently, the Circus Spektakulär was thirty years old and originally set up by a German named Konrad Eichel. When he died seven years ago, Marina Mitchell, who had previously been the circus's fortune-teller, took over as ringmaster. The circus was held not in a traditional circus tent, but in a Spiegeltent, which was a large, colourful structure dating from the late 19th century made from canvas and wood. Apparently, there were only a small number of Spiegeltents left in the world, which made the Circus Spektakulär something of a rare experience.

Already I was imagining what it might look like so that I could paint it.

Hurriedly, I pulled on a light summer dress and some boots, grabbed my coat, and sneaked out of the house as quietly as I could manage. A little rush of excitement ran through me when I got around the corner and speed-walked toward the edge of town. I could see lights flashing up into the sky as I got closer, could hear distant music.

When I reached the usually vacant field where the circus was being held, I had to dodge some bits of mud where the grass had been trodden on too frequently. Old vaudevillian piano music played from speakers that had been set up all around, making you feel as though you were stepping through a portal back in time. I nodded hello to a few families I knew from town and stepped in line to buy a ticket. After I paid, I went to a stand that was selling popcorn and candyfloss. A girl with short brown hair wearing a T-shirt with a cat's face on it smiled at me and asked what I'd like. I bought some popcorn in a paper cone and made my way inside the Spiegeltent.

On the outside, it was a circular structure with a dome-like roof and was painted in red, blue, and yellow. The primary colours. Mix red with yellow, and you get orange. Mix red and blue, and you get purple. Mix blue and yellow, and you get green. I had always been interested in the very simple science of it all.

When I was painting, sometimes I liked to mix random colours together to see what would happen. Often I'd discover a wonderful new shade of pink or purple, while at other times I'd discover that mixing too many colours just gave you an ugly brown or grey.

I thought maybe that was a good philosophy for life. Experiment with your colours, but don't experiment too much, or you'll destroy the natural beauty.

It's like that saying – too many cooks spoil the broth.

The inside of the tent was circular in shape. The stage was a sturdy round platform in the centre with the seating surrounding it. Red and blue stripes lined the ceiling and gathered up towards the dome of the roof. I'd never been anywhere like this before, and I was fascinated.

Sitting down on a seat three rows from the stage, I munched on my popcorn and waited for the place to fill up. Children's excited laughter rang out over the chattering of adults and the vaudeville piano. I heard more mature giggling then, and turned my head to the side to see Delia and three of her friends looking in my direction. So much for her not wanting to go to the circus.

Obviously, they were mocking the fact that I was there alone. My mouth formed a straight line as my gut sank. I felt a momentary flicker of self-consciousness. Was it weird to go to stuff like this on your own? All around me people seemed to be in groups of family or friends. Perhaps it *was* weird. Still, my resolve hardened. Delia really wasn't my friend at all, was she? I needed to add an eleventh item to my list.

Unfriend Delia.

I pretended I was unaware of their mocking and focused my attention straight ahead. After a few minutes, I was almost out of popcorn, and the lights started to dim. I immediately recognised Marina's voice as she announced over the speakers that the show was about to begin. Then a drumroll started up as she walked out onto the stage, wearing a top hat, a red coat with tails, tight black trousers, boots, and her trademark assortment of necklaces. Her lipstick was bright pink, and her eyes were lined with silver and gold eye shadow. However, the most interesting thing about her was that there was a little capuchin monkey sitting on her shoulder.

A monkey!

He had cream-coloured fur on his head and brown fur on his body, and when he jumped off Marina's shoulder and headed towards the audience, I heard a number of children squeal with delight.

"Welcome, everyone, to the Spiegeltent and the Circus Spektakulär! My name is Marina Mitchell, and I'll be your master of ceremonies for the evening. The little guy currently running amok amid the audience is Pierre, my trusty capuchin sidekick. Please keep an eye on your belongings — he has habit of taking shiny things that don't belong to him." She paused to wink at a boy in the front row. "We are a small, independent circus and pride ourselves on giving audiences a unique and magical experience. We have been travelling around Europe, Ireland, and the UK for the past thirty years. Tonight you will see wonders to delight, astound, and thrill. You will see men tame beasts. You will see women dance in the sky. You will see bodies accomplish impossible feats. And yes, you will laugh until your bellies ache as our clowns act out the comical and ridiculous. But first, I give you our Elephant Men, Jan and Ricky."

Applause rang out as Marina took a bow and clapped her hands, and Pierre came running to climb back onto her shoulder. A moment later, two short men with dark hair walked out onto the stage. They were bare-chested and wore matching silk trousers with intricate designs. When one of them made a small gesture, two elephants came trotting out. I smiled widely, my eyes going big as I stared at the magnificent creatures. Playful music came on, "Pink Elephants on Parade" from *Dumbo*. They marched around the stage in a circle, lifting their legs gracefully when prompted or throwing their trunks high into the air.

During the act, the men led the elephants to go up on their hind legs, and at one point, Jan, I think it was, climbed up onto one elephant and sat on its back. Once their act was over, Marina was back out, introducing the Ladies of the Sky, three red-haired acrobats who I thought must be sisters, they resembled one another so closely.

They hung from silky coloured ribbons, twisting, twirling, and diving. My hands itched for a paintbrush as the colours swirled above me. I could have sat there for hours detailing the orange glow of their hair and the lithe, graceful movements of their limbs. I was certain that my Gran, who had been the one who first taught me how to paint, would have loved to be here right now. Unfortunately, she died when I was ten, but I always remembered her teachings, always tried to live by her philosophies, which were so opposite from my mother's.

Make mistakes, Lille. Walk on the cracks. Break the rules that were made to be broken.

Somebody sat down in the empty seat beside me, and I glanced out of the corner of my eye to see the girl from the popcorn stand. She was holding a stick on which was spun a massive cloud of pink candy floss. When she saw me looking at her, she smiled wide, her bright blue eyes sparkling, and asked, "Want some?"

I nodded and eagerly plucked off a wisp before sticking it into my mouth. "Thanks."

"You're welcome. I'm Lola."

"Lille."

"Pleased to meet you, Lille. Are you enjoying the show?"

Again, I nodded, this time more fervently. "Absolutely."

"I'm on my break. Thought I'd come in for the best part. Jack's on next."

Instantly, I recognised the name, and something both nervous and excited squeezed in my gut. Still, I feigned ignorance and asked, "Jack?"

"He's the fire-breather. He also does knife throwing. I swear, every time he throws a knife at someone, I can't be certain whether or not he means to hit or miss. There's this air of danger about him, you know."

I swallowed, more questions on the tip of my tongue, but the low, thrumming rock music that came on interrupted me. The bass hit me right in the pit of my stomach, and the crowd began to cheer. Marina made a passionate introduction for *the* Jack McCabe, fire-eater extraordinaire, and then he was walking out onto the stage, two long metal torches in his hands, the tips blazing with fire. My skin prickled with awareness, and somehow I just knew I was in for something truly amazing.

Two

They crossed a sea of water

He wasn't wearing a shirt, and the way that his large muscular frame moved mesmerised me. He was all hard, toned muscle underneath gorgeous tanned skin. I leaned forward in my chair, because it looked like there was scarring all along his shoulder and half of his back.

"Are those...."

"Burn scars?" Lola interjected casually. "That's what they look like, but nobody knows for certain."

I glanced at her, unsure yet if I was comfortable with this girl. I was by contrast wary and delighted with her instant camaraderie. I'd never had a stranger come up to me and randomly act like we were already friends. For once, I wasn't the eager one. Then again, I thought Lola and I probably came from very different worlds. Perhaps she did this kind of thing all the time.

Thinking of Jack's scars, I wondered if that was why he'd been staring at my burned hand so intensely today. Perhaps it brought back a traumatic memory for him.

My eyes grew wide as he walked to the centre of the stage, holding out the two blazing torches. The crowd applauded when he began to swing them around dexterously, and my body got tense. He swung the torches in swift figure-eights, creating glowing swirls of orange in the dim light of the tent. I was both fascinated and worried that he might hurt himself, or worse, lose his grip on one of the torches.

His movements were almost like dancing. He ran the fire along the length of one arm, and it blazed across his skin before flickering out. He licked at the other flame, then brought the entire torch into his mouth and swallowed the fire. Whoa. Sexily, he lifted a bottle to his mouth, took a drink, tipped a torch to his lips, and spat. Huge, billowing flames exploded outward, making it look like he was breathing fire. It held a terrifying sort of beauty.

I heard quiet chuckling next to me and turned to see Lola grinning, "You're fucking hilarious."

I frowned, unsure whether I should take offence. "What?"

"You act like you've just seen a miracle."

"Well, I've never been to a circus before, so…."

Her eyebrows shot up. "Really? That's mad." Then she dropped her face into the candyfloss and bit off a big chunk. She ate it like a three-year-old would eat a birthday cake, face first.

Hearing delighted noises from those around me, I brought my attention back to Jack to see he was now swinging around pronged metal wheels, the tips all lit with fire. He reminded me of an ancient tribal warrior performing a victory dance, and it was sexy as shit. I felt a chill cover the surface of my skin, my pores prickling. There was something irrefutably carnal about this man, and I was shocked to discover how much he could arouse me without so much as a touch.

Well, "shocked" was probably too strong a word. Since my mid-teens, I'd felt like I was a little preoccupied with sex. I mean, I had an active imagination and daydreamed about it *all* the time – probably because I had yet to find a partner who truly satisfied me. I was desperate to sate the foreign yet familiar hunger inside me. I'd always had this urge to explore, to experience something outside the realms of the normal. I'd had more than enough normal with Henry. Now I wanted more. Just…more.

23

Marina came back onto the stage, declaring that Jack would need a volunteer from the audience for the next part of his act. Needless to say, I was dying to throw my hand up and offer myself, but I had no idea what volunteering would entail. If it was something embarrassing, then half the town would be here to witness it. I shuddered to think of the news getting back to Mum, and I'd already defied her tonight with my backtalk.

So yeah, I craved sticking it to her like nobody's business — I just had to formulate the actual courage to do so. *One step at a time,* I told myself, just as Lola shouted out, "Marina! Over here! I have a volunteer for ya!"

She took hold of my arm and swung it into the air.

"No!" I whisper-hissed, but she only winked at me and pushed me up out of my seat. Before I knew it I was standing, and a spotlight had landed on me, alongside Jack's dark, indecipherable gaze. I stood frozen for a moment, uncertain of what to do, and then Marina was calling me to the stage and my feet were moving one after the other, the traitorous bastards. Okay, so maybe I was going to stick it to Mum sooner than I thought. And really, it was oddly liberating.

Jack held his hand out to me when I reached him, and I placed my palm in his. Without realising it, I'd given him the hand that had been burned. When he gripped it, I hissed in a tiny breath at the sting.

"Sorry," he murmured, but he didn't sound sorry.

"It's okay," I replied as he led me to an upright wooden panel. Taking my shoulders in his big, warm hands, he gently situated me against it, my back flush with the wood.

"I hope you're good at holding still," he said, and his breath hit the side of my neck.

"Why?" I practically whispered. He was incredibly handsome, even more so now that I was seeing him up close, and I felt a little drunk on it.

The edge of his mouth twitched, like he was holding back a smile. With one hand braced above my shoulder, he leaned in as he replied, "Because, blondie, I'm gonna be throwing knives at you, and I'd really hate to make you bleed."

Again, he didn't sound like he meant what he said at all. And I didn't think there was a single pore on my body that wasn't tingling. I remembered items number three and four on my list: Have sex with a stranger and do something dangerous. Perhaps if I could get Jack McCabe to do me, then I could kill two birds with one stone.

I hadn't noticed before, because I was too busy staring at him, but there was a belt attached to the wood. I stood there as Jack took it and buckled it extra tight around my waist. He gave it a firm tug once he was done and smirked. I'm not sure why, but the action caused me to tremble. I think he noticed, too, because his eyes grew darker, if that was even possible.

Surprising me, he placed his flattened-out palm on my belly. I had to try my hardest to concentrate on his words rather than the fact that my libido (the little slut) was willing his hand to move lower.

"This is your core. Visualise it. Focus on it. Keep your body in this exact position, and everything will be fine." There was the tiniest edge of a smile tugging at his lips, and it made me wonder if he was enjoying this, if maybe he was trying to make me nervous.

Sucking in a breath, he continued randomly, "You smell like turpentine." Then he drew up to his full and impressive height, and walked to the other side of the stage.

I knew I smelled like turpentine because I often used it to clean my paintbrushes, and sometimes the smell got into my clothes. That wasn't the part that preoccupied me; that part would be the fact that he'd taken the time to smell me, and I didn't know whether I should be weirded out or turned on.

Okay, so I knew which option my libido was going for. And really, maybe I was just as much of a weirdo, because what I'd wanted to reply was, "You smell like kerosene."

Jack gathered a selection of small throwing knives from the floor and demonstrated the sharpness of each by flinging them one by one into a block of solid wood, where they embedded themselves as though slicing through butter. My heart began to race, and I could feel adrenaline starting to flood my system. I was shaking very slightly all over as I remembered Lola's words.

I swear, every time he throws a knife at someone, I can't be certain whether or not he means to hit or miss.

I was hoping it was the latter. Perhaps I was crossing my "something dangerous" off the list after all. Damn my life. Why couldn't it have been the sexy danger? Jack didn't even announce that he was starting when he stood at least ten feet away from me, flipped a knife in his hand, caught it, then lunged with his whole body and flung the knife right at my head. I squeezed my eyes shut, and a hollow thud sounded at my ear where the knife had, thankfully, hit the board. Sounds of nervous excitement and clapping came from the audience as Jack continued his assault on me. He moved his body with the kind of skill that only comes from obsessive practice.

Adrenaline drowned me, my chest rising and falling rapidly.

A small squeak of fright escaped me when he threw a knife at my hip and it barely missed. In fact, I could feel the hard edge of the steel pressing against me. I was surprised it hadn't cut into the fabric of my coat. Jack prowled around the stage, gaze on me, calculating his next throw. Everywhere his eyes looked, I felt positively laid bare. Molested by disinterest.

I might as well have been a sack of potatoes for all the care he showed as to whether or not he might cut me. Deciding I couldn't take any more, I kept my eyes closed until it was over and all six knives had been thrown.

Thud.

Thud.

Thud.

When I finally opened my eyes, Jack was standing before me, unbuckling the belt that held me in place. I didn't move even after I'd been released, still trying to come to terms with the terror I'd just endured. All of a sudden, Jack McCabe was more scary than sexy.

"That was a close one," he said as he pulled out the knife that had landed just below my ear. I glanced to the side to see a tiny lock of my hair fall to the stage floor. Oh, my God.

"You cut off my hair," I gasped.

"Only a small bit. Don't worry — I didn't leave a bald patch." He chuckled darkly.

I didn't know what to say, but I was momentarily appalled at how cavalierly he was taking all this.

"I could sue you," I said, and then instantly grimaced. I sounded like my mother. It was only hair, after all.

He leaned in, and I thought I saw him bare his teeth for a second. "Go ahead, pumpkin."

He said "pumpkin" with all the disdain most people would put into the word "bitch." I didn't feel safe right then, so I quickly scrambled off the stage and returned to my seat. In all honesty, I felt a bit like going home and having a nice private little cry. Get all the fear and sexual frustration out, you know.

"Have fun?" Lola asked when I reached her.

"Oh, yeah. Big time. Thanks for offering me up for sacrifice, by the way," I said, annoyed.

She laughed loudly. "It's the sexiest thing that's happened to you all year, admit it."

I snorted. She was dead right, but I wasn't going to give her the satisfaction of letting her know it. Forcing myself to get back into the show, I watched the rest of the acts. They included a contortionist named Violet whose eyes and hair matched her name. She had to be wearing contacts. There was also a husband and wife duo of lion tamers, two clowns, and a group of three stuntmen, two of whom stood on the shoulders of the third as he drove a scooter around the stage.

By the time it was all over, I'd just about gotten past the adrenaline rush of having knives thrown at me. I watched as Delia and her girlfriends walked by, giving me snotty looks as they did so.

"Shit, did you shag one of their boyfriends or something?" Lola asked, amused. I'd almost forgotten that she was still sitting next to me.

"Nope. I think they might be jealous that I got to have a near-death experience and they didn't," I deadpanned.

"Ah, I see. Near death at the hands of Jack McCabe is certainly something to envy," she joked, and nudged me with her elbow.

I laughed despite myself. Lola stood and gestured for me to follow. "Come on, you look like you could do with a drink."

I stood, and she linked her arm through mine. Again, her familiarity was odd, but I went with it. I kind of liked her oddness. She brought me through a side passage that led backstage, and I saw the three stuntmen packing up their equipment. Lola waved to them.

"Hey, Lola, who's your friend?" a short, handsome one called.

"My friend is none of your business, Pedro, so you can stick your eyeballs back in their sockets," Lola replied, and gave me a conspiratorial grin.

"Pedro's from Brazil," she explained. "He always uses the accent to get women into bed. You don't want a slice of that venereal-disease-ridden action, believe me."

"Oh," I said, lost for words.

She laughed. "Oh, my God, has anyone ever told you that you have the best facial expressions?"

"Um, no," I said while she opened a door and led me out the back of the tent. There were motor homes parked all about, two large trucks, and a big open-air gazebo with rows of tables and benches. Lots of the performers had gathered there, drinking and eating. Some people I didn't recognise, but I guessed they were the ones who worked behind the scenes. It must take a good deal of manpower to set up the tent and transport everything from one location to the next.

Lola was still linking me by the arm when she brought me to a table where Marina sat with Jack and the husband and wife lion tamers.

"Everybody, I want you to meet my new friend, Lille," Lola announced, pushing me forward to sit in the empty space beside Jack and directly across from Marina. I felt kind of buzzed to be sitting next to him, but was disappointed when he didn't acknowledge me.

The red-haired ringmaster (mistress?) smiled. "We've already met. Nice to see you again, Lille. How's the hand?"

I touched my good hand to the bandage and shrugged. "Sore."

She nodded and introduced the lion tamers. "This is Winnie and Antonio, and you know Jack."

I smiled politely at Winnie and Antonio. Lola poured some red wine into a plastic cup for me and I took it, murmuring my thanks.

"Hi, everyone," I said, feeling stupid, mainly due to Jack's silence. What was his problem? He was flexing and releasing his hand repeatedly, like he wanted to hit something. I took a sip of wine and tried not to look at him anymore. It was difficult, since he was so flipping beautiful, and as an artist I was drawn to memorising beautiful things.

"Give me your good hand, Lille," said Marina, interrupting my thoughts.

I lifted it from my lap, and she took it into her soft, wrinkled fingers. I loved how they felt. Marina had a kind of maternal warmth about her that I'd always longed for in my own mother. And she had a twinkle in her eye that reminded me so much of Gran.

She smoothed her fingers over my palm. "You've got a good distinctive life-line here. See how it's deeply indented? It indicates a certain quality — you'll do lots of living."

"You read palms?" I asked, even though the answer was blatantly obvious.

30

She nodded. "Learned it from my grandmother, the mad old coot."

I smiled.

"How long have you been an artist?" she asked, noting the dried paint stuck under my fingernails.

"Ever since I was little. Funny coincidence, just like your gran taught you to read palms, my gran taught me how to paint," I answered. I thought I could sense Jack looking at me then, but since I was determined not to make eye contact with him again, I couldn't be sure.

"You should come to France with us," Marina went on, like it was a perfectly natural continuation of what we'd just been talking about.

"Um, I don't...."

"You can do your face painting with the children. The punters will love it, and you'll make enough money to live off of. I've been meaning to set up something fun for the kids before they come in to see the show. What do you say?"

"France?" I said, blinking, heart racing. This night was moving way too fast for me. It was confusing.

"We're leaving by ferry at nine in the morning, so you'll have to make a decision soon."

"Oh, my God! You have to come," Lola put in. "I've been dying for someone new to hang out with, and Violet's so bloody annoyed with me all the time. Oh, oh! You could sleep in our camper. We've got a spare bed."

"Shouldn't you consult Violet about that first?" said Jack, finally speaking.

Lola waved him off. "Pffft, she'll be fine with it so long as Lille doesn't get in her way."

"Violet's the contortionist?"

31

"And just about the crankiest woman ever to grace the earth. Seriously, Lille, you'll be doing me a huge favour. I'm gonna crack if I don't get a new roommate soon."

I was flabbergasted. "None of you even know me."

"Ah, but you've got the heart of a traveller," said Marina. "I can see it in those stormy grey eyes. And that's good enough for me."

"Look at you," said Lola, wearing the biggest smile I'd ever seen. She was all lips and teeth. "You're dying to say yes, aren't you?"

"Well, I'd have to run it past my mother first," I said, eyes downcast, and I heard Jack make a sound of derision. "And I have my summer job at the restaurant in town." Why was I being hesitant? This offer was my hot air balloon ready and waiting to bring me on an adventure, and yet I was making excuses. I think I was just suspicious of the randomness of it all. Plus, the sad fact was that I'd probably have said yes right away if it weren't for Jack. He clearly didn't want me around, and I'd just end up feeling awkward every time I saw him. I wasn't sure how obvious it was to him that I fancied him something rotten. Perhaps that was the reason for his disdain. He didn't enjoy being ogled by some dumb girl. He probably had a girlfriend. Probably had several.

"I'm going to go find Violet and ask her what she thinks. She'll say no, of course, but I'll talk her around," said Lola, rising from her seat with a wink.

"The men are taking down the tent tonight so that we can leave first thing in the morning," said Marina. "You'd better go home and start packing."

"I haven't agreed to come yet," I replied.

She only smiled and pursed her lips, a glint in her eye. "Haven't you?"

Winnie gave me an encouraging look, and Antonio told me I'd have a great time if I came. As expected, Jack said nothing. Still, the encouragement of the others spurred me on and I rose, determined to go home and tell Mum I was going to France. I felt like I was walking through a dream. Who makes an offer to some random girl to join their circus? It was crazy, and I was happily drowning in the madness.

Gran would have been proud. She'd had Mum late in life, and before that she'd travelled the world, met with some amazing people. Even though I was only ten when she passed, she'd already made a powerful impression on me. I wanted to be just like her. She was strong in a way Mum wasn't, strong through love and kindness rather than cruelty and control.

I said goodbye to everyone and made my way out of the gazebo. Just as I turned in the direction of town, a strong hand gripped my arm, and I yelped. Aside from a few dim street lights, it was dark out here, and mostly everyone was gone now.

I turned, and my heart stuttered when I found Jack standing behind me, his dark eyebrows drawn into a frown.

"You shouldn't come," he said, voice low.

"Let go of me," I complained, feeling nervous and trying to pull my arm from his grasp. When he realised how tight his grip was, his eyes widened, and he dropped my arm. I turned and began walking again, more speedily this time, wanting to get away from him. No matter how hot he was, I didn't trust being alone on a dark road with a strange man.

I could hear his steady, booted pace behind me, and I didn't know why he was following me. My skin prickled with apprehension, and I pulled my phone out of my bag, pretending to dial my mum and proceeding to carry out a one-sided conversation.

"Hi, Mum, it's me. I'm on my way home now. Yeah. I'm on Frederick Street. See you in a minute."

I'm not sure why I thought letting Jack know that someone was waiting for me would deter him from harming me, but it was the only thing I could think of, and I didn't have anything on me that could be used as a weapon. Plus, I couldn't actually call my mother, since I'd sneaked out to go to the circus and she thought I was still in my room, tucked up safely in bed.

His deep chuckle sounded from behind me as I slid my phone back into my bag.

"Would you like to make a fake call to the police as well?" he asked in amusement.

I scowled and stopped walking, spinning around on him. "It wasn't fake. And why the hell are you following me anyway?" My voice came out high-pitched and frightened. I hated how I sounded.

"Do you always walk home alone at night?" He was frowning again.

"That's none of your business. Now, please stop following me. It's creepy."

He took a step forward, closing the distance between us. "I'm making sure you get home safe. Don't be so ungrateful. How much farther is your house?"

The way he spoke made me feel scolded. I looked back and forth between his eyes, trying to decipher if he was being honest. All I got in return was his smouldering dark gaze and neither honesty nor dishonesty. He was like a vault, locked up tight. I was never going to be able to read him.

"You could have told me that in the first place. Don't you know it's weird to just randomly start following someone?"

He slowly blinked at me and repeated his question. "How much farther is your house?"

"We're almost there. I'll be fine from here. I'm sorry for snapping at you," I said, and began walking again. He kept up the pace beside me. I sighed.

"I don't mean to sound rude, but I'd rather you not know where I live. For my own peace of mind, you understand?"

He tilted his head down at me, a quizzical look on his face, which made me feel like I needed to explain further.

"You're a stranger. A kind of scary-looking stranger, if I'm being honest, no offence. So leading you right to where I live would be dumb, right?"

He almost smiled, and wow, when Jack McCabe *almost* smiled, it really was something to behold. I wasn't sure I could handle a full one. "I'm good scary, Lille. The kind that frightens off bad scary."

I was surprised that he'd remembered my name. I'm not sure what possessed me to say what I did next, and I regretted it instantly. "Pinky promise you're not a psycho killer?" I held out my little finger to him, and he simply stared at it.

"I'm not a psycho killer."

Feeling stupid, I dropped my hand and considered his answer. Perhaps he was trying to be nice and make sure I got home safe. Then another idea struck me. Was he interested in walking me home because he wanted sex? I looked at him as he strode along, gaze straight ahead. It was almost like he'd read my thoughts, because he turned to me then, his voice deep and husky. "If I wanted to fuck you, you'd know about it."

I shivered. I didn't think a man had ever referred to fucking me before, which was sad. And it was even sadder that the first time it happened it was a man referring to the fact that he didn't want to. I let out a long breath and tried not to let my feelings be hurt.

Tugging my coat tighter around myself as we reached my street, I told him, "Well, you don't mince your words, do you?"

He shook his head. "Don't see the point."

"Okay. I'm home now. You've done your duty." I opened my garden gate and stepped inside.

He called after me. "Remember what I said, Lille. You shouldn't come with us. You think it's going to be all fun and games, running away with the circus, but it's not. It's hard work with little sleep and shit pay. It's for people who don't have homes and mothers who worry about them. It's not the life for you."

"I'm not trying to make it my life, Jack. And I never even said I was coming."

"Good. Don't."

"I can make my own decisions."

"So make the right one."

We stared at each other for a long time, almost like we were having a stand-off. I felt triumphant when he was the one to walk away first.

***

I didn't sleep a wink that night. When I got to my room, I sat on my bed, rubbing my hands back and forth over the blanket, my mind racing. I was nearly out of time. I had to make a decision. I mean, running away with the circus was all rainbows and lollipops in theory, but what if

I couldn't hack the reality? I had about four hundred euros in savings to my name and little else. Would I make enough money painting faces to get by?

I was such a coward. The danger was what I wanted. Adventure was something I craved. I had to quit worrying. Steely determination came over me as I pulled out my suitcase and began packing. Of course, I didn't quite get over all of my fear, as instead of telling Mum in person, I decided to leave her a note. Yeah, I was that type of gutless wonder. But my mother was scary in a way that few people understood. I wasn't sure there'd ever be a time when her disappointment wouldn't cut me to the quick.

I was twenty-one. A fully grown woman. I didn't need her permission to do anything anymore.

Now all I had to do was convince myself to believe it.

She was going to blow a gasket when she found my letter. I was hoping I'd be on a ferry halfway to France by the time that happened. I sealed the letter in an envelope and set it down on my dresser. I managed to squeeze the majority of my clothes into my suitcase, and I threw a small duffel with my sleeping bag in it over my shoulder. I wasn't quite sure what my sleeping arrangements were going to be.

If worst came to worst, I could sleep on somebody's floor, right?

I was still wearing the same outfit as the night before when I quietly slipped out of my house at seven in the morning. I could hear Mum moving around in her room, so I knew she'd just woken up. Thankfully, I managed to get out before she noticed. As I hurried down the street, my heart pumped a mile a minute. I loved the thrill of feeling like I was getting away from her. Freeing myself from the prison of quiet desperation I'd been living in.

When I got into town, I stopped by an ATM machine and withdrew all of my savings, shoving the notes into my duffle. I called my boss Nelly and explained to her that I wouldn't be able to work for the rest of the summer. She gave me hell and told me not to come looking for a reference, which I'd expected, but I winced as she spoke angrily down the line all the same.

When I got to the circus, it wasn't a circus anymore. The entire thing had been packed away, presumably in one of the large cargo trucks. All that was left was a field full of camper vans. Marina sat on a step outside her motor home, sipping from a mug of coffee and smoking a cigarette, while Pierre sat on her lap, making cute little noises.

"I've been expecting you," she said, eyes smiling.

I was out of breath when I stopped by her and leaned against the side of the van. I felt like I'd been running ever since I left my house. My heart was still pounding. Mum could be reading my letter right this moment. I could just imagine the vein in her forehead throbbing in outrage.

"You sure you still want me along?" I asked, and she laughed.

"Of course I do, sweetheart. Wouldn't have asked you if I didn't. I've been watching you work in that restaurant all week, and I know a girl desperate for travel when I see one. You'll fit right in with us here."

When Pierre saw me, he jumped off Marina's lap and came ambling towards me.

"He's adorable," I said.

"Don't let the innocent little face fool you," said Marina. "He's as shrewd as they come, is my Pierre." I knew she was telling the truth when Pierre climbed up onto my shoulder, reached down, and pulled an old bus ticket from the breast pocket of my coat. I laughed as he hopped off with his loot, then disappeared inside Marina's camper.

She stubbed out her smoke just as the door to a smaller camper opened and Lola walked out. She rubbed sleep from her eyes, still wearing her pyjamas. "Lille! You came! OMG, I'm so happy right now," she said, and pulled me into a tight hug.

I think Marina must have seen the bewildered look on my face when she said, "Our Lola gets attached fast when she likes someone. It's just her way."

"Yeah, and my way is fucking awesome! Let's get these bags of yours inside, and I'll show you where you'll be sleeping."

I followed her as she led me into her camper van. It was really small and had a kitchenette, and a tiny living area with an equally tiny TV. One door led to a bathroom. The other was closed and led to Violet's room, Lola explained, and then the final one led to Lola's room, which I discovered I'd be sharing with her. There was about a foot of space between the two narrow beds. It was tidy in a messy sort of way. The beds were made, but Lola had stuffed all of her clothes under them. There wouldn't be much room for my things, but I didn't mind. I'd just live out of my suitcase.

"So, Violet agreed that you could stay. This van belongs to her, unfortunately, so she makes the rules. You'll have to pay her sixty euros a week in rent, but you'll make that easily on show nights. All of her food goes in the cupboard to the left and all of ours goes in the cupboard to the right. We get one shelf in the fridge, and she gets two. If you give Marina forty euros a week you can eat in the gazebo with the rest of us for most of your meals. Oh, and don't use any of the toiletries in the bathroom because they all belong to Violet, and she'll go cray-cray if you take anything. I keep all my stuff in a bag and bring it with me when I shower. Keeps things simpler. So yeah, she's a fucking dictator, but you'll learn to live with it. Hey, perhaps me and you could save and get a camper of our own. That'd be cool!"

I laughed. This girl was mental, but I liked it. "Sure, I'll just buy a lottery ticket, shall I?" I joked.

"Ha -ha," she deadpanned, and pulled out a smart phone, fingers gliding across the screen so fast they were almost a blur. "Okay, I'm going to include you in our ferry ticket. Have you got cash?"

I nodded and rummaged in my bag, pulling out some folded notes. Lola took them and finished up the booking. "Great, we're all sorted. You want to sit up front with me while I drive?"

I told her I would, and followed her to the front of the van. I looked out the window and saw Jack helping to load equipment into one of the trucks. It looked heavy, whatever it was, and the way he worked made me feel all fizzy inside. When he was done, he rubbed his hands on his jeans, looking about the field. My heart thudded when he spotted me sitting in the passenger seat while Lola looked over a map. He seemed pissed off when he saw me. Obviously, I hadn't taken his advice not to come. I saw him stomp over to the camper that must have been his and slam the door shut.

Before I knew it, we were off. Lola informed me that we'd be sailing from Rosslare to a place called Cherbourg in France, and that the ferry journey would take almost an entire day. Violet, the contortionist, came out of her room, said a grumpy hello to me, shook my hand, and then went to make herself some coffee.

"A woman of few words," Lola whispered to me as she drove.

"And excellent hearing," Violet called to her. "Seriously, I think you forget how depressingly small this place is sometimes."

When we got to the ferry, we parked the camper below deck and got out. Some people had rented cabins to sleep in, but, like me, most had simply booked seats. I was starving, so I went to buy some breakfast before finding the lounge. It was a cosy room with big cushioned seats. Most people were either sleeping or talking quietly. There were even pillows and blankets if you wanted to take a nap.

I saw Lola waving to me from where she sat beside Violet, who was listening to music on her headphones. I took my seat with them and tucked into my food. I was sleepy when I finished eating, since I hadn't slept the night before, and I was losing the battle to keep my eyes open....

I didn't know how long I'd been out when I woke up because someone was pushing my head off their shoulder. I rubbed my eyes and blinked, seeing Jack staring down at me. Seemingly, he'd booked the seat right next to mine, and I'd clearly just been trying to cuddle up to him.

How embarrassing.

Three

A king fell down who wore no crown

"Sorry," I mumbled, and drew away as far as I possibly could, being that our seats were side by side. I noticed that somebody had covered me with a blanket, but it must've been Lola. My skin prickled as I wondered how long I'd been resting my head on Jack's shoulder. Had it been seconds or hours? I was willing to bet seconds, considering he was roughly shoving me off him.

"I told you not to come. Why didn't you listen to me?" he asked, tilting his head to the side, a subtle edge to his words.

"Oh, I'm sorry, *Dad*. I forgot you had a say in what I do with my life. Please accept my humblest apologies," I said, heavy on the sarcasm. On the inside, my feelings were hurt. I didn't need him to be worshipping at my feet, but the least he could do was be civilised.

His lips twitched as he arched an eyebrow at me. "So, the little princess wants to slum it for a while. Okay, then. Just don't come crying to me when it all goes to shit."

"Why would I come crying to you? I don't even know you," I said, and got up from my seat. Both Violet and Lola were gone. I felt kind of grimy and needed a change of clothes, so I grabbed the small bag I had with me and went to find the showers. I felt a million times better by the time I was done, and when I went back to my seat, I found Jack had left. And really, I was relieved. The man made me feel all weird and jittery in a way I thought I could become obsessed with.

Becoming obsessed with Jack McCabe wouldn't be healthy for me. It'd be like having a crush on a movie star. They were strutting the red carpet, and you were huddled in the gutter. Deciding to stretch my legs, I went for a walk about the ferry, saying hello to Winnie and Antonio and their two daughters, Carrie and Orla. Apparently, they home schooled them while the circus travelled. I thought that must be such an unusual way to grow up, in equal measures difficult and wonderful.

When I reached the doorway that led out onto the deck, I pushed through and was met with a violent gust of wind, my shoulder-length hair going flying all over the place. It was still wet from the shower, so I considered it an unusual sort of blow-dry.

I stared out at the waves and the endless sea that surrounded me, feeling a momentary flutter of pure freedom, and man, did it feel good.

Somebody swore profusely from behind me, and I turned to find Jack trying to light a cigarette. The wind wasn't doing him any favours, and he couldn't get the flame to stay lit. Not wanting him to see me, I began walking swiftly in the opposite direction. I didn't get far when he was suddenly behind me. He looped his finger through my belt and practically dragged me to the corner he'd been standing in.

"What the fu…."

"Stay still," he ordered. "I need you to block the wind."

I didn't have any snappy comebacks, so I simply stood there, amazed by his gruffness. Hadn't anyone ever taught him simple manners? When I looked at him, I thought that maybe they hadn't. I could easily imagine him as a little Mowgli type, being raised by animals in the jungle.

He flicked the lighter and finally got the smoke lit. Inhaling deeply, then exhaling, he watched me all the while. I shivered, and not from the cold. I felt like there was an *atmosphere* between us, but it was more than likely all on my end. I was good at imagining things, especially sexual tension. And I was well-acquainted with the one-sided kind.

"Are my services required further, sir?" I asked with a hint of sass. I mean, I'd been his wind-blocker, and he hadn't even said thanks.

Just like last night, he almost smiled, and I hated that it was wondrous. I could have painted an entire mural of his jaw line alone. He flicked off the ash and leaned back against the wall behind him.

"So, you're staying with Lola?"

"Yes, and Violet."

"That'll be fun."

"Are you being sarcastic?"

"Are you?"

"What?"

"Nothing."

"You're weird."

He took a step forward and stared down at me, teeth flashing as he spoke. "And I bet I could make you like it."

If anyone else had said this to me, I would have thought they were flirting, but not with this guy. No, with this guy it sounded more like a taunt. I narrowed my gaze at him, deciding I was done with this encounter and my unrequited attraction, and returned to the lounge. I checked my phone for the time, relieved that I couldn't get a signal out here. I'd bet Mum was wearing a hole on her dialling pad trying to get in touch with me. I had my fingers crossed that by the time I got to France, she'd have calmed down. If my estimations were correct, we had another eight hours of sailing to do. I pulled a sketch pad out of my bag and began to draw the family sitting in front of me. A little kid played with an iPad while the mother snoozed and the father

44

perused a newspaper. I was so lost in the drawing that I didn't hear Lola when she came to sit beside me.

"You're really good," she commented, and it made me smile. At home my art was always something I had to sneak and hide. I never really got to show it to people, so I appreciated her compliment more than she might have guessed.

"Thanks."

The hours passed slowly, and when we finally arrived in Cherbourg, I was so ready to set foot on solid ground. It wasn't to be, though, as we had another hour and a half drive to Caen, where the circus would be stopping to do a week of shows. It was just after two in the morning, so my first impressions of France were shrouded in darkness. When we reached the site where we'd be spending the next week, it was starting to get bright. I was amazed when the men began immediately setting up the Spiegeltent. Where did they get their energy come from? Perhaps they'd slept for most of the ferry journey.

I spread my sleeping bag out on the bed and crawled into it, deciding I'd get a couple hours of sleep in. Lola was already there, snoring away. Sharing a tiny room with this girl was definitely going to be an experience.

When I woke up, it was mid-morning, and two men were helping Violet connect the camper van to the water and electricity mains on the site. I recognised Pedro, who winked at me (I think because I hadn't put on a bra yet), and one of the other stuntmen. Lola had told me on the ferry that his name was Luan. I thought she might have a thing for him because she gushed a little about what a nice guy he was. He was tall, with tightly cut dark hair and brown eyes.

Apparently, the circus didn't do any shows on Mondays or Tuesdays, because those were usually travelling days where they moved from one site to the next. That gave me a day to find my bearings.

Violet surprised me when she smiled and told me there was coffee inside if I wanted some. I poured myself a cup and took a walk. The newest host to the circus looked like some sort of camping site that was surrounded by trees and greenery on either side. I thought that we must have been situated just outside of town and wondered if we were within walking distance. I would need to buy food and some toiletries soon.

Sitting on the grass, I pulled out my phone to find that Mum had tried to call me a grand total of twenty-five times and left eleven voicemails. The very idea made my stomach twist, so I decided to put off listening to them for a while. Instead, I spent a few minutes reading up on Caen. Everything had happened so quickly that I'd hardly had time to research where I was actually going. The frenzied decision to come here made me feel dizzy with glee. I was breaking free from the monotony my life had been, and it felt glorious.

It turned out that Caen was in Normandy and was the largest city in the region. The pictures that came up showed some beautiful architecture, and I got excited just thinking about going exploring. Perhaps I'd meet a handsome Frenchman, he'd tell me I was beautiful, and we'd enjoy a whirlwind romance. Of course, it would all end in heartbreak when I had to move on to the next city. The idea was surprisingly appealing. I wanted to get my heart broken. I wanted to live through every high and low, because otherwise I wouldn't be living.

I rummaged in the back pocket of my jeans and pulled out my list to add one more item. Grabbing the sketching pencil that was perennially tucked behind my ear, I scribbled down number eleven.

11. Get my heart broken.

Coincidentally, Jack was walking by, lugging a crate of water bottles, just as I finished writing. He glanced at me, then at the paper in my hand. I quickly folded it up and shoved it back in my pocket, sheepish. Jack McCabe was certainly the heart-breaking type. Unfortunately, I didn't think I had a chance of getting close enough to him in order to have my heart broken. Oh, well. If worst came to worst, there was always Pedro.

Jack frowned and continued on his way. He was always frowning at me.

Marina called me over to her camper then and offered me a croissant for breakfast. I took it gladly.

"Tell me, Lille," she said as I sat in the kitchen of her overly frilly motorhome. I swear to God, she had doilies on everything. I wouldn't be surprised if she had them hanging over her toilet seat, to be perfectly honest. "Are you any good with numbers?"

"Numbers?" I asked.

"Okay, so I may have had an ulterior motive for asking you to join us."

The phrase "ulterior motive" sounded positively thrilling to me, so I smiled and nodded for her to continue.

"You see, I heard your boss thanking you for helping her out with her accounts while I was in the restaurant last week. And I desperately need someone to help me with mine. King usually does it, but he's been hitting the bottle more and more lately, so I can't rely on him. Do you think you could have a look at the circus' finances? Clean up the numbers for me?"

Okay, maybe not so thrilling, then. I had no idea who King was, and I didn't ask. "Oh right. Well, I study business at college. I hate it, really, but accounting is probably the part I hate the least. I'm reluctantly good at it. So yeah, I'd be happy to look over your accounts for you if that's what you'd like."

Marina smiled widely. "I'd definitely like that."

And that was how I spent the rest of my day, holed up in Marina's camper, working on spreadsheets. It was a twisted sort of joke. I'd run away with the circus in order to escape all this, and here I was doing exactly what I was trying to get away from. Still, the familiarity of the task soothed me while I tried to get used to the fact that I definitely wasn't in Kansas anymore.

It turned out that the Circus Spektakulär was actually raking in a decent profit; however, the records of those profits were an out-and-out mess. I still had a lot of tidying up to do, but I told Marina I'd continue working on it tomorrow morning. For now, I needed something to eat and some sleep.

It was starting to get dark when I found Violet and Lola back at our camper. They were sitting on folding chairs outside, eating noodles and drinking wine while listening to the soundtrack from *Les Miserables*.

Before I could feel awkward about asking for food, Lola told me to help myself to the last of the noodles in the pot. There wasn't a third folding chair, so I sat on the grass and hungrily shovelled down the noodles in my bowl. They were drowned in some sort of soy sauce that tasted delicious, probably because I was starving.

"I heard Jack and Marina arguing today in the gazebo," Violet said, breaking the companionable silence we'd been sharing. She was looking at me, and I didn't know why.

"Oh, juicy gossip. Do you think they're having a sordid sugar momma/boy toy love affair?" Lola asked with intrigue, and I couldn't help but laugh.

Violet narrowed her eyes at Lola. "Don't be disgusting."

"What? Those two spend an inordinate amount of time together."

"That's because she's, like, his substitute mother figure or something," Violet said before giving me a pointed look. "And no, they were actually arguing about you, Lille."

I almost choked on a noodle. "Me?"

"Yep. Jack was giving Marina hell for inviting you to join us. He said we didn't need the dead weight. Marina defended you. She said you were hardly dead weight since you were fixing her accounts for her."

I hated to admit it, but hearing that upset me a little. "He called me dead weight?"

"Jesus, Violet, have a little tact, would you?" said Lola, elbowing her roughly in the side.

"It's okay — I'd rather know the truth. And I'm not surprised. He's been mean to me since we first met."

"Don't take offence," Lola told me in a soothing voice. "We've got a lot of abrasive characters around here, as you can probably tell." She tilted her head to Violet, who was looking the other way and didn't see her. "Besides, Jack McCabe's always had a reputation for being slightly…eccentric."

That piqued my curiosity. "How so?"

"I've just heard that he's a bit of a kinky bastard. You know, into all that bondage shit."

"Those are lies," said Violet. "Jack's a good guy. People just like to make stuff up to entertain themselves." She took a sip of her wine.

"And then there's what happened to Vera. Nobody knows who did it. It could very well have been Jack," Lola went on, her voice hushed.

Violet seemed to shudder. "Let's not talk about that. And being into bondage doesn't make you a rapist, Lola. For Christ's sake."

My heart hammered at that, and now I needed to know more. "Who's Vera?"

Lola looked to Violet. "She should know, Vi."

"Fine, tell her." Violet waved her away and concentrated on her wine glass.

Lola sucked in a deep breath. "Okay, so, up until about two years ago, we used to do some late-night adult-only shows. Vera was a burlesque dancer. People loved her. She was amazing at what she did. Then one day she just disappeared. She didn't take any of her stuff with her, so we knew something bad had happened. The police got involved, and then two weeks later they found her body buried in the woods. She'd been raped and beaten to death. Needless to say, Marina put a stop to the adult-only shows after that."

I gasped, and my stomach dropped like someone had just dumped a tonne of bricks there. "That's horrific."

Lola grimaced. "Pretty much. They never caught who did it. Most people think it was someone from the town we'd been in. Or a passing traveller. But you know, it could always have been one of us."

"Don't say that!" Violet complained. "I won't sleep a wink tonight now."

Lola only gave her a big toothy smile in response, causing Violet to scowl. My mind was racing, heart beating fast, my skin goose-pimpling. I didn't like Lola's insinuation that Jack might be a murderer. Not because I had any sort of affection for him, aside from thinking he was hot, but because I'd been alone with him the other night on a dark, empty street. If he was capable of doing something like that, then I'd been in a terrible amount of danger and hadn't even realised it. I mean, I craved an adventure, the unknown, but I'd rather the adventure be full of fun and excitement than fear and terror.

It didn't take us long to polish off the rest of the wine, and then we hit the sack. Tomorrow was my first day as a proper circus worker. I didn't like the word "carnie," so I refused to call myself one. I made sure I'd brought my face painting kit with me and then settled into bed. I was tired, so I thought I'd sleep right away, but I didn't. I couldn't stop thinking about Vera and what had happened to her.

The following morning, I awoke to the sound of voices arguing loudly. Violet was complaining that Lola had used up all the hot water for her shower. I winced at her high-pitched screeching. Obviously, showering in the camper wasn't going to happen right now, and I needed to wash. So I gathered my things and made my way to the communal showers on site. Even though I wasn't overjoyed by the idea, I felt a sense of satisfaction to know my mother would be horrified by me using anything that had the word "communal" in front of it.

Take that, Mother, I mused, giving her an imaginary middle finger.

Yes, I was a dork.

The weather was warm, so it wasn't such a hardship to shower in what was essentially the outdoors. There were individual wooden cubicles, one side designated for men and the other for women. I slipped off my shorts and T-shirt quickly, then stepped under the spray, yelping when it hit me because it was freezing cold. Thankfully, though, it heated up after a moment.

I took my time making sure I was squeaky clean, because if I was going to have to shower outdoors for the next week, I wanted this one to last. I was nothing if not economical. When I was done, I reached out and grabbed my towel, wrapping it tightly around my body. It was then that I realised just how many things I'd neglected to bring with me. I'd only brought one towel and no flip-flops. I dried my feet as best I could and then slipped on my Converse.

I was coming out of the showers at an opportune moment, and when I say "opportune," I mean the worst possible moment, because I tripped and fell over somebody's feet. My towel slipped off a little, and I had to fumble to secure it back in place before I ended up flashing the entire campsite. And conveniently, Jack's camper van was parked only a couple of yards away from the showers. He was standing outside, smoking and rubbing a hand across his stubbled jaw, casually watching the whole encounter.

"What the hell," I grumbled, and looked down to see who I'd tripped over. A dishevelled-looking man sat passed out against the wall, an almost empty bottle of whiskey clutched in his dirty hand. He was also snoring loudly. I thought I heard a low, quiet chuckle coming from somewhere close by, and I knew it had to be Jack. I was still looking at the sleeping man, wondering who on earth he was. His clothes were in dire need of cleaning, and his long hair was so thick with dirt and grease that I couldn't tell what colour it was. He also had a beard that covered most of his face.

All of a sudden, he shifted, and his eyes began to blink open. I was startled to be met with eyes so icy blue they almost made him beautiful, despite everything else. And God, did those eyes tell a story. They possessed so many layers I felt like I could have spent a lifetime painting the horrors and wonders in each one and still never get to the bottom.

"The fuck are you looking at?" he asked, accent posh London, those icy blues shooting daggers. I noted his accent was completely at odds with his appearance as I swallowed and stepped away, because there was something about this man that was positively chilling. As I did, my back hit something hard and unyielding. I didn't even need to turn around to know it was Jack, because I could smell him. It surprised me that I remembered what he smelled like: smoke, kerosene, and clove oil.

The man on the ground began to get up, but he was wobbly on his feet and fell over again. His whiskey bottle dropped to the ground, the glass shattering.

"Fuck's sake!" he grunted, and looked at me angrily again, like it was my fault he was so drunk he couldn't stand on his own two feet. I felt the weight of a warm hand land on my shoulder just before Jack murmured in my ear, "This is King. He's Marina's brother. He's also a raging alcoholic. You should try to avoid him if possible."

"What did you say about me, you bastard!?"

"Call me a bastard again, and I'll throw you in those showers. We all know you could do with a wash," said Jack, his voice firm and unwavering. It shut King right up. He mumbled a few choice words that didn't bear repeating and then stumbled away.

I still hadn't turned around, and Jack was still standing behind me, hand on my shoulder. "Where does he sleep?" I asked quietly.

"Outside, mostly. Marina only lets him stay in her camper when we're on the road."

"Oh," I said, and tightened the towel around me again. When I turned, Jack's gaze wandered from my wet temples, along the side of my cheek, and down my neck before finally settling in the region of my chest. I felt touched. Hot and flushed. I looked up at him from under my lashes, and he met my eyes then. There was something intense about the way he looked at me, but again, it could have all been my active and fatally hopeful imagination.

"Got a nice little look at you earlier," he said, and I seriously thought I might die of mortification. My skin prickled with awareness.

"*What?*" I replied, my voice so, so quiet.

He didn't say anything for a second, just hummed low in his throat, and it was the sexiest sound I'd heard, possibly ever. Then he took my hand in his. I'd taken the bandage off, but I still had a red burn mark down the centre of my palm. Holding it up, he seemed fascinated as he ran a finger down it gently. It only stung a tiny bit, and the combination of him touching me and the sting caused a strange tingling between my legs. Yep, my vagina was definitely on Team McCabe, even if my brain was waving around big red BEWARE signs like a maniac.

His mouth moved, and there was something intrigued in his expression, like he'd just figured out he'd aroused me, and it both interested and surprised him. He moved closer, eating up my space…and just *stared* at me.

And man, could he stare. I felt like he was telling me a silent story, and it was captivating.

"Could I get by you, please? I need to go get dressed," I said, breaking the quiet. It could have been minutes or hours that I was standing there, but I'd never know. Time moved in strange patterns when I was around this man.

He said nothing, just dropped my hand and stepped out of the way. I hurried off at an unnecessarily speedy pace and practically raced back to the camper. When I reached it, I slammed the door shut behind me and breathed out a long sigh. It took me a second to realise I wasn't alone. Violet and Lola sat in the living area, Violet painting her toenails violet and Lola eating a packet of potato chips.

"You okay, Lille?" Lola asked as she munched, one eyebrow raised.

"Yeah, just uh…."

"Oh, no, what happened?"

"Jack McCabe."

"Shit," she said, glancing away before looking to me again with mischief. "Did you like it?"

"Well, not much happened for me to like, but, God, I can't tell whether he's indifferent towards me or hates my guts, you know."

Violet let out a little laugh, still concentrating on her toenails.

"Oh, in that case, he probably just wants to fuck you," Lola teased.

Now I was getting manic. "How reassuring. Last night you insinuated he might be a murder rapist, and now you tell me this! Can you see how wrong that is?"

"Is it pretty wrong," Violet put in, agreeing with me.

"Hey, I just say it how I see it," Lola said, raising her hands in surrender.

I pursed my lips and went into our room to get dressed. I'd just finished pulling on my jeans and a top when my phone started ringing. And, as though I'd been blessed with a sixth sense, I knew it was Mum. I still wasn't ready to talk to her, but I figured I should get the agony over and done with.

I picked it up and brought it to my ear, answering, "Hello?"

"Lille! Where on earth have you been? I've been driving myself mad with worry."

"Didn't you get my letter?"

"Oh, I got it all right. I swear, you're trying to put me in an early grave! I mean, a circus of all things. If you wanted to travel, I would have paid for you to go euro railing. Have you any idea the kind of people who work in circuses? And it's not even a chain, it's a flipping independent one, run by some eccentric hippy woman. Bernie from the office told me there was a rape in that circus a couple of years back. A rape, Lillian!"

I'd only been on the phone to her for thirty seconds, and already I could feel my throat constricting, my lungs filling with anxiety. This was the effect she had on me. I tried to summon some composure. "It was actually a murder rape, and yes, I know about it. But it was years ago, and everyone's been perfectly nice," I said, almost telling the truth. King certainly hadn't been nice to me, but he was drunk at the time. I was still trying to figure out what Jack was.

"That's even worse! You need to come home right this minute. Where are you exactly? I'll arrange a flight for you at the nearest airport."

It was on the tip of my tongue to tell her I was in Caen, but I stopped myself just in time. There was no way in hell I was getting on a flight home, and if I told her where I was, I wouldn't put it past her to come looking for me. Or worse, pay some sort of professional intervention people to do it for her. My mother was a strange lady, and you never knew the lengths she'd go to.

"I'm not telling you where I am," I said, trying to sound as calm and steady as I could.

"*Excuse me?*"

"I said I'm not telling you, Mum. I'm not a child, and you can't dictate my life anymore."

"Fine, I'll just have the GPS tracker activated on your phone," she replied, like it was perfectly normal.

My voice raised an unnatural number of octaves. "What?"

"You heard what I said, Lillian."

"You're insane."

"I'm your mother, and I care about you. If that's insane, then yes, I'll accept the title," she replied smoothly.

My pulse ratcheted up a notch as I stood from the bed, hurrying from the room with my phone in my hand. I could still hear Mum complaining down the line as I ran to a quiet spot just outside the campsite and smashed my extremely expensive smart phone into the gravel. The screen cracked, but it wasn't good enough. I began stomping on it until it was broken to pieces. There was no way she could track me now. The thing was practically pulverised, but I still kept going. The more broken it got, the more relieved I felt that Mum wouldn't be able to find me. My chest was moving frantically up and down when I finally stopped, trying to catch my breath, my hands on my hips. My heart stopped when someone started to speak.

"Should I call the nearest madhouse? Because that was the craziest shit I've seen in a long time."

It was Jack. Of course it was.

Four

And Lille's heart surely did falter

He was standing several feet away, an amused smirk on his face as he brought a bottle of water to his mouth and drank. I stomped towards him, grabbed the water from his grip, and returned to the phone, spilling the contents all over the cracked pieces. I felt relatively sure Mum wouldn't be doing any GPS tracking now.

"Did you just steal my water?" Jack asked, blinking at me.

"Yes, but it was for a good cause," I replied.

"So what happened? Did the phone call you a bitch or something? Sleep with your boyfriend? Murder your grandmother?"

I couldn't help it — I laughed. There was something hilarious about his completely humourless tone, plus, I was slightly manic.

"No, actually. My mother was going to try to track my location on it."

"Is your mother James Bond? And what, you couldn't just take out the battery and the SIM?"

"I wasn't sure if that's all it takes."

Jack shrugged and studied me for a long moment. I felt exposed under his watchful gaze, and I didn't like it. I wasn't sure if he was going to say anything at all. Then he finally spoke. "Why don't you want her to find you?"

I sighed and walked over to the kerb before sitting down. Jack caught me off guard when he came and sat down next to me, awaiting my answer. There something very obedient and dog-like about the gesture, which suddenly opened my eyes to another side of him. On the surface he was dark, dangerous, and deeply masculine.

But right now, I could see a flicker of an intrigued little boy.

"Because she's crazy and controlling, and the whole reason I took Marina up on her offer to come here was because I wanted to get away from my mother. No, not wanted, *needed*. Living with her was suffocating me."

He seemed interested as he nodded his head and kept on staring. I didn't understand why I was telling him any of this. Jack McCabe wasn't confidant material. I didn't even think he was friend material, and there was a small likelihood that he was dangerous. Still, I kept on talking.

"She's the CEO for a very successful tech company. I guess the control she has in her job translates over to her dealings with me, because she dictates my entire life. Tells me what I can and can't eat, what I can and can't wear. When I get paid at the end of each week from my waitressing job, she takes eighty percent of the money and leaves me with just enough to get by. If I refuse to give it to her, she threatens to kick me out, and I have nowhere else to go, so I have to follow her crazy rules."

"What about your dad?"

"He left when I was a kid. Perhaps he decided to flee just like I did. I haven't heard from him in years."

Jack didn't comment. I might have been mistaken, but I thought I saw a flicker of empathy in his expression. It was either that or bemusement. There was a quiet between us that suddenly felt awkward, so I dusted my hands off on my jeans and stood.

"Well, I, uh, have to go finish off Marina's accounts now. Wouldn't want anyone thinking I'm dead weight around here," I said before I could censor myself, and winced.

Jack's expression didn't waver. It rarely did, which meant I never quite knew what he was thinking. It was incredibly frustrating. He remained sitting there the whole time I walked away.

Later that day, after I'd borrowed a folding table and two chairs from Winnie and Antonio, I went and set up a face-painting station close to the entrance to the circus. It was a good job I'd studied French at school, because I had decent enough conversational skills in the language to get by. Mostly I just had to ask the kids what they wanted to be. I charged five euros per child and managed to paint ten faces by the time the show began. If I could do the same before every performance, I'd make enough money to see me through the summer.

Jack strode by at one point as I was painting butterfly wings onto the cheeks of a little red-haired girl. He paused, tilted his head to see what I was painting, then continued on his way. It was disconcerting that I got chills every time I saw him. He had this aura, though, like you couldn't tell if he was human or a supernatural being wearing human skin.

Inspiration hit me, and I hurriedly pulled my sketch pad out of my bag, scribbling down ideas. I'd have to keep this piece a secret, of course, because if Jack found out I wanted to paint him, I imagine he'd frown so hard he'd break his own face. This picture would be darker than my usual works. Normally, I drew hearts floating out of bodies as two lovers embraced, or raindrops falling into puddles reflecting a woman carrying a brightly coloured umbrella. This picture would show Jack onstage inside the Spiegeltent, dexterously weaving his flames through the air, his tanned skin glistening, as a fire demon that was possessing his body could be glimpsed through the flames.

I had goose bumps all along my arms just imagining it.

60

The show had been on for about an hour when I slipped inside the tent. The Ladies of the Sky were just finishing up their act, and again I felt a pang of jealousy at how beautifully they could control their bodies. I'd seen all three earlier today, stretching outside their camper. Lola had told me that they were all sisters, with only one or two years between each of them. Their names were Mary, Julie, and Molly and they came from America. I'd wanted to go over and introduce myself, befriend them, but I didn't have the courage. Perhaps another day I'd muster it up.

Their act came to an end, and then Jack was emerging in all his fiery glory. Knocking back a mouthful of fuel, he proceeded to blow an explosive blast of fire from his mouth. I wondered what the chances were of him hurting himself, and if there was any long-term damage caused to his body. Surely putting combustible fluids into your mouth meant you inevitably ingested a small amount over time.

I had so many questions that I wanted to ask him, and if he were anyone else I would, but when it came to Jack McCabe, I found my brain forgetting all those questions in his strange and heady presence. I'd like to say I went away then, back to my camper for the night, but I didn't. I couldn't stop watching until his entire act was over. He did the same knife-throwing bit as before, with Marina selecting a volunteer from the audience. I watched keenly, studying his every move, as he interacted with the woman who'd been selected. I was one-hundred-percent sure I didn't see him place his hands on her shoulders like he did to me, nor did he touch her stomach to calm her or hold her hand as he led her to the wooden panel.

Something fizzy and delightful popped in my belly. Perhaps there had been something different about our encounter, compared to the countless other nights he performed the exact same stunt. Perhaps Jack wasn't as indifferent towards me as I imagined. I delighted in the sense of excitement these thoughts gave me as I went about packing up my face paints and returning the table and chairs to Winnie and Antonio. They told me to keep them, that I'd be doing them a favour, since they had way too much stuff clogging up their small motor home as it was. I thanked them profusely and stored the table and chairs beneath Violet's van until tomorrow, hoping nobody would steal them.

I was sitting in the living area, finishing off the ideas for my Jack painting, when Lola came in looking both tired and energised. She had that way about her. I thought of painting a picture of her, too, with tired grey patches under her eyes and contrasting colourful bolts of electricity spouting from her bobbed haircut.

"Hey, you! Everybody's gathering in the gazebo tonight for a late dinner. Pedro and Luan are cooking feijoada. It's a Brazilian stew. Absolutely delicious. Come on!" she said, grabbing my arm and pulling me up. My sketchpad fell to the floor and she picked it up, taking her time to peruse what I'd been drawing before handing it back, an amused smirk on her face.

"Oh, you've got it bad."

"Got what bad?" I asked, feigning ignorance.

"You're too good of an artist for me not to recognise who you're drawing, Lille. Just take my advice — be careful. I've never seen him with a woman, well, other than casual hook-ups every once in a while. You don't want to get hurt."

Little did she know, I really *did* want to get hurt. It was irrational and probably stupid, but I wanted to feel the pain of having my emotions stomped all over. All of the best creative minds in the world had their hearts broken. It's what made their art genuine, vital, human. It had the potential to elevate me from just a "good" artist into a great one.

After closing my sketchpad and setting it on the counter, I allowed her to pull me out and lead me to the gazebo, which I was learning was a sort of eating/drinking/general hang-out area for the circus performers and crew. Luan, Pedro, and the third man in their stunt group, Raphael, were standing by a portable gas cooker, dishing out bowls of stew to those patiently waiting in line. Once Lola and I had gotten ours, she led me over sit on the floor with Winnie and Antonio's eleven- and thirteen-year-old girls, Carrie and Orla.

We chatted with them about their shared crushes on some boy-band star, while Lola braided their hair into identical French plaits. I felt like we were separate from the adults in that moment, but I didn't mind. I enjoyed being able to observe the interactions from my place on the floor. Jack and King sat by a table in the far corner of the gazebo, a bottle of liquor between them. They appeared to be having a deep conversation, and it surprised me. Judging from the way Jack had spoken to King this morning, I wouldn't have thought they were friends. But it was clear now that they were. Jack listened intently as King spoke, and vice versa. I could have killed to know what they were talking about.

I had three glasses of wine with my stew and ended up feeling sleepy, so I went back to the camper and got into bed. It was only ten o'clock. I slept the whole night through and woke up at five-thirty feeling refreshed and ready to take on the day. It was a day for ticking an item off my list; I could just feel it. After I had a quick shower, this time thankfully within the confines of the van, I had tea and toast for breakfast. After that it was still only six-thirty, so I decided to stretch my legs. I walked twice around the campsite, stopping and admiring the lions in their cages for a time.

They were both sleeping soundly, their purring a deep, melodic rumble that soothed something inside me. I knew that technically these animals were predators, but still, I thought I could fall asleep every night to the peaceful sound of their purring. Their paws were huge and fluffy up close. It was at once frightening and totally adorable. Such beautiful creatures. You could tell they were well taken care of. Not like the lions you saw at the zoo or at one of those chain circuses that looked skinny and malnourished. Winnie and Antonio's lions were clearly very much loved.

I continued my walk. I was just passing by Jack's camper when I stopped mid-stride and hid behind a tree. The door opened, and somebody stepped out. I peeked around the tree to see it was Julie, one of the Ladies of the Sky. Her red hair was messy and her makeup smudged. My gut sank. It was clear that she'd spent the night. And it was even clearer when Jack came out behind her. He stood still as she turned back to him, reaching up and sliding an arm around his neck. She murmured something in his ear, gave him a light kiss on the lips, then sauntered away. My heart was thumping loudly now as it simultaneously sank to the bottom of my boots. It became very obvious to me that I was harbouring a crush on Jack, which was why seeing him with Julie was so disappointing. I bet if someone somewhere did a study on crushes, they'd find that a dishearteningly large proportion of them were unrequited.

I willed him to go back inside so that I could scurry away undiscovered, but he didn't. Instead, he sat down on the deck chair outside his camper and began rolling a cigarette. Just my luck.

I was standing glued to the spot, eyes closed, breathing shallowly and waiting him out, when I heard him call, "I can hear you, you know."

My eyes snapped open, but I remained frozen. Did he know it was me hiding here, or did he just think it was a person, any person? I didn't want to show myself, but there was nothing else for it. He knew someone was here, and he was going to discover it was me sooner or later. Sighing, I came out from behind the tree, and his gaze seemed to sharpen when he saw me.

"Sorry," I said. "I was taking a walk when...God, this is ridiculous. I don't even know why I was hiding. I just didn't want to...."

Jack stood and walked towards me, lighting up and taking a drag of his smoke. If I was any other person, I'd probably advise him to quit, tell him it wasn't good for his health. But I wasn't. I didn't nag people about their personal choices. That was my mother. I didn't want to share any characteristics with her. Still, I worried for Jack. Worried about his lungs. Worried about what the fuel he used in his act was doing to his insides.

"You just didn't want to what, Lille?" he asked. His mouth was a straight line, but there was some kind of amusement dancing in his eyes.

My belly did somersaults when he spoke my name. "I didn't want you to think I was spying."

One eyebrow went up. "You didn't want me to think you were spying...by spying on me?"

"I wasn't! I was just waiting for you to go back inside, that's all."

He blew out smoke, looked at the ground. His shoulder-length hair was down, and a few strands fell forward, shielding his face. When he looked up at me, he was so beautiful I almost couldn't breathe for a second. "You're a strange girl."

"And you're a strange boy," I replied.

One side of his mouth went up, and my palms got a little clammy to have him almost smile at me again. I got the feeling that Jack McCabe didn't almost smile very often.

"Boy," he repeated, a statement, not a question.

There wasn't much that was boy-like about him, but I liked how me calling him one seemed to rile him up some. I simply looked at him, not knowing how to reply.

"So, what brings you out here so early this morning? Taking another shower?" he asked, his gaze growing softer as he reached out and took a strand of my dark blonde hair in his fingers. "Damp," he said, voice low.

"No, I woke up early, decided to explore the campsite. The lions are just beautiful."

Jack nodded. "Pip and Skip."

"Huh?"

He took another drag. "The lions. Those are their names."

"Oh, right!" I laughed nervously. "Pip, like in *Great Expectations*. Do you think Winnie and Antonio named him after the character? It's my favourite Dickens book."

"I don't know," he said, withdrawing a little then. There was a moment of silence, during which I struggled with whether or not to go or stay. Yes, I wanted something to happen between Jack and me, however unlikely it was. The problem was that whenever I was around him, I got all antsy, like I was experiencing fight-or-flight syndrome and my brain wanted me to flee even though my body begged me to stay.

"Have you seen the elephants yet?" Jack asked, surprising me.

I shook my head, then jumped a little when he reached out and took my hand. His was big and warm, and I luxuriated in the feeling of his skin on mine, even in such a small way. I tried not to think of what he had just been doing with Julie. I wanted to live in a bubble of denial for a while. He led me to the far side of the campsite, where there was a large grassy field. This was my first experience of feeling not quite right about the way the circus used animals for entertainment. Yes, they were out in the open, the sun was shining, and there were huge pails of water for them to drink from and troughs of cabbage for them to eat.

But technically they weren't free, were they? I couldn't stop staring at the locks around their ankles. They reminded me far too much of the emotional chains my mother had been placing around me my whole life. Similar to the elephants, I was fed, provided with shelter, but I wasn't free. Jack saw me frowning and gave me a questioning look.

"They're prisoners," I said, suddenly realising that although they had seemed peaceful and beautiful to me as they slept, the lions were prisoners, too.

"Not prisoners," Jack replied. "More like property."

"It doesn't feel right."

"No. Very little in this world is right, Lille. All we can hope for is to make it less not right. See these elephants? They might be chained up, but at least they aren't in a cage all the time. At least Jan and Ricky only do the basic sort of stunts that don't require so much cruelty in the training."

I let out a long breath. One of the elephants was drinking water through its trunk. I wasn't one of those overly righteous people who waxed lyrical about how all animals should live in the wild. I'd never been to an anti-fur protest, nor had I ever given much thought to the cruelty of animal testing. Yet being here, being forced to see their captivity with my own two eyes, made my heart pound. And I was certain it was far from the worst kind of captivity that was out there. I guess it's easy to ignore things when they're hidden from your view.

Jack was watching me intently, perhaps trying to figure out what I was thinking. And really, I didn't want to be thinking about the lives of these elephants anymore. I didn't want to feel sad wondering whether or not they were happy, so I changed the subject.

"Your girlfriend is so beautiful," I said gently. "I'm completely in awe of her and her sisters. They must have been training to become acrobats ever since they were little."

His eyebrows moved closer together, creating a broody sort of expression on his face. "Julie," I said, and he stayed silent, so I clarified, "The woman I just saw leaving your camper?"

"I don't have a girlfriend," he replied simply.

Oh, so it was a temporary thing. I can't say I didn't feel a small measure of relief. I should have known, though, since Lola did say she only ever saw Jack with casual hook-ups.

"Sorry. My mistake. So, where are you from? Originally, I mean? Dublin?" Christ, I was getting nervous now, thus the sentence of many questions. Jack nodded a *yes* to Dublin but didn't give me any details. I decided his moment of chattiness was over, so I sat on a rock and watched the elephants. It was an interesting visual when Jack picked a stalk from their feed and approached one of them. He was wearing a T-shirt that looked like the sleeves had been carelessly cut off, underneath a worn dark brown waistcoat, his tanned, muscular arms showing. He was tall enough that he could reach up and run a hand along the elephant's large body. Then he held out the stalk for it to eat.

Wow. The sight of such a strong, vital man feeding a strong, vital animal was kind of arousing in strange way. Then he started to walk away.

I cupped my hands around my mouth and called after him, "Where are you going?"

He turned around and shrugged. "For a walk."

I knew it wasn't an invitation to join him, but I followed anyway. I wasn't beyond forcing my friendship on Jack. He was mysterious and intriguing enough for me to step out of my comfort zone and be the aggressor. To me, some people feel like the lives they've lived are novels. With Jack, I wanted to get my hands on the book and feverishly work my way through the pages until I got to the end.

The direction we walked was away from the campsite, where there were fields upon fields that bled out into the distance. A countryside landscape. Silently, I walked side by side with Jack through the grass. The weather was warm and the ground dry, which kept my shoes from getting muddy.

I breathed in the fresh, summery air and felt peaceful. Then a fly landed on my shoulder, and I could have been imagining things, but I thought it might have bitten me through my thin T-shirt. I slid my hand under the fabric and scratched at my skin, soothing the itch. I remembered that this was the exact spot I'd planned on getting my tattoo. I couldn't believe I'd forgotten about my tattoo!

Determination formulated. I would find a parlour in the city and have my tattoo done today. I'd tick an item off my list. There were no Shay Cosgroves here in Caen to deny me what I wanted. Nobody knew who I was, nor were they afraid of inviting my mother's wrath. I only realised Jack had been watching me as we walked when his voice broke through the quiet.

"What are you smiling so happily about?"

I was still smiling when I answered. "I just thought of something fun to do today. Want to join me?"

I'm not sure why I asked him that. In all honesty, this was one thing I wasn't sure I wanted Jack to be around for. It would be scary enough letting a stranger repeatedly stick a needle in me. I didn't need the added tension of having Jack in the room with his broody eyebrows and intense black eyes, the mask on his face that constantly shrouded his thoughts.

He stopped walking and turned to face me, reaching over my head and plucking a leaf from an overhanging tree. His attention was almost unnerving when he looked at me closely and ran the leaf down the side of my face to my neck. It tickled, and something tightened in the pit of my stomach.

"Fun?"

"You're acquainted with the idea, yes?" I said, closing my eyes for a second and doing my best not to stammer. He was just so close now, close enough to smell. Close enough to feel his potent energy.

He tilted his head to the side. "Are you poking fun at me, Lille, insinuating I don't know how to have fun?"

"Well," I continued bravely, "generally, people who frown as often as you do don't have a lot of it."

"Shall I show you how I have *it*?" he asked, and stepped closer so that my chest was brushing off his. I wasn't a short person, but Jack McCabe had a presence, a presence that could make someone feel positively tiny. I sidestepped away from him, putting some distance between us, and began walking again, practically tripping over my own feet. I could tell he was just behind me, following.

"I'm not in such dire straits that I need to be taught how to have fun by frowning Jack McCabe," I said, trying for casual. "But if I ever run out of other options, I'll give you a call. Like, say, if Angela Merkel isn't available, you'll be next on my list."

I was pushing my luck now, and I knew it. I really didn't know what had gotten into me, but I was in a teasing mood. There was a beat of silence, and then I heard him chuckle. It was scary to know how much his reaction relieved me. You just never quite knew with this guy which way he'd react, and there was still that lingering doubt in the back of my mind. The story of Vera and the fact that Jack could have been the one who killed her was unnerving. Ever since Lola told me the story, I'd been trying to convince myself it wasn't anyone from the circus. That the murderer being a stranger from a nearby town was much more plausible.

It was the only thing that allowed me to sleep at night and embrace this adventure of mine.

"I'm confused — do you want me to come with you or not?" Jack said. "I still don't know what it is you have planned. So, you know, feel free to enlighten me any time."

I looked back at him then. He was still holding the leaf, and he winked. My heart thudded. A wink from Jack

McCabe. This morning was turning out to be one for the diary. If I had a diary, which I didn't. I did, however, have a sketchpad, and I had a feeling I'd be sketching elephants and leaves and winking black eyes for many nights to come.

It was like masturbation for artists: draw the thing that turns you on.

Not that elephants turned me on....or leaves, for that matter.

"I'm going to get my first tattoo," I told him finally, and he let out a little snicker.

"Is this an attempt to defy Mother, Lille dear?" he asked, and I didn't like the touch of mockery in his tone.

"No, actually. I've been planning it for a long time. And I've just decided I don't want you there."

"Oh, no, but I want to come now," he said flatly. Was that sarcasm?

I stopped and turned to face him. I didn't think he was expecting it, because he faltered a little before halting. "Do you know what, Jack? You don't always have to judge people just because they might have had it easier than you. We're all struggling in our own way."

"Lille...." he began, but I didn't allow him to finish. Instead, I brushed past him and strode off, arms folded across my chest. It was obvious that he thought I was some pampered little brat out to slum it with the carnie folk. He probably even thought I looked down on the people who worked in the circus, and he couldn't have been farther from the truth. I envied them, respected them.

When I got back to the camper, Violet was cooking breakfast, and Lola was blow-drying her hair with the tiniest travel hair dryer I'd ever seen. I sat down on a chair and waited for her to shut it off, then asked, "Do either of you want to come into the city with me today?"

Violet shook her head. "Sorry, I can't. I have to practice for tonight's show."

Lola nodded enthusiastically. "I'm in. What are we doing?"

I smiled and answered, "I'm getting a tattoo."

Lola clapped her hands together in excitement, and I went to find my hot air balloon drawing. Soon enough, we'd eaten and were on our way into town, walking along the roadside. Cars passed us by, one or two honking at us. I wasn't sure if they were "get out of the way" honks or "hello, ladies" honks, but it pleased me to believe they were the latter. Then I heard someone call out from behind and turned to see Jack running towards us, waving his hand in the air for us to wait for him.

Five
A tattoo Lille got but Jack did not

"What the hell...." said Lola in confusion. I took this to mean that Jack wasn't normally the kind of man who chased after people. It was more likely that they chased after him...or ran away from him in fear, my brain provided.

"I think he wants to come with us," I replied in puzzlement, perhaps even more confused than Lola.

When Jack finally reached us, he bent over for a second to catch his breath before drawing himself upright. "You left without me." Oh, wow, the way he was looking at me hit me right in the chest, like *thump*. He was just so striking physically that any extremes of emotion in him were quite...arresting.

"I thought you made it clear you didn't want to come."

One eyebrow went up as he shook his head. "I never said that."

We stared at each other for several seconds, almost in challenge, before Lola interrupted with a laugh that seemed to hold secret knowledge. "Okay, you two. Let's start walking, or you'll be having that staring contest all day."

Jack was still looking at me when I fumblingly turned on my heel and followed Lola. Strangely, all the way into town he walked behind us rather than beside us. Lola and I chatted away, and the only sign of participation from Jack was the odd grunt or low chuckle. I really didn't understand why he was insisting on coming with us, because he'd seemed so sardonic about the whole idea earlier.

As we searched for a tattoo parlour, we came by a little curiosity shop selling all kinds of pretty ornaments and trinkets. Lola and I stood by the window, admiring the display. Just behind a big purple vase I spotted a small object and gasped, taking it as a sign. It was a little hot air balloon forged in copper. I pulled out my drawing and unfolded the paper.

"It looks just like my tattoo design. See?" I said, holding the picture out for Lola, aware of Jack looking just over my shoulder.

"Okay, that's spooky. I officially have goose bumps. Go ahead, feel my skin," Lola declared, and held her arm out to me. I obliged her by running my hand over it, and it was true, she did have them. I craned my neck to try to make out the price tag on the ornament. There on the little old-fashioned handwritten price tag it read seventy euros, which was way too pricey, considering I currently had less than four hundred to my name, and I was responsible for supporting myself for the entire summer. It must have been an antique.

"Yeah. I'd buy it, only it's way too expensive. Maybe if I make enough money before the week is through I'll come back for it." I sighed wistfully.

"Sounds like a plan," said Lola before linking her arm through mine and leading me away from the shop window. I turned a little to see Jack still standing there, staring at the ornament. Or maybe there was something else in the display that had caught his eye. A moment later he began following us again.

It took another twenty minutes to find a tattoo parlour, where a French girl with a septum piercing and an undercut told me in broken English that she could do the tattoo, but I needed to have something to eat first. We left her to practice sketching my hot air balloon and went in search of food.

I was delighted when we came across a crepe stand that also sold waffles covered in chocolate syrup – so obviously I went for the waffles. It also surprised me when Jack ate with us, because it felt like he was there to perform some sort of strange guard duties rather than to actually spend time with us. I think his silence put Lola on edge a bit, because at one point she leaned close to me and whispered, "This is…weird."

I only nodded, not saying anything because I thought Jack had heard her, and in a strange way I didn't want to hurt his feelings. I made eye contact with him for a second, trying to convey that I really didn't think it was weird. In fact, there was something both soothing and exciting about his presence. He possessed a stoic sort of strength I felt like I could somehow siphon off for myself. I definitely needed some of his bravery if I was going to go through with the tattoo.

I was happily full of waffles and chocolate syrup by the time we arrived back at the parlour. When we reached the door, Lola went in ahead of me, but Jack cut me off when he put an arm out to stop me.

I turned to see what he wanted and gasped when he lifted his thumb up and dragged it over the corner of my mouth. His lips curved at the edges.

"You had some chocolate there," he explained.

I arched a brow. "You could have just told me, and I'd have gotten it myself." His touch had thrown me off kilter, and I think he knew the effect he had on me, which was why I was getting snippy. It was like he enjoyed the tease, knowing it was never going to lead anywhere. Kind of like the way a cat might toy with a mouse.

He had both hands braced on either side of the doorframe now, penning me in. Bravely, I made eye contact with him, holding my head high.

Out here in the bright light of day, his eyes looked the colour of whiskey. They weren't really black at all. They softened, went all "bedroomy," but you know, I didn't think he realised just how bedroomy his eyes went at times. I think I might have even seen him giving Marina bedroom eyes the other day. So yeah, he definitely didn't know. It must have been one of his default settings.

"And where's the fun in that?" he asked, teasingly. *Okay*, maybe he did know about his bedroom eyes…which only made the Marina thing all the more unsettling. Did he use them on every woman?

"Are you playing with me?" I asked outright. I didn't want to fall victim to the games of his strange and unexpected flirting. I wanted him to know I was onto him. Because, you know, I was such a cool and experienced woman, and I didn't take any shit.

If only.

He feigned a small look of shock. "Me? Never?" His gaze trailed to my lips then, and I recognised a definite expression of interest.

"Stop it," I said.

"Stop what?"

"Stop…what you're doing," I sputtered. "We don't have time for this, and I – I have a tattoo to get."

"Are you sure you want to do this?" he asked before placing a hand on my shoulder and running it down my arm. "Are you sure you want to mark this untouched skin?"

"It's just skin," I answered, shivering, and then winced, remembering his burn scars. Perhaps he couldn't understand why someone would choose to mark themselves in this way. Ridiculously, I felt like apologising to him. It was actually surprising when I noted that he didn't have any tattoos himself, because he looked like the kind of person who would have them.

"Skin is important, Lille. Some marks last forever. You have to decide if they're worth it."

My eyes flickered back and forth between his, somehow feeling like he wasn't talking about tattoos anymore. I swallowed, mustering determination, and stepped backward, pushing the door open with my bottom and escaping his unnerving closeness.

"I believe this is worth it," I said to him with conviction, then turned to greet the tattoo artist. The parlour had an open-plan layout, which meant you were sitting right there for all to see, rather than in a private room. I thought that maybe they only went to the back room to tattoo bottoms, or penises, or something. I didn't even have a penis, and I still grimaced at the idea of having one inked.

Ouch.

Lola sat on a couch, casually flicking through folders of artwork, but Jack didn't sit. Instead, he stood by the wall, folded his arms, and watched me. Great. Like this wasn't going to be nerve-wracking enough already.

The tattooist, whose name was Jasmine, instructed me to lie down stomach first on a mechanical chair that she'd flattened out for me. I realised the error I'd made when choosing what to wear today, because the only way to expose my shoulder and back was to pull my T-shirt off halfway, holding the front to my chest. It was a good job I could turn my head to the side and face away from Jack to hide my blush.

I was probably imagining things, but I swore I could feel his eyes on my body, trailing down my spine, over the flare of my hips. A tingle made its presence known right between my legs. Jack's attention had such an exhilarating effect, even if sometimes I wasn't sure I wanted it.

Jasmine cleaned my skin first, then pressed a stencil of my tattoo onto my back just below my shoulder.

"You look in mirror, see if you like," she encouraged me with a smile. I climbed from the chair, holding the T-shirt firmly to my chest. I frowned at Jack in annoyance when he gave me what could only be described as a lascivious grin. He knew I felt awkward being the semi-clothed centre of attention. Perhaps I should have done the wise thing and come alone.

"It looks great, Lille," Lola enthused, looking up at me from her place on the couch as I turned to inspect the stencil in the mirror. I think she saw me glancing nervously at Jack when she said to him, "I don't have a disease, you know. You can come share this lovely big couch with me. You won't catch anything."

Jack very subtly arched his brow, arms still folded over his chest. "I'm fine where I am."

"Oh, for Christ's sake, sit down! You're putting us all on edge, standing over there like the angel of death."

I sputtered a laugh at her wry expression and made my way back to the chair, telling Jasmine it all looked good. I heard Jack let out a long breath before he finally gave in and took a seat beside Lola. The buzzing sound of the tattoo gun came on, a sound I recognised well after my many days spent hanging around the parlour back home, hoping Shay Cosgrove might offer me a job, i.e., the position of girlfriend.

Looking back on it now, my crush felt so juvenile. I glanced at Jack just before Jasmine brought the needle to my skin. Yeah, I'd definitely moved on to bigger and better things. And sadly, more unattainable, too.

It was painful at first – a sharp, dragging sort of pain that was uncomfortable but at the same time tolerable. I clenched my teeth and shut my eyes, trying to meditate. When I shut them, though, all I could see was Jack's whiskey eyes from earlier, staring at my mouth and giving me grandiose notions that he might actually have wanted to kiss me.

Jasmine was almost done when she asked, "You like your boyfriend fill in the last dot of blue here? Some couples, they like to do that. The intimacy," she explained as best she could, a look on her face like she was doing me a wonderful favour. I was struck speechless for a second and was about to set her straight as to my boyfriendlessness when Jack spoke up.

"Yeah, I'll do it." He stood and walked to the chair. What the hell? I glared at him furiously, my expression distinctly telling him no, it wasn't going to happen. But then he knelt down and put his hand on the base of my spine, and I lost the ability to think. "How are you holding up, baby?" he asked deviously, and I heard Lola let out an amused squawk of laughter.

"Just fine," I bit out, and then Jasmine was presenting the gun to Jack and showing him how to hold it. She was basically doing all the work, her hands on top of his, but I supposed this was something certain couples would class as "fun." A special moment, even.

A second later it was over, and I had no idea why I didn't tell them to stop, that I didn't want Jack to be involved. Maybe in the back of my psyche, I did want him to do it. I certainly knew my libido was a fan. Jack's eyes blazed when I sat up, because my T-shirt slipped a little, exposing the top of my breast. I was irritated only for a second before Jasmine showed me my finished tattoo, and I gasped. It was beautiful, almost identical to the picture I'd given her, and it bore the distinct mark of my own work. I felt like I'd just painted onto my own skin, and it would last for the rest of my life.

Incredible.

I was in a daze as Jasmine talked through the aftercare and handed me a card with detailed instructions. She covered the tattoo in cling film, and it stung a little when I reached up to put my top back on. I sucked in a breath, and before I knew it, big, warm hands were tugging the T-shirt down over my head. I stood there, frozen, as Jack set my top back to rights. It was strangely intimate, like we were two lovers who'd just had sex and he was helping me dress afterwards.

I thought I might be dreaming when he leaned close, lips brushing my ear, and whispered, "You've got me under your skin now, Lille."

The way he said it wasn't cocky or teasing; his tone was sombre, regretful. And I was shivering again. I widened my eyes, and Lola gave me a look that asked frantically, *What? What did he say?*

I'd never felt more like the mouse in the whole cat/mouse scenario than I did right in that moment. I could hardly meet his gaze on the way back to the campsite. We stopped at a shop to pick up a few items we needed and then continued on our way. Things seemed quiet at first when we arrived back, but as we got deeper into the campsite, I heard someone yelling. Turning a corner around one of the camper vans, we discovered a heated argument going on between Winnie and Julie.

Drama practically sizzled in the air, and almost the entire circus was there to witness it.

"That lion almost bit my hand off!" Julie screamed, tears streaming down her face while one of her sisters held her back.

"He doesn't bite unless provoked," Winnie countered angrily. "You provoked him, you stupid, bored little girl! You go poking sticks into my animal's enclosure, what else do you expect to happen?"

"I expect you to have *fucking* trained it properly so that it.wouldn't.try.to.attack.me!!" Julie yelled, enunciating each word with a vicious bite.

Winnie turned to Marina, who was standing nearby. "She is an immature spoiled imbecile, and I have had enough. This is not the first time I've had trouble from her."

"She's a lying bitch," Julie cut in, throwing her body forward like she might swing for Winnie, but her sister continued to hold her back. "I've been nothing but nice to her."

"Oh, you call trying to seduce my Antonio nice? Yes, I love it when women pathetically throw themselves at my husband." Winnie laughed disdainfully.

Marina watched the argument unfold quietly, and I couldn't tell if she was bored or angry, or maybe just amused.

Julie gave Winnie the most disgusted look before spitting, "You think I want your husband? He's, like, a hundred years old, and has more hair on his chest than he does on his head. I'm sorry, but I find that laughable."

"What a load of bull," Lola, who was standing right next to me, whispered under her breath. Then she stepped forward, siding with Winnie.

"I have to intervene here and agree with Winnie. I've seen you come on to Antonio with my own two eyes, Julie. We all have."

I glanced at Jack for a second, expecting his attention to be on the women, but he was looking at me, frowning. I wondered if he felt embarrassed that I'd seen Julie leaving his camper this morning, since it was now quite clear she was a just a little bit of a bitch.

Beautiful, yes, but also the kind of woman who goes after other women's husbands and provokes lions.

"Thank you," said Winnie, nodding gratefully at Lola and putting her hands on her hips as she returned her attention to Julie, who proceeded to burst into tears. When she spotted Jack standing there, she ran to him, throwing her arms around him in distress. He stood still, seemingly not knowing what to do for a second. It would almost be funny if it hadn't made me so jealous. He patted her hair, and I saw Marina give him an exasperated look. He just shrugged and led Julie away.

Suddenly, I realised that there was a whole history among these people that I knew nothing about. A whole set of intertwined relationships, feuds, and allegiances. It made me feel a little like an outsider.

"Okay, everyone, back to work. The drama's over. There's nothing more to see here," said Marina, shooing the circus workers away. She went and spoke a few quiet words to Winnie, placing a hand reassuringly on her shoulder. When she saw me, her eyes lit up in a smile.

"Lille, how are you? I have to thank you for all the work you've done on my accounts. Everything's so organised now, it's like a dream. Come, have tea with me."

I allowed her to lead me back to her camper, where she sat me down on the couch and went about turning on the kettle. There was a loud thump on the door, and when Marina went to answer it, I heard a gruff male voice muttering to her, sounding annoyed.

"You'll find no alcohol here, King, so you're out of luck. It's about time you sobered up, anyway."

I heard rather than saw it when he slammed his hand into the side of the camper and swore loudly. My heart jumped in my chest.

"Just give me a fucking drink, Marina. I swear, just one more, and then I'll quit. *Please*."

There was a struggle in her voice as she said, "No, I won't. I can't enable you anymore. Now please go. We've had enough drama on this campsite for one day."

She slammed the door shut and took several deep breaths before turning back to me. "Sorry about that. He's my brother. I love him, but the man is going to kill himself if he keeps drinking."

"It must be difficult," I said sadly.

She sighed and walked to the kitchen, lifting the kettle and pouring the boiled water into a teapot. "It is difficult. King's lived a bizarre life. If you could have seen him in his day, you'd never connect the man he was then to the man he is now. He's not a bad person, but his addiction makes him horrible to live with at times."

Her words had my mind racing with questions I wanted to ask, but I felt it might be rude. I went with something simple. "King's a very unusual name. Is it a nickname?"

She shook her head and set the teapot down on the table, pouring us each a cup. "No, it's his surname. His given name is Oliver, but nobody ever calls him that anymore."

"But your surname is Mitchell."

"That's right. We're only half-siblings. Same father, different mothers. That's why there's such a large age gap between us."

"So you weren't raised together?"

Marina lifted her cup to her mouth and took a sip. In contrast to how distressed she'd been a moment ago, she now seemed relaxed and open. "Oh, goodness, no. King and I had very different upbringings. My mother was a lounge girl...King's mother was a concert pianist. British upper crust. So you see what I mean when I say life used to be a lot different for him."

Well, that was certainly interesting. I wondered what great tragedies must have befallen him to bring him so low. Not that living with the circus was low, but he didn't even have a camper van. From what I could tell, he slept rough most nights. A small pang of emotion swept over me as I considered the loneliness of an existence like that, the pain he must be going through.

I thought back to the first time I'd seen him the other day, and how I'd felt like his eyes held a multitude of experiences, sinner and saint all rolled into one. I was about to ask her more questions when I realised that King wasn't really the person I wanted to learn about. Jack was just as much of a mystery, one that pulled at my curiosity far stronger than anything else.

As we drank our tea, I tried to figure out a casual way to work him into the conversation, but then I didn't need to. Marina did it for me.

"I saw you show up with Jack today while Winnie and Julie were arguing," she said, and her observation made me self-conscious. It felt like Marina saw a lot more than most people. I tucked a strand of hair behind my ear.

"Yeah, he, uh, came into town with me and Lola."

"Really? Did you ask him to come?"

I wasn't sure what she was getting at, but I answered anyway. "Um, yes. Well no, actually. I invited him, but then he was rude, so I withdrew the invitation. Then he decided he'd come anyway."

"You know," said Marina, plucking a biscuit from the plate on the coffee table and taking a bite, "I first met Jack a number of years ago in Dublin. He was practically still a boy back then. Had been performing fire tricks on the street for passers-by. His skill at such a young age was incredible. I'd never seen anything like it. So I waited until he was done and expressed an interest in recruiting him into the circus. I tell you, I'd never come across such a mistrustful creature as I did when I first met young Jack." She paused and chuckled.

"He was angry at me, came right out and said he wasn't a gigolo. He thought I was trying to buy sex from him when I'd made the suggestion of work. It was a terrible misunderstanding. I left, but returned the next day and tried to convince him that I wasn't a madam or some washed-up old woman looking for sex, but that I ran a circus and I thought he'd be ideal to perform with us. Still, he wasn't having any of it. I gave him a card with my information, and every time I saw him chuck it in the bin. I knew real talent when I saw it, and I wasn't going to give up on him. So I came back every day for a week until he finally agreed to have lunch with me. And the rest, I guess, is history. But my point is, Jack doesn't trust easily. I've seen him in your company a number of times now, and it's heartening. The fact that he's letting you in means something." Reaching across the table, she took my hand and gave it a soft squeeze. "Promise me you'll be careful with his trust, Lille."

There was genuine affection in her voice, and I knew that, for whatever reason, Marina cared a great deal for Jack.

"I will be, I promise."

"Thank you, love."

A moment of quiet went by before I spoke. "You know, he may not be as mistrustful as you think. I've seen him with Julie…."

Marina cut me off with a sound of derision. "Jack doesn't trust Julie. I think we both know what that relationship is all about. It's a friend he needs, not a pair of open legs. You, Lille, are his friend. He needs a friend."

What she said took me by surprise. Was I his friend? I wasn't sure my feelings for him were entirely friendly. In fact, I was certain they weren't. Still, there was such hope in Marina's eyes that I felt I needed to make an effort to be his friend. Whatever had happened to him to make him so untrusting of people must have been horrible, so I supposed, despite his behaviour sometimes, he deserved a friend he could trust. I resolved myself to being that person. It would also allow me to tick an item off my list. I'd thought it contained only selfish endeavours, things that would make me feel better, make *my* life better, but I was now seeing that wasn't the case at all. I could use my list as a means to make better the lives of those around me, too.

Yes, Jack would be my number seven:

Make a new friend.

Six

Jack's brother was in the paper

"I wish I could have a flower for a nose and butterfly wings for ears," said the little girl whose face I was painting red like a ladybird. Her name was Bea, and she was the daughter of one of the circus workers. She seemed to always be running around the place unsupervised, so I tended to spend a lot of time with her, mainly because I worried she might get lost or hurt if left alone. I was a worrier like that, which was why my lofty dreams of adventure often didn't pan out.

"I don't like the way noses look. They're ugly. Ears are ugly, too."

I laughed loudly. How could I not? The things children came out with sometimes were just crazy. "I tell you what," I said fondly. "I'll paint you a portrait, but instead of a nose, you'll have a flower, and instead of ears, you'll have the prettiest little butterfly wings anyone has ever seen."

She blinked at me and cocked her head curiously. "What's a portrait?"

"It's a picture of you. Like, the same as if someone took a photograph, except it's a painting."

This explanation seemed to excite her. "Really? You'll paint a picture of me? Do you think Daddy will let me hang it up on our wall?"

"Maybe. You'll have to ask him," I answered as I coloured in the black dot on her cheek.

Bea grinned widely and wiggled happily in her seat just as Pedro and two other men stopped by. They were labourers who assisted with various things around the circus. To be honest, I didn't really like the look of them.

They had hard eyes, and their personal hygiene left a little to be desired.

Perhaps one of them is Vera's murderer, my brain put in. I hated that I thought it, because I was judging them purely by the way they looked.

"Lily white," said Pedro flirtatiously. "You look very sexy today. Maybe you'd like to come join me and my friends in the gazebo for a drink."

"I'm busy with Bea at the moment, but maybe some other time," I replied, nervousness formulating in my gut. I was uncomfortable and just wanted them to move along. There was something about the interest in Pedro's eyes that unsettled me, like he'd already stripped me naked, had his way, and disposed of me all in the space of a moment. It kind of made my skin crawl. Also, he and his friends were drinking cans of beer in the middle of the day, which just felt off to me. Not to mention one of them was smoking what was clearly a joint. I tried to focus back on Bea, wishing they'd just leave, but they kept standing there, bantering back and forth.

"I have to go pee now," Bea said, and hopped off her seat. I'd finished painting her face, but I'd been drawing it out, hoping to look busy to Pedro & Co. I swore under my breath when one of the men grinned and said, "Looks like you're free now. Come on, let's go have some fun."

"That's very kind of you to offer, but no, thank you," I replied politely, focusing on putting away my paints.

Pedro chuckled and looked to his friends. "She's so fancy, isn't she? We don't get fancy around here very often, Lily White."

I swallowed, fiercely disliking the nickname he'd given me, but didn't comment on it. I felt like engaging them in any way would only lead to trouble.

"I like fancy," said one of the men. "Nothing tastes sweeter than fancy pussy." He smacked his lips together, and I cringed inwardly. Coming from a small town and living with an overbearingly strict mother, I wasn't used to lewd talk, especially lewd talk directed at me. A sick feeling grew in my belly.

Stuffing all my things in my bag, I slung it over my shoulder and made a move to leave, but Pedro stopped me. I was actually a couple of inches taller than he was, but he had muscle on his side, and there was something distinctly intimidating about him despite his smaller stature.

He gripped my arm, and it wasn't friendly. In fact, his fingers dug into me in a painful way.

Cocking his head, he asked, "You think you're too good for us, huh?"

I swallowed. "Of course not. I'm just very busy, that's all, and I don't usually drink alcohol during the day, so…."

"You looking down on us for drinking, eh?" Pedro bit out, and turned to look at his friends, his fingers still digging into my arm. "Pity fancy is usually snobby, too. I should teach her a lesson. Stupid fucking uppity bitch." The alcohol on his breath told me he'd had quite a bit to drink, so maybe that was the beer talking. Still, the way he spoke was upsetting. I could feel tears catching in the back of my throat, apprehension clenching in my gut. I wished someone would come by and help me, but we were at the front of the tent, and most people were in their motor homes or at the gazebo having lunch at this hour.

"Let go of me," I pleaded, trying to keep my voice even.

Instead of letting go, Pedro pulled me closer so that our bodies collided. His grip was like steel. "You're gonna come have a drink with us as an apology. Make things right. Then we'll let you go."

He dragged me forward, and I stumbled over my own feet. Pedro slid his arm around my waist, still holding tightly. I suspected he wanted to make it look like I was going with him willingly to the people in the camper vans we passed by. I tried to break out of his hold again, but he only gripped me harder, held me closer.

We were passing by a van that I realised was Jack's when I heard a low voice swear, "What the *fuck*."

"Jackie boy, we're going to have some fun with this one. Want to come?" one of the men asked. I turned my head, desperation in my eyes when I looked at Jack, and I saw the anger plain as day on his face. He strode forward, fuming, and used both hands to push Pedro away from me. "You don't fucking touch her, you hear me?"

I stared wide-eyed at the scene that unravelled. "Are you serious, bro?" Pedro asked, wearing an indignant expression.

Jack looked at me. "Did you want this dickhead's hands on you?" he asked, and all I could manage was a fervent shake of my head. "Yeah, I didn't think so. And I'm not your bro. Are you so hard up you're forcing women to spend time with you now, Pedro?"

Pedro spat on the ground and grinned viciously. "She wants it. Just needs a little convincing, that's all. Bet she'll be a nice tight little fuck."

In a blur Jack swung for Pedro, laying a hard punch to his jaw, and I heard an awful *crack*.

"Oh, Jesus fuck, did you just break his face?" one of the men exclaimed, looking bleary-eyed.

Pedro was grunting in pain, kneeling on the ground and holding onto his jaw. "I'm going to fucking kill you, McCabe," he seethed.

Jack stepped forward and towered over him, flashing his teeth menacingly, his threat low and eerily calm. "Try it."

For the first time, Pedro looked genuinely frightened as he crawled to his feet, still holding his jaw. "Come on, boys, let's get out of here."

They all scurried away, and I stood there, several feet between me and Jack. Once they were gone, he seemed to deflate, running a hand through his long hair and cursing under his breath.

"Thank you," I whispered. The tears that had been clogging my throat made my eyes grow watery. I was so unbelievably grateful for what he'd done, but there was an air about him that made me wary. I wanted to hug him in gratitude, but my body remained frozen and stiff. Jack advanced on me then, but stopped just when his chest brushed mine. His voice softened considerably when he lifted his hand and ran his knuckles down the side of my face.

"I told you. I told you coming with us was a bad idea, but did you listen? No, you didn't. You put your trust in a bunch of strangers. Can't you see how stupid that was, Lille? For all you knew, we could have had some kind of human-trafficking gig going on the side and sold you into a life of slavery or prostitution. You never would have seen your family again." He swore, dragging his fingers through his hair yet again, and looked to the side. When he turned back to me, he met my eyes dead on. "You have to learn that you can't trust people."

I swallowed down all of the emotion that had formed like a ball in my throat and met his eyes. "I just wanted to escape," I whispered so, so quietly.

"And you could have been escaping, only to be captured. This work, this place, it's not safe for women all alone."

What he said irritated me. "What about Lola? And Violet? They're alone, and they've survived just fine. Look, this whole thing was just a bit of bad luck. Pedro and his friends were drunk and acting stupid. I'll know to stay away from them in future. But thank you for helping me. I'm not sure what might have happened if you hadn't, and for that I owe you one."

At this I shocked even myself when I threw my arms around his neck and pulled him in for a hug. I heard him suck in a breath as I pressed my body to his and rested my face against his hard chest.

Hug me back. Please, hug me back, I silently urged him.

He was still for a second before I felt him accept my embrace, his arms going around me, returning the hug almost too tightly. We stayed like that for a long time, standing on the grass outside his camper, birds chirping in the trees nearby. In the distance, I heard one of the elephants make a noise with its trunk that reminded me of a brass horn.

Jack's face moved, and I could have sworn I felt him press a kiss to the top of my head, his lips in my hair. Then he murmured, "Come on. I'll walk you back."

He pulled away first, and we began walking. I kept my eyes on my shoes, embarrassed and wondering if he felt awkward that I'd hugged him. When we got to Violet's camper, I asked him if he wanted to come inside. I didn't expect him to say yes, so when he nodded and followed me in, I had to stifle my surprise. Lola was sitting on the sofa, earphones in as she watched YouTube videos on her phone. She saw us and smiled, greeting us loudly, "Hey, you two!"

I gestured for Jack to sit down, and poured him a glass of water. He hadn't even asked for it, but I felt like I had to offer him something, and I had nothing else. I sat across from him at the table and a few minutes of semi-awkward silence passed, Jack and I looking at each other and then intermittently looking away. Lola started talking, pulling her earphones out, completely unaware of the tension between us.

"Oh, my God, you have got to see this, Lille. I've been watching this guy's videos for the past hour. He's amazing. Everyone online is going crazy for him." She came and pulled up a chair beside me, laying her phone on the table and hitting "replay" on a video. The caption read: **Jay Fields Amazes Yet Again!!**

In the video, a tall, attractive man with light brown hair and lots of tattoos stood on the street, shuffling a deck of cards in a way I'd never seen before. The cards practically did somersaults as his lightning-fast fingers simultaneously spun them into the air and effortlessly caught them again. He approached a woman standing in front of him and held out the deck.

"Okay, darlin, pick a card, any card."

I was so engrossed in the video that I startled when Jack's chair squealed across the floor and he stood abruptly.

"Hey, what's wrong?" I asked in concern. His face was pale, and he looked like he'd seen a ghost.

"I have to go," he said, turning and exiting the van in a rush.

Lola and I exchanged a bemused glance before I got up and followed him out. I called after him, but he kept stomping away. We'd reached his camper by the time I caught up with him, reaching out and tugging on his arm.

"What the hell is wrong with you?" I said, trying to catch my breath.

Jack stood by the door to his camper. His shoulders sagged. "Just leave me alone, Lille."

He turned to me then, and there was such sheer agony in his eyes that my heart almost broke. Marina was right — Jack did need a friend, and I was determined to be one for him.

I reached down and slid my fingers into his, my voice soft as I said, "Let me be your friend, Jack."

My words seemed to strike a chord in him, because I'd never seen him look at me so fiercely. A raindrop landed on the tip of my nose as a light shower started to fall.

"Can we go inside?" I asked, indicating the falling rain.

Jack seemed to struggle with whether or not to let me in, and then finally he nodded and tugged on my hand as he opened the door. Inside his camper was warm, and it smelled so strongly of him it was almost dizzying: clove oil, mint, and something that was a lot like burnt embers. The living area was tidy but worn; the whole place was very much lived in. I saw the door to his bedroom was open; a navy blanket lay messily on top of the duvet, and on the floor was a stack of old books. I tilted my head to try to read the spines, but before I got a chance, Jack pulled the door closed. I startled, embarrassed to be caught looking in his room. My cheeks heated, and without being invited I went and sat down on the sofa, which, like in most of the campers, was built into the furnishings. It was upholstered in a dark green tartan.

"Do you like living here?" I asked, my palms growing sweaty. The camper felt so small, but that was probably just because Jack had such a presence. He had this way of filling up empty space like no one I'd ever known before.

He rubbed at his stubbly jaw, finally coming and sitting down beside me. "Ah, it's hardly a palace, but it does the job."

I nodded, eyes roaming the space so I wouldn't have to look at him. There was an intensity about his demeanour that I found difficult to absorb head-on.

"You should see the room Lola and I share. It's so tiny you can hardly fit between the beds without standing sideways. And she has so much *stuff*. I swear, I'm going to go crazy from all the clutter pretty soon."

Jack gave me a soft smile, and I continued to ramble, joking, "She thinks Violet is grumpy, but I wonder if it's just because she's had to live with Lola for so long. She talks in her sleep, too. Some nights I wake up thinking she's trying to talk to me, but it just turns out she's mumbling nonsense to herself."

"I could see that getting old very quick," Jack offered, and my heart leapt that he was engaging me.

I laughed. "Oh, yeah, big time. You don't have a spare bed, do you? Maybe I could come and live here if it all becomes too much."

When I looked at him, his gaze grew heated. "No spare bed. Just mine."

I gulped down a wad of saliva and endeavoured to change the subject. "So, eh, anyway, why did you run off back there?"

He stared at me, a thousand stories passing over his face. I was fascinated by him and all his layers. When he didn't answer me for a long time, I began to worry if he would at all.

"I just thought…." He sighed and ran a hand down his face. "Fuck, it was just time for me to leave, you know."

Well, that was a lie if ever I heard one.

"You seemed upset."

He arched a brow, his arm resting along the back of the seat, his fingers almost touching me. I wished he'd touch me. I loved it when he touched me.

"Has anyone ever told you that you pay far too much attention, Lille?"

I laughed gently. "Actually, no, it's more the opposite. Mum always says I've got my head in the clouds. I feel like I'm oblivious a lot of the time." I went quiet, practically whispering the next bit as I looked up at him from beneath my lashes. "But when something *really* captures my interest, I notice every detail."

My words caused a reaction in him. Surprise, maybe? His body seemed to lean closer. "Outside," he began, "you said you wanted to be my friend. Is that true?"

"Of course. I'd very much like to be a friend to you, if you'll let me."

He seemed to be considering my answer, and while he did so, I couldn't stop staring at his mouth. It was wide and masculine, the bottom lip fuller than the top.

"I feel like I could tell you anything," he said then, shocking the hell out of me. "I watched you a lot back at your job in the restaurant. There was something about you…I don't know. Your face was always so…open."

My heart literally plopped right out of my chest at what he said, and I was a goner. Gruff, moody, boorish Jack McCabe was opening up to me, and it felt like I might be dreaming.

"You watched me?" I said quietly.

"All the time."

"I never saw. I thought I was the one who watched you."

"You were. That's why I started watching back." And there it was again, one of those almost smiles that gave me tingles all over. The idea of him watching me while I worked brought on strange, foreign emotions. I didn't know what to think. It was almost overwhelming.

"And what did you see?" I asked, inching closer.

He moved the arm that was resting along the top of the seat, took a strand of my hair, and rubbed it between his fingers. "I saw a girl who smiled at everyone like they were her best friend. It made me worry for you, because the world eats up that kind of openness, Lille."

"If you're not open, then no one can ever come inside," I countered, not really knowing what I meant. I realised Jack read some kind of innuendo in my words, because his nostrils flared and his eyes grew heated. "Tell me why you went away before. Did something bother you?" I asked, bringing the conversation back around again. When his expression went guarded, I knew I was on to something, and I just couldn't let it go.

"You can tell me anything. You can trust me," I urged him, reaching out for his hand, and he let me take it. It was so big and heavy that my hand felt encapsulated. He watched me like a wild animal sussing out another wild animal in the jungle. It felt like I was waiting for years for him to say something. When he finally did, it wasn't at all what I expected.

"That video Lola was showing you of the magician," he began, and I nodded for him to continue. "That's my brother."

"Really? The American guy? That's so cool. So performing must run in your family then," I said, and Jack's brows knit together in consternation as he shook his head.

"No, you don't understand. He's my brother, but I haven't seen him in over sixteen years."

A quick breath escaped me. "Oh, right." A pause. "Are you estranged?"

He looked away, his gaze focused on the raindrops clinging to the window, the weak ray of sunshine breaking through the clouds. "Something like that."

"You can talk to me, Jack. Whatever you say will never leave this room, I promise," I said, and squeezed his hand in mine. For a tiny second, I saw a man crying out for comfort, for somebody to confide in. It was such a stark contrast to the stern, stoic person he came across as most of the time.

Crossing one foot over the other and shifting his body on the couch, he started to tell me his story. "When I was ten, my family's house burned down in a really bad fire. It's where I got my burn scars from."

He stopped and a long quiet followed. I wasn't sure if he was going to continue, but when he finally did his voice bore a distinct strain. "The fire killed both my parents and put me in a coma for almost a year. When I woke up, I was all alone, and when I was well enough to receive the news, I was told that my parents were dead and my brother had been taken to live with my uncle in America. They wouldn't give me any more details than that, but I overheard the nurses talking. They spoke of my uncle and how he'd reacted when he saw how badly injured I was. He told the medical staff that he didn't have the resources to care for a sick kid, so he only took my brother, who hadn't been hurt so badly by the fire. I was put in foster care, and the rest is history."

I swallowed, trying to absorb his sad, terrible story. Thinking of him as a boy all alone simply broke my heart in two. "You never saw your brother again? But how do you know this magician guy is really him?"

"Fields was our mother's maiden name. I can understand why he took it, because he hated our father. Long story short, Dad was a violent drunk, and Jay took the lion's share of the beatings because he was older. When I aged out of the foster care system, I had nowhere to go. I'd always felt too proud to try to locate my uncle and ask for help, but this time I was desperate. When I called him, he was cold and dispassionate on the phone, telling me that neither he nor Jay wanted anything to do with me. I backed off, angry. Then, some time later, I saw a story in the news about how my brother had won this big legal battle against some tabloid that had been slandering him, and I knew it was Jay from the picture. He'd become famous. He had all the money and resources in the world at his fingertips, and he still hadn't tried to come look for me. I could forgive him before because he was just a kid, but not now. So that's what upset me. I don't like being reminded that I have a brother who couldn't give a shit about me enough to check if I was even still alive."

"That's...wow," I breathed, unsure what to say. "Thank you for telling me all that."

His eyes were on my lips when he replied, "Thanks for listening."

The air between us thickened just as somebody knocked on the door of the camper. Then a male voice called, "Jack, you have a rehearsal in twenty minutes."

"I'll be there," Jack answered, and I saw Antonio pass by the window as he continued on his way.

Seeing Antonio reminded me of the fight earlier between Winnie and Julie, and I couldn't help but ask, "How was Julie today? She seemed really upset."

Jack cocked his head towards me. "Do you really want to hear about Julie, Lille?"

"I'm just concerned, that's all," I lied. The look in his eyes told me I wasn't fooling anyone.

"She was fine. The tears come at will for her," he said as he stood and went to pull a drawstring bag from the closet.

"What does that mean?"

He chuckled low. "She knows how to manipulate people, is what it means."

"Oh."

Opening the bag, he began to pull out the torches he used in his act, running his hand along their lengths as though inspecting them for damage. I was still hung up on what he'd said about Julie. I didn't want to voice the thoughts in my head, but I couldn't seem to hold them in.

"If that's how you feel about her, then why are you with her?"

I probably sounded horribly jealous, which I was, but it just made me angry to think someone like Julie could have Jack in the way I wanted him. Yes, I'd set out on a path to be his friend, but that didn't mean I didn't still find him attractive, intensely so.

Jack's brows drew together as he set the torches down on the table. "I'm not with her. I will never be with anyone, not in the way you mean."

"You don't ever want to fall in love, have a family?" I asked, sorrow seizing my chest.

"All of that isn't meant for the likes of me," he answered as he slotted the torches back in the bag. "The things I desire most are not something I'm sure I could ask another person to give."

I didn't really get what he was saying, but the overall sentiment made me sad. No person wants to end up alone. "Everybody deserves love. They just have to find the right person."

He grew agitated all of a sudden. "Christ, let it go, Lille."

His dismissive tone irritated me, and I stood. "You don't have to talk to me like that." I folded my arms and waited for an apology, but none came. He simply indicated the door.

"I have to leave now," he said, and what he didn't say was clear. *You have to leave now.* I felt like I'd broken such ground with him today, only to have him close down on me again. I hated to admit it, but it hurt.

Without giving him another look, I walked by him and out the door.

Seven

Under the sun, Jack watched Lille paint

Since I'd destroyed my phone, that night I convinced Lola to lend me hers so I could look up Jack's brother. I felt like a bit of a dirtbag doing it, but my curiosity was too much to bear. This Jay Fields must have been some piece of work to abandon his sibling like that. Wikipedia told me that he was a stage illusionist with a growing cult following, but aside from a tiny paragraph about his personal life, there wasn't much else in terms of details. There was definitely no mention of a younger brother that he had all but left for dead.

I was more interested in hearing him talk than watching his tricks. I needed to see his personality so I could determine what kind of a person he was. Despite Jack indicating he was done with his brother, I had a feeling he was harbouring a lot of pain on the inside. I hunted down an interview and hit "play." The interviewer was a woman, but you couldn't see her because she was off camera.

"What's most important to you?" she asked at one point. To which Jay replied, "My family, always my family."

I paused on that bit, frowning, and replayed it a number of times, looking closely at his face to see if he was lying. If Jack's story was anything to go by, he had to be. The problem was, all I could read from him was sincerity, and it made me feel like there was more to this than met the eye. If not, Jay Fields was an exceptional liar. He was certainly charismatic enough to pull it off. He had a frisky sort of charm that Jack didn't. Looks-wise, they didn't resemble each other much, either. Jay wasn't as dark as Jack; however, there was something in his mannerisms that was similar, in his facial expressions and the way he moved his body.

The interview was only a couple of minutes long, and the interviewer mostly asked him questions about his magic show and his new wife. Still, I didn't get the feeling that he was a bad person. There was a warmth about him that made me think he wouldn't do something as callous as abandon Jack. Then again, people did all sorts of unexpected things in life. I pondered on the matter for a while until I was too tired to think anymore. Then I gave Lola back her phone and went to bed.

***

The next morning, I went into town early and visited an art shop to buy some supplies. I was running out of face paints, but I needed supplies for my paintings, too. There was an easel for sale in the corner of the store, but it was too expensive. I stared at it longingly and settled for some cheap paintbrushes, oil paints, and a few small canvases instead. I longed for the day when I wouldn't have to care about storing things and could buy canvases as big as I liked. If that day ever came.

When I got back to the campsite, they were serving lunch in the gazebo, some kind of paella. I took a bowl and ate quickly. Jack was sitting with King again. He met my eyes for a prolonged moment, and I felt an intense shiver. As soon as I was finished, I left. I had something important that I needed to do.

The other day I'd spotted some disused bits of wood lying around at the back of the circus tent, and I thought maybe I could salvage a few pieces and fashion a makeshift easel. It was a long shot, but I had nothing else to do with my day anyway. Unfortunately, I didn't count on the wood being so difficult to carry. I had to split it into two runs. On the second, as I made my way back to the camper, I felt the muscle in my arm spasm, and I had to set the load down for a moment.

"What are you doing?" Jack's voice came from behind me.

I dabbed the sweat from my brow and turned to face him as he approached. "Oh, I need the wood to make something. Don't worry, I'm not up to anything sinister."

He smirked a little and stepped forward, easily hefting the wood up with his big arms and looking to me for direction. "Where to?"

"Violet's camper. Um, thanks. You don't have to...."

Jack cut me off with a chuckle. "You're going to do yourself a mischief if you try carrying it the rest of the way. And I'd rather not have to rush you to the hospital just because you're too stubborn to ask for help."

Scowling a little, I walked alongside him, having to work to keep up with his long strides even though he was the one carrying the load. "I'm stubborn? You're the most stubborn man I've ever met."

He flashed me a rare smile, laughing, and when we made it to the camper, he laid the wood down on the grass for me.

"So are you going to tell me about this big secret project or what?" he asked, rubbing his hands on his thighs.

I tried not to stare in that general area, which was difficult. Going to lean against the side of the camper, I folded my arms. "Well, I had this hare-brained idea that I could make an easel out of it, you know, to paint on. It might be a little far-fetched, though, because I don't have any tools."

I must have had a hopeful look in my eye, because he let out a long sigh. He didn't seem annoyed, though. He seemed playful, which I hadn't seen on him before, and it was very appealing. "Is this you hinting for me to make the easel for you, Lille?"

"Well," I said, "you were a little snippy with me yesterday. This could be the perfect way for you to make it up to me."

His smile was fading now, but there was still a hint of it playing on his features. He took a step forward and gazed down at me. "I can think of a few other ways that'd be much more fun," he murmured, and ran his hand down my arm. I swallowed visibly and started to blush, my eyes fixing on the toes of my worn Converse. The quiet between us dragged out for a long moment before he moved away, calling over his shoulder, "I'll be back in a few minutes."

When he left, I could finally breathe again. God, why hadn't I just grabbed him then and kissed him? He was obviously being suggestive. I hated how I was always so hesitant.

Friends, I reminded myself. I was supposed to be trying to be his friend.

Deciding to make the most of the sunny weather, I set up a chair and brought out my sketchpad to start outlining the portrait I'd promised Bea. I thought I had her face memorised well enough that I could do most of it without needing her in front of me. I was lost in the drawing when Jack arrived back, carrying a toolbox and a saw.

He definitely looks good with tools. He'll probably look even better when he's using them, I thought to myself as he set to work. I had something of a dirty mind of late. His fault, obviously. About two hours passed, and somewhere within that time I'd set aside my sketchpad in order to watch him. The view was *pretty fine*. He was wearing the T-shirt with the sleeves cut off again, his muscles moving as he hammered a nail into a length of wood. His skin glistened with beads of sweat.

His back had been turned to me the entire time, which was why I got a little fright when he asked knowingly, "Enjoying the view?"

I didn't even bother to act coy. "Uh, yeah. I am, actually."

I could tell from his profile that he was smiling. Wow, Jack really was in an unusually good mood today.

"Can I get you some water? You must be thirsty."

"I've only been waiting about an hour for you to ask that, so yeah, I'd like some water, Lille. How did you last so long as a waitress, huh?" The teasing lilt in his voice put a bit of a spring in my step as I went inside to get the water. Perhaps we were turning over a new leaf. When I came back out, I handed him the bottle, and he knocked almost the entire thing back in one long gulp, keeping his eyes on me the whole time. It was disconcerting, to say the least. He'd just about finished the easel, and I was taken aback by what he had achieved. It was probably better than the one they were selling back at the art shop.

I walked over to inspect it, running my hand lightly over the wood. "This is so good. You could be, like, a carpenter if you wanted."

"My one true dream," Jack replied with no small amount of sarcasm.

"Okay, whatever, fire boy. I still think this is amazing. In fact, I should probably pay you." I dug in the back pocket of my jeans for my wallet, but he stopped me with a hand.

107

"No payment needed. Think of it as an apology. Like you said, I owed you for being a dick yesterday."

And now I was thinking about dicks, his in particular. Where was my mind today? Oh, right, in the gutter, obviously. Jack put the final touches to the easel, and I invited him inside for a sandwich. It was the least I could do. And since Violet and Lola weren't around, I knew we wouldn't have an audience. Lola was always watching me with Jack, a glint in her eye, like she knew something I didn't.

There was a small Breville toaster in the kitchen, and I went about putting together some cheese sandwiches for us. After sitting in the sun and watching Jack work all day, I'd built up quite the appetite. For food, of course. Well, other things, too, but the likelihood of those happening was slim. I must have been overly eager to get to my sandwich, plus, I hadn't used this toaster before, because I touched the metal part by mistake. It was burning hot and two of my fingertips came away red and raw. I hissed at the pain as I pulled them to my chest, hurrying over to the tap and holding them under the cold running water.

"I'm such a fucking klutz," I complained just as I felt Jack's warmth behind me. When my fingers were about to turn to icicles, he reached past me and shut off the tap. Taking my hand, he dried it off with a dish towel and then led me over to the lounge. His silence put me slightly on edge, but then again, Jack wasn't the sort of person who talked just to fill empty space. He spoke only when he had something to say.

He pulled me down to sit next to him, and we were so close I was practically on his lap. I realised oddly that this was the second time I'd accidentally burned myself in front of him. It was just my luck that I'd keep doing that in front of someone who had almost died in a fire when he was a kid. Someone who had burn scars on his body that would never be healed. He cradled my one hand in both of his, then rubbed his thumb down the centre of my palm. I sucked in a breath at the contact. It still had a mark from where I'd touched the frying pan at work, but it wasn't sore anymore.

All of a sudden, I became aware that Jack was unusually fascinated by the burns. I remembered him back at the restaurant when he'd stared at me with those intense eyes of his, a stare that made me come over all hot and sweaty. I'd thought he was trying to soothe me now, but he wasn't. Well, not in the way I imagined. He was looking at the burn mark and my singed fingertips like they were a work of art, and he was completely captivated. He was so absorbed his eyes practically glowed with it. My mouth felt dry, and my stomach was doing somersaults. The camper van felt so *quiet*. All I could hear was his breathing, which was slightly quicker than usual.

Finally, I broke the quiet when I whispered his name. "Jack."

It was like my voice had reminded him that he wasn't alone in the room, just him and the work of art, because his gaze shot to me, and God, it burned more than the damage I'd done to my hand. In a split second he pushed me back so I was lying on the sofa, and he moved so that his hands were braced on either side of my shoulders. He held himself above me, barely touching me, chest rising and falling with his quickening breaths. My eyes flickered down, and I was startled to see the thick length of his erection outlined against his jeans.

He was turned on. Whoa.

His eyes flickered back and forth between mine, as though asking for permission, and I must have given it to him, because he began moving down until he reached my belly. He pushed my shirt up to just below my breasts, revealing the pale skin of my stomach and abdomen. Starting at my ribs, he began planting kisses downward, and I gasped at the sensation of his warm lips on me. When he reached the waistband of my jeans, he nuzzled the soft part of my belly, then shocked the hell out of me when he slid his hands over my hips and around to squeeze my backside. Quick as a flash, he lifted me and buried his face between my legs. A small yelp escaped me, tingles radiating down my spine and culminating everywhere he touched.

I think I could have come from that alone. He eyed me from below, moving his face back and forth, his nose hitting just the right spot, and I trembled with pleasure, reaching down to sink my hands into his hair. I felt him take a deep breath as though drinking in my scent, and I swear my entire body turned to jelly.

We were so lost in one another that I didn't hear the door open and Lola step inside. I glanced up just as she turned and saw us there in the lounge, and my cheeks grew insanely red.

"Oh, wow, um, sorry to interrupt," she said, and the moment Jack heard her, he pulled away from me like someone had given him an electric shock. I fell back into the seat when he dropped me, instantly missing the warmth of his hands…and his face. When I looked at him, he was standing, striding past Lola and straight out the door. I lay there in confusion, trying to comprehend how we got from me making sandwiches, to his face dry humping my vagina, to him skulking away like he'd just realised what a mistake he'd made.

"Crap, Lille, these sandwiches are completely burned," Lola complained as she unplugged the toaster and sat down in a chair. A moment of awkward silence elapsed between us. In the grand scheme of things, we didn't know one another very well, and she'd just walked in on quite the scene.

"I'm sorry. I'll clean it up," I said, still feeling entirely discombobulated.

"Fuck, I'm so sorry for walking in like that," she apologised, and then a cheeky smile lit her face. "You two should have put a sock on the door handle or something."

"What you saw, it wasn't exactly planned," I told her, fixing my top in place.

"No? So, do tell me, how did it come about? Because I swear, that is one of the hottest things I've seen in a while. He looked like he wanted to devour you from the inside out."

I screwed up my mouth at her description and thought about her question. I didn't really know how to answer it. *Well, Lola, I burned my hand, and Jack got so turned on by it that he practically jumped on me.*

Yeah, I definitely wasn't telling her that. In all honesty, I still didn't know how I felt about it.

"We were sitting on the couch, and it just kind of happened," I lied, shrugging.

"I knew that he liked you, I could sense such a *vibe*," she said, looking happy with herself. "Just remember what I said. Be careful. Enjoy the ride, but don't let your heart get involved, and everything will be fine."

She got up then and began putting some food away in the cupboards. I contemplated what she'd told me with a small feeling of dread. I felt like I'd already allowed my heart to become involved, and he hadn't even kissed me yet. Just over twenty-four hours ago, he'd had another woman in his bed, and I was letting my heart get involved.

I couldn't tell if I was being very, very reckless or just very, very naïve.

Sigh.

Of course, getting my heart broken was on my list, but it felt different in theory. Now that it was a real possibility, I was afraid, afraid of the pain I might have to endure once Jack discarded me. He seemed to be enjoying my company right now, but I wasn't under any illusions that it was going to last.

Would I be able to pick myself up and move on? Be a better person for having the experience? I had no answers to those questions.

The next morning, the sun was shining again. I took a shower on the campsite and managed to get back to the camper without bumping into Jack. I left my hair down to dry in the sun and wore a simple sky-blue dress. I felt light and airy on the outside, but oh, so heavy on the inside.

Setting up my new easel, I placed a fresh canvas on the wood, adjusted the height, and then sat down to paint. Sometime later, a hand swept my hair along the back of my neck, knuckles brushing lightly across my skin. Pleasurable shivers skittered down my spine, and I closed my eyes for a second, savouring the touch, instinctively knowing it was him without having to look.

"That's an odd picture of Bea you're painting," he commented, gripping my neck for a moment before letting go. I swallowed, watching as he went to grab a folding chair that had been resting against the side of the camper and sat down. I was secretly thrilled I'd done a good enough job of depicting her likeness that he knew right away it was Bea. He had a bottle of water with him, unscrewing the cap and taking a long drink. Staring at his profile as he drank made me feel flush as I remembered the previous evening, how he'd kissed his way down my stomach.

"She asked for it. I think it's pretty," I replied, ogling him and dabbing my paintbrush into some yellow paint. I wasn't sure why he'd decided to hang out with me, but I was pleased by the turn of events. A tiny part of me relished the fact that I never quite knew what he'd do next. We sat in companionable silence for over an hour. Jack alternated between watching me paint and reading a dog-eared paperback he'd brought with him. At the angle I was sitting, I couldn't see the cover to tell what it was.

Violet had parked her camper van in a quieter spot on the site, so not many people passed by. Then I heard women chatting and some feminine giggles approaching us. I turned to find Julie and her two sisters strolling along, arm in arm. I'm not sure why, but I got really self-conscious and itchy, like I was doing something wrong by spending time with Jack. I knew that he and Julie weren't a couple, but still my anxiety wouldn't abate.

"Hi, Jack," Julie called to him with a little finger wave. I pretended to focus on my painting as they drew nearer, while at the same time listening intently to the conversation that followed. Out of the corner of my eye, I saw him nod to the sisters and return his attention to his book. They stopped, and Molly asked, "What are you reading, Jack?" There was a flirtatious tone to her voice. "I do love a man who reads." The other two giggled.

When Jack didn't answer her, she ducked her head to see the cover and laughed. "*The Hardy Boys*? You do

113

realise those books are for children, right?" All of a sudden, her tone was mocking rather than flirtatious, and I grew tense. When I glanced up, I saw that Julie's blue eyes were trained on me while her sisters focused on Jack. Her mouth had formed an unhappy thin line. Swallowing, I kept dabbing my brush to the same part of my canvas, hoping she'd lose interest in me.

"Fuck off, Molly," Jack replied, all matter-of-fact, and she let out a squeak of outrage.

"No need to be rude! I was only teasing."

"Being a bitch, more like," said Jack dismissively.

"You're the face-painter girl, aren't you?" said Julie, walking around to look at my canvas. I felt uncomfortable under her attention and had never really liked people looking at my half-finished works. She was so petite and well-formed, slim but muscular in an attractive way, that I felt myself deflate. How the hell could I compete with that?

I mustered a smile for her. "That's me."

She glanced at my painting, found nothing of interest, and then stepped away again. I soon discovered that she wasn't a woman to beat around the bush when she waggled her finger between Jack and me. "So, what's going on here?"

I was opening my mouth to say something, I wasn't quite sure what, when Jack addressed her firmly. "Lille is painting. I'm reading. The three of you are interrupting."

"Well," said the third sister, Mary, "we know where we're not wanted." She tugged on Molly's arm and the two walked away, but Julie remained.

"That's not what I meant, and I think we all know that."

Jack set his book down then and stared at her head on. He didn't have to say a word, because the look he gave her

114

was silencing enough. In a split second, she completely changed her tack, taking a strand of hair and twirling it around her finger.

She coughed to clear her throat. "Well, um, will I see you around the gazebo later? We're having spaghetti bolognaise tonight, I think."

"That's where I usually eat," said Jack.

She skipped forward, leant down, and placed a kiss on his cheek. "Okay, great. I'll see you later, then."

Her attention flickered warily to me one last time, and then she left. I nearly laughed when I saw Jack roll his eyes before they slid to me and he frowned. "Sorry about that."

I raised my eyebrows. "No need to apologise. It's none of my business."

The look he gave me seared me to the core, his voice dropping so low I almost didn't hear him. "The fact I can still smell you on me says different."

I'm sure I flushed bright pink at his words. My paintbrush had been levelled on the canvas, and I'd completely messed up Bea's butterfly ears. I tried to keep my voice steady as I whispered, "Don't play games with me, Jack."

He ignored what I said, his face taking on a contemplative expression. "I wonder if we hadn't been interrupted yesterday, would I have been able to make you come like that?"

I swallowed deeply and glanced at him. His eyes held a thousand dark, carnal promises, and I felt completely lost, had no idea how to respond. He made a noise that sounded a lot like a growl then as he came and knelt before me, his hands cupping my knees and spreading my thighs apart so he could get between them. Next, he began running his hands up and down my thighs; they were so much warmer than the afternoon sun, and I was suddenly melting.

"Do you come sweetly, Lille? Do you shake? Do you moan and beg for release?"

I licked my lips and moved my attention from his eyes down to his mouth. I was so worked up I felt like pushing him to the grass and taking my pleasure from his perfect, beautiful body without asking for permission. I knew I'd promised myself I'd be his friend, but maybe I could be his lover, too. You didn't always have to sacrifice one to be the other, right?

I drew my gaze up to his eyes again and told him honestly, "You're embarrassing me, Jack."

His thumbs rubbed at my inner thighs, and I trembled.

"Am I making you wet, too?"

Air left my lungs in a single *whoosh*, and I closed my eyes, unable to look at him as I answered, "Yes."

In the next second, his hands were travelling up to my neck, sinking into my hair, and my entire body felt a pull towards him like he was a magnet and I was a piece of metal. My face fell to his neck and I breathed him in, savoured the warmth of his skin. His arms went around me and pulled my body flush with his. I wrapped my arms around his shoulders and hugged him tight. When I pressed a kiss to his skin, my mouth open, tongue slipping out to lick, I felt him shudder in my arms. It stunned me to know my touch could affect him so. Had he been yearning for me the same way I'd been yearning for him?

"Your smell," he growled, breathing deeply. "It drowns me."

If my heart could have exploded out of my chest, it would have.

"Kiss me, Jack," I begged, forcing myself to ask for what I truly wanted for once.

"I can't," he replied with a sigh of frustration.

"Please," I whimpered desperately.

"When I kiss you, it will be everywhere. When I kiss you, I won't stop there. If I taste you, I'll want to taste everything."

I fisted his shirt in my hand, silently cursing the fact that both Lola and Violet were inside the camper at this very moment and Jack's camper was too far away. "Jesus, you're killing me."

His hands roamed my back, my thighs, my neck. All he had to do was slip his hand beneath my dress, and he'd be able to feel me, feel how much I needed him.

With a deep sigh he drew away, his jaw working like it took great effort to restrain himself. "Tonight, after the show, will you come to my place?" he asked, eyes hopeful.

"Yes." There really was no other reply I could have given him. I felt hot and flushed all over, from my temples to the tips of my toes. I'd never been so worked up before in my life.

He brought his forehead to mine and breathed out, the air hitting my skin and strangely cooling it. "Thank you."

Standing, he went to put away the folding chair he'd been sitting in and picked up his book. I frowned, remembering how Molly had mocked him for reading a kids' book. I wanted to know why he was reading it. I mean, I knew adults read kids' books all the time, but this was Jack. He was the last person I'd expected to be into stories like that.

I nodded to the battered paperback. "Is it any good?"

He grimaced, as though remembering that I now knew what he'd been reading. Was he embarrassed? For the first time since I'd met him, he seemed lost for words.

Scratching the back of his head, he finally replied, "Yeah, it's…uh, Marina gave it to me. Well, she gave me a whole bunch of them."

"Oh, right. That was nice of her."

"Yeah. I have to go now," he said abruptly, and turned on his heel. I watched his long strides as he walked away, not knowing what to think.

Eight

Under the stars they came together

I wondered after Jack's abrupt departure whether or not he still wanted me to come by that night. Then I wondered about what he planned on doing with me when I got there, and I became tingly all over. The idea of being with him frightened me a little, but I sucked it up. This was freedom, and I was determined for it to taste good.

The show that evening went over a storm, and there was a buzz in the air. I went to the gazebo with Lola for something to eat, and there seemed to be a bit of a party going on. There were some local women who had obviously come to see the show and were now enjoying an after party. I felt a little grimy in comparison. I was still wearing my blue dress from earlier, and it had paint stains all over; my hands were covered in paint, too, and my hair felt messy. I hadn't had the chance to run a brush through it since that morning.

A space had been cleared for people to dance, and music was streaming from the speakers, some kind of French rap. It was curious. I only caught the odd word here and there, but the basic gist was pretty racy. I guessed that was why Julie was dancing all by herself wearing a tiny slip of a dress. In fact, I thought it might actually *be* a slip. Huh. She shook her hips and threw her hands up into the air before seductively running them down her body and swaying from side to side.

"Excuse me while I go pour some bleach in my eyes," Lola deadpanned before steering me towards a table where Luan, Pedro, and Raphael were sitting. Air got caught in my lungs when I saw how half of Pedro's face was bruised up. Lola sat beside Luan, chatting amiably, and I went to

119

the opposite end of the bench, as far away from Pedro as I could possibly get.

He glanced at me, brown eyes hardening, then knocked back a gulp of whatever drink was in his glass. I got the distinct feeling he wasn't done with me yet, and my throat ran dry.

"Don't mind me," came a hard yet humorous voice from behind me, and I jumped, turning to see I'd almost sat on top of King. I'd been so focused on Pedro that I hadn't noticed him skulking in the corner.

"Sorry," I apologised, and sat down across from him. His eyes weren't as bloodshot as usual, and you could actually make out the colour of his hair now. It was an attractive shade of dark blond. Almost the same colour as mine. Somebody must have forced him to take a wash. I wondered if it was Jack. His clothes were still pretty worn and dirty, though.

His long hair and beard obscured half his face, but I thought he had probably been a very good-looking man at one time. I couldn't really tell what age he was. It was difficult to pin down, due to his appearance, but he could've been anywhere between thirty and forty years old. And his eyes, man, I still couldn't get over them. They were so beautiful and yet so sad.

"I don't think we've properly met yet," I said, holding my hand out to him. "I'm Lille."

His icy blues narrowed on me somewhat warily, but he didn't shake my hand. "I know who you are, love," he said, then looked away over my shoulder where Marina sat with Winnie and Antonio, muttering under his breath, "Stupid meddling old bitch."

There was a harsh, cutting tone to his words that surprised me. He must have seen the wide-eyed look on my face when he went on to explain. "Not you. My sister. The bitch has everyone watching me. Can't get a fucking drink around here to save my life. What's the point of living in a shithole like this if you can't have a drink every now and again, eh?"

"Everywhere's a shithole to you, King," came Jack's voice as he threw his leg over the bench and sat down beside me, his breath whispering over my ear when he said, "Hey."

I glanced at him, getting goose bumps. "Hi."

"Yeah, well, this place really is one," King griped, and pressed his fingers to his skull. "Shitting cock bastards, I feel like someone's trying to drill a hole into my cranium."

Jack laughed. "Your mouth is a real thing of beauty. And the hole drilling would be what the rest of us who actually stop drinking every now and again call a hangover."

"I wish somebody would hang me," King complained. "Do you know that's where the word comes from? Hangover? Historically, when there was a hanging, there'd also be a big street party, everyone boozing it up. Then the next day, when the hanging was over, they'd all feel like a steaming pile of shit, hence the now commonly used term. Kind of fucked up when you think about it. Having a party while some poor old sod gets hung." He paused, his sad eyes growing even sadder. "People are depraved."

"Look at you, using your words. Seems like the alcohol drought is doing you well already," said Jack, and King grumbled. I thought that maybe Jack was the only person in this whole place who King allowed to tease him like that.

All of a sudden, the music got louder, and we all turned to see that Julie had gotten up on a table to dance. The straps of her dress had fallen down and hung low around her arms, showing more cleavage than before, along with the top of her black lacy bra.

"Red's putting on a show for you, McCabe," said King, letting out a cynical laugh that then transformed into a painful-sounding cough. Sleeping outdoors must have been wreaking havoc with his body. I shot him a sympathetic look, which he didn't appear to appreciate.

Jack waved him away. "She puts on a show for everyone. Nothing special there."

King began coughing again, and Julie continued to dance her way across the tables, finally reaching ours. Her eyes were honed in on Jack as she swayed, then came to a stop in front of him. She licked her lips and ran her hand over her collarbone, then down her chest. I felt myself grow incredibly uncomfortable and a little bit upset. She was pulling out all the stops to get Jack's attention, and it must have been working, because he was staring back at her. I couldn't read his expression, but still, the fact that he was looking at her made me feel about two inches tall.

Invisible, really.

"*Licence my roving hands, and let them go,*" King began loudly over the music, "*before, behind, between, above, below.*" The way he spoke made me think he was quoting from somewhere, but I didn't recognise the lines. Julie turned to him and scowled. He was ruining her performance.

"*Before, behind, between, above, below,*" he repeated. "But if you let them all go, what is there left for anyone? What is there left for you?"

He was talking in riddles, but Julie still seemed annoyed. She kicked her leg out in a calculated move that hit King right in the shoulder. He went flying backwards and almost fell off the bench.

122

"That's right," he coughed, "hit a man when he's down."

Julie narrowed her eyes and leaned over to him. I was the only one close enough to hear her whisper-hiss, "You're no man. I bet your cock is necrotic by now."

When she turned around she was smiling again and I sat there in shock. She definitely didn't know that I'd heard her. What a cruel, cruel thing to say. King might not have been the most pleasant person in the world, but it was obvious that he was the way he was because he was suffering.

I looked at him and saw genuine hurt on his face. Without thinking, I reached across the table and took his hand into mine. I don't know why I did it. I guess I was just driven to comfort people when they were in pain.

"Don't listen to her," I told him, and at the same time he swiped his hand from my grasp.

"I don't need your sympathy, girl," he said, then got up from the bench and walked directly to a table of men who were drinking cans of beer. There was a half-full bottle of whiskey sitting right there in the open, and I was the only one who saw King swipe it, tuck it inside his coat, and walk right out of the gazebo.

Julie was still dancing in front of Jack. She sashayed down to her haunches, then climbed onto his lap. His hands went to her hips to steady her as she gyrated for him. Ugh, I really couldn't take much more. Standing, I took a leaf out of King's book and left. The campsite was dark, lit only by the lights that shone from inside the camper vans.

A chill ran down my spine, because the silence out here seemed punctuated by the loud music in the gazebo beyond. My throat felt tight and my eyes watered, emotion clutching at my chest. The past few days with Jack and me growing closer had really done a number on me. I'd gotten my hopes up. But what was the point in hoping when there were always going to be women like Julie throwing themselves at him?

I felt lost.

When I finally reached the camper, I sat on the grass outside, burying my face in my hands. Nobody could see me out here, so I let all of my pent-up emotions flow free. In other words, I cried. I was feeling so strange, an odd mixture of homesickness and lovesickness. I didn't want to go home. I didn't want to have feelings for Jack, and yet I found myself drowning in both of those things. I longed for the comfort of my own bed, but I didn't want to be anywhere near my mother. I yearned for Jack's strong arms to surround me, but I didn't want to deal with the way he made my lungs feel like there wasn't enough air to breathe.

Footsteps crunched on the grass, and I looked up to see a tall figure approaching. When he came into view, I saw it was Jack, and he seemed agitated. He'd clearly come looking for me. Just as he was about to knock on the door to the camper, he heard me sniffle. Turning his head, he saw me sitting on the grass. Our eyes met, held.

"Lille, fuck," he swore, and came towards me. Reaching down, he grabbed me by the elbows and pulled me up to stand. It was a little rough, but I didn't think he realised that. He pushed me back against the camper and stared at my tear-streaked face, his brows drawn together in either concern or annoyance. I couldn't tell which. Bringing his thumbs up to my cheeks, he wiped away the tears. For a brief moment, he seemed fascinated by them. His chest met mine, and I felt his breathing accelerate.

"Why did you disappear?" he asked, eyes flickering back and forth across my face.

I shrugged and tried to calm my breathing. "Does it matter? I already felt invisible."

His brows drew together. "What? Because of Julie? You left before seeing me lift her off my lap. I wasn't enjoying it, if that's what you thought."

"I don't get you at all. How could you not be enjoying it? You had sex with her the other night. I can't see how so much has changed in so little time."

"Everything and nothing has changed," said Jack, levelling his hands on either side of my face. "Why are you crying?"

"I'm not crying."

"Not anymore. You were a minute ago. Tell me why."

My entire body slumped back against the camper, my energy draining like sand through an egg timer. "I'm just overwhelmed. This life is a lot different to what I'm used to." I was evading answering honestly, but I really was far too embarrassed to admit my feelings for him. I barely knew him, and already he was all I could see when I shut my eyes at night.

"I warned you it wasn't going to be fun," said Jack. "It's dangerous out here for women on their own."

"Don't start that again. It pissed me off enough the first time you said it. I might be a woman and I also might technically be alone, but I'm surviving just fine."

His mouth moved in a way that made me think he was amused. "Yeah, you're surviving just fine, thanks to me. Or was it you who put that pretty bruise on Pedro's face?"

"Oh, whatever," I sighed, and looked away. I knew he had me there. Plus, I couldn't handle his handsomeness up so close.

"Whatever," Jack mimicked before his voice dipped low. "You sound so petulant when you say that. Why are you being petulant, Lille? Sexual frustration?"

I snorted. "You wish."

He cocked his head. "Yeah, I do. And I think you're lying." He brought his mouth to my neck and kissed me tenderly, then again and again, his kisses whisper-soft but growing harder each time. Breath escaped me, and I sighed in reluctant pleasure. There was no way I could resist him. The feel of his mouth sent wonderful tingles all the way down my spine. He rose back up and gripped my neck in his hand.

"Your pulse is racing. I can feel it fluttering against my palm, so fragile, like butterfly wings," he rasped, then brought his mouth over mine. His tongue slid languidly past my lips, licking at me, taking everything without asking permission. I fisted his shirt, unsure whether I was pulling him closer or endeavouring to push him away.

Losing myself in sensation, I melted right there next to the camper, standing on the dampening grass. Night sounds drifted about us, and I became aware of his lips leaving mine, trailing across my collarbone and then falling away completely as he bent to kneel on the ground. I looked down and he stared up, hands rubbing the outsides of my thighs, pushing the hem of my dress higher and higher until my underwear was showing.

Like before, he pressed his face to me and breathed in. I don't think I'd ever seen anything more erotic. The look in his eyes as he stared at me was worshipful, and it felt like my heart had gotten stuck in my throat. Then he put his hand to the back of my knee and lifted my leg, throwing it over his shoulder. I held on to his other shoulder for balance just as he began lowering my underwear. Cool air hit my most intimate parts, and I hissed in a breath.

Now he wasn't looking at me anymore. He eyes were focused intently between my legs as he ran a single finger down my slit. I gasped and waited, needing more.

"Touch me," I pleaded.

"Touch you or kiss you?"

"Both. Please," I said, and then his mouth was on me, soft and wet at first before his tongue licked at my clit and I trembled. His hand ventured further, fingers finding me and plunging inside. I shivered at the invasion, feeling myself clamp tight around him. I felt stripped bare, seen entirely, as his hand dug into my hip, his fingers fucking me and his mouth laying siege to my most sensitive parts.

My orgasm hit me quick and fast, and Jack growled in appreciation as I braced his shoulders for support. His lips and tongue and fingers drew out every last wave until I was entirely spent. He fixed my underwear back in place, pulled down my dress, and took my mouth again in a hungry kiss filled with a thousand unspoken words. I could taste myself on him, which was oddly intoxicating.

Then, on a physical level at least, I felt him withdraw. Just before he left, he kissed the shell of my ear and murmured, "You have never been invisible to me, flower. You're all I see."

As he walked away, I tilted my head up to look at the sky, and the stars seemed to shimmer like polished silver.

***

Even though he left me there all alone, I was still on a high the next day. Jack had gone down on me, *outside*. The whole time it was happening I felt electric, alive. I noticed that I wasn't the only one who'd gotten some action, because Lola's bed remained empty the whole night. She arrived back the next morning, still wearing the same clothes and a satisfied look on her face.

I didn't ask questions, but I knew it must've been Luan who put the satisfied look there. I hadn't really spoken to him much, but he seemed like a nice guy. Still, the fact that he was good friends with Pedro put me off slightly. I just hoped he wouldn't turn out to be a sleaze, because Lola didn't deserve that.

Violet was in the lounge, and I was sitting at the table, eating a bowl of cereal, when she came in.

"Well, well, well, where have you been, Josephine?" Violet asked in an uncharacteristically chipper voice.

Lola scowled and went to our room, shouting over her shoulder, "Don't call me that."

Violet snickered and returned her attention to her magazine.

"Josephine?" I asked.

She arched an eyebrow. "You didn't actually think that Lola was her real name, did you?"

I shrugged. "I hadn't really thought about it."

"Yeah, well," she replied pointedly. "It isn't. Circuses like this attract lots of girls looking to run away, escape their realities, you know. Giving yourself a new name is all a part of it, I guess."

"In that case, I think I'll rename myself Methuselah," I joked. "It sounds all mysterious and exotic, right?"

Violet raised an eyebrow at me. "If you say so."

Deciding to get out for a while and get my mind off Jack, I went for a walk around the campsite, stopping when I saw Winnie. She had Pip and Skip out of their cage, and my heart stuttered for a moment. When I watched them from the safety of the audience or from behind the bars of their cage, I felt safe. But here, out in the open, I became

128

aware of their size and the danger they presented. Winnie held nothing but a long wooden stick as she walked alongside Pip, alternating between petting his mane and giving him little taps on the side. Skip sat on the grass, head resting on his paws, absently surveying the scene.

When Winnie saw me standing there, she smiled. "You want to come meet my boys?" she asked, and I hesitated before venturing closer. Pip watched me, assessing the new person, his eyes almost human. His thick, golden mane shone in the sunlight, and I yearned to reach out and touch it.

"They're so beautiful," I said in wonder. "I hope what happened with Julie won't get them taken away from you."

Winnie nodded and petted Pip's head again. "She's not making any official complaints. Julie is the little girl who pulled the legs from spiders, the one who poked at dogs until they turned vicious. I'm not saying my animals would never hurt someone, because at their core they are predators, but Julie was provoking them. My Carrie witnessed the whole thing. Julie had been sticking a pole inside their cage, trying to get a reaction." She paused and laughed wryly. "I heard her wail, and came out to find Skip had broken the pole and was clawing at her through the bars. You don't mess with him."

"I can't understand why she'd do something like that," I said, and sat down to admire Pip. He seemed to have determined I wasn't a threat, because he wasn't paying attention to me anymore. "I mean, how is that fun?"

"Some people have warped ideas of fun," said Winnie, her voice growing hard. "Pip and Skip are brothers. We've had them both for a long time, since they were just teenagers. Not in all that time have they harmed a person, and Antonio and I pride ourselves on that fact. If I catch that girl going near my animals again, it will not be the lions she should be afraid of."

I absorbed her words, suddenly understanding that although Winnie looked like a completely harmless woman to the casual bystander, there was a warrior lying underneath who would stop at nothing to protect the ones she loved.

"Well, I doubt she'll try anything again. I'm sure Pip frightened her enough the first time. If she does, she'd be pretty dumb."

Winnie laughed. "Have you seen the girl? I would hasten to say that dumb is her middle name."

I laughed along with her, but I wasn't quite sure I agreed. Julie wasn't dumb; she was cruel. The way she spoke to King last night told me that. And really, I hated to think she'd been with Jack, had put her mouth on him. The knowledge alone made me shudder.

A few minutes passed, and I watched Winnie interact with her lions in such a way that made me truly believe she loved them dearly. At one point, she encouraged Skip to roll over onto his back, his paws in the air as she took one in her hand and massaged it. I never thought I'd see a tiny little woman render a beast into a kitten as she rubbed his feet for him.

"Do you think he'd let me pet him?" I asked shyly.

"Of course," she replied. "Come here."

I went to her, and she showed me how to approach him. Before I knew it, I was running my hand over his mane, delighting in its softness. Getting to touch the animal excited my curiosity, and I went on to bombard Winnie with questions.

What do you feed them?

How long do they sleep each day?

Do they ever fight one another?

How old are they?

How many years do they live?

Don't they need to have sex with a lioness every once in a while?

She was very patient in answering all of my questions. By the time we were done talking, I found I was starving, so I headed for the gazebo to see what they were serving for lunch. Tomato soup and bread was the name of the game, as it happened. I spotted Jack, King, and Marina sitting at a table together. Pierre sat on Marina's shoulder, watching her as she ate her lunch. I saw him try to swipe for a piece of bread, but she caught him before he could grab it. The little monkey's antics made me laugh.

As I passed them by, Jack reached out, grabbed my wrist, and pulled me into him so that I was sitting on his lap. His eyes zoned in on my hair like we were completely alone. I looked down to see there was a clump of green paint in it, and he had started picking it out. He hadn't said a word in greeting, just spun me onto his lap like it was the most natural thing in the world.

The intimacy of it all made my heart squeeze.

My eyes wandered to Marina, and I found she was watching me with an odd mixture of warmth and curiosity. I took it to mean that Jack didn't often do this sort of thing. It felt a bit like a social show, like when men put their arms around their girlfriends' waists to show other men they were taken. He was absorbed in picking the paint from my hair as I turned my head a little to face Marina.

"Winnie let me pet one of the lions," I said with excitement.

"Aren't they just exquisite?" Marina replied, giving Pierre a little pat on the backside. He jumped off her shoulder with a screech before scurrying to the other side of the gazebo. "Back when I was just starting out, I was with a big circus. The tamers would work with about five or six lions and a couple of tigers all in the one act. You could tell the animals were treated terribly — they just looked so sad. It felt unnatural to see these big, powerful animals sitting perched on stools like housecats."

I tried to concentrate on listening to Marina, but the way Jack's fingers worked through my hair, his knuckles brushing my collarbone, was highly distracting. I remembered him from the night before, staring up at me like I was the centre of his universe, worshipping me with his mouth, and squeezed my thighs together tight. I really didn't need to be remembering how good he was at that.

King, who had been sitting slumped over the table asleep with his head in his arms, awoke suddenly with a groan.

"Where the fuck am I?"

Marina gave him an almighty clip 'round the ear. "You're in hell. Now tell me who gave you the whiskey last night?"

An argument ensued between the two, and I looked back to Jack, whispering, "I think you got all of it."

He didn't stop. "I like your hair."

"Thanks."

His voice got low and quiet as he leaned in and spoke into my ear. "I like your pussy, too."

"Jack," I gasped.

"It likes me back."

"You're crazy."

He shrugged. "You wouldn't be the first person to say that."

"What are you doing today?" I asked, shifting on his lap. I thought I could feel him stirring to, uh...life, but I couldn't be certain.

"Practice. Then show. Then sleep. And tomorrow we move on."

"I can't believe we've been here in Caen a whole week. Where do we go next?"

"Orléans. It's just over three hours away. You can ride with me."

I thought about a three-hour journey with Jack alone in his camper and grew fidgety. What would we talk about? Would we just sit in silence? Strangely, I kind of enjoyed being quiet with him, and usually I felt the need to chatter to fill quiet periods.

"Okay," I replied, finally.

Nine

Lille lost her way

The rest of the day was a flurry of activity, and I was proving my mother right by walking around with my head in the clouds. It was all Jack's fault. His attention made me feel constant flutters and giddiness, and I was sure I had a perennial dreamy look on my face.

I went to see Bea and give her the finished painting. She squealed with delight when she saw it and proceeded to pester her dad to hang it up on her bedroom wall in their camper. Her dad, Aiden, was a single parent and a general labourer for the circus. He had a decent, unassuming sort of personality. I was constantly seeing him lugging heavy equipment about. It certainly didn't look like an easy job, but I still had this itching need to tell him that he shouldn't let Bea run around by herself all the time. I tamped the need down, because I didn't want to come across as judgemental.

When I was leaving their camper, I saw Julie walking my way. She took me in, eyes narrowing ever so slightly. I thought she was going to say something mean, but then she surprised me when she plastered a polite though obviously fake smile on her face and said, "Hey, Lille, is Aiden in there?"

"Yeah, he and Bea are watching television," I answered. She only nodded and walked by me before disappearing inside the camper.

Once the show started, I was busy painting faces outside by the entrance. I found that the more French people I interacted with, the better I became at speaking the language. This trip was doing all sorts of great things for my life. I was speaking a second language, doing art every single day, and receiving orgasms from the sexiest man alive. Well, one orgasm, but I had high hopes for more.

I slept like the dead that night and awoke early to the noise of the men taking down the Spiegeltent. My bed was on the side of our tiny room with the window. I wiped away the condensation and peered out to see Jack vaulting up a pole as he assisted with the dismantling of the tent. It looked like doing such a thing came so easy to him. Well, he certainly wasn't afraid of heights. I watched him for longer than normal, fascinated. Plus, he was so sexy when he was working.

Finally dragging myself away, I had a quick shower, making sure not to use all of the hot water for fear of facing the wrath of Violet, then dressed in some jeans and a yellow knit jumper. Violet was sitting by the table, eating toast, one leg thrown over her shoulder (I know, weird) and wearing a T-shirt that read, "Warning, Gymnast: Could flip at any moment." It made me smile.

"What's with the top?" I asked. "I thought you were a contortionist."

"An ex-boyfriend bought it for me. He thought it was a funny jibe at me having a short temper. Well, it was ironic that I did flip when I saw he didn't even get my profession right. I have a mean left hook."

"So you punched your ex-boyfriend and you're still wearing the T-shirt?" I said, amused.

She shrugged. "Pretty much."

I gave her a wide-eyed look. "Fair enough."

Lola came out of our room then, scratching her head, her short hair sticking up in every direction. "Shit, it's moving day today, isn't it? I feel like absolute crap, Vi. Could you drive this time? I don't think I'm up to it."

135

"You do realise the only reason I let you live here is because I hate driving this thing, right?" Violet threw back, one eyebrow arched.

Lola coughed, then sniffled. "Seriously, I'm not faking just so that I can beg off. I think I have a temperature."

Violet made a huff of annoyance but didn't respond. I walked over to Lola and put my hand to her forehead, only to find she was burning up.

"She's not lying," I said. "She definitely has a temperature."

"Oh, wonderful!" Violet groaned. "It better not be the flu. I can't afford to get the flu. Get back in your room, Lola, and stay there. We don't want to catch what you've got."

Okay, so it was official. Violet had just about the worst bedside manner I'd ever encountered, and I grew up with the ultimate ice queen mother who never gave hugs or cups of cocoa or petted my head when I was ill.

"Come on, let's get you back to bed," I told Lola. "I'll make you some soup, and you can try and sleep it off."

And that's how I spent the rest of my morning, taking care of Lola and making sure she was comfortable. I was just washing my hands when I saw Jack pass by the window of our camper. He was pulling along a large trunk full of equipment. When he saw me watching him, he raised a questioning eyebrow, as if to ask, *Are you riding with me today or not?* I got a fizzy sensation in my belly to think he'd been waiting for me to come over.

"Lola's all settled. She should be fine until we reach Orléans. I'll be riding with Jack," I told Violet, who was sitting in the driver's seat, drinking a cup of coffee.

"Cool. Just make sure you don't let him talk you into a blowjob on the drive. We don't want him crashing," she teased, and I gave her a narrowed-eyed but amused glare.

When I got outside, I practically raced all the way to Jack's camper. I knocked on the door and heard him call, "It's open."

Stepping inside, I found the place clean and tidy, the same as before. There was something that warmed my heart about how lived in and threadbare everything felt. I'd grown up in a house with expensive carpets and designer couches, where you had to take your shoes off as soon as you stepped in the door. Mum never let me eat in the living room or in my bedroom. It was always so tense. Everything had to be perfect.

Jack's camper felt like pure comfort in comparison; it was the kind of place where I could sit back and relax, completely be myself.

"Hi," I said, going to take the passenger seat beside him at the front. "What time do we leave?"

He glanced up to look at me, his eyes moving from my face to my chest and then down. I relished how he completely soaked in my appearance like that. There was something so…excessive about it.

"Good morning, Lille. Five minutes. I was beginning to wonder if you'd show."

I let out a sigh. "Sorry about that. Lola's fallen sick. I think it's a cold. Anyway, I had to get her something to eat and tuck her into bed."

Jack seemed perplexed by this. "Who are you? Her mother?"

"Definitely not. In my experience, that isn't how mothers act."

He stared at me for a long moment before looking away again. There was a faraway tone to his voice when he said, "No, nor in mine."

"Ah, something we have in common, then? Though I take it your mum never tried to track your location against your wishes using GPS."

I winced when I remembered that his mother had died in a house fire when he was little. How fucking tactless could I be sometimes? Christ.

Jack contemplated my statement for a while. It was probably only seconds, but it felt like forever. "Well, I only have a handful of memories of my birth mother. She was loving, caring, you know, everything a mother should be. Unfortunately, I have more memories of my foster mum. She was the exact opposite."

My lips turned down in a frown. "I'm sorry."

He glanced at me and seemed genuinely confused as to why I would say that. It was what anyone would say, but I was learning that Jack wasn't like everyone else. He dealt in blunt statements of fact, not platitudes and empty expressions.

"Why would you be sorry? You weren't there," he said plainly.

"It's just something people say."

Bea's father, Aiden, walked in front of the camper then and waved his hand in the air to signal it was time to leave. I watched quietly as Jack started the engine and began to pull out of the campsite behind the truck in front of us. Watching him drive was kind of sexy. He was so big and muscular, and even though his camper was one of the larger ones, it felt small with him in it. The mid-morning sun warmed my face as I sat back and got comfortable. Deciding to make the most of three hours in Jack's company, I pulled out my sketchpad and began to draw him.

He was focused on driving mostly, but after about twenty minutes, I saw his attention flicker between me and the road, his head turning every once in a while, craning his neck to see what I was drawing. My lips curved in a smile as I crossed one leg over the other and tilted the sketchpad to obscure it from his view.

In the end, he huffed out a breath of irritation and asked gruffly, "What are you drawing?"

"You," I answered honestly. There really was no point in lying. I was willing to bet he knew I was a tiny bit fascinated by him at this stage.

"Me? Why are you drawing me?"

I stewed on that one for a moment, trying to think of the best way to answer. "You've got an interesting face. I like interesting."

Another huff of irritation. "I can't see how drawing me driving would be very interesting."

"I'm not drawing you driving. I'm drawing you on stage, weaving fire around your body. Having you in front of me for the physical characteristics is helpful. I can use my imagination for the rest."

His brows shot up, and he appeared to be taken aback by my answer. He let go of the steering wheel and held a hand out for the sketchpad. "Let me see."

I shifted back a little. "Nuh-uh. You don't get to see it until it's finished. And maybe not even then."

He made a speedy move, grabbing for the sketchpad, but I was quicker and shot out of reach. "Hey, now, that's a dirty tactic," I said, laughing nervously.

In all honesty, I was self-conscious about showing him. I didn't think I'd ever put such effort and detail into drawing a person before, and it was perfectly evident. It was also perfectly evident by the sheer amount of detail that I was obsessed with him. And, let's face it, nobody wants the object of their obsession to be aware of it. Then you just end up feeling weird and itchy and a little bit like a creep.

"Lille, you have five seconds to hand me that sketchpad, or else," he warned me. My heart stuttered in response to his harsh tone of voice, and my skin prickled in a way that made me wonder if I liked it.

"Not going to happen," I said, sticking to my guns.

"Fine," he replied a moment before he abruptly turned the steering wheel, bringing the camper over to the side of the road. The vehicles behind us honked their horns in annoyance while Jack casually pulled over and stopped. The rest of the circus party drove on ahead of us, and I saw a few people staring out of their windows curiously. I almost burst into laughter when Violet sped past, casually mimicking a blowjob with one hand as she drove.

I knew I was in for it when Jack undid his seatbelt and came at me. Quick as a flash, I was out of my seat and running. Though, since we were in the camper, there wasn't really anywhere for me to run to.

I dashed inside his bedroom and slammed the door shut, pressing my body against it and holding down the handle to keep him from getting inside. And yeah, it was a futile mission because, let's face it, my strength was no match for his. I was no dainty little thing, but still, Jack got the door open in record time, and I found myself stumbling backwards, my arse hitting the floor painfully.

"Ouch, my coccyx," I whined, rubbing at my lower back.

Jack stood in the doorway, expressionless, for a moment before he began a slow laugh.

"What did you just say?"

"I hurt my coccyx, the lower part of my spine. I think I might have done some serious damage," I complained, scowling up at him. "I'm glad to know you're finding it so funny, though."

He held his hand out to help me up and I took it, my sketchpad long forgotten on the floor. "I'm sure your coccyx is fine, Lille," said Jack, towering over me. Then his voice dipped low. "But just to be sure, let me check."

Slowly, he took a breath and reached around me, encapsulating me in his arms. He found my spine and gently ran his fingers downwards. When he reached the base, he started to rub in slow circles. I drew in a gulp of air, tingling all over from his closeness.

"How does that feel?" he murmured.

It felt incredible.

"G-good," I managed, and glanced up at him.

He held my gaze and continued massaging for a full minute. It was perhaps the best minute of my life, all eye contact and gently probing fingers. I was a little disappointed when he drew away. "Better now?"

I swallowed and nodded. "Mm-hmm, much better."

"Good," he said, and before I could react, he dove for my sketchpad, picking it up and flipping through the pages, trying to find my most recent drawing. I swiped for it, but he held it above his head, and yeah, there was no way I was going to reach it. I briefly considered hopping on his bed for the extra height, but I had shoes on, so I thought that might be rude, even though he was being epically rude by nosing at my pictures without my permission.

I accepted defeat and stood back, folding my arms and leaning against the door while he examined my drawings as though they were curious artefacts. I got a little dry-throated just watching him. There were a lot of half-finished works in there, and I really did have a fear of my incomplete drawings being seen. I wasn't sure why, but his opinion was important to me. I didn't want him to dismiss my work as airy-fairy and pointless like Shay Cosgrove would have.

"You see a lot of light in the world," Jack said finally, his face drawn into a perturbed expression. He flipped to the next page, and I knew he'd come to the drawing of him because he paused, dark eyes taking it in. I bit on my fingernails, waiting.

He tilted his head to the side and held the sketchpad out to look at the picture from a different angle. Then he glanced at me and back to the sketchpad before cocking a brow.

"This is how I look to you?" he asked.

"Uh, yeah," I croaked.

He was staring at the picture again, and almost in slow motion, I saw his lips curve into a smile. It was the most goose-bump-inducing, belly-tingling, heart-fluttering smile I'd ever witnessed. He closed the sketchpad and handed it back to me, then placed a kiss on the top of my head.

"You're a great artist, Lille," he said, and then made his way to the front of the camper without another word. I was still standing there when the engine started running and we were on the road again. I stumbled a little and steadied myself on the bed before sitting down. What he said had been so simple, and yet it felt like just a few words from him, telling me that I didn't actually suck, had legitimised me. For the first time in my life, I felt real.

I could officially tick number nine off my list. Wow.

I didn't know how long I'd been sitting there when I finally managed to draw myself out of my thoughts. Looking around Jack's room, I saw a tall, narrow wardrobe, some drawers, and a couple of shelves built into the wall. On the shelves was an array of books. I leaned closer to read the spines and found that they were all books for kids and teenagers. Adventure novels. Fantasy. Science Fiction. The only book that wasn't a novel was a big, hardback, well-worn Oxford English dictionary. Randomly, I pulled out a paperback and flipped through the pages. It was curious that there wasn't a single adult book in his entire collection.

I noticed that certain words had been underlined with a pencil. Words like "abolish," "eschew," "contrite," and "gregarious." They were the kind of words you wouldn't really consider using until you were older and more learned, but still, any fully grown adult would at least have a decent idea of what they meant. It struck me that Jack must have been underlining them so he could go and look them up later.

Then, out of the corner of my eye, I spotted another book on his bedside dresser. It was a brand-new copy of *Great Expectations*, and I immediately remembered how I'd told Jack it was my favourite work of Dickens. I picked it up and found that a receipt had been tucked into the inside cover. It was for a shop back in Caen, the date showing he'd bought it just a few days ago. The bookmark told me he was just over a hundred pages in. Had he bought this because I'd mentioned it? The thought made my chest feel too full.

Slotting the book back onto the dresser, I went and joined him, sitting down in the passenger seat.

"You took your time," he noted, glancing at me sideways.

"Yeah, well, I'm a little put out by you bulldozing your way into my artwork," I said with humour.

The shape of his lips told me he was almost smiling. "You're very talented, Lille. You don't need to be self-conscious about it."

"Hmm, that doesn't make me feel much better about the invasion of privacy," I sniffed, heavy on the dramatics, while on the inside I was delighted. I had a feeling that compliments from Jack McCabe were few and far between. And what was seldom was wonderful in my book.

"Stop being moody," he chastised me playfully, and then went quiet for a second. "What are you going to do with the picture of me when you're done with it?"

"I hadn't planned that far ahead yet."

A frisky gleam came into his eye. "I think you should hang it over your bed. For inspiration."

He said this with such a straight tone that I didn't get his meaning at first. When I did, I blushed like crazy and focused my attention out the window. "You know what, Jack McCabe, you're a sneaky little flirt sometimes."

He seemed to enjoy my assessment, because he was smiling full-on now, never taking his eyes off the road. A little while passed in quiet before I spoke again.

"I saw all your books in your room. You must really love reading."

His face grew wary, and he shifted in his seat, hands flexing on the steering wheel. "Reading helps to kill time when I'm on the road."

I nodded. "You also underline the words to look them up later, right? That's a really good idea. I hate it when I come across a word I don't know but forget to look it up."

Jack let out a long breath. "That's not really it."

"No?"

He shook his head. "I have gaps in my education. Well, not so much gaps as one big gap. My schooling basically stopped after my parents died. I only really began reading again a couple of years ago, so I look up the words I haven't come across before."

I furrowed my brow. "But how can that be? You went to live with a foster family. Didn't they send you to school?"

"Not exactly."

"What does that mean?" I shifted closer in my seat, giving him my full attention now. I felt like I was being nosy, asking all these questions, but I couldn't seem to hold back my curiosity.

"I went to school some days, but Frances never really enforced it, and if you tell a teenage boy he doesn't have to go to school, more often than not he isn't going to go. Other days, Frances kept me at home for other reasons." He trailed off, staring dead ahead. I got the feeling he was somewhere else for a moment.

My face must have shown my incredulity, because I seriously couldn't believe what I was hearing. "That's completely fucked up. I don't understand how she got away with that."

What I really wanted to do was ask about those "other reasons," but I had a feeling he'd evade answering me. Plus, there was something in the way he said it that gave me a sick sensation in my belly.

"Frances got away with a lot of things. Until she didn't anymore."

There was a chilling tone to his voice that put me on edge. I opened my mouth to ask another question, but no words came. Somehow, I felt like I didn't want to know the rest of the story. I went quiet and was surprised when Jack spoke.

"I read those books to improve my writing and grammar, but also because they're an escape. They're not like real life. In the stories I read, the bad people get what's coming to them. In the real world, that's not always the case."

I stared at him, a lump in my throat, and my heart broke a little. He was a small boy again, the one I caught glimpses of every now and again before the strong, impenetrable man returned.

"That's true. You know, I can read *The Witches* by Roald Dahl over and over again, and it never gets old. It's like the perfect comfort read, a hug in a book."

He shook his head in amusement at my use of "hug in a book" and kept on driving.

"I also saw you're reading *Great Expectations*. I feel like I should warn you that there isn't exactly a happy ending to that one. It's a little bit tragic, actually."

His body tensed for a moment, but all he said was, "Yeah, okay."

I wondered if he was embarrassed for me to know he'd bought it because I'd said it was my favourite. He had no need to be, but still, I let the subject drop all the same. We were a little bit behind the others due to our unexpected stop, but I could see the long string of campers and trucks in the distance, so I knew we were almost caught up to them.

When we reached Orléans, I stared out the window in fascination at the buildings and the old stone bridge with arches beneath that crossed over the river. The view made my heart excited. It was just so French. Right then I wished

I hadn't destroyed my phone because I wanted to look up the city, read about what there was to see here. I guessed Jack knew just as little as I did about the place, even though I suspected he'd been there before, because when I asked him the name of the river we were crossing, he only shrugged.

Everywhere was just another place to him. It made me a little bit sad.

In a complete contrast to the last site we'd been camped in, which was on a country road, we were now smack bang in the middle of civilisation in what appeared to be a large empty car park.

"Can I use your phone for a minute?" I asked Jack as he pulled in behind Marina's camper.

He glanced at me, and then without a word opened the glove compartment and rummaged through it, fishing out his phone. When he handed it to me, I realised I wouldn't be doing any Googling, because it was at least ten years old.

"Who are you calling?" he asked.

"Um, nobody. Never mind," I replied, and handed it back to him.

He frowned. "What's wrong?"

"I wanted to use the Internet, and your phone is from the Stone Age, Jack."

"Well, it's a phone, isn't it?"

His simple reply made me laugh, and when I saw his face, I realised he thought I was laughing at him.

"Being a snob doesn't suit you, Lille."

I quickly sobered and reached for his arm, but he drew away. "That's not what I was implying. I actually think it's refreshing. Everybody's so over-connected these days."

"Yeah, well, I wouldn't know anything about that, would I? I'm just a barely literate slumdog living in the fucking Stone Age."

I stared at him, mouth open, not understanding how he could take offense so easily, how his mood could turn so swiftly. Was I being snobbish? If I was, I hadn't meant to be. He got up and walked to the back of the camper, opening the fridge and pulling out a carton of orange juice. I made my way toward him as he drank, and said quietly, "I'm sorry."

He pulled the carton from his mouth, swallowed, and glanced at me. "You should probably go check on Lola. See how she's feeling."

Well, I knew dismissal when I heard it. A lump forming in my throat, I shot him a final apologetic look before turning and leaving the van. When I got to Violet's camper, Lola was fast asleep in our room, snoring loudly, and Violet was on the floor in the lounge, her body bent into a crab position. It looked almost painful but was clearly effortless to her. She only gave me a nod in greeting. I was beginning to learn that, like a lot of the people in this circus, Violet was an odd character. Sometimes she'd have a conversation with you, even joke around, and then other times she wouldn't talk to you at all.

Later that night when I went to the gazebo for something to eat, I chatted with Marina for a while, letting her know that Lola wasn't well and that I'd fill in for her if she wasn't up to working tomorrow night. I noticed Pedro watching me again from the other end of the long table, his face hard like before. He sat by himself, eating a bowl of stew and listening to us as we spoke. I didn't see any sign of Jack, but I did get a death glare from Julie as she passed by the table with her sisters. Today was definitely not my day.

Infamy, infamy, they've all got it in for me.

As I was leaving, I filled a bowl for Lola and brought it back to the camper van. She was awake when I got there and had just enough energy to eat before she fell asleep again. It was definitely looking like she had the flu, and I resigned myself to sleeping on the sofa that night, since I didn't want to catch it.

After the way I'd left things with Jack, I felt unsettled. I couldn't seem to sit still, so I decided to go find him and make amends. Running what I'd said about his phone through my head again, I realised that I had been a bit of a snob. His camper van was dark on the inside, and when I knocked on the door, I got no answer. I wished I had a phone so that I could call him and made a note to buy a cheap one in town the next day. Disappointed, I started walking back when I caught sight of him leaving the gazebo, headed towards the street.

Picking up my pace, I followed, cupping my hands around my mouth and calling out his name, but the traffic was too loud, and he couldn't hear me. He was so tall that I could easily pick him out in the distance and so I kept following him. The tricky part came in when I reached a large open square that reminded me of an Italian piazza. In no time I'd lost him and found myself standing in front of a restaurant. Some men sat outside, smoking cigarettes and drinking fancy European-looking beers. They wore business suits, their ties loosened, signalling that they were off duty.

When one of them gave me a look up and down and called me over, I began walking away hurriedly, not wanting the attention. I already felt vulnerable, all alone in a strange city at night with no phone and very little money. When I tried going back the way I came, I realised I must have made a wrong turn somewhere because I didn't recognise the street. A group of teenagers walked by me, and I knew I appeared distraught because they gave me curious looks. In usual teenage fashion, though, none of them offered to help.

I had a vague feeling that I was going in the right direction, but I realised I was wrong when I'd been walking for ten minutes and still didn't recognise where I was. Why the hell had I left the circus without even asking what street we were on?

I stood outside a newsagents, folding my arms across my chest because it was getting cold and I had no coat. I was just about to stop a woman I saw approaching me and ask for help when a hand landed on my shoulder. I yelped at the unexpected contact and turned around, relief flooding me when I saw it was Jack.

That relief only lasted a moment when I saw the look of anger on his face.

Ten
An attack led them astray

"What do you think you're doing?" he fumed, his hand on my shoulder steering me across the street where a tram was just pulling up to the stop. Jack led me onto it, pushing me right up into the opposite door and glaring down at me. My back hit the glass, my heart going ninety. The carriage was by no means full, but there were a couple of people giving us wary glances.

I was focusing on looking anywhere but Jack's eyes because they were scary right then. So black. I noticed he had a plastic bag dangling over one arm that contained a carton of milk, bread, and a packet of cigarettes. So yeah, I'd obviously been following him on a trip to the grocery shop and had gotten myself lost in the process. Still, I couldn't understand why he was this mad. Mild irritation I'd expect, but this level of pissed off was way over the top.

Telling him I'd been following him would only worsen his temper, so I lied. "I was taking a walk. I wanted to see the city."

"You wanted to see the city at eleven o'clock at night? Wouldn't it have been wiser to wait until morning?"

I bristled. "Probably."

"And if you were only taking a walk, then why did I find you huddled outside a newsagents looking like you were ready to have a panic attack?"

As he spoke, his body moved closer and closer to mine. Now his hips had me penned in place, one arm braced above my head and his broad chest in my face. I tried to keep my tone light-hearted.

"'Huddled' is a bit of an exaggeration, isn't it? And okay, I may have lost my way. I was just about to ask for

151

directions when you showed up. Lucky that," I said, and winked at him. Winked. At. Him. Why the hell did my brain think that was a clever thing to do? Jack frowned at me, a look I was beginning to recognise as him thinking I was being weird. Then he let out a long breath.

"You don't know this city. Next time you want to go for a stroll, ask me to take you. Then, once you know where you're going, you can wander all you like, though *not* at night. That's just asking for trouble."

There was something about the way he spoke to me that ruffled my feathers. Maybe I just didn't like people telling me what to do. I stood straighter, lifted my chin, and pushed him out of the way. His body moved, though I was certain that if he hadn't wanted to, my pushing would have been pointless.

"I'm not an idiot, so don't talk to me like I am," I said firmly. I'd spent my entire life being spoken down to by my mother. I wasn't going to start letting someone else do it. Especially not Jack.

"Well, you sure seem to act like one sometimes," he shot back, and I saw red.

"Excuse me?"

"You heard me."

I stared at him without blinking, and he stared right back. My arms were folded tight across my chest like steel, and I had the distinct urge to make a fist so I could punch him. This man was so aggravating.

"Are you being mean because of what I said earlier about your phone? Because if that's the case, then I apologise again. I didn't realise you were so sensitive."

Okay, so I was goading him, but he had it coming. In an instant he was in my space, and this time the tension practically radiated off him. His hands went to my neck, his thumbs stroking my throat, and God, I was already turned on. He had that effect on me. Hell, maybe I got off on fighting with him. It really wouldn't surprise me if I did.

He bent to bring his face level with mine and spoke slowly. "'Sensitive' is the last word anyone would use to describe me, flower, but keep poking, see how long it takes for me to snap." His voice was low and cutting, but so erotic, and the subtle edge of a threat had my every pore alight and tingling.

"Seems like you've snapped already," I whispered so quietly I'm sure he only heard because he was so close.

"If you think that's snapping, then you don't know me at all."

"That's right, I don't." I paused before continuing bravely, "But I want to."

His mouth twisted, and he began to shake his head; for a second there was a tortured expression on his face. "No, you don't."

"Don't tell me what I want."

He dropped his shoulders so his forehead rested against mine, and I could feel him breathing. "Seeing you like that, alone, panicking, pissed me off, okay? I'm sorry for lashing out."

His protective instincts were not entirely unexpected; however, they did surprise me. I was just a girl he knew. Yes, one he had the urge to go down on, but still just a girl. Would he really be that bothered if something were to happen to me? His words from the other night rang in my head.

You're all I see.

Maybe he would be bothered. Maybe he would be very bothered. The thought made me shiver.

I didn't know what to do. His mood had changed so swiftly. In the end, I just stood there, breathing him in, until the tram stopped and the door started to open. Jack laced his fingers in mine and led me off. We turned a corner, and there was the circus, the foundations of the Spiegeltent being laid out already. I had an idea for a three-part painting of the tent in its various stages of being built, the final complete one full of colour and light, people coming to see the show.

Sometimes it felt like I had so many ideas but never enough time to make them happen.

"What are you thinking about?" Jack asked, and I realised he'd been watching me.

"Oh, you know, the usual. How our lives are finite and we'll only ever get to fit so much into them. How it doesn't feel like enough."

Jack gave me a thoughtful look and was silent a moment before he spoke. "Would it make you feel better to know that we all get the same number of hours in a day, days in a year? Some people might be rich and some might be poor, but none of them can buy time. It is one of the fairest systems in the world."

"Yeah, but most rich people live longer lives than the poor."

Jack shrugged. "I'm not talking about lifespans. I'm talking about time. And what makes you a good judge of what is enough? Maybe stop thinking of enough and just live in the moment. Then you won't worry — you'll just be experiencing."

"It's hard to change the way you think when you were raised to measure everything in comparison to everything else."

"Well, that sounds like a depressing way to live your life."

"It is."

"Change, then."

There was a forcefulness to his words, like he really cared. I stopped walking, my hand slipping from his. He paused two steps ahead of me and turned, arching a questioning brow. He was so beautiful. I loved looking at him in the dark and then in the light, noting the contrasts, realising that he was exquisite in every setting.

"Jack," I breathed.

He looked wary. "Lille?"

"You're kind of beautiful, you know that?"

Staring at me, he seemed caught off guard. He definitely hadn't expected me to say that. His face appeared to be battling a war within itself over whether or not to smile or frown. In the end, I got something that was neither one nor the other.

"Only kind of?"

I let out a loud bark of a laugh and teased, "Well, you're no Gandy."

Jack shot me a confused glance. "And thank fuck for that. Who wants to look like a little old bald man with John Lennon glasses?"

My laughter spilled out and was impossible to control. When I finally regained the ability to speak, I said, "David Gandy the male model, not Gandhi the father of Independence in India. And technically, John Lennon stole the spectacles from him, since Gandhi came before Lennon."

His face was what I could only describe as amused affection. "So, let me get this straight: I don't look like a male model. Okay, I think I can live with that." He said this with such a deadpan tone that I began laughing all over again, and it had just started to die down. What was even funnier was the fact that my comment was intended to tease and rile him up, but it hadn't riled him up at all. And the truth of the matter was that he could've wiped the floor with a whole room full of male models. Jack's beauty was far beyond anything quite so flat and one-dimensional.

I took two steps towards him and placed my hands on his chest. He watched my every move intently, like I was a strange animal and he didn't know what I was going to do next.

"No, you don't. You're still beautiful, though," I whispered before rising up on my tiptoes and pressing my lips to his. I was being uncharacteristically forward. There was something about being out in the dark that made me feel less inhibited than usual. Jack stood still, an immovable living statue, letting me kiss him. I got a vibe of curiosity, like he was waiting to see where I was going with this.

Good luck with that.

I didn't even know where I was going.

I was trying to live in the moment, like he said. Experience rather than measure. My hands explored his hard, warm chest before moving up to his neck and sliding around to sink into his hair. All the while he did nothing, and there was some sort of triumph in that. I felt like he was surrendering, letting me take what I wanted. It was a gift, I knew, because Jack McCabe wasn't a man to surrender often.

Pressing my body along the length of his and feeling just how much he wasn't indifferent towards me by the thick hardness at his crotch, I slid my tongue into his mouth and felt him shudder. Wow. I tugged on his hair a little and was rewarded with a deep, masculine groan that originated in the back of his throat and made every tiny hair on my body stand on end.

I broke away from his mouth long enough to whisper, "Touch me back."

He didn't give in immediately, but after a moment or two, his arms went around my waist, tightening and pulling me closer. His mouth began to move, his tongue tangling with mine in a soft, sensual dance. I felt like I was trying to drink him in but would never quite get enough. My hands were everywhere, feeling every place I could reach, while his remained in place, never venturing anywhere other than my waist. His hands were balled at my hips, fisting my shirt tightly. I adored how solid he was, how immovable.

Just as I was falling into him, getting lost out here in the dark, a sharp, violent scream rang out, and I pulled away, startled.

"What was that?" I asked, breathless, right before a second scream sounded. Jack grabbed my hand and tugged me forward, my body propelling faster than I'd be capable of on my own. The screaming continued and it made my heart pound, my skin growing tight. We followed the noise right to Violet's camper. The light was dim, but it was bright enough for us to make out a figure leaving through the door in a hurry. It was definitely male.

"Hey!" Jack shouted, letting go of my hand to chase after him. I hurried inside to find Lola crouched over, tears streaming down her face. The covers had been yanked off the bed, and it looked like someone had kicked a hole in the wall. Blood was running down her chin from her lip, and there was a look of terror in her eyes that I knew I'd never forget.

"Lola, what happened?" I asked, breathless and frantic as I went to sit by her and wrap my arm around her shoulders. The moment I touched her, she instantly jumped away, her hands shaking and tears filling her eyes.

"Don't," was all she said.

"I'm sorry," I replied, moving away and picking the blanket up off the floor. Carefully, I draped it around her shoulders, and she gripped it tight. Her eyes were bloodshot, and she continued to shake. I wanted to ask her what had happened again, but I didn't feel like I'd get an answer. Leaving her for a moment, I went outside to find Jack walking back towards the camper, breathing hurriedly.

"Fucking lost him," he said between breaths, and nodded to the van. "Who's inside?"

"Lola. She won't answer when I ask her what happened, but it looks like someone assaulted her. She won't stop shaking, Jack."

He swore and slammed his hand into the side of the camper in frustration. Over his shoulder, I saw a shadow move in the darkness a moment before King stumbled forward, his trademark bottle of liquor in his hand.

"Keep the noise down, would ya?" he grumbled, and brought the bottle to his mouth for a drink. Jack swiped it away from him and held it out of reach.

"You been hanging around here all night?" Jack asked.

"Hey! Give that back," King complained, trying to grab for it.

"Answer me and then I'll give it back," said Jack, voice stern.

"Been around, yeah."

"Did you see anyone go inside this camper?"

King frowned, his brows drawn together as he thought about it. "Nah, don't think so."

"Yes or no, King."

"Fuck's sake. No, I didn't see anyone," he shouted then, words slicing from his lips like razor blades. His arctic-blue eyes seemed to glow in the dark, and for a moment I was frightened. What if King was the one who attacked Lola? He had been hanging around all night. But then, we did see someone running away, someone fast enough to outrun Jack, and I didn't think King was capable of that in his current state.

Jack scowled and finally handed him back his bottle. "Marina's gonna chop your balls off when she finds out you've been drinking."

"Bitch can have them. I've no use for them anymore," King spat as he hungrily grabbed the bottle and stumbled away.

I glanced at Jack. "Can you come and try talk to Lola? She won't tell me anything."

He cocked an eyebrow. "And you think she'll talk to me? She's just been attacked by a man, and I'm not exactly the gentle type. She'll freak if I go near her."

He sounded like he had experience with this type of thing, which only made my stomach twist further. What kind of things had this man seen in his life? I already felt uneasy and upset thinking of my friend sitting in her room, traumatised.

Turning, I went back inside to find Lola had calmed down a little and was no longer shaking so much. I sat at the end of her bed and laced my fingers together. There was a lump in my throat that I couldn't seem to swallow, and my eyes filled with tears.

"We need to call the police, Lola."

Her eyes flared and she reached out, grabbing my wrist painfully. "No! No police."

159

I didn't understand her. "Why not?"

Fingers digging into my skin, she pleaded, "Just don't call them. Please. I'm begging you."

"Okay, I won't. I promise, but you need to tell me what happened."

She let out a long, shuddering breath and then locked eyes with me. Hers were still so bloodshot that it was almost difficult to look at them. She was still sick. "I was sleeping and all the lights were out. I didn't hear him come in. All I know is that I woke because I felt like I couldn't breathe. He was leaning over me, pressing all his weight into my chest. It was too dark to see his face, but I thought he might be wearing a balaclava, because I felt something woollen brush my skin. I started to scream, and he punched me hard in the mouth." She stopped, weeping now, and brought her hand to her bloodied lips.

I wanted to go to her so badly, but I didn't. I knew she didn't want to be touched by anyone. Not yet. All of a sudden, I became aware of a presence behind me and turned to see Jack standing just outside the door, listening. Thankfully, the door was mostly closed, so Lola couldn't see him. He'd been right. His presence was far too foreboding sometimes. He was so big and male, and Lola was very likely to freak if she saw him right now.

I took her hand in mine and urged her to continue with my eyes. Her words tumbled out again. "He yanked the blanket away from me and I tried to struggle free, but this time h-he…he punched me in the stomach. The pain was so bad that I couldn't move for a minute, and he pried my knees apart and put his hands on me." She paused and almost whispered, "Between my legs. I got just enough energy up to start screaming again, and I must have been loud, because he ran."

A painful kind of fear clutched my chest. "Did he say anything? Did you hear his voice?"

She shook her head. "No."

A silence elapsed, but I could still sense Jack standing outside the door. I made my voice as soft as possible when I asked, "Lola, why can't we call the police? This guy is still out there. He could do it to someone else."

She groaned like she was in pain, more tears streaming down her cheeks. "Lola's not my real name, Lille."

"I know. Violet told me."

The confession that came next completed unexpected. "There's a reason for that. I can't be found. And if I tell the police my real name, he'll find me."

"Who?"

"My husband."

My jaw dropped. Lola had a husband? It was hard to believe, because she was only a year older than me. At least, she'd told me she was twenty-two.

"You know why I liked you right from the get-go?" she asked, reaching out to run her fingertips lightly down the side of my face. "Your eyes. They haven't grown hard yet, and there's no malice. When I got away from him, I promised myself I'd try my hardest to surround myself with people like you. Gentle people. People who don't hurt others. Then I'd never go back to what my life used to be."

She hadn't said anything explicitly, but she didn't need to. Her husband had hurt her, and that's why she needed to get away.

"Derek is the filth," she said, using London slang for police. "He has connections. If my name shows up, he'll find me. That's why we can't call them."

"But we're in France," I began, and she interrupted,

161

"It doesn't matter. He'll find me. I can't let that happen."

Behind me, I could hear Jack swearing and pacing around the living area.

Lola's brows drew together. "McCabe's out there?"

I nodded. "Yeah, he was walking me home. We heard you screaming and saw your attacker leaving. Jack chased him, but he couldn't catch him."

"Oh."

Some kind of relief showed on her features, and my stomach twisted again. I knew what she'd been thinking. For a moment she'd wondered if her attacker had been Jack. I felt like defending him, but she hadn't said anything outright, so I couldn't. I barely knew him, really, and already I wanted to tell everyone that he wasn't a bad person, that he might actually be a great person. One of the best.

Yeah, I had it bad.

I heard the camper door opening and Violet's recognisable voice questioning Jack as to what he was doing there. Seconds later she practically exploded into the room, taking in Lola's appearance and hurrying to her, asking her if she was all right. On a normal day, these two were at each other's throats, but now that something bad had happened, Violet looked just about ready to murder someone. It was an awful situation, but for a second my heart warmed to see that Violet actually genuinely cared for Lola.

I knew that Violet was aware of Lola's past when she didn't ask if we'd called the police yet. She knew that we hadn't. Couldn't. I glanced at Jack and could tell that he was seriously pissed off about this, but he didn't try to force his hand. The camper was small. He'd obviously heard Lola and derived the same conclusions I had. I left Violet to comfort Lola and stepped out of the room, closing the door softly and coming face to face with Jack. He ran his hand through his hair in frustration.

"This whole situation is fucked," he said. "Whoever did this is dangerous, and he's out there free to do as he pleases."

For some reason, his anger surprised me. I'd expect anyone to be pissed about not calling the police, but Jack was outraged. I felt like he had some kind of personal investment in this that I couldn't understand.

"You heard Lola. She doesn't want her husband to find her. I didn't even know she had a husband."

Jack growled and sat down on the couch. "Everybody here has a past they're trying to run from. That's why we feel the need to travel, keep moving so we'll never be found. This circus is particularly appealing because we only advertise when we reach a destination. We don't have a website or a tour schedule that's accessible by the public. Marina likes it that way, mainly because she says she hates computers, but I personally think she might be afraid of them. She has a tonne of books about conspiracy theories in her camper."

For the first time since we discovered Lola had been attacked, his face showed something other than severe anger. He was clearly very fond of Marina. I gave him a small smile. I'd actually seen those books when I'd been holed up in her place doing her accounts.

What Jack said gave me another realisation, something that had been niggling at me. In the back of my mind, I'd very much expected for my mum to have shown up by now. I put it down to her not being able to take the time off work, but now I knew differently. She couldn't find me because the Circus Spektakulär wasn't listed. The thought made me feel so much better, a tension leaving me I hadn't even known was there.

"I'm not looking forward to spending the night on this couch," said Jack, perusing the living area, his words breaking through my thoughts.

"Huh?"

"I'm staying here tonight. I can't take the risk of the attacker coming back."

I scratched at my neck awkwardly. "Um, I was actually going to sleep there, since Lola's sick. I don't want to catch her flu."

The moment the words left my mouth, Jack's gaze grew hot, his eyes smouldering. I never thought smouldering was actually a real thing until I met him.

"You can lie on top of me if you like. Better yet, just sit on my face."

I stared at him in silence, mouth hanging open. He was so…lewd sometimes. It unsettled me to think that if anyone else had said that to me, I'd be disgusted. But Jack managed to make the stark obscenity sound appealing. I flushed, and a tingle radiated down my spine.

"That's…that's…that's a really inappropriate thing to say to someone."

I could feel his gaze right then like it was a physical touch. "True, but you're not just anyone to me."

"Who am I to you?" I asked, unable to help myself.

He looked at me for a long, endless moment. "Someone."

I wasn't even sure what that meant, but it still made me feel hot all over. My heart beat hard just for him. It felt euphoric to be someone to Jack, and I knew from deep within me that I wanted to be his only someone. I wasn't his only someone, though. There was still Julie with her bitchy looks and cruel words that hid behind her pretty face and fake beaming smiles.

"You're someone to me, too," I whispered into the quiet. We stayed like that for a long time: me standing in the middle of the room, him sitting on the chair, having a silent conversation until Violet came in, completely unaware of the tension.

"Lille, Lola's asking for you," she said, and I grabbed onto her words as an escape. Otherwise, I'd never be free of the prison that was Jack McCabe's sexy stare.

***

Despite my plans to do otherwise, I ended up sleeping with Lola in her bed, her small frame wrapped up in my arms. She'd been so distraught and jittery that I decided I'd put up with catching the flu because she needed me, and I didn't want to leave her on her own. I knew that if I were in her place, I wouldn't want to be alone, either. Violet had to be healthy for her performances this week. I was much less vital to the circus and therefore could afford to get sick. And I had a strong immune system, so maybe I wouldn't catch it.

I woke early, Lola still in my arms. Gently extricating myself from her, I got out of bed and headed to the bathroom, needing to pee. I caught sight of Jack on the couch, still sleeping. I'd given him my duvet last night, and felt warm and fuzzy inside to think of him being able to smell me on the fabric. His deep breathing filled the camper and it was a gorgeous sound. With my dad out of the picture, I'd never really experienced living with a strong masculine presence.

My bladder felt full and heavy, and it was a relief to finally go. When I was leaving the bathroom, only wearing

165

a T-shirt and a pair of sleep shorts, my gaze flicked to Jack to see he wasn't asleep anymore.

He lay with his arm behind his head, watching me. His legs hung off the edge of the couch because he was so tall. I cringed to think of him hearing me pee, which was ridiculous, because it was a perfectly natural bodily function. There should be no shame in peeing.

His eyes ran down my body, from my face to my neck to my chest, lingering on my bare legs the longest. I thought I had nice legs. They weren't too fat, or worse, too thin, and they were long enough to be considered attractive. I felt myself blushing hotly and staring at the carpeted floor like it was fascinating.

"That was by far the worst night's sleep I've ever had," he said, his deep voice hitting me deliciously at the pit of my stomach. Yeah, I definitely enjoyed listening to Jack speak first thing in the morning.

"That's because the couches in these camper vans were built for hobbits, and if you lived in Middle Earth, you'd definitely be one of the elves," I shot back, and received the most delectable low chuckle in response. It sent a thrill right down to my toes. I felt his eyes on me as I walked to the kitchen and popped the kettle on.

"Do you want a cup of tea? Or coffee, maybe?"

He sat up and rubbed his hand along his jaw, where there was an attractive bit of stubble growing. "Coffee. Thank you."

I glanced at him briefly, allowed myself a second to enjoy his naked chest, then focused on making his drink. I'd seen him topless before, of course, but that was when he was onstage, or from afar as he helped build the Spiegeltent, not up close in a tiny camper van, his presence soaking up all the oxygen. Perhaps that was why I was suddenly having difficulty remembering to breathe. I heard the floor creak, and then a moment later I felt his heat behind me as he brought his hands to my hips and rested his chin on my shoulder.

"Hey," he murmured in my ear, all gravelly. I swear I was wet already. His voice, his closeness, his subtle touch — it all worked to soften me, make me a welcoming host for whatever he wanted to give.

"Hi," I squeaked, spooning instant coffee into two cups and trying to focus on keeping my hands from trembling. Then his lips were on my neck, his hot, wet, open mouth sucking my skin, and I ended up dropping the spoon, coffee granules spilling over the counter.

"Jack," I protested, but my voice was more air than sound, and it did nothing to stop him. I gripped the edge of the counter for support, my legs growing weak. His deft hands spun me around to face him, and his mouth left my neck. He stared down at me, eyes roaming my face, my mouth in particular.

"You've got pretty lips," he said, cupping my jaw, then lifting his thumb to my mouth. I stood there, immobile, as he rubbed across my lips and dipped inside. Jack groaned as his thumb went in, watching with rapt attention, and I shuddered at the invasion. He started to move it slowly in and out, and I swallowed back a moan. My tongue touched his thumb and he hissed, hips pressing into me, his erection hard and hot against my stomach.

I surrendered completely, body limp, as he invaded my mouth, and I welcomed it every time he went deeper. I imagined doing this to his cock, taking all of him in, and the dark, simmering look in his gaze told me he was imagining the exact same thing.

I broke away from him abruptly the second I heard Violet's bedroom door creak open. Jack retreated back to the couch and casually sat, like nothing had even happened.

"Whoa, McCabe, put a top on, would you?" said Violet, giving him a cranky glare. "I don't wanna see that shit first thing in the morning."

And she sounded like she genuinely didn't. It boggled my mind, because I couldn't imagine any heterosexual, red-blooded female *not* wanting to see a topless Jack first thing in the morning. Topless Jacks were what mornings of dreams were made of. Then again, I had just been enjoying his thumb in my mouth, so perhaps I was biased.

Silently, I returned to making the coffee, cleaning up the spilt granules and making a third cup for Violet. Much to my disappointment, Jack pulled on a shirt, and we sat drinking, getting our caffeine fixes and quietly discussing how to go about dealing with what happened last night. There wasn't much we could do, given that Lola wouldn't let us call the police, but Jack said he'd let Marina know and inform the others, make sure they were on the lookout for any strange activity.

Every time I looked at him now, I blushed. I mean, he'd gone down on me outside just the other night, and somehow I was more embarrassed about what had happened this morning. There was something about the stark daylight and the raw sexuality of how he touched me that made me feel too hot under my skin.

When he left to go back to his place and take a shower, I finally felt like I could breathe again. Violet made a few back-handed comments about unresolved sexual tension, which only served to put my nerves well and truly on edge. If Jack could get me this worked up by barely touching me, then I shuddered to think how it would be if we had sex. I needed an outlet, a bit of stress relief, so I set up my easel outside and started painting.

I'd sketched an outline of the painting I planned of Jack, but I wasn't in the right place to tackle it properly yet. He was taking up enough space in my head already. Instead, I started my three-part painting of the Spiegeltent, which was a much easier subject, given the current state of my emotions. After a while I heard someone approach, and I knew it was him. It was almost like I recognised how his eyes felt watching me, which was downright weird. He sat on a folding chair with a book in his lap, quietly reading just like the last time. Was this going to become a habit?

Oddly enough, I hoped it would.

A couple of minutes passed before I asked, "Do you ever think about what your life would be like if your parents hadn't died in the fire?"

He looked at me for a long moment, but I couldn't read his expression. "Feeling like inflicting a little light emotional torture today, flower?" His words held both a bite and a certain level of tenderness.

"I'm just curious. I mean, I'd think about it if I were you. Don't you ever feel like contacting your brother? Talking to him?"

"He left me. What's there to talk about?"

I shrugged, looking at my painting because Jack's stare was too intense right then. "I dunno. I just feel like believing the words of two random nurses and an uncle you never met before is foolish. You should hear it from the horse's mouth. People make mistakes all the time. Perhaps the nurses got it wrong. Or perhaps your uncle was lying. You never contacted Jay directly. Not once."

"Don't say his name. I don't want to hear it," said Jack, a warning in his voice.

I went quiet for a minute, then said, "Thinking about him hurts, doesn't it?"

Jack's jaw tightened as he stared off into the distance. I didn't expect him to answer me, so I was surprised when he bit out, "Yes."

"Letting it fester won't help anyone. Believe me, I know. I've spent years letting my mother's meanness fester. All it does is eat you up inside. About a year ago, I started writing letters, telling her just how much she'd hurt me. I never intended to send them, but writing it down helped. The burden wasn't so heavy afterwards."

"What are you saying, Lille? That I should write my brother a letter, tell him how much I fucking despise him, is that it?" he scoffed.

I gave him the most sincere look I could muster as I replied, "If you think it will help, then yes." I paused, summoning up the courage to whisper, "I care about you, and I don't want you to hurt on the inside."

His head turned, and he looked at me for a moment that dragged on forever, like my words had meant something to him. I saw a war wage within his black eyes before some of the tension went out of him in a long exhalation.

"Go get me a pen and paper," he said, and I literally felt my heart leap. He was actually going to do it. I couldn't have been more shocked if he told me he had a penchant for wearing women's underwear every now and again.

Not saying a word, I went inside and checked on Lola for a minute (she was sleeping), then tore a few pages out of my notebook and grabbed a pen. Going back out, I handed them to Jack, our fingers brushing absently, then returned to my painting. He sat there for a long time, fiddling with the pen, before he began to write.

My belly was all aflutter as I watched him. I tried to focus on my painting, but I couldn't help it. I was dying to know what he was writing. It was private, though, and I wouldn't pry. I got lost in my painting for a while, working on the details of the stained glass windows of the Spiegeltent, and how they caught the light.

"*Fuck*," Jack swore, startling me out of my concentration. I looked up to see him stand from his seat, scrunch up the paper he'd been writing on, and throw it in the bin. "This is bollocks." He glared at me, and I felt my throat tighten. Jack McCabe was not the kind of man anyone wanted glaring at them, and I certainly didn't relish being the recipient of said glare.

"I never said it worked for everyone. Maybe writing stuff down just isn't cathartic for you like it is for me," I suggested quietly.

"Why'd you even bring it up, Lille, huh? I told you about Jay because I trusted you. That doesn't mean you have permission to start discussing it all casual like you're commenting on the fucking weather."

He kicked the side of the camper in frustration, which caused Violet to stick her head out the window, looking pissed. "What the fuck, man?"

Jack gave her a withering stare, and she shrank in on herself, muttering something under her breath that sounded a lot like "psycho" before she retreated back inside and shut the window tight. I stood and strode toward him, reaching out and pushing his shoulder. "Hey, that was uncalled for. I was only trying to help you."

He grabbed my wrist, clutching it harshly, and I sucked in a breath. "From now on, my past is off limits. We don't talk about it. You understand?"

"You're angry. People that angry need to sort their shit out, Jack. You can't just keep ignoring it. Burying your head in the sand just leaves you with sand in your eyes."

He arched an eyebrow, and okay, yeah, what I'd just said sounded stupid, but I didn't know how to get through to him. I also didn't know why I felt it was so important that he come to terms with his feelings about his brother's abandonment. All I knew was that it made me sad to think of what he might be missing out on. From what I'd learned about Jay Fields, he was an amazing person, and Jack deserved to have someone like him in his life.

Something about Jack's story just didn't ring true, and it had been niggling at me for a while.

"Stay out of my business, Lille," he said finally, voice harsh but eyes sad, as he let go of my wrist, turned around, and walked away. I stood there even after he was gone, wondering if I'd just ruined whatever we had before it had even begun.

Then my eyes landed on the rubbish bin, where Jack had thrown his scrunched-up paper. My curiosity was about to get the better of me.

Eleven

In secret Lille stole Jack's letter

Tears stung my eyes and ran down my face.

I didn't know what I thought I'd find when I read Jack's letter, but I certainly hadn't expected to feel like someone had just buried a bullet in my chest. I was bawling as I crouched behind the camper for privacy, holding the uncrumpled sheet of paper in my hands. Even the way he wrote broke my heart. He used short, simple sentences, with frequent misspellings, and I remembered him telling me about the gaps in his education. You could tell simply from the lines he'd written.

When I woke up I wondered wer u wer 1st.
The last ting I remembered was suffocation and smoke.
Not being able to breathe is the scariest ting.
I cryed when they said Mam and Dad were dead.
I cryed when they said our uncle took u and not me.
I still hate hospitals.
Being alone feels worse when ur a kid.
Life seems endless. Endless loneliness.

U have no 1 and they give u to people and the people don't want u but they do want u becos they can get mony for u and they want the mony and they're all so greedy and they take everything until you have nothing and they don't even care.

I've done bad tings.
I thought about u every day.
Remember u taught me how to throw plastic knives?
U were so much better than me.
I'm probably better than u now.
Sometimes I want u 2 see.
But I hate u.

173

I hate that I still love u.
Why didn't u come back for me?
Why did u leave me?
Why did u leave me?
Why did u leave me?

Those last lines became harder to make out the more he repeated the question, like he'd stabbed the pen in so harshly it tore the paper, a manifestation of the pain he felt inside. I read it so many times the letters started to blur, mostly because I was still crying.

I hate that I still love u.

That was the line that made me cry the most. Jack still loved his brother. Even though he hated him, he still loved him. The declaration was so raw, I could almost feel the hurt like it was my own. Somehow I had to figure out a way to help him. I smoothed out the letter more, then folded it neatly and tucked it in my pocket. I had an idea, but it was so fucking risky. I definitely wasn't Jack's favourite person right now, but if I did this, I could ruin things between us completely.

Would it be worth it to reunite him with Jay?

Inside the camper, Violet gave me a look as if to ask, *What the hell was all that with Jack earlier?* Then she saw my reddened eyes and kept quiet. It was clear that I'd been crying. Lola was groggily eating tea and toast in bed. She still wasn't over her flu, and last night's attack had only worsened matters. I asked how she was, then asked if I could use her phone. Weakly, she told me I could use it whenever I wanted, that I didn't have to ask.

It didn't take me long to find two mailing addresses for Jay Fields. One looked like a P.O. Box, and the other was for a hotel in Las Vegas. I decided to use the latter, because who knew how many adoring fans sent letters to his P.O.

174

Box, and mine would only get lost amid the masses. I was incredibly nervous as I composed my message to him, and I still questioned if I even had any right to be doing this. My heart fluttered like an electrocuted butterfly. It was completely dodgy, but I couldn't sit back and do nothing. Something in my gut told me this was the right thing to do. I had to sacrifice what little Jack and I had in order to give him something more.

Dear Jay,

You don't know me. My name's Lille Baker. Very recently I met a man named Jack. Our relationship isn't an easy one to explain, but I feel very protective of him. I want to help him, even if he doesn't know he needs it yet.

He confided in me. Told me about how his parents died in a house fire and how his brother abandoned him.

I think that brother is you. And somehow, I feel like there's more to this story than meets the eye. Jack's feelings are still all messed up, so I encouraged him to write you a letter telling you how he feels. We never planned on sending it. It was supposed to be therapeutic. After he wrote it, he got upset and threw it away.

I picked it out of the rubbish and decided to send it to you.

He doesn't know I'm writing this. He's a performer with the Circus Spektakulär. We're currently doing shows in Orléans in France; next week we move on to Lyon, and after that I'm not sure. I think you should come find us. Come see your brother after all these years, Jay. He's an incredible person, and I've been fascinated by him since the very first time we met.

I hope you read this letter sooner rather than later.

Yours sincerely,

Lille.

***

I walked to the post office and sent the letter right after I'd written it, because if I waited, I knew I'd lose my nerve. After that I explored the city for a while, visiting an old church and browsing in the shops, mostly in an effort to calm my beating heart. Sending that letter could either turn out to be the best thing I'd ever done, or the worst.

I found an electronics store and bought a cheap phone, then sat in a little café by the river and had something to eat. When I arrived back at the circus, there was only enough time for me to give Lola some flu medicine before I had to go and cover for her at the refreshments stand. It was much harder work than painting faces, and by the time the show was over, I had blisters on my feet from standing for so long.

My stomach complained about not being fed, so I made my way to the gazebo to see if there was any food left from dinner. There wasn't. In fact, I briefly considered leaving right away because there was a wild party going on, lots of local men and women mixed in with the circus workers. It was a little too rowdy for my tastes. Still, seeing King sitting by himself in a corner, nursing a bottle of cheap-looking vodka, I went and sat beside him. He didn't smell so great, which made me all the more curious about my urge to be in his company. Even though he was drunk all the time, and even though I was a tiny bit scared of him, there was something about him that made me feel like he saw the world more clearly than any of us sober people.

"Your boyfriend's over there," he muttered, his head turning lazily to me, eyes bleary and bloodshot.

I looked in the direction he gestured, and saw Jack sitting with a group of men and women. He held a can of beer in his hand and wore a blank stare as a brunette spoke in his ear, alternating between touching his arm and running her hand along his leg. My heart lurched possessively to see another woman all over him, especially considering what had been brewing between us. I swallowed back the emotion, trying not to let the pain I felt inside bubble to the surface.

"If he was my boyfriend, he wouldn't have some French tart all over him right now," I said, my skin prickling with jealousy.

King laughed loudly, which garnered Jack's attention. His eyes found me immediately, blazing with some kind of emotion. His gaze darkened, and then all of a sudden he wasn't blanking the brunette anymore. He put his hand over hers on his leg and spoke into her ear now, returning her attention.

"Fucking hearts, who'd have them, eh?" said King in a surprisingly sympathetic voice, nudging me with his elbow.

I looked to him, and he seemed like he was actually trying to make me feel better. It made my heart squeeze. Here was a man at his lowest ebb, drowning in his own addiction to alcohol, showing me kindness. "Sometimes we don't get a choice in the matter, unfortunately," I replied.

King raised the bottle to his mouth and drank. A long quiet elapsed and I got the feeling he was somewhere else in his head for a moment. "Yeah, you're right about that," he finally whispered.

I was distracted when I heard someone coughing. At a nearby table, I saw Pedro with Luan and Raphael, and he looked a little worse for wear. He'd clearly caught the same flu as Lola, which got my mind racing. Was he the one who'd attacked her last night? Given his previous behaviour, it wouldn't surprise me to discover it was him. Then Luan blew his nose with a tissue, and my theory cracked. Luan and Lola were close. I didn't know all the details of their relationship, but it would make sense that he caught the flu from Lola and Pedro caught it from him.

My attention went to Jack again. This time the woman was straddling his lap and kissing her way down his neck. And he was just sitting there, letting her, while he stared at me. My stomach twisted, and all of a sudden I felt sick. This situation was so messed up.

"Ah, the push and pull," said King. I was so focused on Jack that I couldn't pay much attention to King's words; my head was too preoccupied trying to figure out what he was playing at. His behaviour was so confusing. Maybe he was some sort of sociopath who got off on making girls think he had feelings for them and then pushing them away completely. Because that was clearly what he was trying to do now, letting some strange woman grope him while I watched. He might as well have been pissing all over my emotions.

I stood, made sure to concentrate all the disdain I had inside me into a single look, gave that look to Jack, then strode out of the party. I was proud of myself. I might have been feeling like crap on the inside, but at least I'd kept my dignity. I hadn't gone over and started shouting at him like a jealous lunatic. When I reached the camper, I stood outside, my hand on my heart. This shit hurt so bad. I was dangerously close to ticking off item number eleven, and it felt truly awful.

Perhaps my list was just a load of bullshit after all.

***

The next morning, I made my way to the gazebo to get some breakfast for Lola. I had to pass by Jack's camper to get there, and I hurried my pace as I approached. Much to my dismay, he was already outside, hair damp from a

178

shower and a mug of coffee in his hand. I muttered some choice words to myself and plastered on a brave face.

"Good morning," I said to him curtly, and continued walking.

"Lille," he called after me, and I stopped, turning around. It would be just my luck that he'd want to torture me, make this so much worse than it already was. The sad thing was that even after last night, I still cared for him immensely. Perhaps I was being foolish, but I couldn't seem to turn my emotions on and off like he could.

"Yes?" I replied, glancing over his shoulder and inside his camper. My heart was thumping fast as I wondered if the woman from last night was there. I wondered if he'd taken her into his bed and let her touch him in places I wanted to belong only to me. His gaze followed mine, and he frowned.

"What are you looking at?"

"Just checking to see if the latest notch on your bedpost is still hanging around," I bit out, and instantly wanted to take the words back. Now he knew he'd succeeded in hurting me.

He knocked back the last of his coffee, ran a hand through his hair, and looked away. "She's not here."

"Oh, kicked her out after the deed was done, did you? How gentlemanly."

Now he looked at me, and the expression on his face made me shiver. "There was no need to kick her out. She was never here."

I folded my arms and rolled my eyes. I was so pissed off, and I think he knew it. "Even more gentlemanly. Gave her a knee-trembler behind the gazebo, then?"

His lips twitched before he let out a chuckle. "A knee-trembler? Only fifty-year-old men are allowed to use that term, Lille."

I scowled at him and turned to leave. I'd only gotten a few steps away when he caught my arm to stop me. My back was to his front as he locked my arm out and held it firmly to his chest. His breath hit my neck as he said quietly, "I wasn't with her, okay? How can I possibly be with anyone else when you've taken over my every thought?"

I closed my eyes and swallowed hard. His question melted my insides. The way his voice shook slightly told me he was telling the truth and that it was hard for him. All the strength went out of me as my body sank into his.

"You can't say stuff like that if you're going to do things like you did last night. You can't keep pushing me away, then pulling me back all the time," I whispered.

"I know," said Jack, his big, warm body pressing into mine. "That's why you need to stay away from me." He loosened his grip on my arm and I stepped back, turning to face him.

"I don't want to stay away."

His eyes scorched. "If you knew the truth, you would."

"The truth? What truth?"

"About the things I want to do to you. With other women I can restrain myself, but with you, I'm not sure I could. That's why it will never work between us. The way you look at me, Lille, like you'll let me own you, all I have to do is say the word. You don't want to be owned by me."

I frowned at him, remembering how he'd said something like this before.

"And what if I do want to?"

"You don't. Life twists some of us in strange ways, ways that shape us to always be alone, and I'm one of them."

I didn't know what to say to that, so I just stared at him. Our staring contest ended when Julie sauntered by wearing a tiny sundress, her hair curled like a fifties pinup.

"Looking good this morning, Jack," she said sweetly. I felt like telling her to piss off, that she was interrupting a private and perhaps monumental conversation. She gave me a narrow-eyed glance, then focused her attention back on Jack. He barely even registered her presence, just kept on staring at me with an intensity that was far too overwhelming. I couldn't take much more, so I turned and went.

He didn't follow.

Four days passed by in a blur. A good deal of the circus workers had fallen ill with the flu, so we were all working double time in an effort to keep everything afloat. When I felt the beginnings of it coming on myself, I took a whole bunch of vitamin tablets, made sure I got a full night's sleep, and that seemed to work in staving it off.

By the time we were moving on to Lyon, Lola had recovered; however, she still wasn't back to her usual self. I'd often catch her with a haunted, faraway look in her eyes, and I knew she was thinking of the night of her attack. I couldn't blame her. It was at the forefront of my mind, too. I was constantly wondering about the attacker's identity. Was it just some random person? Or was it the very same person who'd killed Vera, the burlesque dancer?

Violet offered to drive the four hours it took to get to Lyon, which was out of character, but I guessed she was still wearing her kid gloves with Lola. When we arrived at our destination, it was outside the city, in a gorgeous countryside setting quite like when we'd been in Caen, just more majestic somehow. It wasn't far from the city, though, and was easy enough for people to reach if they wanted to come see the show.

Lola had spent most of the journey in our room, so I went to see how she was doing. When I stepped inside, I knew instantly that she'd been crying, because her eyes were red and her lips were all puffy. She seemed embarrassed when we locked eyes, so I didn't mention her appearance. Instead, I decided to try to cheer her up. I'd been working on a painting of her the last couple of days, and now was as good a time as any to give it to her.

"I have a present for you," I said. "Stay there."

I went to retrieve the painting I'd done on a small ten-by-ten-inch canvas. The picture was very Andy Warhol inspired, and showed a colourful caricature of Lola's face on a background of popcorn and candyfloss. I set it on the bed in front of her and stood back to take in her reaction.

"Well, what do you think?" I asked, biting a little at my fingernails.

She picked up the canvas and stared at it for a long time. Her voice was all breathy when she finally spoke. "Honestly, Lille, where did I find you?"

"In a boring old town in the back arse of nowhere," I replied humorously, and she smiled.

"You're too much. I think my guardian angel sent you. He must have known I needed a friend."

"Your guardian angel's a man?"

She gave me a little wry look, and for the first time in days, I saw a hint of the old Lola coming back to life. "Of course. I like to imagine he's hopelessly in love with me, but we can never be together because it's against the rules."

I laughed. "Sounds like a book I wouldn't mind reading."

She smiled at me, a full-on happy smile, and I felt something in my chest untighten. "It does, doesn't it?" A short silence elapsed before she said, "Seriously, though, I love this painting. I'll treasure it always."

What she said had me walking towards the bed and taking her into a long, tight hug. I knew the memories of what had happened would always haunt her, but if I could make her feel a little bit better, then I'd done my job.

***

There was an air of excitement about the circus as the workers set up camp in Lyon. When I went to the gazebo, I found Winnie and her two daughters putting up decorations, and I asked if it was somebody's birthday.

"No, dear," said Winnie. "It's the anniversary of Konrad's death, the founder of the circus. We have a celebration every year to mark the day. Marina insists on it. Did you know they used to be lovers?"

Her daughters giggled as they untangled some frilly ribbons at her mentioning Marina having a lover.

"Really?"

She nodded. "They were together for a very long time. Never married, though. Konrad was forever asking her, but Marina always said no, said that it wasn't because she didn't love him, but more that she didn't believe in the institution of marriage."

"Oh. That's kind of romantic, actually."

"You think so?" Winnie questioned curiously.

"Well, yeah, staying together for love is better than staying together because of a piece of paper. The paper is the prison. Making the choice to stay with someone without the prison feels more like true love to me."

Winnie grinned and gave me a perceptive look. "Your parents divorced, didn't they?"

I only shrugged before I heard recognisable laughter from behind and turned to see Marina approaching. Her red hair was up in an intricate French twist, and she wore a long black dress that would have looked like Victorian mourning garb if it weren't for the bustier and cleavage. On any other woman her age, I would have said the cleavage was excessive, but somehow it suited her.

"I knew there was a reason why I liked you," she said as she came to stand beside me. I felt a little embarrassed to be caught talking about her, but I knew she didn't mind after she squeezed my hand and gave me a wink. I caught a quick flash of Jack walking by, his eyes meeting mine for a fraction of a second before he was gone again. This was how things had been the past few days. Catching glimpses of him, but no real contact. He was keeping his distance, and I constantly felt like my lungs were burning.

I wanted to reach out to him, but feared being pushed away again. I'd been agonising over what he'd said, trying to figure out what it all meant, but I knew deep down he'd been purposefully vague. He didn't want me to know the truth, whatever it was.

So tonight was all about celebrating. I decided I was going to force myself to have a good time, even though my heart had other ideas. The stupid thing wanted me lying in bed, agonising over Jack and his sudden distance. And no way was I letting that happen.

When I arrived back at the camper, I found Lola and Violet in the living area, doing each other's hair and makeup. This whole attack thing had really brought them closer together. It was heart-warming to see their friendship evolving, and, let's face it, my heart definitely needed a bit of warmth these days.

For the party, Lola talked me into wearing a tight little black dress she owned but never wore because it was too big for her. Surprise, surprise, it fit me perfectly, and I hardly recognised myself as I examined my appearance in our tiny bathroom mirror. Violet had done my makeup all smoky and dark, which made my blue-grey eyes look brighter somehow, and Lola curled my straight blonde hair into flowing waves.

"I have to say, we all look hot as fuck tonight," Lola declared as we stood in the kitchen, passing around a small bottle of vodka and taking turns knocking it back. Violet and I both looked at each other and laughed. Our Lola was back, and it felt really good to see her being her old self again.

I knew choosing to wear heels was a bad decision when I stepped outside onto the grass and felt the vodka take hold. Thankfully, Lola linked her arm through mine for balance before I could stumble to my knees. When we arrived at the gazebo, I recognised some of the circus workers had formed a band; one guy played the accordion, one played an acoustic guitar, and the third beat his hands on a wooden barrel he was using as a drum. The music they played was loud and rhythmic, and it made me feel excited.

"Fucking show-offs," I heard Violet mutter grumpily, and my eyes wandered in the direction she was looking. Just to the right of the gazebo was a tall tree, lit up in the dark by dozens of tea light candles nestled at its base. Its branches spread out like veins fifteen feet high in the air. From the branches hung three women in various poses, and I instantly recognised it was Julie and her sisters. They hung from the silk they usually used in their act, but unlike inside the Spiegeltent, none of them were moving.

It was certainly a striking scene, and though I wasn't exactly fond of Julie, I thought that what she and her sisters had created was beautiful. Mary's limbs were spread out like a starfish, while Molly wrapped her body around the silk, clinging to it like a koala. Julie's pose was the *pièce de resistance*, as she hung elegantly in the middle, the silk holding her at the waist.

"Don't be so cynical, Vi," said Lola, nudging her with her elbow. "It's performance art. I think it looks pretty."

"It's a pity none of them are pretty on the inside."

"Okay, so Julie might be a bitch, but Mary and Molly are okay," Lola conceded as she followed Violet over to a table of drinks and party food. I stood in place, still taking in the scene. They'd chosen the strongest three branches to hang from, and they were so still I began to wonder if they were even breathing. It was mesmerising, and I hated to admit it, but I'd give anything to have a couple of hours right now to paint them.

I felt rather than saw the movement to my left, and out of the corner of my eye I saw Jack standing there. His eyes weren't on the sisters, they were on me, and I felt positively violated as they wandered from my face to my chest and then all down my body and back up again. He was definitely noticing my more glamorous than usual appearance, and I so desperately wanted to know what he thought of it.

Did he like this me better than the everyday me?

Did glamour and makeup mean anything to him?

I got the distinct feeling that it didn't. I mean, sometimes he wore eyeliner as part of his act, but that was all just for dramatics, to make him look as dark and mysterious as the art he performed. I wouldn't be surprised if Marina had suggested it to him. I just couldn't see Jack thinking to wear eyeliner on his own.

I felt suspended in time and space as I slowly turned to him and gave him a look of acknowledgement. It said, *I know you're there, and I know you're not going to talk to me.* I pulled myself away and went to find Violet and Lola. They were sitting with the Brazilian stuntmen, which was just fantastic, since I'd promised myself I'd keep my distance from Pedro. The place was crowded and there wasn't anywhere else to sit, so I sighed and gave in, taking a spot across from him. He openly leered at me, his seedy gaze contradicting the fun-loving, carefree image he tried to present to everyone else.

He said something under his breath that I didn't quite catch, but I got the distinct sense it wasn't friendly. My hackles rose instantly, and I was about to give up on this party before it had even started when somebody slid onto the bench next to me, making it a very tight squeeze. His smell was so familiar, and the tension inside me loosened just to have Jack close.

How could he ever think he was a danger to me when he made me feel this safe?

I was frozen in place, felt too exposed to acknowledge him, but the outside of his thigh pressed up against mine and our shoulders were touching. Such sweet relief it was even to have this small, impersonal amount of contact.

"Her saviour arrives." Pedro spat disdainfully before picking up his beer and taking a long swig.

Lola passed me a plastic cup with red wine and I took it gratefully, glad to have some small distraction from Jack's closeness. I wanted to say something to him, even make polite small talk, but I couldn't seem to find my voice.

My attention was distracted when people began cheering and clapping as Marina took to the makeshift stage where the band was playing. There was no microphone, but somehow her voice carried well around the space.

"As many of you who knew him will agree, Konrad was one of the best people the world ever thought to spit out. He was a marvellously twisted human being, and so perfect in his madness. That madness took him in the end, and, like many who came before him, he put out his own flame. But in his life he created all of this," she said, spreading her arms out, "and so, on this day I will always think of him, and I will always thank him for leaving behind such beauty in my memories." She stopped and brought a shot glass to her mouth, knocking it back in one go. "Here's to the love of my life. May he wander between the worlds until we meet again."

Her words were so heartfelt, so full of emotion, that even though I never knew the man, I felt my eyes grow wet. It was clear from what she said that Konrad had taken his own life. My emotional state was only worsened when the guitar player began to pick at the strings and Marina started to sing "Starry, Starry Night" in a surprisingly appealing voice.

I knew in that moment that I was going to paint this scene. It struck me so powerfully that I'd never forget it: Marina standing there, a vision in black, her hair so red and her eyes so sad. I was lost in the song when I realised someone was staring at me, and I turned my head to find Jack's eyes blazing fiercely.

"You're crying," he murmured, and reached over to wipe away my tears with his fingertips.

"It's sad," I said, feeling strangely exposed and self-conscious. "How much she clearly misses him, I mean."

"Have you ever missed someone that much?" he asked, voice intense.

"No," I answered honestly, wanting to tack onto the end that if I'd spent as many years with him as Marina had with Konrad, then I'd probably die of the pain from missing him.

"You're lucky, then," he said.

I knew the meaning behind his words. I was lucky, but he was not, because he'd probably missed his brother like Marina missed Konrad. God, how I hoped Jay would read my letter and come find him. The laughter and talk that surrounded us was loud, but I still felt like I was in a bubble with Jack, his attention all-consuming.

"You shouldn't be sitting here, looking like that," he said, and I furrowed my brow.

"Why not?"

He leaned in close and my heart stuttered, his lips touching the shell of my ear as he whispered, "Because the wolves are circling, and I could be considered one of them."

Twelve

With courage Jack threw his mask away forever

I shivered, but before I could react to his words, the music changed, the band belting out a fast-paced number. Lola grabbed my hand to pull me up from my seat. I was still reeling after what Jack had said to refuse dancing with her, and before I knew it, I was crowded amid a sea of other bodies in the middle of the floor.

Lola clapped and stomped her foot in time to the beat and I copied her, trying to get into it as my eyes sought out Jack. I couldn't spot him over all the moving heads, and the loud music was distracting. A moment later, we were joined by a smiling Luan, who put his hands on Lola's waist and matched the tempo of her movements with his own. Violet was to my right, and I couldn't help laughing when Pedro tried to dance with her. She completely blanked him and instead focused her attention on a tall blond guy I recognised from around the campsite. My laughter cut off abruptly when I saw his attention land on me, and he began moving through the gyrating bodies.

Before he reached me, I felt warm, familiar arms go around my waist, and my heart fluttered. The moment Pedro spotted Jack, he scowled and turned away. My head swam with relief. I soaked in being close to him for a moment before he bent down and spoke into my ear.

"I won't always be here to be your good wolf, Lille. What will you do about the bad ones then?"

I turned my body and stared up at him. His mouth was so close, and I missed it. I was looking at his lips while I replied, "If you're my good wolf, then why do you think you're bad for me?"

A wall went up behind his eyes. "Because I am."

I leaned closer, moulding my body to his. I knew he felt how perfectly we connected by his sudden intake of breath, my breasts pushing into his chest. "That's not a good enough answer," I told him, then bravely went up on my tiptoes to brush my lips over his. It was a handy thing I was wearing heels now, because it meant I wasn't at too much of a disadvantage in height.

"Don't," he said pleadingly, but I wasn't feeling very charitable. I missed him, and something told me he missed me, too. It was ridiculous to keep fighting it, so I kissed him. I ran my tongue along the seam of his lips, then dipped inside, my body straining against his, because whenever I got to taste him, it always felt too good. I was breathless when I broke away for air.

"If you don't want this, then I want a better reason, Jack." I wasn't sure what it was, perhaps the mix of vodka and red wine, or maybe the dark of the night and the feeling of recklessness this party of death brought on, but I was feeling braver than I'd ever felt before.

He gripped the back of my neck, then brought his mouth down on mine with a hard, fierce hunger that caused my bravery to waver. In that moment, I knew that when we'd been together before, he'd been holding back a great deal of himself. In fact, he still was, and I shuddered not unpleasantly to think of what it would be like to have him unleash his entire self on me.

I moaned as his fingers dug into my neck, his tongue worshipping my mouth and his erection thickening against my thigh.

"Jack," I gasped, and though I could feel several stares on us, I didn't have the ability to focus on anyone else but him.

He took my hand in his then and dragged me away from the dancing. The music became less loud the farther away we got, and soon we were past the campers and trucks and heading towards an empty field.

"Where are you taking me?" I asked, voice thick with arousal and curiosity.

"Somewhere I can give you a good enough answer. I won't pull you in completely until you know everything. Then you can make your own decision," he bit out, and my arousal vanished in a heartbeat. My curiosity remained, but it was now tinged with apprehension. I stumbled on my heels, and Jack stopped walking to bend down and relieve me of my shoes. He held them both in one hand while scooping me up with the other. I startled and gripped his neck, holding on tight as we walked through the long grass until he reached a cluster of bushy trees. I slid down his solid, hard body, and my feet touched the earth.

"Why are we here?" I asked as I glanced all about, voice hushed. There was hardly any light here, just a greyish-yellow cloud from the city in the distance.

He rubbed his jaw and paced, then looked back at me. "I needed to go somewhere away from listening ears to tell you this, but I'm starting to wonder if I should confide in you at all."

"You said before that you trusted me. You trusted me enough to tell me about your brother," I whispered. *And you betrayed that trust, Lille. He just doesn't know it yet,* my conscience whispered back.

"Yeah, and look where that got me," he replied, and I flinched. He didn't know the half of it. Still, I wanted to know more. I wanted to know everything about this enigma of a man.

I took three steps forward until I was in front of him, close enough to take his big hand in mine and place it over my heart. "You can still trust me, Jack. Whatever you tell me will stay between the two of us. I just need to know why you think we can't be together. I don't know about you, but I've never felt anything like this before. I've never had a man make me feel the way you make me feel."

My voice felt louder, more pronounced in the quiet darkness, and I could just make out the shine of his eyes as he stared at me. He cupped my jaw in his hand and seemed to sigh.

"I feel it, Lille. Maybe even more than you do."

I gripped his shirt in my hands, my mouth a hair's breadth away from his. "So why not let it happen, then? Sometimes I lie awake at night, unable to sleep, because I can't stop thinking of you, can't stop fixating on how empty I feel and how I want you to fill me up."

He groaned as the words left my lips, then swore, low and guttural. "*Fuck.*"

I started to plant kisses along his neck, my hands travelling down his flat torso. "I love how you feel, Jack." Yeah, I was definitely running on alcohol-fuelled courage tonight.

"Wait," he breathed, and caught my wrists, stopping their descent.

I shivered, my skin prickling with the nighttime cold. Jack must have noticed, because he let go of me and took off his work shirt before draping it around my shoulders. There was something about the way he did it that made me fall for him a little. How he could be so caring was completely at odds with his gruff, masculine exterior. He tugged me over to a tree and sat down, pulling me between his legs so I was sitting with my back to his front, his arms cradling me in warmth.

I moved against him, and he groaned again. "God, you're horny tonight."

"It's your fault," I said fitfully.

He growled low and his fingers danced along my thigh, tapping out a silent rhythm. It was unexpected when he began to speak. "This isn't a pretty story, Lille. In fact, it's going to make you feel sick beyond belief. And after you hear it, you'll probably feel sick just to look at me."

"That's not possible," I argued, and he went silent for a moment.

"I told you a little about my foster mother, Frances, though calling her a mother is being very generous. She wasn't a nice woman, and taking young boys into her home was a money-making scheme, pure and simple."

All of a sudden, I didn't want to hear his story. Especially if this was him giving me a good enough answer as to why we couldn't be together. At the same time, I needed him to tell me so that I could disprove it, counter it with all of my own reasons as to why it didn't matter.

"Do you mean so she could get government support?" I asked, keeping my voice low and soft.

"Partly. But more so that she could pimp us out." His stark reply made me startle, and I twisted in his arms so I could look at him. For a moment I thought he might be messing with me, but then, if I knew anything about Jack McCabe, it was that he didn't beat around the bush. No, he was telling the truth, and I was shocked and disgusted as it all sank in.

"You're not lying, are you?" I whispered, and he shook his head. I remembered Marina telling me about the first time she'd met Jack on the street, and how he thought she was trying to solicit him for sex. Now it all made sense. The horror of his reality struck me silent as I gripped onto his arm, too tight, almost. Then I began to move my hands to his face, touching him tenderly, like he might break any second as I murmured, "You poor, poor thing."

For a long time we just sat there, staring into each other's eyes. Mine said, *This doesn't change how I see you.* His said, *How can it not?*

"I was thirteen when it all started. At night, men would come into the room I shared with two other boys. Sometimes women, though more often than not it was men. You can't believe how small your world becomes when you depend on one person to survive and that person has no mercy. How it feels like there's no escape but to suffer in silence. The years went by, and I started to become numb to sex. In the beginning I was aroused against my will, but by the end I felt nothing. I retreated inside my head. I didn't even want to be with girls my own age because everything connected to my sexuality made me feel sick. I hardly ever masturbated.

"Frances used to call me Freaky Jack because of my burn scars. Sometimes she'd forbid me from wearing a shirt around the house and would periodically poke at my scars, saying how ugly they were, how I was lucky she took me in because nobody else would want a disfigured boy. Her words rang true. My uncle didn't want me, and neither did my brother. When I was sixteen, I came home one day, and the house was empty except for Frances. She was in the kitchen making lunch, a pan of oil heating on the cooker. When she saw me, she made some cruel comment. I can't even remember it anymore, but it was the last straw. I completely snapped, picked up the pan of oil, and threw it in her face. I'd never heard screaming like it — her agony as she wailed was satisfying to me. I didn't feel horror, I felt justice, I felt pleasure. I left her there, disfigured even worse than I was, packed my stuff, and left. I'm not sure if she reported me to the police, but no one ever came for me. I've been on my own ever since."

My brain was still trying to piece together all the information when he continued talking. "To this day, I've been obsessed with burning. Obsessed with fire and heat, and what it can do to people. When I was a child, it always frightened me, reminded me of the horror of losing my family and almost dying. Somehow, by harming Frances, I'd turned it into my medicine. I'd burn stuff all the time. It was addicting. You can't believe the relief it brought me. Then I began learning how to breathe it, how to eat it, and the performance followed. It's still the only thing that gives me complete sexual gratification, Lille."

Suddenly, what he was trying to say made sense. I understood why he'd told me his sad, horrific story. It was to make a point. That point said this was his reason. This was his proper answer. *You have to stay away from me because being with me means you'll get burned, literally.*

Two memories struck me at once, how I'd burned my hand back home in the restaurant and how Jack couldn't take his eyes off me afterwards. How it had happened again in Violet's camper, and that was the first time he'd been overtly sexual towards me. It had turned him on.

"So, you're into sadomasochism," I said quietly, and I wasn't sure if I meant it as a statement or a question.

"More like erotically fixated with burning. Does that frighten you?" he asked, eyes seeking. He was tense as he awaited my reply.

"A little bit," I answered honestly, and saw him wince. That's when I knew he'd been holding out hope that I wouldn't reject him. That he could show me all his flaws and have me accept them. "No, don't do that," I said. "Don't pull away. What that woman submitted you to was unforgiveable. She was a monster, and I would never judge you for what you did to her. By all accounts, she deserved it."

"But it turned me on, Lille. I told you experiences shape us, twist us, and mine have twisted me in ways not meant for women like you."

Desperately, I grabbed his hand and placed it on my breast. His breathing grew shallow. "Does that turn you on?" I whispered, and he nodded as he swallowed. I bent and pressed my lips to his throat. "Does this?" Again, he nodded, and I felt the evidence of his arousal in how he hardened against my inner thigh. I smiled as I spoke into his skin. "Then, quite frankly, Jack, I have to ask, what exactly is the problem?"

Abruptly, he turned us so that I was no longer in the power position. He crouched over me, pulling my legs around his waist and growling in my ear, "The problem is that it makes me want to pour wax over your skin, press hot matches to your thighs. It makes want to leave marks all over your body until no man can refute that you're mine."

I moaned and pulled him closer, and I wasn't sure who was more surprised by my reaction, me or him. I couldn't understand why, because he was telling me he wanted to hurt me, but I'd never been more aroused in my entire life.

With only a few deft movements, he had my legs parted wide, his hand sliding under my dress, beneath the fabric of my underwear, and discovering how wet I was. A strangled cry escaped me as he thrust two fingers into me, and I bit his neck, causing a deep, masculine groan. His body was so magnificent, I wanted to bite and lick him everywhere. He buried his face in my neck, breathing raggedly, and muttering lovely worshipful swear words into my skin.

Fuck, fuck, fuck, you feel good, you're so wet, shit, I love how you feel, Christ, Lille, I've dreamt about this.

His fingers moved in and out, his thumb finding my clit and applying just the right amount of pressure to make me whimper. The sweet relief of his touch was ecstasy. I tried to remember to be frightened, to be scared of what he wanted to do to me, but I couldn't. The overwhelming urge to have him inside me outweighed everything else until I was nothing but a needy pile of flesh and bones.

I grabbed a handful of his hair as he travelled down my body, his hand still working me into a frenzy as his mouth met the rise of my breasts. His other hand came up, pushing the top of the dress down urgently to reveal my nipples. His mouth was on me in an instant, alternating between licks, sucks, and bites and I felt my body coil tight. I was going to come so fast it was almost embarrassing.

"Jack," I cried out as my orgasm hit me quick. I was blushing all over as his eyes raked my body, and then he kissed me in a way that was almost more indecent than what his hand was doing. The slow slide of his tongue was dirty and erotic, and I knew I could become addicted to the way he tasted me.

This was nothing like the sex I'd had before. It was in a whole other stratosphere, it was *more*, and it wasn't even sex, not yet. He rose up on his knees and dragged my underwear down my legs. A moment later they were gone, tucked into his pants pocket. He leaned down and kissed me again before breathing a ragged warning, "I'm going to fuck you now, and it won't be slow."

I felt more like a spectator than a participant as I watched him move. The way he undid his belt buckle was too sexy for words. I soaked in every inch of him when he pulled himself from his boxers. He withdrew a condom from his pocket, tore open the packet, and began rolling it down his length. Eyes levelled firmly between my legs, he moved my thigh aside and tilted his head, just looking at me, and I knew I was blushing again. I felt something rattle as he reached inside his pocket a second time and pulled out a packet of matches.

The next time our eyes met, there was a question in his, requesting permission, and I didn't hesitate a moment in giving it. I wanted this. Even though he was going to hurt me, I knew that he wouldn't *hurt* me. He'd told me he trusted me, and now I was trusting him right back. I watched in fascination as he flicked the match along the edge of the box and a flame sparked to life. It lit up his face, such handsome features, his eyes liquid black as he stared at the fire with such enchantment. Then he blew it out, and he was a work of light and shadow again. Smoke rose from the match as he took it between his teeth, then bent over me, his mouth going to my breast.

I yelped when I felt the hot sting against my nipple as it met the tip of the match, but it was instantly soothed by the soft, wet lick of his tongue. It happened once more, and once more he gave me his tongue to temper out the burn. It was actually...exciting. I felt his cock nudge against my lips, and then he was pushing into me, the invasion deliciously sweet. I felt tight around him. It had been a while since anyone had been inside me, and it showed. Jack's groan filled my ears as he thrust his hips, and he was suddenly embedded deep.

Our gazes locked, and it felt like in that moment, we both had the exact same thought.

Wow.

His eyes grew hooded as his hands held my hips, and his movements were hard and fast. He'd been right to warn me, because there was nothing slow or soft about this. Yet, still, it was strangely tender.

"Jesus," he hissed when I clenched around him, a light sheen of sweat forming at his brow. My eyes had long since adjusted to the dark, and now it felt like I could see every inch of him. Every pore and crevice.

Somehow, by joining our bodies, we lit each other up.

The long grass was soft beneath me as I stared up at him, mouth open, sounds I never knew I was capable of making coming out of me in a rush. I loved how his defined, muscular hips jutted in and out, almost violently, in his need to go deeper, harder. He wore his hunger on his face, and my heart squeezed knowing it was all for me. I felt like the centre of his universe right then, and there was no denying that he was the centre of mine.

Suddenly, he was picking me up and flipping us over so I was straddling him. His hips hammered up into me from below, and the pleasure was so much more intense for me this way. From the searing look he gave me, I knew that had been his intention. His hands massaged my breasts as I rode him.

"Fuck, you should see yourself right now," he growled, and then our movements grew more frenzied as we raced toward release. I took his hands in mine, lacing our fingers, not breaking eye contact as I felt myself contract around him. His noises filled my ears and were branded into my memory as he came, long and hard, and I collapsed on top of him, savouring the feel of my naked breasts on his skin.

His arms went tight around me, and I closed my eyes as I nestled my face in the crook of his neck.

Our hearts beat in time; I could feel his fluttering beneath me. Mine was racing, too. I was fascinated by how something that felt so delicate could reside inside such a hard, impenetrable body.

"That was…holy fuck…Lille," he said breathlessly, making me laugh gently, my eyes still closed. He laughed, too, and it was the most glorious sound. When it quietened down, I found myself listening to his heartbeat again, savouring the feeling of connection in the moment, happily drowning in it.

I wasn't sure who fell asleep first, but it wasn't long before the soothing sounds of the night were pulling me under.

Thirteen
Julie showed Lille her true colours

I woke up to a chill that came from the cool morning air surrounding me rather the hot, lean body beneath me. Sometime during the night, Jack had pulled my dress back in place, and I missed the feel of his skin. His shirt was draped over my back, and I nuzzled into his neck, savouring his heady masculine scent.

I couldn't believe we'd slept the entire night outdoors. I'd been so blissed out by our lovemaking that I hadn't cared. I didn't want to leave, not even now that the day had arrived, the sun lighting up the deeds of the night before. Unable to resist, I began planting soft little kisses on his neck, hoping he'd wake up to them. I felt him move a little before his eyes flickered open. He looked down at me, seconds drifting by as he remembered what we'd done, and then his arms tightened around me.

"You make a good blanket, flower," he said, voice all raspy.

"And you make a delectable bed," I giggled quietly in reply.

His smile lit up his face, the sunlight shining on his dark brown eyes, making them swirl with flecks of honey gold. We stayed like that for a while, me with my head on his chest, gazing up at him, and him tracing the contours of my face with his fingertips.

"We should probably get up," I said, even though I didn't want to. "Somebody might come by and see us."

"Somebody might," Jack replied, but it still took him a long few moments to move. He sat up, bringing me with him, and his shirt fell off my back. As he helped me to stand, I turned my neck from side to side, feeling an ache.

My legs and arms felt achy, too, but it was a satisfying sort of ache. I liked knowing that spending the night with Jack was what gave it to me. We stared at one another as we righted our clothes, silly happy grins on our faces. Then Jack laced his fingers with mine and led me back to the campsite. I walked in my bare feet, the grass ticklish on my soles as I held my shoes in my hand. I wondered what I looked like, and considering the heavy makeup I'd been wearing last night, it was probably smudged all over my face. Jack didn't seem to care, but I wanted to go clean up before breakfast. Reaching Violet's camper, he backed me up against it and gave me a long, scorching kiss goodbye. I was weak in the knees by the time he withdrew, and it took all my strength to climb the steps into the van.

Lola was eating breakfast when I went in, the tiny television playing the morning news. A loud snore rang out from Violet's room, so I knew she was still sleeping.

"Where did you disappear off to last night, ya dirty little stop out?" Lola asked excitedly as she took in my appearance.

I went straight to the kitchen and poured myself a glass of water, knocked it back in two long gulps, then turned to face her, fidgeting. "Um, Jack and I sort of…."

"I fucking knew it!" she interrupted me. "What was it like?"

Her question encouraged a stupid dreamy look to come over my face, which must have spoken volumes, because she was laughing, and Lola had a real dirty laugh. I kind of loved hearing it.

"That good, huh?"

I sighed. "Pretty much."

She huffed. "Some girls get all the luck."

For a moment, I felt awkward as I remembered all that Lola had been through lately. Did it make her uncomfortable to talk about sex? If it did, she didn't show it. I told her I was going to take a shower and left her to finish her breakfast. Half an hour later, I was clean and dressed in fresh clothes, a loose cream top and some washed denim jeans. The top was oversized and kind of fell off one shoulder, showing my black bra strap. I thought my choice in clothing was indicative of how I felt, all lazy and sexed up.

I left my hair down and pulled on my shoes before heading to the gazebo in search of a hot breakfast. I was starving, and the tea and toast back at the camper wouldn't be enough to sate my appetite. When I got there, it seemed like half the circus was sporting a hangover as they chowed down on sausage and eggs. I loaded my plate up, and as I went in search of a seat, I felt someone tug on the end of my top.

I hadn't spotted Jack sitting there, and had almost walked right past him. He gave me an affectionate, sexy look, taking my plate from me and setting it on the table before pulling me onto his lap. I must have felt the ferocity of her stare, because my gaze was drawn in the direction of Julie, who was sitting at a table a few feet away, glaring daggers at me.

Whoa.

"Hey," Jack murmured in my ear, distracting me from the eye daggers with one hand on my thigh as he ran his nose down the side of my neck.

I glanced at him and teased, "So, is this how it's going to be? By night you're my bed, and by day you're my chair?"

His voice lowered, and his eyes heated up, "If it means I get your arse cushioning my dick, then yeah."

"You've got a frisky mouth," I said, turning and reaching for my fork.

I let out a tiny yelp when I felt his teeth graze my bare shoulder. "All the better to bite you with." His warm hand grasped my shoulder, and his thumb slid beneath the strap of my bra, causing me to shiver. I almost didn't hear him when he growled low, "This is a good look for you."

My tummy gurgled and I blushed, finally giving in and shovelling some food into my mouth. Whenever I was close to Jack, it was always so tempting to just lose myself in him. His thumb brushed discreetly over my nipple as he asked, "How are you feeling this morning? Any soreness?"

The memory of his mouth on me with the hot matchstick between his teeth hit me, and I shivered. My nipple was a little sore, along with a whole range of other parts, but it wasn't unpleasant.

"A small bit," I answered.

His eyes grew hooded as he playfully leaned in and said, "What I did to you last night was child's play, Lille. The next time I can't be quite so gentle."

Wow. If he thought last night was gentle, then I shuddered to think what he was like rough – in a good way.

A loud clatter sounded close by, and my attention was drawn to King as he stumbled into the gazebo. He knocked into Julie's table where she sat with her two sisters, causing their cups and plates to tumble over. Julie rose from her seat, her voice shrill as she focused the glare she'd been giving me earlier on King.

"You fucking imbecile, look what you've done!"

King held his hands in the air. "Sorry, sorry, wasn't looking where I was going."

"That's your problem," Julie spat. "You never do. Seriously, what is the point of you? I really don't understand why Marina even lets you stay here."

I felt Jack lift me from his lap, about to go and intervene, when Marina suddenly appeared. She stood between Julie and her brother, a look of eerie calm on her face as she sized Julie up.

"This is my circus, girl. You'd do well to remember that. King apologised for his actions. Now, if I ever hear you speak to him like you just did again, I'll kick you and your sisters off the lineup so quick you'll have skid marks on your backside."

Julie swallowed, her face growing red, restrained fury in her eyes as she silently sat back down. Her sisters anxiously worked to clean up the mess on the table. Marina turned to King and placed her hand on his shoulder, murmuring something to him that nobody else could hear. His entire form seemed to slump miserably as he nodded to her, then turned and left.

There was an air of tension amongst those present as Marina strode away, her five-foot-two height seeming taller and more foreboding all of a sudden. I glanced at Jack to find him seething, and it took me by surprise. He was staring at Julie, and it was clear to me that he was pissed off by how she treated King. I think she misinterpreted his attention as the positive kind, because she gave him a sultry smile. The woman needed to get a clue.

I put my hand on Jack's thigh and rubbed it in an effort to calm his temper. Marina had already put Julie in her place; there was no need for him to still be riled up. I wondered at his anger, since he'd spoken harshly to King himself in the past. But what happened today had been an accident. King had apologised. And something told me that

Jack felt an affection for the man; he could relate to him on some level, and that was why he also felt a protectiveness towards him.

I leaned close and gave Jack a peck on the cheek, which seemed to distract him. He gave me a tender look, and then we ate the rest of our meal in companionable silence. After breakfast I sat in the back of the Spiegeltent, doing sketches as Jack practiced some new additions to his act. I was supposed to be using it as an opportunity to do some work on my picture of him, but found myself simply sitting back and watching mostly. The way he moved was so careful and practiced, seamless, really, and it was hard to look away. The fiery torches weren't quite so dark and dangerous-looking in the light of day, but Jack still managed to make them fascinating.

I wondered about his obsession with the element, how it had become something he needed to be around all the time in order to get through the day. It struck me as strange at first, but then when I thought on it more, I realised it was no stranger than people smoking cigarettes because they craved nicotine, or drinking coffee to sate their hunger for caffeine. It was an addiction, simple as that. Burning gave him relief. He associated it with the one time in his life he felt truly liberated from being a victim. I thought I should be more appalled by what he'd done to his foster mum and by what she had done to him, but I wasn't.

It was all just a part of life's darkness. And without darkness, there would be no light.

I didn't see him as a damaged little boy; I saw him as a unique, wonderful, yet very breakable grown man.

***

Later that day I was walking about the campsite in search of Bea. I hadn't seen her for a couple of days, and I was beginning to worry. Perhaps she'd caught the flu that was going around. I was just making my way past the back of the Spiegeltent in the direction of Aiden's camper when I suddenly felt myself propelling forward, a sharp pain shattering through my skull. My hand went to my head as my breath left me all in a rush. I could feel a wetness, and as I moved my fingers in front of my face, I saw they were red with blood.

It took me several beats to find my bearings as I turned and found Julie standing in front of me, wielding a broken plank of wood. My eyes moved from the wood to her and then back again as my brain tried to compute the fact that she'd just whacked me with it.

"What the hell?!" I yelled at her, and she dropped the wood before launching herself at me. Adrenaline flooded my system as she grabbed my throat in her surprisingly strong grip and slammed my body back into the hard frame of the tent. Pain shattered down my spine, my head still thumping. She was shorter than I was by about three or four inches, but she had the muscle tone of a professional athlete, hence her strength.

Acrobats be crazy.

First King and now me. She really was on a roll today.

"You're going to stay the fuck away from Jack, or the next time, I swear I'll end you," she hissed, crazy eyes piercing me. My entire body had broken into a cold sweat, and my throat was constricting from her grip. When I didn't answer, she tightened it more, and I broke into a fit of choking. My heart was trying to beat its way out of my chest, and I was genuinely in fear for my life. With just the hold she had on my neck, she pulled my body forward, then slammed me back into the tent again.

"Say it!" she demanded.

My voice came out scratchy and broken. "I'll s-s-stay away from him."

She looked me up and down, disdain clear in her expression. "I had him long before you came along. Don't you know you can't just show up, all fucking innocent and clueless, and take what doesn't belong to you? That's not how it works," she spat, and the spray hit me right in the face. "There are *rules*."

"I didn't know you were together, I swear," I said, and her grip started to loosen. I was lying through my teeth, of course, but I'd never experienced an attack like this, and I was scared witless. She was obviously mentally disturbed, and I couldn't believe I didn't pick up on it sooner. It was startling to think that this woman could do such beautiful things with her body, perform in a way that provoked such emotion in her audience, yet be so thoroughly, certifiably insane.

Her hand left my throat completely, but only to slap me hard across the face, so hard it was going to leave a mark. My mind reeled, and my body began to shake as tears ran down my cheeks. Slaps across the face were Mum's signature move, and suddenly I was stuck in countless memories.

I felt so small.

Wretched and unimportant.

Clutching my cheek in my hand, the sting echoing through my jaw, I looked back at Julie to find her still seething at me. "You're a liar. If I see you with him again, I'll break your face. And if you tell a single person about this, I'll cut out your tongue."

With that parting threat, she stomped off, leaving me feeling like I'd just entered an alternate universe where everyone was evil, and women you thought were just bitches were actually psychopaths.

But then I remembered what Winnie had told me back in Caen, when she'd let me pet her lions.

Julie is the little girl who pulled the legs from spiders, the one who poked at dogs until they turned vicious.

Suddenly, I wasn't so shocked anymore, and her behaviour made perfect sense. Winnie had spent years observing Julie. She knew what she was like far better than I did. And then there was the indignity she suffered this morning when Marina told her off in front of the entire circus. Attacking me was clearly her way of offsetting the shame and frustration she felt.

I sank to the grass, sitting there for God knows how long before I finally picked myself up and stumbled back to the camper. Violet and Lola were out, and after I'd cleaned myself up in the bathroom, I went straight to bed, changing into my pyjamas and climbing under the covers. I was completely spaced out, my body still humming from the attack. My head ached, and beneath my hair where I'd cleaned away the blood, I could feel a soft, mushy bump rising. My throat was raw, and I knew I'd have bruises on my neck tomorrow from where she'd choked me.

I cried for so long that it drained all of my energy, and I eventually fell asleep.

When I woke up, it was dark out. Lola was entering the room and came to sit at the end of my bed.

"Hey, are you all right, hon?" she asked, her face etched in concern as she took me in. I obviously seemed out of it.

I wanted to tell her about Julie, but I was frightened. If I told her, Lola would go find Julie and confront her, and I couldn't have that. I had no doubts that Julie would follow through on her threats, and I didn't want to be on the receiving end of her crazy ever again.

"I'm okay. I just have a little bit of a headache," I said, sitting up.

"Well, that's a relief. For a second there, I thought you might be coming down with what I had. You missed tonight's show. Oh, and Jack was looking for you."

I swore under my breath as I realised I'd be short on money, since I hadn't worked today. What happened with Julie had completely messed with my head, literally and figuratively. I hadn't even thought about working.

A knock sounded on the front door, and Lola went to answer it. I sank back under the blanket when I heard Jack asking for me. Lola murmured a reply, and then a moment later she was peeking her head back in the room.

"It's Jack. He wants to see you."

I swallowed thickly with nerves. I wanted to see him so badly, but Julie's threats were still ringing loud in my ears. I didn't know what to do. "Could you tell him I'm not feeling well and that I'll see him in the morning?"

She frowned but nodded. "Sure."

I heard her repeating my excuse to Jack and his tone grew stern, but since the bedroom door was shut, I couldn't quite hear what he was saying. Then loud footsteps sounded on the floor and a moment later his frame filled the doorway, a look of worry on his handsome face.

Lola came after him, complaining about him pushing by her, but he slammed the door, shutting her out, and hurried to my side. Before I knew it his hand was on my forehead, feeling for a temperature. I shifted uncomfortably in the bed and met his eyes.

"What's wrong, Lille?" he asked, voice soft and concerned.

211

"I'm just a little bit under the weather," I croaked. "It's nothing to worry about."

"If you're sick, I want to see you. You don't send Lola out with excuses, okay?" he said firmly, and all I could do was nod.

"Good. Now come here." He pulled back the blankets and lifted me onto his lap. I knew I shouldn't let him, but being close to him was my weakness. I was feeble in the face of his affection. My legs went around his waist, my arms around his neck as I hugged him and he took a deep breath, inhaling me. I was still shaky from earlier, and I think he noticed, because he pulled back and frowned down at me.

"You're freaked out by what I told you last night, aren't you?"

I shook my head. "No, of course not."

"Then why are you so on edge?"

"It's just been a long day, and I think sleeping outdoors drained my energy. My muscles ache." The moment I said it, his practiced hands found my thighs and began to massage. He looked like he wanted to kiss me, but he didn't; he only stared.

"That feel good?"

My answering sigh said it all, and his expression darkened.

"You've been on my mind all day."

I whimpered when he began rubbing the inside of my thigh and his knuckles grazed between my legs. My body sagged into him, completely at his mercy, and he chuckled low. "Too much, flower?"

"Not enough," I answered, biting my lip.

I let out a gasp of surprise when he full-on cupped my vagina and caressed me. Honest to God, I was done for. I

212

briefly considering telling him about Julie being a nutjob, but I was far too lusty in that moment to speak. I moaned into his neck, and he gathered my hair in one hand, using it to tug my mouth up to his.

I winced slightly at the pull, because it sent a sting to the bump Julie had inflicted. It wasn't enough to deter me, though. His tongue slid along mine, our mouths not yet meeting fully. His hand wandered inside my pants and beneath my knickers, seeking. When his thumb flicked across my clit, I shook as a wave of pleasure consumed me. I bit his full bottom lip, eliciting a low growl, and before I knew it, I was on my back, his fingers moving in a slow, tantalising rhythm.

His kiss matched the tempo of his hand, playing my body like he knew it intimately. I was nothing but a map, and he knew every single sweet spot. His thumb began to rub circles around my clit, agonisingly slow, and my hands scrambled for the buckle of his jeans. I was too lost in feeling to get his pants off, so I settled for palming his cock and loved the guttural hum that rose from deep in his throat in response to me touching him.

"Shit, I'm gonna come," I gasped, and his lips curved in a sexy smile.

"Come then, beautiful."

And I did. It was spectacular. His slow touches had teased me, made my orgasm so much more intense. I trembled beneath him, and his hands went to my face, pushing strands of hair away from my forehead.

"Fuck, who sent you?" he murmured reverently, and I swear my heart exploded. I nuzzled below his ear, then pressed my face to his chest and inhaled. I hated Julie even more in that moment, because she was ruining the most perfect thing I'd ever had. Jack kissed my temples, then unexpectedly, he rose from the bed.

"Sleep, flower, feel better, and I'll see you in the morning."

He was gone before I had the chance to reply. It would have been pointless anyway, because my throat was too thick with suppressed tears to say a word. I wasn't sure I had it in me to stay away from him, but I was going to have to try, at least in public.

And at least until I figured out what to do about Julie.

Fourteen

A storm fell over the lovers

The following day, avoiding Jack was something of a tactical endeavour. I didn't go to the gazebo for breakfast, and instead of sitting beside the camper to paint, I wandered outside the campsite and found a quiet spot beside some sweet-smelling bushes. I didn't get anything of much substance done because I was so angry at Julie. I hated feeling blackmailed like this. By lunchtime I grew hungry, and I cursed myself for not thinking to bring a packed sandwich.

So much for tactics.

My injuries felt far worse today than they did yesterday. My head thumped constantly, and I had to sneakily borrow some of Lola's makeup to cover the red mark on my cheek and the bruises on my neck.

I was almost at the camper when I heard Jack call out my name, so I quickened my pace.

"Lille! What the fuck?" he called in that way he had of sounding both stoic and pissed at the same time. The next thing I knew, I was being spun around as he grabbed hold of my arm.

Nervously, I glanced up at him. "Oh, hi, um, how are you?"

I sounded stupid, and it was clear as day that there something going on with me. His face was incredulous.

"Did you just ignore me?"

I shook my head fervently. "What? No. What are you talking about?"

"Unless you've gone deaf in the last twelve hours, then you were fucking ignoring me, Lille, and I want to know why."

"I swear to God, I wasn't ignoring you, Jack. I must have been daydreaming, because I didn't hear you."

He moved closer, like a panther, dark eyes narrowing. "Didn't hear what? I never told you I said anything, so clearly you're lying."

I gestured with my free hand. "You said the thing about me being deaf. It doesn't take a rocket scientist to figure out you said something that I didn't hear."

"Flower," he said quietly. The term of endearment didn't sound the way it usually did. In fact, it sounded a little threatening. "If you lie to me one more time, you won't like what happens next."

The bloody nerve of him! I used every ounce of strength I had in me to shove him away. Any other time I wouldn't have had such a strong response to his threat, but combined with Julie's blackmail, what he said was the last straw.

I pointed my finger at him. "Don't you dare fucking threaten me, Jack McCabe."

He stared at me, eyes hard, and for a moment we were locked in a standoff, a silent battle of wills. The silence was broken when somebody's footsteps crunched along the grass and I turned to see Marina approach, Pierre ambling alongside her as she carried a stack of flyers in her arms.

"Ah, just the two able-bodied young people I wanted to see," she said, smiling innocently like she hadn't a clue about the argument we'd just been having. Jack's gaze cut to her, and it was far from welcoming. Marina barely gave his hostility a second glance, and I wished I could have even half her impassivity when dealing with him.

216

"I need you two to head into town and leave some of these advertisements in the shops. We didn't sell as many seats as usual last night, so we need the extra publicity boost."

"Kind of busy at the moment, Marina," Jack grunted as I walked to her and took the flyers out of her hands.

"I can do it. I wasn't feeling well last night and couldn't make it to the show. This can be my way of paying you back. Jack doesn't need to help."

"You won't be able to manage it alone," said Marina. "Jack *will* help you."

There was a steeliness to her voice that brooked no argument, and Jack let out a grunt of annoyance before coming and taking the last of the flyers. Seeming satisfied, Marina sauntered off with Pierre, leaving us alone again. I was having a hard time looking at Jack, but I could feel him practically boring a hole into my skull.

"Our conversation isn't over," he called after me as I went inside the camper to grab a bag for the flyers. When I emerged, he stood there, all cranky and foreboding, and I hated that he still looked sexy as you fucking please. Christ, I was going to have to tell him about Julie, wasn't I? I mean, if nothing else, she couldn't just be left to run around kicking the crap out of her love rivals. I had to summon some courage and be brave. Yes, I was going to tell him.

Just…not right this second.

With a heavy silence between us, I followed Jack to a bus stop just outside the campsite, and we stood a few feet apart as we waited for one to come by. Thankfully, it only took a few minutes. Not so thankfully, each of those minutes felt like an hour. I could feel him watching me, studying me, trying to figure me out. When the bus finally arrived, there weren't any seats available. I stood beside a window while Jack hovered close to me, his arm raised up and holding on to a bar above my head. An electricity hummed between us, but not a word was spoken. Minutes went by, his attention on me like a physical touch. His smell filled my nose, and it was so divine it took all of my willpower not to rest my head on his shoulder and breathe him in.

"Last night you said you were sick when you weren't, and today you're avoiding me like the plague," Jack said, keeping his voice low so the other people on the bus couldn't hear. "I take it you've had more time to think about being with me, and decided it's not what you want." A sadness tinged his words, and guilt seized my chest. "I can't say I'm surprised. I knew the truth would change how you saw me."

No, no, no, my mind screamed, while on the outside I didn't know what to say. I placed my hand on his arm, half to comfort him and half for balance. "That's not it at all."

"What is it, then?" he asked, a flicker of hope flashing as his eyes scanned my face.

Before I could answer, the bus shuddered to a halt, and it was time for us to get off. My head was dizzy all of a sudden as I stepped onto the busy city street. I had to stumble to a nearby wall to steady myself. The spot where Julie had struck me was giving me trouble, and I wondered if I was having some sort of delayed concussion. I remembered that you weren't supposed to sleep after being hit on the head and inwardly cursed myself, because I'd gone straight to bed after. What an idiot.

Warm hands covered my shoulders. "Lille, are you all right? You've gone pale."

I breathed deeply and righted myself. "I'm fine. Standing on the bus just made me a little bit dizzy."

"Do you want to sit down for a minute?"

A twinge of pain hit me again, and I nodded. "Yes, please, just for a minute."

Slipping his arm around my waist, Jack led me to the nearest café and lowered me into a seat. He went up to the counter, and before I knew it, a sandwich and a glass of fresh juice was in front of me. *That* was it. My blood sugar was low because I'd missed lunch, and, combined with my recent blow to the head, my sudden bout of illness was totally understandable.

Jack slid into the booth next to me and gestured for me to eat the sandwich. I took an eager bite and almost groaned at how good it was. Ham and melted cheese.

"When was the last time you ate?"

I scratched my head. "Um, last night. I forgot breakfast…and lunch. I've had a lot on my mind."

His mouth formed a sad little frown, and he looked out the window, all broody. God, did that come out wrong or what? He thought I meant him. That *he* was the lot I had on my mind. It couldn't be further from the truth. In fact, when all was said and done, my feelings for Jack were quite simple. It was everything else that was complicated.

He flexed his hand as I ate, forming a fist, and I recognised this as a sign that he was on edge.

"Like I said on the bus," he started to say, "I understand. Shit, if I were you, I'd be running a mile."

I placed my hand on his before he had the chance to form a fist again. "You're wrong. That's not what this is about. I'm worried about my mother trying to find me, and well, I've been having trouble with someone on the campsite."

The moment the words left my mouth, he turned his entire body to face me as he tilted his head at an angle.

219

Those thick, dark eyebrows drawing together made his expression a little unsettling. "What do you mean? Has someone been hassling you? Was it that little Brazilian twat again?"

"No, no," I breathed, placing my hands against his chest. "It wasn't Pedro. It's…it's…well, it's Julie."

His eyes widened a tiny bit in surprise. "What did she say?"

"It wasn't so much what she said as what she did."

He didn't breathe a word, but he didn't have to. His face said it all. He wanted to know what she'd done, and he wanted to know now.

"Yesterday when I was out looking for Bea, Julie followed me to the back of the tent. There was nobody around, and she had this plank of wood she must have gotten off one of the cargo trucks. I didn't even know she was there until she clocked me with it."

"She what?" Jack eyes flared black murder.

"She hit me with it, then tried to choke me out," I said, tentatively tugging down the collar of my T-shirt and wiping away the makeup to show him my bruises. "She really hurt me. And honestly, I think she needs help. I mean, giving me evils in the gazebo is one thing, but attacking me is another entirely. She's off her rocker, Jack. She told me you two were together and warned me to stay away from you. She said if I told anyone what she did, she'd cut out my tongue. That's why I didn't say anything last night. I was in too much shock."

He absorbed my words and my bruises with a scary intensity. "She'll regret this." His hands went to my head, searching for the wound she'd inflicted with the wood. He hissed when he found it, and I winced. I felt squeamish just thinking about the mushy lump.

Pulling my body close to his, he clenched his jaw, and I could tell he was having a hard time with all this. It made me melt just a little so see how angry someone hurting me made him, and I regretted not telling him as soon as it happened. A long time passed before he pulled away and looked at me, tucking a loose strand of hair behind my ear.

"We travel great distances. However, sometimes living in close quarters with so many people can be stifling. I love the circus, but this life can make people go a little odd. I've spent a couple of nights with Julie, but those nights were spread over months, and I never gave her any reason to believe there was anything other than sex between us. Saying that, I really shouldn't have touched her in the first place. She's always been a wild card."

I absorbed his words, our faces close as we spoke quietly. The sandwich I'd just eaten, alongside the idea of Jack and Julie together, started to make my stomach feel a little queasy. "Did you ever, you know...*burn* her?"

Hesitation flickered in his gaze before he answered, "Once, but it didn't work out. Julie is more suited to being the one doing the burning. She doesn't like to be made weak. Being with her was like masturbation, Lille, staving off a need, that's all."

I glanced away, cheeks heating. He took my chin in his fingers and turned me to face him again. "The first thing we do after we leave here is go to the police station and report her. I've had enough of letting shit go, and the fact that the prick who attacked Lola is still out there makes me want to break something. Then we'll do the flyers. Then we go home. If you see Julie, you will not, I repeat, you will not act like you're staying away from me. You'll hold my fucking hand and show her she's not winning. The police can deal with the rest. I also want you to stay at my place

221

for the next few days. She won't dare touch you again with me around."

His plan was a good one…especially the suggestion I stay with him in his van. But still, the idea of reporting Julie, of causing drama for the circus, made me nervous. I was only just beginning to feel like a part of the community, and now I might end up alienating myself. I looked at the dark, brooding man sitting next to me, though, and knew it could be worse. At least in this scenario I got to have Jack.

He ordered another sandwich and shared it with me, but he ate most of it. I wondered absently just how much a big guy like him had to eat every day. I bet it was a lot. If he were a dog, he'd be a malamute or a German shepherd. And those things packed away the grub like nobody's business.

Even though I had to do most of the talking, I never felt alone while we were at the police station. Jack was close to me through it all, giving me subtle touches or looks to show his support. It struck me that I felt so much stronger when he was with me. He'd worried that being with him would be bad for me, when really the opposite was true.

By the time we left the station, I was exhausted, but we still had to do the flyers. We started on a street with lots of little boutique-style shops. Most of them employed women, and most of those women practically wet themselves when they saw Jack. It began to grate on my nerves, having to suffer through them flirting with him, and in broken English at that. One blonde in her mid-twenties seemed to be fluent, though, and that was the most uncomfortable of all.

"Would you mind if we left some of these with you?" Jack asked, handing her a stack of flyers. "We're with the circus just outside of town."

She leaned across the counter and fluttered her eyelashes, her V-neck shirt showing a healthy dose of cleavage. I didn't even think she realised I was there, standing by the door, uncomfortably holding my jealous/awkward girl of the year award.

"Of course not, *mon cher*, you look tired. Have you been on your feet all day? Come and sit down — I'll make you some coffee." When she reached for his arm, Jack moved out of the way.

"There's no need. We can't stop. We have more shops to visit, and it looks like the weather's turning."

The woman pursed her lips, and at his mention of "we," she suddenly became aware of my presence. Her narrow-eyed look wasn't too different from the ones Julie had been giving me of late, and I wondered if this was what I'd have to contend with from now on. Women hating me because I was with Jack.

Was I with him? It felt like we'd come to some sort of mutual understanding, but neither one of us had put into words what we were or what we were doing.

Jack was right about the weather. I glanced out the window to see some dark clouds forming, blocking out the sun, and I knew were in for some kind of storm, heavy rain at the very least.

After we finished visiting each shop on the street, we went to some of the local public spaces, and Jack stapled flyers to any free signage boards we could find. Man, he looked hot when he hammered a stapler into cork board. I think I might have drooled a little just from watching him.

The next time we stepped outside, I felt a drop of rain hit the top of my head. Moments later, it was pouring down. Jack took my hand in his and pulled me along, but we still got drenched. It was summer in France, and neither one of us was wearing a coat. Stupid unpredictable weather. Running didn't stop us from getting soaked, and our clothes were saturated when Jack tugged me under a bus shelter with him, both our chests heaving as we tried to catch our breaths.

His long sleeved T-shirt was glued to his chest, and I had a hard time looking away. I glanced up at him for a second and caught him smirking. A small, nervous giggle escaped me, and he laughed softly, looking across the street and brushing his long, wet hair away from his face. I actually thought he looked a little bit shy for a second. It made him seem so young.

"How old are you?" I blurted, and he gave me a sideways glance.

"Twenty-six." He must have seen the surprised look on my face as he continued, brow arching, "How old did you think I was?"

"You know what, I'm actually not sure. Sometimes you seem young, then other times you seem really wise and, I don't know, sort of unreachable."

He stared at me for a long time but didn't say anything.

I shivered in my damp clothes as the rain continued to pound down on the roof of the shelter, and I knew, I just knew by the way Jack's gaze was growing heated that my nipples were peeking through my top. I couldn't even bring myself to look, so I simply folded my arms across my chest to hide my embarrassment. An old lady came and stood under the shelter, lowering her umbrella and shaking out the rain. She peered at us and muttered something in

French about us catching our death with no coats on. Because she looked a little bit like my Gran, my mind wandered and I imagined her looking down on me, proudly watching my circus adventure unfold.

A moment later Jack was in front of me, his hands, which were surprisingly warm, cupping my neck, his thumbs massaging into my throat.

"Sorry you got wet," he said, and his words dripped with sexual undertones.

I shrugged, trying to play off how his expression alone was practically drying all my clothes. His eyes scorched, and I couldn't stop staring at his mouth, silently begging for his sensual lips to kiss me. An engine sounded to our left, and I turned to see a bus approach.

"Will this one take us back to the campsite?" I asked.

Jack nodded and laced his fingers through mine, pulling me onto the bus. The driver seemed annoyed that we were dripping water everywhere, but Jack just stared at him, unconcerned, and paid both our fares. He tugged me down to sit on his lap, and his arms went around my waist, his face pressing into my shoulder as he exhaled. His breath was hot, warming up my skin through the fabric, and a pleasurable shiver danced along my spine. My wet jeans were starting to itch. Add that to my urgent need for Jack simmering between my thighs, and I was about ready to combust.

I reached up and began running my fingers through his wet hair, trying to get out some of the tangles. He seemed to melt into my touch, and I savoured the simple act of grooming him. When his eyes met mine again, they were full of affection, and I thought he liked me touching his hair. I made a mental note to do it often.

It was still raining when the bus dropped us off at the campsite. Startling me, Jack scooped me up and deftly swung me onto his back. I wrapped my arms tight around his neck as he ran fast, and even with me on his back, it felt effortless. The rain sailed past us, or was it us sailing past the rain? With Jack, I felt like even the laws of physics could be broken.

My heart beat wildly. There was something intoxicating about being so close to him, being cared for by him, because I got the feeling Jack had never been like this with a girl before. It made it all the more significant, made my heart feel sore and not sore all at once. I suspected Jack's encounters with women in the past had been unemotional and quick. All about the sex. The shame he felt about the desires he held and what they arose from had kept him from getting too close to anyone.

I wanted to wash away that shame, show him that though things could be born of darkness, with the right person you could make them light.

When we reached his camper, he pushed open the door and stepped in, gently lowering his body so I could climb off his back. I looked around, unsure what my next move should be, when all of a sudden he bent to one knee and began carefully untying my laces. As I watched him, the air left my lungs and my heart felt fuller.

I was falling.

"There are towels in the bathroom that you can use. The water should be warm," he said, and then stood once he'd relieved me of my shoes and socks. He wanted me to take a shower. Wordlessly, I went inside his bathroom, which was larger than the one in Violet's camper. Well, it was still small, but at least here I didn't keep knocking off the sink when I tried to get to the toilet. I could hear him moving around outside as I shut the door, and my pores tingled as I stripped out of my sodden jeans and top. Jack's proximity to my naked skin made me clench my thighs together with longing. I yearned to see him totally bare so I could kiss and lick and suck every corner of his glorious body.

I turned the shower on and waited for the water to get hot, and when I stepped under the spray, my throat felt tight as I silently wished for him to come inside and join me. I felt like I'd been waiting forever, but the door never budged. Sighing in disappointment, I wrapped up in one of the clean, dry towels that hung from a rack and stepped out into the living area. Having used the shampoo and shower gel in his bathroom, I now smelled like him. I breathed it in, and it smelled like home.

I stopped when I saw him by the sink, using some paper towels to dry his face. God, even with the burn scar, his back was perfect, all broad and muscled, his skin deeply tanned. All he had on was his boxer shorts, his clothes discarded.

He turned when he heard my footsteps on the floor, and his eyelids grew hooded as he took me in.

"Feel better?"

I nodded and concentrated on the drops of rain trickling down the window, the beat of it as it hammered onto the roof of the camper.

"What's wrong?"

I cleared my throat, my voice a self-conscious whisper. "I thought....it's silly, but I thought you might join me." Could I be blushing any more furiously right now? "In the shower, I mean."

His lips twitched and a smile formed, and I knew he hadn't expected me to say that. "Have you seen my shower?"

I frowned. "Uh, yeah."

"And have you seen the size of me?" he went on. Some dirty part of my brain made my mind wander to things other than his height. "It's painful to admit, but that is not a two-person shower, Lille," he said, taking a step toward me until his hands were warming my shoulders. "If it were, I'd have been there, fucking you against the tiles with my tongue."

Jesus, now there was a visual. All of a sudden, my head was full of his mouth between my legs, his tongue sliding inside me, all wet and warm and delicious. I trembled, and he growled as he backed me up until I was stepping over the threshold of his bedroom. My thighs hit the mattress before I fell backwards onto the thick navy blanket.

"Tonight, my bed is your bed. Get some rest. I'm going to clean up."

I lay there, watching him leave and close the door behind him. Okay, that was not how I envisioned this playing out. My chest was still heaving with anticipation when I heard the shower come on. Frustrated, I turned over onto my belly and buried my face in his pillows. Of course, they'd have to smell of him, and of course that only functioned to raise my frustration levels even higher. I'd just washed, but I could feel that I was wet between my legs. My clit begged for his mouth, my nipples aching for him to do that thing with the match again.

Jack had said that was child's play, and already I felt like I was ruined for sex with anyone else.

Despite my frustration, it had been a long day, and I began to grow drowsy, my heavy eyelids falling closed. I'd almost nodded off when I heard the door open and shut with a soft click. Suddenly, I was wide awake as I listened to Jack turn off the lamp, shrouding the room in darkness before I heard the scraping flick of a match, the sizzling blaze of the flame. Out of the corner of my eye, I could see him light two expensive-looking candles that sat on the bedside dresser, and I swear every single muscle in my body tensed. All he wore was a pair of black lounge pants.

I pretended to be sleeping when he turned to look at me, and a low chuckle vibrated from his chest. That sound was going to be my undoing one of these days. "I can hear your breathing, Lille. I know you're not asleep." The mattress dipped down as he sat at the foot of the bed.

"I was about to be," I mumbled into the pillow, "until your loud elephant feet clomped into the room and woke me."

He continued laughing, low and quiet, and then I jumped a little when he took my bare foot into his hands. His fingers found just the right spot to rub, and I moaned involuntarily. God, that felt good.

"You're wound up tight, flower," Jack whispered as his hands slowly began to make their way to my ankle, then my calf. It was like he knew every muscle and chord intimately, knew just how to rub to turn me into a melting pile of hormones and need.

Before I knew it, he was kneeling between my legs and massaging my thigh as I made loud and very embarrassing noises that the pillows did nothing to muffle. His deft fingers were so close to my vagina that I had to bite down on said pillow just to keep from grabbing his hand and placing it where I wanted him to touch me the most.

"Your skin," he said, and his voice sounded pained. "Your fucking skin."

His fingers skimmed over the rise of my arse, then fluttered feather light less than a centimetre from my folds. *Touch me*, my mind begged, *God, Jack, please touch me.*

He emitted a long, agonised groan before he pushed the towel off me, and then his mouth was on my arse cheek, biting. I let out a strangled yelp as he nuzzled where he'd bitten with the tip of his nose. I felt his hand move, and then his fingers were trailing across my wet lips, giving no pressure at all. He was trying to torture me.

"Please," I begged, and he grunted, nipping my cheek again with his sharp teeth, then rising up and pulling the towel off me completely. I was naked, and I could feel the soft cotton of his pants brush my skin as he bent over me and palmed my bottom.

"Seeing this every day kills me, do you know that?" he growled, and I shook with the pleasure of his deep voice and heated words.

"I need...."

"Tell me what you need, flower."

"I need you to touch me."

"I am touching you."

"Somewhere else."

A smirk. "In time."

His hand went to my shoulder and lightly caressed the skin. My tattoo was almost healed, and his touch reminded me I had it. Since it was in a place I couldn't easily see, I often forgot it was even there.

"Your ink is beautiful," he murmured, and his fingers danced along a particular spot. "This is the part I filled in. I feel so fucking proud when I see it, like you have my name on you or something."

I sighed, my every pore tingling with his possessive words. Then I felt his weight leave the bed, and a moment later he was back, straddling me as I lay on my stomach. I didn't know what he was doing until I felt something hot and wet brand the base of my spine.

"Ahhh," I cried out. "What was that?" My words were more air than sound as I felt him harden and lengthen against my bottom.

The burn hit me again, right on the cusp of too much and not enough. It stung, but, combined with my heady arousal, the sting was euphoric. In fact, I wanted more.

"It's hot wax, Lille," Jack said, and his voice sounded electric right then, full of pent-up desire that was slowly finding its relief. "How does it feel?"

Instead of answering his question, I simply pleaded in the tiniest voice, "Do it again."

The deep, erotic sound of approval that followed melted my bones, and I felt the wax drip along my back and pool around my hip. I hissed in a breath and then let the air out in an audible groan. Jack began to move his hips against me, his erection rutting hard into my arse. His fingers found the wax near my spine and rubbed, and then his body was covering me completely as his face fell to my neck. His tongue snaked out and licked all along the shell of my ear.

"*Fuck*," he swore, and the word had never sounded more carnal. A second later, his arm wrapped around my middle, and he was pulling me up onto all fours. He knelt behind me, his hands caressing my thighs as the head of his penis nudged against me. There was nothing between us, no condom, and in that moment I had a crazy wish that he wouldn't put one on. The moment his bare erection touched me, an addictive surge ran through my body, indicative of the heaven it would be to have him inside me raw.

He took the back of my neck in his hand, twisting so that our eyes could meet. All in a matter of seconds, as his cock continued to nudge teasingly at my entrance, almost going in but then not quite, his eyes asked a question, and my eyes replied with the answer.

Yes.

Perhaps all that hot wax was making me crazy and reckless, but I wanted to feel all of him, and pregnancy wasn't an issue because I was on the pill. His grip on my hair fell away for a second, and then it was back again, this time on my neck, holding on tight as he sank his thick length inside in one delicious thrust. The feel of him, the sensation, the connection, was overwhelming, and my vision blurred.

He withdrew, and I whimpered before he rammed himself back in. His fingers dug into my neck, erasing Julie's bruises with his own, marking me as his. Never in my life had I wanted to be owned so badly. His movements grew frenzied, his fucking hard and precise. Soon, his thrusts began to blur into one, and I was nothing but sensation. My brain shut off, words no longer held meaning, and I was only pleasure.

I was my senses and no more.

All I could hear was him.

All I could smell was him.

All I could taste was him.

All I could feel was him.

All I could see was him.

With his grip on my neck, he drew my body up, and pumped his hips sharp and quick. I shuddered and moaned as he reached around my body to palm my breast. His hand dug in hard as it travelled down my belly, over my mound and to my clit, where his fingers started to rub, not slow like the other night, but fast. This was all about making me come.

"I want to feel your muscles contract on my cock," he rasped into my ear before biting down hard on my neck. A loud, strangled sound escaped me as his length slid in and out, the rhythm of his fingers coaxing me, raising me up into the sweetest possible release.

"You smell like me. Do you know how much that drives me crazy? God, you're perfect, too perfect. You make me feel so wretched. I want to consume you, steal your light and make myself a little bit more. You're more, Lille. I want to be more, too."

His words came out harsh and ragged, his breathing filling my ears, and I wasn't sure if this was the sex talking or if it was sheer, unrestrained, terrifying honesty. I felt my stomach tighten, and his pumps became harsher, his fingers more desperate.

"Come with me," he grunted, and it was like the words in themselves were an aphrodisiac, because I shattered right there under his practiced touch and he came, his cock pulsing as he emptied himself inside me.

As one, our bodies collapsed onto the bed. His weight on top of me was almost crushing, but then he flipped us so that I lay stretched out on his chest. It was just like the other night, when we'd fallen asleep together under the stars. Now the storm raged on outside our peaceful, spent little bubble, rain pounding the roof. Jack stared at me like I was an apparition, a spectre about to disappear as I ran my fingers through his gorgeous hair, let my eyes memorise every inch of his face. His lids fell closed and his breathing evened out, his arms still clutching me tight. I knew he'd fallen asleep when his breaths grew deep, and I felt brave enough to utter the words that were trying to break their way out of my very soul.

"I think I'm falling in love with you, Jack McCabe."

Fifteen
A picture lost was then found

"Get the fuck out here and face me now, you bitch!"

I woke to somebody screaming, adrenaline flooding my system as I shot up in the bed. Jack's warm body wasn't under me anymore, and I looked around to find him standing by the window, rubbing the sleep from his eyes as he peeked through the blinds. A bang rang out, and it sounded like the person who'd been screaming was now trying to kick the door in.

I sat up in the bed, heart racing, and Jack's attention landed on me as he saw I was awake.

"What on earth is going on?"

He'd pulled on his lounge pants, but he still wore no shirt, and from the tired look of his eyes, he'd just woken up moments before I had. He came over to the bed and cupped my face in his hands before leaning in and pressing a kiss to my lips.

"Good morning," he murmured. "I'm sorry she's ruining everything. I wanted to wake you with breakfast."

"It's Julie, isn't it?"

Jack nodded. "By the looks of it, the police paid her a visit. She's like a raging bull out there. I'm going to go out, but I need you stay in here. Okay?"

"Yeah," I whispered. "Sure."

"God, you're beautiful. I like waking up with you next to me."

A small laugh escaped me. "You sound surprised by that."

He scratched his head as he rose and gave me a sexy, perplexed little smile. "I'm am, kind of."

A moment later, he'd thrown on a shirt and was gone, out to face the wrath of Julie. I buried myself further under the blankets, wishing that I could bury myself so deep she'd disappear and this wouldn't be happening. Unfortunately, the walls of the camper were thin, and I could hear every word that was said.

"What the hell do you think you're playing at? You've got five seconds to leave, or I'll make you leave." Jack.

"Your fucking whore went to the police, telling lies about me. Get her out here now. I want to see her." Julie.

"Lies? Are you fucking shitting me? Why does she have a head wound, then, huh? Why are there bruises on her neck from your malicious little hands?" Jack.

"I never touched her. She's trying to come between us." Julie.

"Come on, Jules, let's go. You're making a scene." Mary or Molly, I couldn't be quite sure.

"Get off me. I'm not leaving until that bitch comes out here and faces me."

A lump formed in my throat. I knew this wasn't going to end until I went out there. Jack must have left my clothes to dry on the heater by the window last night because they were resting on it, now dry and toasty. I pulled on my jeans and top, then slid my feet into my shoes. I just wanted to end this. Jack looked like he was seeing red when I stepped out of the camper, and he immediately came to stand in front of me, shielding me from Julie.

"Go back inside, Lille," he instructed me, chest puffing out. I glanced around to see that half the circus were hovering close by to take in the disturbance. There was nothing like a fight to garner people's attention, and around here it seemed that Julie was always the centre of the drama.

"You stupid bitch!" Julie screamed as she lunged for me. I ducked behind Jack, who held his arm out to fend her off. She clawed at him before her sister pulled her away. "They didn't arrest me," she said snidely as she glared daggers at me over Jack's shoulder. "Not enough evidence and no witnesses, obviously, since I didn't *do* anything." Wow, she actually sounded like she believed that as she turned to face the onlookers. "I say we all take a vote to kick her out. She can't just go around making false accusations, and I refuse to perform another night while she's still here."

My heart pounded at her declaration, and tears began to form in my eyes. I didn't want to leave. Not now. It felt like Jack and I had only just found one another. There were some murmurings among the onlookers as Jack balled his fists.

"You're being a spiteful bitch, Julie. Let it go."

I tugged on his arm, and his eyes came to me. "It's okay. She's a headlining act. I can't stay if it's going to cause trouble with the shows," I whispered, my voice choked.

His responding tone was firm as he cupped my cheek. "Get off your cross — you're going nowhere." He stared Julie down. "*She* just needs to chill the fuck out and stop being a temperamental violent fucking lunatic."

Julie's eyes flashed red, and her mouth formed a thin, sour line. "You're taking her side!? You've known me for years and you've known her for a couple of weeks, but still you'd believe her over me?"

At this Winnie stepped forward. "The fact he's known you for years is the reason he believes her. He knows what you're like. We all do."

"You can stay out of this," Julie hissed.

"I thought you wanted us to have a vote," said Winnie.

"I do," Julie scowled.

"Well, then, let's vote. All those who believe Julie's version of events stand by Julie, and all those who believe Lille, stand by Lille." Immediately, Winnie came to stand by me, taking my arm and squeezing it to show her solidarity. In that moment, I felt unendingly grateful to her. I didn't know what to expect, but after a couple moments of hesitation, everyone began to come and stand with me and Jack. The only ones standing with Julie were her sisters, and even they seemed a little unsure of their sibling. My heart filled with emotion. These people barely even knew me, and yet they were standing up for me. It was like a strange big family of misfits, and they were making me truly feel like one of them. I didn't know what to say.

"This is ridiculous!" Julie wailed just before she cursed everyone out and stormed off. Looking uncomfortable, her sisters went after her.

Jack turned to me and took me in his arms, his chest moving with a deep inhalation. I looked up at him, anxious. "Is she going to quit? Marina will be mad at me if she quits."

"I can't count the number of times Julie's threatened to leave. She's not going anywhere."

"More's the pity," Winnie put in, then gave my shoulder a gentle pat. "I'm sorry you had to go through that. If she ever tries to lay a hand on you again, you come to me, and I'll set her straight." The way she said it made me feel like she genuinely meant it, which caused me to become even more emotional.

Jack's arms tightened around me. "It won't happen again," he said darkly. "I won't let it."

A few minutes later, those who'd gathered to take in the drama had dispersed, and Jack and I returned to his camper. He made me a breakfast of peanut butter and chopped bananas on toast, and we sat close together on his couch as we ate. It was strange to see such a big, sexy, mysterious man carrying out a mundane task like making breakfast, but I loved it.

Still, I was in a contemplative mood, Julie's spiteful claims continuing to echo in my head. If she wasn't leaving the circus, then that meant she was staying, and that also meant I'd have to be around her for the rest of the summer. Despite Jack stating firmly that she wouldn't lay a hand on me again, I didn't know how he could be so sure. And quite frankly, I was scared. Julie was definitely not the full shilling, and I had no idea what she might try to do next.

Jack kissed me long and passionately right before I was leaving to go get some clean clothes. The ones I was wearing were dry, but they smelled damp from the rain. His kiss put me in a little bit of a daze as I left his camper. I was strolling along, unable to keep a stupid grin off my face, my worries about Julie momentarily forgotten, when I saw King walking ahead of me. He was doing his usual half-drunken stumble, muttering to himself, as he reached into his pocket and pulled out a small bottle of liquor. As he did so, a piece of paper fell to the ground, and I hurried to pick it up for him.

It was a photograph, and had fallen blank side up. I held it in my hands and turned it over to find a picture of a woman at the beach. She was smiling widely, her teeth white and straight, and she wore a red bathing suit that showed off some enviable curves. Her hair was dark brown, her skin a pale olive, and her eyes were almost as dark as Jack's. She looked like maybe she had some Greek or Italian blood in her, and she was certainly very beautiful.

I turned the photo over again to see someone had written on the back in pen, but it was nearly faded to nothing. It read: *Alexis, Rome, 2009.*

When I looked back up, King had gotten a good distance ahead of me. I was about to run after him to return the photo when Lola suddenly appeared, her face a mixture of excitement and concern.

"Is it true? About Julie?" she asked, a little breathless.

I nodded, shoving the picture in my pocket to return to King later as I filled Lola in on everything that had happened.

"That little psycho. I swear, I always knew she was a bitch, but I didn't know she was a crazy bitch," Lola exclaimed as we reached the camper. We both stepped inside and found the bathroom door open as Violet stood by the mirror in her underwear, dyeing her hair. Her roots had been growing out a little, and she was topping them up with more purple. We stared at her for a moment. She gestured with her gloved hand, irritated. "What? I don't want to get dye on my clothes."

Lola gave her a pointed look. "I think that's what coveralls are for."

"Oh, whatever. Nobody has time to buy coveralls."

"I think you'll find they do. Shall I compile a list? Plumbers, painters, welders, matchstick makers…."

"Seriously, Lola, shut up and tell me the news. You came in with a gossipy gleam in your eye."

Nude hair dyeing forgotten, Lola immediately began to regale her with the Julie gossip as I went to change into some fresh clothes. I also packed a small bag to bring with me to Jack's. I wasn't being presumptuous. He'd asked me to do it before I left. I'd barely been away from him an hour, but already I was itching to see him again. After I'd taken care of a few tasks, I made my way to the Spiegeltent, where he told me he'd be rehearsing.

The place was empty when I walked in, save for Jack standing on the stage. He brought a bottle to his mouth and drank, then spat it back out in a spray. It hit the lit torch he was holding, and the flame blew massively. My skin prickled with awareness. There was something so primal about him when he breathed fire. It was his element, the balm that soothed his damaged soul, and the way he worked with it was captivating.

He saw me come in and sit by the edge of the stage, giving me a heated smile that made my tummy flutter. Now that I knew about his bedroom preferences, even *seeing* fire reminded me of sex. And sex with Jack was something that branded itself into your memory like hot steel permanently marking your skin. His eyes wandered over my body. I was wearing a dress today, a light summery one that showed off my arms and stopped above the knee. Unlike yesterday, the weather was hot and dry, so I thought I could get away with showing a little more skin.

His lips formed a smirk as he called over, "Like your dress, flower."

I blushed but didn't respond to the compliment. Instead, I asked, "What's in the bottle?"

He took a few steps towards me. "It's kerosene. I never use gasoline or alcohols. They're too dangerous."

I scrunched up my nose. "Does it taste okay?"

"Not at all, but I'm not exactly savouring it when it's in my mouth, Lille." He laughed low and gave me pointed stare. "In fact, I practice having it there for the shortest time

241

possible to minimise the chances of ingesting. You can do a lot of damage. It's a risk."

"Is the risk a part of the thrill?" I asked quietly.

His boots sounded against the floor of the stage as he took the last few steps to reach me. Then he went down on one knee, eyes flickering over my face as he took my chin in his hand. "Perceptive little thing, aren't you?" he whispered.

I stared at his mouth, the air thickening between us. "When it comes to you, yes. I think breathing fire makes you feel alive, and I think you take the risk because it's your choice and no one else's. You're the master of your fate, and whether or not you get hurt is all down to whether or not you fuck up."

His smile grew slowly. "I like the way you see me."

I smiled back. "I like seeing you."

The moment was broken when a noise sounded at the entrance and a couple of circus workers came in carrying equipment. Jack eyed them, then rose and went to gather his things. "Looks like Julie and her sisters are going to be rehearsing soon. We'd better leave." I got a little jolt to be reminded of her and stood, following him to the back of the tent. When we were in the backstage area, he kept sneaking glances at me as he slotted his torches into a duffle bag.

"What?" I said, self-conscious.

"Nothing."

I elbowed him. "Don't lie. You were thinking something, and I want to know what it is."

His smile was provocative. "I was thinking that you're in a very good mood after last night, and I was also wondering if I asked you to do something, would you say yes or no."

I absorbed his reply for a moment, then said, "Ask me to do what?"

A second later, he was crowding me into the wall and murmuring in my ear, "To get down on your knees and take me in your mouth."

I blinked nervously and stared up at him. It surprised me how much his request turned me on. "Well" —I swallowed— "that all depends."

His eyebrow rose. "On?"

"On whether or not you mean here or back at your camper," I answered in the most seductive voice I could manage, which probably sounded like I was getting a chest infection.

With his thumb brushing along my throat, he replied, "And what if I said here?"

God, why did he have to sound so sexy when he spoke? It wasn't fair. "Then I'd say you're pushing your luck."

"I like pushing my luck with you." His voice was pure gravel, and his body was pressing heavily into mine now, his arousal firm at my belly. I was fascinated by how quickly he could get it up. Okay, fascinated, and also flattered that I was the catalyst for his speedy readiness.

"There are people around," I protested.

His hand stroked my hair away from my neck as he bent to place an open-mouthed kiss below my ear. "No, there aren't. Nobody ever comes up this end. Not at this time of day."

My eyes flickered between his uncertainly, and I was embarrassed to admit even to myself that I wanted to do it. I wanted to taste him. I wanted the power of knowing I could give him that kind of pleasure.

"You don't have anything to burn me with here," I said, voice weak with the need to taste him.

His head tilted, and he smiled darkly. "I have my memories from last night. For now, those are enough. In fact, thinking of last night is what gave me the bright idea."

He kissed my neck again, his tongue darting out to lick, and I let out a breathy sigh, my hands wandering eagerly to his belt buckle. I had it undone within seconds, and before I knew it, I was lowering my knees to the wood-panelled floor and pulling his thick length from his pants. He was hard and beautiful; I whispered my lips over the head of his cock, and his whole body shuddered.

"Christ," he hissed in a sharp breath.

I let my tongue slip out, giving him teasing little licks, and his hands went to my hair, my face, my neck, tracing my skin with a look of wonder in his eyes. That look made me feel powerful, and I held his gaze in mine as I slowly lowered my mouth onto him, taking him in inch by inch. He groaned, one hand fisting in my hair, the other caressing my cheek. I took in as much of him as I could, bobbing my head slowly up and down. Somebody's laughter sounded from outside, and it made my heart pound. We might have been doing this in a dark corner backstage, but it still wasn't private. Someone could walk by at any moment.

A pleasurable thrill ran through me at the thought. I knew that giving someone head in a public place wasn't exactly on my list, but right then it felt like it should be. I was high on the act. On Jack. On being here with him in the moment.

This felt like *living*.

I swirled my tongue around his head, and he swore profusely, the deep, raspy words fuel to the fire of my arousal. I pressed my thighs together in an effort to relieve some of the ache, but it was pointless. The only antidote to this torture was Jack's touch. I let him fall from my mouth to catch my breath and ran my tongue along his length. He had one hand braced against the wall behind us for support. When I took him back in, he growled and cupped my jaw tightly.

"I wish you could see how you look."

I held his gaze, and his eyes grew hooded as they travelled over my form before fixing on my mouth again. "Touch yourself," he urged in a deep, naughty whisper.

I breathed in sharply through my nose at his command, and there was something in the way he looked at me that made me feel beautiful and sensual enough to do it. I let my hand fall to my thighs, then under my dress. Jack's attention scorched as he watched me find myself, watched me soothe some of the need he was inciting.

"That's it, flower, feel it."

I moaned on his cock as I found my sweet spot and rubbed, desperate for release. For some reason, it made my desire to make him come grow even stronger, and my mouth moved on him in earnest. I slid two fingers inside myself and sighed. The air felt slow and thick like honey, like I was in a waking dream. My mouth and my fingers grew frenzied as I felt my own orgasm building as well as Jack's. I could tell by how he became even harder in my mouth, how his growled words and whispered sentiments began to merge into one.

I never looked away from him when I came with startling intensity, and a few seconds later, hot liquid hit my mouth. I swallowed before I could think about it as Jack pulled me up to stand and wrapped his arms around me tight. His pulse was racing.

"That was incredible, thank you," he said, a little breathless, his voice full of gratitude. Then he began to softly laugh. It wasn't a mocking sort of laughter; it was a gentle, tender kind. "That's going to be etched into my memory for the rest of my days, Lille. Just looking at your lips is going to be a struggle."

I wasn't sure why, but thinking about that made me smile.

***

Later that day, we were just arriving at the gazebo for dinner, hand in hand, when a loud ruckus sounded. I'd thought the scene Julie had made this morning was enough drama for one day, but seemingly not. People stood nearby as King bulldozed around the space, tossing over tables and chairs, fury and misery melding into one as angry tears ran down his face. He was on a rampage and drunk beyond measure.

"Where is it?" he growled, the rumble of his voice making the tiniest hairs on my arms stand on end. "Which one of you took it?!" He glared at those standing by, pointing accusatory fingers at anyone who dared make eye contact. My heart pounded and I swallowed deeply, wondering what the hell had happened.

"I swear to God, I'll burn this place to the ground if I don't find it," he threatened. His body lost some of its tension as he slumped forward, bracing his hands on a table. "Thieves! You're all a bunch of thieves! Will you try to steal everything from me? Strip every last pound of flesh from my bones until there's nothing left?" Now he stopped pointing fingers at those around him and looked up to the sky as though talking to a higher power. "Have I not suffered enough for you? Have I not paid yet for my sins?"

The stark suffering and woe that encapsulated him despite his anger made my eyes prick a little with tears. A moment later, Marina was hurrying to him. He turned away when he saw her, as though ashamed of his behaviour, and she reached out to place a hand on his elbow. As she tugged on his arm, he slowly turned around, icy blue eyes full of heartache.

"What's wrong, brother?" Marina asked in a surprisingly tender voice. "What happened?"

"They took it," he said, spittle flying from his mouth as he spoke. "Somebody took it."

Marina began to rub his arm in a soothing manner. "Took what?"

"The picture. It's all I have of her and now it's gone."

As I listened to him speak, my entire body startled with a sickening jolt. Oh, God. The picture. I still had his picture. I'd been meaning to give it back to him all day, but Jack had been distracting me so much that I'd forgotten. I felt for it in my pocket, fingers sliding over the worn edges of the paper. I didn't know what to do. I felt like if I stepped forward now, King might try to attack me, thinking I stole the picture, when really I'd just found it and had every intention of giving it back.

"Jack," I whispered, and his attention fell on me. "I think I know what he's talking about. I think I have his picture."

He stared at me for a moment before comprehension lit in his eyes and he held his hand out. "Give it to me."

I pulled it from my pocket and did as he asked. "I didn't steal it. I found it."

"Don't worry, Lille," he said, looking down at the picture and taking in the image of the beautiful woman. "I'll take care of it."

With that he walked towards King, holding the picture out to him. "King, mate, look, is this what you're searching for? I found it today. I've been looking for you to give it back."

King's eyes darted to Jack, and the moment he saw the picture, he swiped it from his hands. It was almost like everything else faded away as he held it close, peering down at the image. He blinked a few times, tears still on his face, as his body slumped to the ground and shook as though in agony. I frowned at the scene, my curiosity building to almost uncontainable levels. I wanted to know desperately who the woman in the picture was. It said on the back that her name was Alexis, but there were few other details. I had the feeling this woman had something to do with why King was the way he was. What on earth could have happened between them to bring him so low?

After a moment, Jack assisted Marina in helping King to stand, and they led him out of the gazebo. A couple of minutes passed before everyone had fixed the tables and chairs back in place, and then it was like nothing had even happened. It was more than a little bizarre. One of the women who did the cooking — I didn't know her name, but I recognised her face — came and asked me if I'd like some stew and I nodded, asking for a bowl for Jack, too. I thought he'd be back as soon as he was done with King.

I was halfway through my bowl, my mind still fixating on King and the mystery of his photograph, when a shadow fell over me. I looked up to see Jack. He sat down across from me, and I told him the extra bowl was for him.

"Thanks," he said, fitting his feet around mine beneath the table, but it seemed like his mind was elsewhere.

"Is…is King okay?" I asked.

"Marina put him to bed in her camper to sleep it off. He'll be fine."

"Do you know who the woman in the picture is?" I couldn't help blurting.

He shrugged. "Some old flame of King's, I think. When he's really wasted, he sometimes talks about losing the love of his life, how it was some guy called Bruce's fault. I don't know many more details than that. He doesn't make a lot of sense when he's drunk, and he's drunk more often than he's sober."

I pondered his answer, wondering if the love of King's life had died or if she'd just left him.

"What did he do before he came here?" I asked. "Marina once said something about his life being very different before."

Jack met my gaze as he chewed on a piece of bread he'd dipped into the stew. "You're very curious about King, Lille."

"Yes, I am," I said, not bothering to deny it. "There's something fascinating about him. I'd actually really like to draw him."

Jack tilted his head, now taking a swig from a glass of water. "Do you want to draw him for the same reasons you want to draw me?"

I scrunched my face up. "No, of course not. I like interesting subjects. And different people interest me for different reasons. King interests me."

He absorbed my answer and continued eating for a while before he spoke again. "In answer to your question, from what Marina's told me, King used to be really rich. Some big successful banker or something, but he got involved in some shady stuff and lost everything. Marina thinks he was being blackmailed, but who knows if that's true."

"Oh my God, that's awful."

"Yeah. In the end whatever he was doing caught up with him, and he lost everything. And like a lot of fallen men, he hit the bottle."

"Wow."

Jack cocked an eyebrow. "Wow?"

"Yeah. I mean, to have it all and then lose it is kind of epic. It's like the ultimate tragedy."

He let out a deep, cynical chuckle. "If you say so."

The smile that shaped his lips told me he found me amusing for whatever reason, and I scowled at him playfully. "So how come you don't know more about him? You two seem to talk a lot."

Jack shrugged one shoulder. "We do talk a lot, about lots of things, but never his past. He obviously doesn't want to discuss it." He paused and got a faraway look in his eyes. "I guess we have that in common."

I reached over and squeezed his hand, feeling a deep sense of gratitude that he'd entrusted me with his past. I had a feeling no one else knew the full story of Jack McCabe, and it was humbling.

Before I knew it, it was time for the night's performance, and people were flocking in from the city to see the show. My hands were stained with all the colours of the rainbow by the time I was done, but I felt satisfyingly tired. I'd transformed kids and even some adults into a whole variety of creatures, from real to mythical, and I was so looking forward to sleep.

Jack had given me a key for his camper, so I tiredly trudged my way there. Lola walked with me, then continued on to Violet's. I must have been caught up in all the activity after the show, because when I arrived, Jack was already inside. He lay on his bed, reading. All he wore was his black lounge pants, and his long hair hung wet at his shoulders. I came in quietly and set my things at the foot of the bed. We smiled at one another, not saying a word, and I went to kick off my shoes and leave my sketchpad and face paints on the dresser.

"I need a shower," I sighed.

Jack glanced up from his book, a quizzical arch to his brow. "What does Teutonic mean?"

His question caught me off guard, and I scratched at my head, trying to remember. "Oh, I think it's similar to Germanic, or relating to an ancient race of German people called the Teutons. Don't ask me for more details — I was always crap at history."

A little smile graced his mouth as he plucked a pencil from behind his ear and scribbled down a note. "Thanks."

"No problem. So, is it okay if I shower?"

When his eyes came to me again, they were heated. "Only if you promise not to wear a towel when you get out."

I laughed and shook my head as I turned for the bathroom. "We'll see."

I noticed his eyes had been flickering to my sketchpad when I was in the room, so it wasn't a surprise when he called after me, "Can I look at your pictures?"

I hesitated a moment in the hallway. I was self-conscious about my work, but Jack had already seen most of it, so I shrugged and answered, "Yeah, sure." And honestly, I was a little bit flattered that he wanted to look at them. When I emerged from the shower, I considered his no-towel request, but I wasn't ballsy enough to go through with it. Instead, I pulled on my sleep shorts and tank top, which really didn't leave much to the imagination anyway. And technically, I was fulfilling his request, since I wasn't wearing a towel.

All thoughts of towels fled my mind when I stepped inside his room again to find him with my sketchpad open on his lap. He wasn't looking at the sketches, though. He had a piece of paper in his hands, his eyes scanning the words as he read.

It was my list.

Sixteen

A discovery made Lille's heart pound

Oh, God. I'd tucked it into my sketchpad the other day and forgot about it. Now Jack was holding it in his hands, reading it, and my mortification was palpable.

His attention landed on me, but I couldn't read his expression, couldn't tell what he was thinking. The list made me look like a silly little girl, I knew that, but I didn't care because I'd never planned for anyone to read it but me. It was my comfort blanket, something to remind me of my goals and ambitions, ridiculous though some of them might seem. I took a steadying breath and swallowed.

My voice was tense when I held my hand out and requested, "Can I have that back, please?"

Jack stared at me, and the numbered items ran through my head. I knew them off by heart. Aside from numbers 3, 6, and 11, there wasn't anything on there to embarrass me too much. Still, I felt exposed.

1. Dump Henry Jackson.
2. Get a tattoo.
3. Have sex with a stranger.
4. Do something dangerous.
5. Visit a place I've never been before.
6. Fall in love.
7. Make a new friend.
8. Quit my degree.
9. Become a real artist.
10. Move out of my mother's house.
11. Get my heart broken.

The first thing Jack said was not what I expected at all. "Who's Henry Jackson?"

I let out a long breath and came to sit beside him, running my suddenly sweaty palms against the fabric of my shorts.

"You shouldn't be reading that. It's private." I knew I was being a little unfair, since I'd read his discarded letter to his brother, but I couldn't help my annoyance. I tried to convince myself that turnaround was fair play, and my irritation slowly deflated. Plus, if I had found a similar list among Jack's things, I was pretty sure my curiosity would have gotten the better of me, too.

Jack reached out and pulled me close, tucking me under his arm as he continued to hold the list in front of him. I rested my head on his chest and could feel the steady rhythm of his heartbeat. It was reassuring somehow.

"I thought it was a sketch," Jack explained.

"Mm-hmm."

A beat of silence elapsed. "So, who is he?" If I wasn't mistaken, there was a note of insecurity in his tone, and I was taken aback. Jack was jealous of the idea of me with someone else. At the very least, he wasn't thrilled to be thinking about it. My little beating heart and its ever-growing feelings for him was over the moon.

"My ex, obviously," I answered, peering up at him speculatively.

"How long were you with him?"

"Two years, but it wasn't serious. He was...I don't know. Safe, maybe? You know how sometimes you'd rather be with anyone over no one?" Jack's nod was infinitesimal, but it was there. I guessed he was thinking of Julie and how his loneliness, at least physically, had propelled him to being with her because she was available. His finger scrolled down my list until it stopped at number four. "This one is stupid. Why would you willingly put yourself in harm's way?"

I let out a tiny laugh. "Coming from the guy who risks his life every night as part of his job?"

He only stared at me, hard. I swallowed, shrugged, and finally answered, "To feel alive, I guess. My life growing up has consisted of a sequence of straight lines. I wanted to throw in a couple of curves and dips, you know. Take a risk, the same as you."

"It's not the same, but I see your point."

"Anyway," I went on teasingly, "I think I've ticked this item off my list. Being with you is pretty dangerous, right?"

My humour was lost on him; in fact, I'd never seen him frown so hard. "Is that how you see me? As a little dip in your straight line? Because if you're angling to get hurt by me, I'll put you straight right now. It won't happen. I will not be your number eleven, Lille. My hesitancy to be with you was indicative of my apprehension as to whether or not I could control myself. Yes, I get off on giving you a little pain, but I will always be controlled, highly so. If I hurt you, it will be momentary, and it will be followed by pleasure. This is the promise I've made to myself. And I will never burn you in a way that would cause permanent physical damage. You may be left with a few marks, but they'll be the kind that heal. I don't want to feel like a monster, not anymore." He paused his passionate speech to take my hand in his and bring it to the scars on his shoulder. "You will never wear scars like I do, Lille, do you understand?"

I blinked at him, my throat suddenly dry as my heart pounded in my chest. For years this man had been living under the assumption that he was sick, that there was something wrong with him on the inside, when really he was just different. Changed by experience. And really, he was far more noble than most. Far more worthy of trust, and I didn't think for a second that he would ever hurt me, not intentionally anyway.

We fell into a strange sort of quiet, still resting close, still touching.

"You've completed almost all of these," Jack said then, and I realised he was talking about the list again.

"I know. It feels crazy. I never thought I'd actually do them all. I thought they'd each take a great effort, but by deciding to join the circus, one thing just kind of followed the other." He made a little grunting sound, and I glanced at him. "What?"

Instead of replying, he reached for the pencil that was tucked behind his ear, the one he'd used earlier to scribble a note in his book. He brought it to the list and drew a distinct line through number three.

3. Have sex with a stranger

"You're not doing that one," he said, voice a firm growl.

I couldn't contain my grin. "Oh, yeah, well, maybe I already have."

I swear to God, his expression went so dark I was a little frightened. I really needed to start learning what I could and couldn't tease him about. "Excuse me?"

"With you, you idiot! You're my stranger." I nuzzled affectionately at the spot just below his ear.

Almost as quickly as it came, all of the tension went out of him. His thumb brushed my shoulder, while the other hand spread out warm and tingly on my belly. He was practically purring now. "I am far from a stranger to you. In fact, that night you knew me better than anyone."

I closed my eyes for a moment, savouring his purring cadence. His voice was pure sex sometimes, so intimate. God, I wanted him inside me, but I was so tired my muscles ached. My body was at once begging me for sleep and squirming for Jack's cock. I think he saw the thought pass over my face, because he gave me a slow, lazy grin.

"You want me inside you, flower?" he asked in a seductive whisper, tongue licking at the shell of my ear and sending tingles all the way down my spine.

I stared at his bare, muscular torso and groaned, "Yes, but I'm so tired."

He moved so he was on top of me, pulling my legs around his waist. "That's actually perfect. Tonight, I want to give rather than take."

I knew he had to be referring to our tryst backstage in the Spiegeltent earlier today, where I'd gone down on him. The memory gave me a pleasant shudder, and at the same time I wondered about his statement. If he didn't want to take tonight, then what did he want to give? I watched with rapt attention as he reached over to his bedside dresser and pulled open a drawer. He retrieved a small black leather box and set it on the bed beside me. I got the sense that he wanted me to open it, so I picked it up and lifted the lid. Inside were several pieces of metal. One was long and thin, like a small wand, and the others were silver hoops, both equal in size.

"What are they?" I asked, taking one of the hoops and looping it through my fingers.

"Toys," Jack answered, studying my reaction with care. "They're quite specialist, actually. They're new, too. I haven't used them on anyone else."

"What do they do?" I asked breathily as my eyes rose to meet his.

His gaze darkened. "Would you like me to show you?"

Quietly, I nodded, and he took the hoops from me. Grabbing a lighter, he lit one of the candles from the other night. I noticed they were specialist, too, as I read the label. They were sex candles, for lack of a better word, designed specifically for pouring wax onto your lover. They must have been less damaging to the skin, because the marks that had been on my lower back were almost completely gone by morning.

Jack held each metal hoop over the flame for several seconds, then instructed me to strip. Within moments my pyjamas were off. The room was dark, and the glow of the candles made me feel lazy and pliant. Jack studied my body for a long time, his gaze alone making my nipples harden as he brought the hot metal to me and ran it over my skin. I hissed in a breath at the warmth, and it felt a little like when you place your hand against a radiator that's too hot. The metal was so thin, though, which made the sting bearable. He ran each hoop up and down my stomach before grazing them leisurely over the peaks of my breasts, until they rested around the circumference of each nipple. My breathing was heavy, my heart racing in anticipation.

"The metal holds the heat for about ten minutes," Jack said, eyes all aglow as he absorbed the sight of me lying there, hot and needy. My breasts had never felt fuller with sensation. My nipples were almost painfully hard, the metal hoops sending thrilling spikes right to their tips.

"How does that feel, flower?" Jack asked as he rubbed my belly soothingly with his big hand.

I squirmed and let out a sound of undiluted pleasure. My words were choppy. "K-kind of m-mind-blowing."

He chuckled. "I'm not done with you yet." Moving down my body until his head was between my legs, he spread my thighs wide, bent forward, and licked lightly at my clit. All the while, his eyes moved from the hoops on my breasts to my face and then back again.

I could tell from the intensity of his gaze that the sight was giving him an immense amount of pleasure. His tongue lapped at me, going deeper each time until he found my entrance and slid inside. I fisted the sheets, my hips rising at the soft, silky feel of him. With the metal on my skin, several of my erogenous zones had been awakened. I'd never felt anything like it before. Jack's mouth worked my body to a crescendo, every lick focused and intent on making me come. His fingers replaced his tongue inside me, pumping in a mesmerising rhythm, while his thumb went to my clit. He kept licking until I shattered, my body bucking and my skin tingling, as wave upon wave flooded me. I moaned long and hard, and was vaguely aware of Jack moving away from me, but I was too lost in my orgasm to pay too close attention.

When he came back, he held the wand in his hand. He ran it along my shoulders, and it was hot to the touch, just like the hoops. I closed my eyes and breathed deeply, just feeling as he ran along every dip and curve, over my hip, down my thigh, along the back of my knee. His breathing was slow and focused, like he was concentrating on every tiny detail, every minuscule reaction the hot metal elicited from me. I watched how his arms moved, how the muscles contracted and released, and it was way too sexy. I could have come again if I wasn't so exhausted. Soon, as the wand continued its voyage around my body, my eyes drifted closed. The hot sting started to feel like a warm caress, and that caress was lulling me to slumber.

"That's it, go to sleep, beautiful," I heard Jack whisper before exhaustion pulled me under.

***

The days began to blend into a sequence of shows, spending time with Jack, working on my art, travelling, and having earth-shattering sex that involved heat and pleasure and pain, and it was blowing my mind. Jack and I grew quietly closer. I say quietly, because when we were around each other, it was never long before our eyes met, before our bodies were touching in whatever small way we could manage.

But still, we spoke no words. We didn't apply any labels, and it was oddly reassuring. I didn't feel like I needed to chain him down and plaster a "boyfriend" sticker over his forehead. I felt like he was with me because he wanted to be, and if he didn't want me anymore, then I'd know about it.

Julie kept her distance, mostly because it felt like all eyes were on her now. Ever since news had travelled of her attack, people became wary. Marina had given her a firm and final warning, so she was on her best behaviour. One thing was for certain, her performances never wavered. I marvelled at how she could be so crazy, yet it never translated over into her art. Or perhaps she was so good at her art *because* she was crazy.

The circus had moved its way through France and was now stopping in the city of Turin in Italy. Having lived on an island my entire life, it was amazing to think how we could be on the same land, yet move into a whole other country. One moment you're in France, the next you're in Italy. Turin was an impressive city, with beautiful architecture that was overlooked by the Alps. It was perhaps the most majestic place we'd been yet, and the shows were selling out every night.

I was putting away my face paints as the music I recognised for Jack's act played inside the tent. I smiled at the edgy rhythm as I went about my task in my own little bubble, until a familiar voice broke through and almost stopped my heart from beating.

"Hurry up, Benjamin, we haven't got much time," my mother snipped as her PA hurried to try to keep pace with her. There was only one thought in my head as I stood there, frozen in place.

She found me.

This thought was followed by a number of expletives, and a distinct and tangible feeling of dread. Her heels clicked on the wooden panels set out at the entrance to the tent. The sound of those heels clicking would forever remind me of her, and was probably the reason why more often than not I chose to wear flats. My throat tightened, my skin grew clammy, and though I was out in the open, I suddenly felt like I couldn't find enough air to breathe.

I couldn't decide whether I should hide or go right up and confront her. She had no right to be here, and if she thought that somehow she was going to bring me home, she had another thing coming. A month ago I would have hidden, and even though in the grand scale of things a month was not a very long time, I wasn't the same person I had been then. I felt stronger, less naïve. Yes, I still wanted to have an adventure, but I now knew that with every adventure came very real dangers, and I couldn't simply throw caution to the wind like I used to think I could.

Maybe living life also meant doing things that were hard and sometimes scary. And confronting my mother right now was definitely scary. Before I could hesitate a moment longer, the word was out of my mouth.

"Mum," I called.

She turned on her heel, straightened out her pencil skirt, and swung to face me. Her expression ran the gamut of surprised to relieved to angry in a heartbeat.

"Lillian!" she exclaimed, and began walking towards me. "Have you any idea of the trouble we've been through trying to find you?"

"You shouldn't have come," I said, folding my arms and standing my ground. I made a concerted effort not to stutter. Benjamin gave me a cynical look up and down. He'd been working for Mum for years and was the kind of sycophant who kept her thinking she was a wonderful person, instead of what she truly was, i.e. cold and mean.

"We're taking you home," Mum said, coming forward and grabbing a hold of my arm. "Our flight leaves in a couple of hours, and we don't want to miss it."

I jerked away from her. "I'm not going anywhere."

As soon as the words left my mouth, she looked like she was about to burst a blood vessel. "We just spent over four hours on a plane to come here. Don't be so ungrateful. If you're worried about not having enough money for the flight, there's no need. I already booked you a ticket."

I laughed involuntarily. "Oh, a whole four hours, what a sacrifice. And it's not about the money. I'm staying here because I want to. I'm happy."

Her impatience was clear on her face. "You're supposed to be starting back at college in a fortnight. You might as well come home now. It's the best solution for everyone."

And that was exactly why she was here. It wasn't because she genuinely cared about my well-being. She just didn't want me dropping out of college and making a show of her in the process. I was sure if she'd really wanted to, she could have come and found me long before now. But no, this sudden intervention was because the new semester was just two weeks away, and Mum wanted me there in the lecture hall, playing the part of her studious little daughter.

"I'm not going back to college," I said in a steady voice, holding my chin high.

"Don't be ridiculous. Of course you are. This is your final year. Quitting now would be a waste." Jesus, it was like she wasn't even listening. Like she didn't care enough to listen. As far as my mother was concerned, her way was right, and everyone else's way was wrong.

"No, the last three years of my life have been a waste. I should never had agreed to go to college in the first place. It's not what I want. It's not my passion. Yeah, I'd probably make a lot of money when I eventually got a job, but I wouldn't be happy. What's the point of being successful if you're going to be miserable? I'd rather be penniless and happy any day of the week."

Mum rolled her eyes to the heavens, like my little speech was a cliché she didn't have time for. And okay, perhaps it was a cliché, but it was *my* cliché, and I was determined not to give in. I wasn't going to be spineless and bend to her wishes anymore. I was going to lead the life I chose.

"You say all this now," said Mum, "but wait another few months, and you'll be whistling a very different tune. Wait until you can't afford clothes or food, or a place to live, and then let's see how happy you are. You're used to a certain lifestyle, Lillian, and eventually you'll miss the comfort."

"I won't," I gritted.

"For Christ's sake, stop being a brat. I've lived longer than you have. I know better. Now come, let's go collect your things and be going. I want to have enough time for something to eat before we get on the plane."

Before I could respond, I heard hard footsteps approach and then Jack's deep, questioning voice asking, "Lille, what's going on?"

My mother turned to face him, her eyes taking him in as she crossed her arms over her chest and raised a speculative eyebrow. Okay, so she had never exactly been a nun, and I hated to say it, but Mum had a thing for handsome younger men. She always kept it away from our home life, which was at least something I was thankful to her for. But over the years, I came to learn that she liked to use her hard-earned money to wine and dine toy boys. Needless to say, it wasn't really something I liked to think about very often.

Jack had clearly just come off the stage, because he was using a towel to wipe sweat from his neck, and he wasn't wearing a shirt. I cringed when I saw how my mother appreciated the view. It was just plain wrong. Benjamin let out another impatient scowl and tapped his finger to his watch. I scowled right back while Mum ignored him, her attention all on Jack.

"Hello," she said, stepping forward and holding out her hand. "I'm Miranda Baker. Lille's mother. I came to take her home, I'm afraid." She smiled urbanely, her last words mixed with amused laughter, like this was all a little misunderstanding. Like I was a five-year-old who'd wandered into the neighbour's back garden and needed to be retrieved. My hackles rose as I gritted my teeth. Jack stared her hand, then arched a dismissive brow, making no move to shake with her.

"I told you, I'm not going home," I said, loud and firm.

Jack's gaze travelled from me to my mother and then back again. There was a beat of silence before he took a few steps to stand next to me.

"You heard her," he said to my mother, cocking his head and giving her a placid stare.

Mum waved him away. "Oh, don't mind Lillian. She has her head in the clouds most days. What kind of mother would I be if I left her here to fend for herself?"

"I've been fending for myself just fine," I said, and Mum glanced at me, taking in my crumpled, paint-stained T-shirt and the long gypsy skirt I bought at a market last week.

"Your appearance says otherwise, darling. What on earth are you wearing?" she replied with just the tiniest edge of mockery in her tone. Now I felt Jack straighten, and his fists were flexing, a familiar sign that he wasn't a happy camper.

"You need to leave," he ground out as his arm went around my middle. Within seconds, my mother took in the dynamic. She may have been mean and controlling, but she wasn't dumb.

"Ah, I see," she said, pursing her lips before reaching into her designer handbag and pulling out her wallet. "You're clearly attached to my daughter in some way and would be put out to have her leave." Wow, I'd almost forgotten the knack she had for saying things without actually saying them. Her tone did it all for her. She had deduced that Jack and I were having sex and thought he'd be "put out" if I were gone.

"I don't want any trouble, and you're clearly a *big, powerful* man," Mum went on, placing firm admiration in the words "big" and "powerful." She was trying to sweet-talk him, stroke his ego so that she could get her way. "So, name your price," she finished. "How much will it take for you to back off and let me extract my daughter in a hassle-free manner?"

My heart pounded and my face started to get red, I was so furious. She spoke about me as if I were a product she wanted to buy. And if I was furious, Jack was positively livid. He moved me so I was standing behind him, then took a step closer to my mother. She drew in a startled breath at his advancement and stumbled back a little, eyelids fluttering in surprise.

When he started to speak, his voice was low and menacing, "Listen to me, Miranda, and listen good. There is no price you could pay, no words you could speak, no threats you could spew that would make me let you take the woman I love away from me. Your daughter is worth more than what you think of her. She is one of the most beautiful, intelligent, talented, caring souls I have ever met, and she deserves better than you. She is not a commodity to be bought and sold, and she is not your property." He paused before finishing firmly, "Not anymore."

All of a sudden, I was finding it hard to breathe again as his voice echoed in my ears.

The woman I love.

That's what he'd said. I swallowed hard and focused on Mum. She was staring at him like he was a foreign language she couldn't translate. At long last Miranda Baker had come up against somebody she couldn't buy or intimidate. Time seemed suspended, until I finally regained the ability to move. I took a few steps forward and slid my fingers through Jack's to convey our solidarity. Mum's mouth scrunched up in distaste, and she was no longer looking at Jack with attraction. He'd gone down in her estimation by the simple fact of being in love with her daughter, and if ever I needed proof that I was doing the right thing by severing myself from her, then this was it.

Benjamin began to grow uncomfortable as he fidgeted where he stood, probably because he thought Mum might expect him to go up against Jack. And yeah, her PA possessed about as much brawn as a Barbie doll.

I expected Mum to throw some thinly veiled insult back at Jack, but she didn't. Instead, her attention landed on me. She let out a long, exasperated sigh, like this was all such an inconvenience to her and we weren't discussing my entire life here. "I have tried, Lillian, but if this is what you want, then I suppose I can't force you to come home. But know this, I will not try again, and when it all goes belly up, do not expect me to come to the rescue. You're on your own now."

I stared at her head on, my focus never wavering, and continued to hold my chin high. Her threats wouldn't work to cow me anymore.

After imparting her final words, she turned to Benjamin, nodded for him to follow her, and left. My mother's PA shot me one last retreating glance, like I was some kind of imbecile for not coming home with them, and then he was gone, too. Muted music streamed from inside the tent, and I stood hand in hand with Jack, a heavy tension resting between us. My heart felt full and light at the same time, my lungs drowning in emotion. I had never felt so much love for another human being in my entire life as I did for him in that moment.

He'd helped me stand up to Mum. But not only that, he'd shown her that I was worth something. He told her that although she considered me a burden, a helpless little bird she had to continually spoon-feed, that was not how he saw me. That in his eyes I was brilliant just as I was.

I turned my body to his and pulled him into my arms. My heart was beating double time as I soaked in the feel of his hot, silky skin and his long hair tickling my chin.

"Your mother is awful," he murmured into my neck.

"You told her you loved me."

"I told her that because it's true."

I pulled back and stared up at him. "Is it?" My words were so quiet, I wasn't sure he heard them at first. He seemed amused rather than insulted by the question.

"You don't believe me?"

Flustered, I backtracked. "No, no, that's not what I meant. I just…this is going to sound stupid, but I need to know if you meant what you said or if you said it simply to stick up for me."

He smiled down at me tenderly and brushed a tear I hadn't realised had fallen away from my cheek. "I don't say things I don't mean, flower."

All in one go, the air in my body left me. I was weightless as I sank into him, gripping his shoulders in my hands. And suddenly I felt shy, as his dark eyes penetrated me, flicking back and forth between mine as though trying to read my thoughts. I blushed hard and looked at the ground over his shoulder. God, how could I be shy about this when I knew he loved me, too? I had to say it. I couldn't just let him put himself on the chopping block without putting myself on there with him.

"I love you, too," I whispered, eyes trained on the grass. Even in the dark it looked so green, or maybe that was just my thumping heart amplifying the colour.

A deep, low chuckle escaped him. "What was that, flower? I didn't quite catch what you said there. Also, you need to look at me. Don't rob me of your eyes."

Swallowing for courage, I moved my gaze to his. "I said, I love you."

A wide, glorious smile shaped his mouth as he bent down to place a gentle kiss to the edge of my lips. "Yeah, that's what I thought."

Loud clapping startled me out of my trance before I had the chance to pull him in for a proper kiss. Whatever act that had been on inside had just ended, and the audience was cheering. I decided to pretend they were cheering for us. For me and Jack and our quiet little confession of love.

He brushed his thumb over my lip and tugged on my hand. "Come with me — I want to give you something."

Curious, I allowed him to lead me past the tent and back to the campers. When we reached his, he pulled me inside, then disappeared into his bedroom. I heard him opening and shutting a drawer before he returned with a small cardboard box in his hand. Pulling me down to sit, he placed it in my palm and told me to open it.

I pushed open the top and saw something bundled up in bubble wrap. Retrieving it, I began to strip away the plastic until I discovered it was a tiny hot air balloon forged in copper. Only a second passed before I remembered it. I'd seen this ornament before. It was from the curiosity shop back in Caen. It had been sitting in the window display while I admired it and pointed out to Lola and Jack how much it resembled my tattoo.

"You bought this back in Caen, didn't you?" I said, my voice airy, emotion causing my voice to catch.

He pulled me onto his lap and rested his head on my shoulder as I traced my fingers over the copper.

"Yes."

"Why?"

I felt rather than saw him shift, as though self-conscious. "I wanted it because you wanted it. There was something about the way you looked at it, like it was magical, that made me need to buy it. I wanted to possess that kind of magic, but more importantly I wanted to give it to you because I knew it would make you happy and I liked to see you smile. So I went back the next day and bought it."

A small, affectionate laugh escaped me, while at the same time my eyes grew watery. It was just a little ornament, and yet, it meant the world to me. It meant everything to know Jack had been so thoughtful to buy it when I couldn't afford it. I turned in his lap and stroked his jaw. "You bought it for me?"

His laugh matched mine. "Yes. I suppose I thought it'd endear you to me."

"I was already fascinated by you. Endearment wasn't necessary," I told him, hoping he could see the love in my eyes. "Why did you wait so long to give it to me?"

His arms slid around my waist, and his voice vibrated deep into my core. "I got a little attached to it for a while, but I don't need its magic anymore. I've got you now." He said the words simply, like all this was completely obvious, and my heart squeezed as I twisted and planted a kiss on his mouth.

"You, Jack McCabe, are the magic one," I said before setting the ornament down and reaching up to lift my shirt over my head.

Seventeen
And two bleeding souls were reunited

It had been an extremely humid day, and I was taking a break from face painting to sit in the refreshment stand with Lola and press a cold water bottle to my forehead. The show had just started, so Lola's customers were slowly trickling out. She wouldn't get busy again until the intermission. I eyed her speculatively. She seemed to be doing quite well now, and I never caught her crying or looking sad anymore. But still, I thought about the night of the attack all the time, wondered who it had been. It made my skin prickle with eerie awareness.

I also wondered about her life before the circus. About her husband Derek, who had treated her so badly she'd run away and assumed a new identity.

"What age were you when you came here?" I asked as she wiped down the service counter. I had graduated from pressing the bottle to my forehead to opening it up and gulping down its soothing coolness.

"Eighteen," she answered without having to think about it.

"Eighteen?" I said. "And you were already married?"

"Yeah, well, you know I'm kind of impulsive. I have this habit of meeting people and latching on right away. I did it with you." She paused and gave me a smile, which I returned. "The problem is that sometimes I latch onto the wrong person. Derek was twenty-five when I met him. He was a policeman, had his own place, and owned a car. I thought he was so sophisticated," she said, rolling her eyes at herself. "I never questioned it when he proposed to me after only two months seeing each other. We married a month after that, and I moved in with him. That's when the hitting started. I'd forget to wash his uniform on time or I'd be late having dinner on the table, and he'd beat me black and blue. I had to escape. The circus was in town, and I saw it as my opportunity. I applied for a job, and the rest is history. Derek hasn't found me yet, and if I play my cards right, he never will."

I nodded, absorbing her story and thinking of how scared she must have been to run away like that. How strong she was now in the little life she'd made for herself.

"I'm sorry, but you wouldn't know where we could buy a ticket, would you?" A voice cut through my thoughts, and Lola stepped over to the counter again to help the customer. I glanced at the woman, taking in her long dark hair and light blue eyes, her pretty heart-shaped face and stylish clothes. I normally wouldn't have paid such close attention, but this woman had an Irish accent, which was an unusual thing to hear when you were in Italy. She looked to be in her early to mid-twenties, and smiled at us with straight white teeth.

"Yeah," Lola began, and pointed to the ticket booth just across the way, "you can get tickets over there."

"Thank you," said the woman, just before a man called out,

"Watson, for crying out loud, is it impossible for you to wait up for me?"

The man behind the voice appeared a second later, and the moment I saw him, my entire body broke out into a cold sweat. He was tall, about the same height as Jack, had gorgeous hazel brown eyes and an undercut, the top part a touch dishevelled. He wore a tailored suit jacket with a band T-shirt underneath and dark jeans. Basically, he was drop-dead gorgeous; he'd barely spoken, and already I was being hit with a whack of the charisma stick. Jack had the same effect, but it was rough around the edges, and he was often unaware of it. This guy knew exactly the effect he wielded, and his charm was practiced and honed to a "T."

I'd recognise him anywhere. This was Jay Fields, Jack's brother, and I couldn't believe he was standing in front of me. I couldn't believe my letter had brought him here. I also couldn't believe that I'd basically forgotten I'd even sent that letter. In recent weeks, I'd been so wrapped up in Jack that it had completely slipped from my mind.

He wrapped his arm around the petite woman's waist, his jaw tight. There was an air of tension about him that put me on edge. I only realised I was staring at him with my mouth wide open when Lola nudged me with her elbow and muttered under her breath in amusement, "Close your mouth, Lille."

Her words made me blink, snapping me back to attention.

Jay glanced at me and frowned. "Hey, are you okay, darlin? You look like you just saw a ghost." He was staring at me hard now, attention flickering over my features as though he was thinking rapid thoughts.

"You're Jay Fields," I blurted out stupidly.

"A-ha!" Lola exclaimed. "I knew I recognised him from somewhere. You're mad talented, mate. I can't believe you're here at the circus. I was just showing Lille your videos a couple of weeks ago. What are the chances, eh?"

Jay was still staring at me when a light bulb set off behind his eyes. "You're Lille," he breathed, stepping forward with his arm still around the woman. "Lille Baker?"

I swallowed hard and nodded, unable to find my voice. Jay shoved his hand in his pocket and pulled out some folded papers. He unfolded them, and with a sudden pang of dread, I recognised both my and Jack's handwriting. Jay pointed to my letter. "You wrote this?"

Again, all I could do was nod. I was sure my eyes were just two big round saucers at that stage.

"Where is he?" Jay asked, running a hand anxiously through his hair. He seemed pumped, full of nervous energy. "Where is my brother?"

"Jay," said the woman, turning in his arms and placing her hands to his chest. Her voice was gentle, soothing. "Relax. Take a breath. We don't even know if this is real."

Jay closed his eyes and took a deep breath as instructed before speaking again. "That's why I came here. I need to find out. I need to know if he's alive."

Whoa, hold up a second, what? Jay thought Jack was dead? I had no clue what was going on, but I did know that I needed to push back my nerves and deal with this situation. Jack had always been clear that he had no desire to see his brother ever again, but here he was, and it was all my doing. If I didn't get a handle on it quickly, then this whole thing was likely to blow up in my face. Jack was going to *hate* me when he found out what I'd done. Why on earth had I done it again? Oh, yeah, because I'm a sentimental idiot.

I quickly left the refreshments stand and went around to meet them, calling over my shoulder, "Lola, can we go to Violet's for a little bit?"

Lola seemed confused. "You want to take these two to Violet's? Why?"

"I'll explain everything later. But right now I need to take care of something really important."

She shrugged. "Yeah, okay, go ahead. Violet won't be back until later after the show anyway."

I gave her a thankful look before turning to Jay. "Can you come with me, please? I need to talk with you. Jack can't know you're here, not yet."

There was suspicion in his eyes, but after a moment he nodded and gestured for me to lead the way, taking the woman's hand in his and following me. I quietly led them both to Violet's camper and opened the door, standing back and gesturing for them to go inside.

They sat down in the lounge, and I stood there for a second, not knowing what to do. I moved my feet one after the other and went to put on the kettle. Then I went to sit across from them. The woman was smiling at me in a friendly manner while Jay continued to regard me with suspicion.

"I'm Matilda, by the way," she said, holding out her hand. "Jay's wife."

I noticed she was wearing a beautiful engagement ring and wedding band before I took her hand and shook it.

"I'm Lille, Lille Baker, but you already know that," I replied, my voice shaky. I stared at my hands. "So, um, as I said in my letter, Jack has no idea I wrote to you. In fact, well, I don't know how else to say this, but he doesn't want to see you. I apologise for being blunt, but he kind of hates you."

Jay leaned forward, resting his elbows on his knees as he tilted his head at me. "He hates me?"

"Well, yes, you see, it's because your uncle told him you didn't want to see him. And he was all alone for so long, and people treated him so badly, and he was just hurting so much. He's still hurting, but he pretends he doesn't care. As you can tell from the letter, he does care — he just doesn't want to admit it." I was rambling, but I couldn't seem to stop.

Jay sat back, like it all suddenly made sense to him, and I wondered what I'd said that explained things. I didn't have to wait long before a dark look came over his face, and he began shaking his head back and forth. "My uncle. My fucking dipshit of an uncle." A silence elapsed before he turned to his wife. "Can you fucking believe this?"

"Jay, calm down," she whispered, but her plea only seemed to set him off worse. He turned to her, furious.

"Calm down!? Calm fucking down? Not only did that evil bastard rob me of a decent childhood, but he also robbed me of my only brother. He told me Jack was dead, Matilda. Dead! What kind of sick fuck does something like that?" He punched his fist into the sofa, and it all quickly started to make sense. All of my misgivings about Jack's story were not unfounded. I'd been right. Something fishy had been going on. Jay didn't abandon Jack — he'd thought he was dead because that's what his uncle had told him.

Once Jay had relaxed a little, Matilda pulled him into her arms. His body shook and I knew instinctively that he was crying. I thought I should have been more stunned by such a big, handsome, confident man crying, but I wasn't. I felt his pain, his loss. I felt it all through my connection with Jack.

Matilda looked at me over Jay's shoulder, and we exchanged concerned glances. I had no idea where to go from here. I mean, how would I explain all this to Jack? I wasn't sure I was brave enough to just go right up to him and be all, *Hey, Jack, funny story, but I stole the letter you wrote to your brother and sent it to him. Now he's here, and, well, you're welcome.* Yeah, I could see that conversation going down like a lead balloon.

My eyes went to the clock on the wall, and I noticed it was almost time for Jack's performance. Perhaps that was the way I could get around this. If I brought Jay into the audience, he'd be able to see Jack, have proof that he was alive from a distance, and then I could figure out where to go from there.

After a minute, Jay pulled away from his wife and turned to study me again. His eyes were a little blotchy, and his face stern. It was clear that he still didn't trust me. I was wearing my summer dress and a loose cardigan, my battered converse on my feet. My hair was up in a dishevelled bun that I'd secured with a wooden paintbrush, in lieu of a proper hair tie. I was forever losing those things. I desperately wanted to know what he thought of me, and deep down I wanted him to like me because he was Jack's brother and I was in love with Jack.

"How do you know my brother?" Jay asked, sitting up straight now and levelling me with his full attention. And whoa, the full attention of Jay Fields was more than a little intense. My skin was prickling slightly, and I felt like I was on trial.

I glanced away for a second and nervously scratched at my wrist. "I'm, well, I'm kind of his girlfriend."

Jay's eyebrow shot up, and for the first time something that resembled a smile shaped his lips. "Only kind of?"

My throat felt tight. "Well, yeah, I'm head over heels in love with him, but it's all very new."

Now he gave me a proper smile, and there must have been something in the way I said it that rang true, because all his suspicions melted away.

"Yeah, it looks like you are, darlin." His eyes moved over my form. "My brother has good taste." At this his wife elbowed him in the side, but she was smirking. "Stop

277

flirting with your brother's girlfriend, Jason," she scolded playfully, and he raised his hands in surrender. "What? She's cute. I'm just noticing that my brother has a cute girl, no harm in that." He went quiet for a second, and some of his tension returned as he ran his hand down his face. "My brother," he whispered to himself. "Fuck, this is crazy."

"Would you like to see him now?" I asked gently, and his response was fervent.

"Hell, yes."

Standing and smoothing down the skirt of my dress, I said, "Come on, then. He should be on stage right about now."

As I led them both out of the camper and towards the tent, Jay asked, "So, you mentioned in your letter that Jack's a performer, but you never said what kind?"

We were almost at the tent now, and I could hear Marina's voice echoing through the sound system as she introduced Jack's act. When we reached the side entrance, I took a deep breath and turned to face him. "I think I'll let you see for yourself."

Jay and Matilda stepped in ahead of me just as the music began to play and Jack made his entrance onto the stage, the flame-tipped metal wheels spinning on his bare, muscular arms. The audience cheered wildly, and I found my attention wandering to Jay as he stood there, frozen. His jaw was tight, his hands clenching into fists, and I could see his Adam's apple bob as he swallowed. His eyes blazed fiercely as his attention fixed on Jack, and I desperately wanted to know what he was thinking. Did he recognise him after all this time? What was he feeling right now to see his brother? A brother who for years he thought was dead but was in fact very much alive. And man, was Jack alive. As he moved about the stage, his very being practically pulsated with life and vitality.

Jay's hand went to his mouth, emotion overtaking him, as Matilda wrapped her arms around him for support. All of a sudden, it looked like the strength went out of him, and if it weren't for his petite wife, he might have crumpled to the floor. A wave of emotion hit me just watching him. My throat was heavy with tears, my lungs burned, and my heart beat hard and fast.

My attention wandered back to Jack, who was now spewing flames around the stage and soliciting noises of fear, awe, and excitement in his audience. He looked magnificent, so strong and fierce. And he had no idea that his brother was in the audience, his brother who up until a half hour ago had been convinced that he was dead. I was frightened of Jack discovering what I'd done, but at the same time, I knew it was the right thing. Both Jay and Jack had been mistaken about their past, and by putting myself on the line, I was reuniting them.

His act went on for about fifteen minutes, and several times throughout I saw Jay try to pull out of his wife's arms and run towards the stage. He wanted Jack to know he was there. Fortunately, each time Matilda pulled him back and murmured in his ear, her words working to subdue his eagerness and distress.

What do I do now?
What do I do now?

The question was still echoing in my head as I began to panic, no answers forthcoming, when suddenly Jack was performing his final trick. He tilted his head back and dipped the torch deep inside his mouth before swallowing the flame. The moment the music cut out and the crowd began to cheer, Jay was pulling out of his wife's hold and taking big, hurried strides toward that stage.

I heard him call out, "Jack! Jack!" but his voice melded into the noise of the cheers. Jack walked from one end of the stage to the other, taking a bow each time. When he rose from the final bow, he must have heard something, because his attention flickered across the audience. Then, as though in slow motion, his attention landed on Jay, who stood in the middle of an aisle, just a few feet shy of the stage. Time stood still, and my heart thundered in my ears as Jack stared at his brother, eyes dark and uncomprehending.

"Jack, it's me. It's Jay," he called, but still Jack didn't respond. A flash of anger passed over his face, his entire body coiling tight before he swung around, turning his back on his brother and disappearing through the curtains. Seeing Jack flee, Jay jumped up onto the stage quick as a flash and chased after him. Matilda and I exchanged glances before we both began moving through the audience to follow them.

I could hear Jay calling out, "Jack! Jack! Wait a minute!" We followed his voice until we were out in the back of the circus, where many of the camper vans were parked. Jay finally reached his brother and grabbed him by the shoulder to stop him. Jack spun around and glared at Jay, his eyes blacker than obsidian in the dark. The lights from inside the Spiegeltent flashed through the stained glass windows, casting the brothers in alternating shades of red, green, yellow, purple, and blue.

"Don't fucking touch me!" Jack hissed as he glared daggers at his brother.

"Let me explain," Jay pleaded, chest heaving from the effort exerted in chasing down Jack.

"There's nothing to explain. I have no idea how you found me or what you're doing here, but you need to leave. I don't want to see you."

Jay was fumbling in his pocket, and my gut sank when I saw him retrieve my letter. "I got this letter in the mail. It told me where you were," said Jay, right before Jack snatched the paper from him, his eyes flashing with fury as he scanned the words. He seemed confused for a moment as he put two and two together. Then he glanced to his brother, gaze flickering back and forth, brow furrowed. I was hit with the weight of a thousand bricks when suddenly Jack's eyes landed on me. Those eyes were heavy with betrayal and accusation, and for a moment I found it difficult to breathe. He strode toward me with purpose and tossed the letters at my feet.

"How could you do this? I trusted you, Lille, I fucking trusted you!"

"Wait, Jack, listen. It's not what you think," I pleaded but he cut me off.

"Not what I think? So you didn't steal this letter I wrote and send it to my brother without telling me? It just so happened to find its way to him by magic, did it?"

"No, but you have to understand, I did it all because I care for you. I wasn't trying to hurt you. I was trying help you." Tears were streaming down my face as I moved to touch him, but he flinched away from me.

"I told you I hated him. I told you how he abandoned me, how fucked up my life was after. How in the hell could you be trying to help me by bringing him here?"

Before I spoke, Jay cut in. He was now standing right behind his brother. "I didn't abandon you, Jack. You have it all wrong."

Jack spun on him. "Shut the fuck up! I don't want to hear it. I don't even want to look at you." He took a pained breath and shoved Jay back with both his hands. Jay took the hit without reciprocating. "Just stay the hell way from me, you selfish fuck!" His voice had become choked, and before I knew it, he was looking at me again with those pained eyes, and I felt my heart breaking, shattering into a million tiny pieces.

"You know what drew me to you from the very beginning, Lille? It wasn't your pretty face, your big grey eyes, or your beautiful smile. It was because for the first time in my life I felt like I was looking at a person I could trust. Someone so open and without malice that they didn't even possess the ability to betray, but I was wrong. And how wrong I was is destroying me inside."

His words made my stomach twist and my throat tighten in agony.

"Jack, please," I begged, trying to grab for him again, but he wouldn't let me touch him.

"Hey, look, you need to calm down," Jay interjected while Jack glowered at him hatefully. "I never abandoned you. Listen to me for one fucking minute, would you?"

Jack's chest rose and fell with his anger, but he didn't speak. Instead, he waited for Jay to finish. "Up until I got this letter, I thought you were dead. That's what our sick fuck of an uncle told me. I should have questioned it, but I didn't. I was only a kid. I didn't know you were still alive until your girl sent me this letter, and still I thought it was someone playing a sick joke, but I had to find out for myself. Then I come here and I see you, and it's really you, but you fucking hate me. You have to understand that everything you thought was true was a lie. I was told you died in that fire with our parents, Jack. That's why I never came for you. Because if I thought there was even a single shred of a chance you'd still be alive, then I would have destroyed the entire world to find you. You're my brother. I love you. Please understand that none of what happened was within either of our power to change."

Jack stared at Jay, and little by little I could see the fight go out of him as he absorbed the words. He swallowed hard, and the tension left his body, only to be replaced with sheer agony. He turned away from Jay, his back broad and tanned in the darkness, shoulders moving up and down as he tried to compose himself.

"You're lying," he said, the words so quiet I barely heard them. "This is all a lie. You're trying to manipulate me," he went on, voice small and choked with emotion.

"I'm not lying, Jack," Jay said, taking a tentative step forward until he was right behind him. I saw him notice the scarring on Jack's shoulder, his face contorting with sympathy and pain at the sight of it. It was a reminder of the house fire, the catalyst for all they had been through.

"Don't touch me," Jack pleaded, right before Jay threw his arms around Jack's shoulders and hugged him from behind. Jay held on for dear life while Jack fought the hug, straining in Jay's arms, but Jay held firm.

"It's the truth, Jack," he murmured. "It's the truth. You're my brother, and I love you. And I swear to God, from this day on, you'll never be alone again."

All of a sudden, the tension left him, and Jack sagged in his brother's arms. I could tell from the way his chest moved that he was crying. I thought Jay might be, too. I'd never witnessed such a scene before in my life, and I was completely undone by it. Two big, strong men, shattered by their pasts, so wholly ruined by it, embracing one another. Tears rolled down my face until I could taste the saltiness against my lips. When I looked at Matilda, I saw that she was crying, too.

"I'll never let you go again," Jay said, right before Jack turned and embraced him properly. My heart squeezed to see him do it, and even if Jack could never forgive me for what I'd done, I'd always have this memory. I'd always have the knowledge that my actions had brought two broken, hurting souls together. And perhaps by reuniting him with his brother, Jack would truly learn how to heal.

I felt soft, cool fingers touch against mine and looked down to see Matilda take my hand in hers. We both watched the brothers for a moment before she murmured gently to me, "Come on, let's leave them alone for a little while. I've a feeling they're going to have a lot to talk about."

I nodded solemnly and allowed her to lead me away. Before I knew it, we were back at Violet's camper, sitting on the steps and staring off into the night.

"I can't believe their uncle would lie like that. I mean, where's the payoff?" I said, not really expecting any answers.

Matilda took a breath and then started to speak. "I'm not sure there's a payoff, not in the traditional sense, anyway. Jay's told me a lot about his uncle Killian. After their parents died, he was the one who took Jay in and raised him, though his idea of raising a kid was fairly skewed. He was a professor of behavioural science and had this big important position at Harvard. But he used to get off on messing with people's heads. He was constantly playing mind games on Jay until he'd finally had enough of it and ran away. I guess telling Jay that Jack was dead was just another one of his mind games. He got a kick out of separating them, I suppose."

"He sounds like a sociopath," I said, appalled by what she was telling me. By the sounds of it, just like Jack, Jay hadn't had it so easy, either.

"That'd be about the size of it," Matilda said, smoothing her hands over her skirt.

There was a stretch of silence before I spoke again, and this time my voice was laced with misery. "Jack hates me for what I did. I don't think he's going to forgive me."

Matilda made sympathetic noises as she leaned close and put her arm around my shoulders. "No, that's not true. What you did was incredibly brave. You sacrificed yourself in order to reunite him with his brother, and I for one am unendingly grateful to you. Family means the world to Jay, and seeing his brother again after all these years is the biggest gift anyone could ever give him. Jack will forgive you — you just need to allow him time to process everything. It's a lot to take in."

"Yeah," I said, sniffling.

We were quiet for a long time. Usually I'd feel awkward being silent with someone I'd just met, but with Matilda, that wasn't the case. In a way, she was having all the same feelings as I was right now. She just didn't have the prospect of losing the man she loved dumped on top of it.

I was starting to feel a little less emotional when Matilda spoke again. "Jack is kind of beautiful, isn't he?" she said, her voice awed. "I mean, Jay is, too — it's just that Jack was always the little one. The younger brother. Now he's bigger than Jay. Such a man, and wow, when he's on the stage, he just shines. It's incredible to see."

I stared at her, curious. "You knew Jack when he was a kid?"

She nodded. "Yeah. I used to live next door to both of them before their house burned down. Jay and Jack didn't have the best of upbringings even before all that. Their dad was a violent drunk, and they'd be left hungry a lot. I used to give them food and stuff." She shrugged as though it was no big deal.

I mustered a smile for her. "You must have been a very kind child."

"It wasn't really intentional. I just liked being around them, helping them, you know. I must have made an impression, because Jay always remembered me. It's kind of a long story, but he came back for me when he was grown."

"Will you tell it to me?" I asked quietly. "I'd like to hear about you two. I don't care if it's long. It'll take my mind off Jack."

Matilda gave me an empathic smile, then began to recite her tale. I sat back and listened to the story of how she and Jay were reunited. A story of mystery and revenge and falling in love. It was truly exhilarating. And all the while I hoped my own love story hadn't yet come to an end.

Eighteen

Mystery came knocking once more

I barely slept a wink that night. After sitting and talking with Matilda for more than two hours, we exchanged numbers, and she called for a taxi to bring her back to her hotel. When she called Jay, he told her that he was in Jack's camper and that he wouldn't be returning until late. He didn't give any more details than that, which was frustrating. I desperately wanted to know what was happening and how Jack was feeling, but I forced myself to be selfless. This wasn't about me, this was about the brothers.

I stayed the night in Lola's room. The past few weeks I'd basically started living at Jack's place, but I knew I wasn't welcome there right now. If not because he and Jay needed time alone with one another, then because he considered me a Judas. He thought I had betrayed him, and I didn't know if just because he was embracing Jay that he'd forgiven me, too. I finally fell asleep in the early hours of the morning/passed out from emotional and physical exhaustion. Take your pick.

When I woke up, Lola's bed was empty, and the alarm clock told me it was past one in the afternoon. I shot up in the bed and hurriedly pulled on some clothes. I didn't even stop to grab breakfast. Instead, I made my way directly to Jack's camper. I knocked on the door a number of times but received no answer, and when I peered in the window, it didn't look like anyone was home. Dejected, I returned to Violet's, where I found Lola in the lounge, reading some magazines.

"Wow, you look like someone just told you your cat died," she said, taking in my appearance. "So, what was all that last night with Jay Fields?" she went on curiously. I let out a long sigh, sat down across from her, and recited the tale from beginning to end. By the time I was done, Lola was staring at me with her jaw hanging open.

"That's some crazy story," she said, and then her eyes took on a mischievous gleam. "Okay, so is it wrong that I'm visualising some brother-on-brother action right now? Because that's one sexy threesome opportunity right there."

I threw a cushion at her head. "Lola! That's so wrong — firstly because it's incest, and secondly because Jay is a married man."

"Oh, fine, go and piss all over my fantasies, why don't you?"

I just shook my head at her, a tiny smile shaping my lips. The girl had a knack for making me feel better even when I was at my lowest. My smile faded quickly, though, and Lola noticed.

"He'll forgive you, Lille. Quit fretting about it. That man is head over heels for you. I've seen it with my own two eyes."

I glanced at her, praying she was right. The rest of the day passed restlessly for me. I tried to concentrate on some sketches, but it was no use. I even offered to wash the outside of the camper van for Violet and Lola. Violet looked at me like I needed mental help for wanting to do such a thing, but she let me clean it all the same. Losing myself in scrubbing the dirt off the van occupied my mind for a little while, but as soon I finished I was itching to find Jack again.

I tried calling his phone but got no answer. This wasn't too unusual though, because he often forgot to carry it on him. When I called Matilda she told me that Jack and Jay were spending the day together, and that she was hanging out at the hotel by herself. She offered for me to come and join her, but I declined. I wouldn't have been good company right then.

I sat on the steps of Violet's camper, sipping on a mug of red wine (she didn't own any glasses) to soothe my nerves, when King ambled up to me and sat down. It was unexpected, but I didn't question it. My emotions were all over the place, so I merely accepted his company for what it was.

"It doesn't help, you know," he said and I glanced at him.

"Pardon?"

He nodded to the wine. "It numbs but it doesn't heal. It numbs you just enough every time to make you forget that it doesn't heal. It's like Western medicine, treating the symptom and ignoring the cause. So, forget about the symptom and look at the cause," he stopped and pointed his finger harshly into my arm to drive home his point. "That's where you'll find the cure."

What he said made perfect sense, but still, it irked me that he didn't take his own advice. "If you know all this, then why don't you treat your cause? Why do you continue to medicate the symptom?"

"Ah," he said, letting out a long, weary sigh. "Some of us are too far gone for all that."

A silence elapsed as the noise from the crowds coming to see the circus began to grow louder. I decided I wasn't going to work that night; I wasn't in the right frame of mind. I did, however, know what I was in the right frame of mind for.

"King," I started and he turned to me. I swallowed. "You know that picture you have of the woman?" He nodded, eyes narrowing warily. "Could I...I mean, would you like me to paint it for you?"

I shivered as I waited for his response. I wasn't even sure why I wanted to do it, but for some reason I thought he'd like to have a painting of his Alexis that he could keep.

"That way, if you ever lose the photograph again, you'll still have the painting."

More silence, and then, ever so slightly and without breathing a word, he nodded his head. Digging into his pocket, he pulled out the worn photo and handed it to me. I took it with care and then went to gather some of the supplies I still kept in Lola's bedroom. King sat and watched me as I set up and began to paint. I painted well into the small hours of the morning, as the grey light of the coming day began to slowly filter into the sky.

Wiping the perspiration from my brow, I stood back and took in my work. I was satisfied with the end result, and felt like I'd managed to capture the happiness on the woman's face as she stared into the camera. Without my realising it, King had come to stand beside me, and when I looked at him his pale blue eyes were watery with tears. Even though I'd been the one to create the painting, I felt like this was a private moment for him, so I went inside to scrub my hands. When I returned, both the painting and King were gone.

He'd taken it, and that was good enough for me. I'd made something that held meaning for him, and it gave me a sense of peace. When I finally went to bed, I found that I'd exhausted myself enough to sleep.

***

The next day I woke up to my phone ringing. Checking the time, I found it was past two in the afternoon and my heart jumped to know I'd slept half the day away. I noted that it was Matilda's number flashing on the screen, and when I answered she asked me if I had any dinner plans. Apparently, Jay and Jack were still getting reacquainted with one another, and she wanted some company.

It filled my heart with good feelings to know the brothers were still bonding, which soothed some of the ache inside me. I told her I'd love to, and we hung up with plans to meet in a couple of hours at the restaurant beside her hotel. Lola forced me to take a shower and gave me a loan of some clothes to wear, which consisted of an emerald green skater dress and a navy cardigan. The green was surprisingly complementary to my skin tone, and after blow-drying my hair with Lola's tiny travel hair dryer, I felt a little better about myself.

I had enough cash to spare, so I took a taxi into the city, getting out when I arrived at the restaurant. Running my hand through my hair and hitching my bag up on my shoulder, I stepped inside and was immediately hit with the sound of male laughter. I was drawn to that sound, and as my eyes scanned the space for Matilda, I found her, but she wasn't alone. She sat at a booth-style table beside Jay, and Jack sat on the other side, wearing a long-sleeved black T-shirt and with his hair down. My stomach tightened when I saw him, and I got the distinct sense that this was an ambush. I stood there, taking in the scene, as Jay made some kind of joke, smiling widely across the table at his brother, and Jack smirked at whatever he said.

"I swear to God," Jay exclaimed, gesturing animatedly with his hands. "I'm standing in front of this chick, asking her to pick a number between one and twenty, and she starts telling me about her yeast infection. I'm like, and I need to know this why? Selecting random people on the street can be fucking weird sometimes."

Jack laughed low and deep, and when he glanced at his brother with genuine affection in his eyes, my heart did a little somersault. I couldn't believe the turnaround since the other night. The atmosphere between them had completely transformed. I didn't move until Matilda's eyes landed on me and she gave me a warm, welcoming smile. Stepping forward, I reached the table and just about managed to find my voice.

"Uh, hi."

Jack's back was turned to me, but I saw him tense the second he heard my voice. Yeah, he definitely didn't know I was coming. I wasn't sure whether I should be thanking Matilda or chewing her out for tricking me. Jay saw me and smiled, then gave me a little wink.

"Hey, darlin.'"

"Lille," said Matilda, "I'm so glad you could make it. You look gorgeous. Love your dress. Come, sit down."

Anxiously, I slid into the booth next to Jack, but he didn't acknowledge me. Making sure to keep several inches of distance between us, I frowned and stared at the menu that lay on the table, trying to decide whether or not I should stay. He clearly didn't want me here.

"Jack," I said quietly as I took in his handsome profile. Upon hearing his name, he turned to me, and when he met my eyes, it nearly took my breath away. They held such stark emotion that I was sure was mirrored in my own. "H-how are you?" I asked, trying for casual and failing. His gaze travelled from my face to my shoulders, and then down. I felt hot and itchy under his stare, and I could have killed to know what he was thinking.

"I'm good, all things considered," he answered finally, and I couldn't read him at all.

Jay leaned down and whispered something in Matilda's ear. She narrowed her gaze and elbowed him in the side. "No way, Jay. I already told you no, so quit pestering me."

I tried to focus on them, but I was still hyper aware of every little move Jack made, every breath he took.

"Oh, come on, Watson. You need to live a little."

"What's this?" I asked, not really caring what they were talking about. I just needed to distract myself from the tension that was radiating off Jack.

Matilda leaned in, sighed, and rested her elbows on the table. "My husband, the horndog, has been trying to convince me to join the mile-high club. I swear to God, every time we take a flight, he's at it. Like a dog with a bone."

Jay barked playfully and leaned in to nip her earlobe with his teeth. Seeing them both so much in love made my current heartsickness feel that much worse. Jack was right beside me, but it felt like there was an ocean between us. I turned to look at him again and saw his lips twitch slightly at his brother's antics. I could see in his eyes the love that was there; it even seemed like he looked up to Jay. Hardly two days had gone by, and already the dynamic they'd had as kids was returning. I imagined they must have done some serious amount of talking.

The waiter appeared at our table then. He was a handsome Italian guy with dark eyes and dark hair, and he spoke very good English. I wasn't even hungry and the menu was practically gibberish to me, but I forced myself to pick something. When it was my turn to order, I glanced up at the waiter for help. "Um, what is the *Milanese di pollo?*"

"It's a breaded chicken breast with salad," he answered, giving me a warm, interested smile. Something about the way he looked at me told me he liked what he saw, and I grew uncomfortable, mainly because Jack was right beside me.

"Oh, right, okay, that sounds good," I said. "I'll take that."

The waiter must have sensed I was ordering it for convenience, and he was right, because I wasn't a big fan of breaded chicken. He leaned down and took the menu in his hands, holding it in front of me. "You tell me what you like and I'll choose, yes? What is your favourite: steak, seafood, pasta?"

"I like seafood," I offered.

"Ah, so how about the *zuppa di pesce*? It is a fish stew."

"That sounds good, thank you," I replied, smiling gratefully.

"It is my pleasure, *bella ragazza*," he said, and placed his hand on my shoulder for a second. All of a sudden I felt heat at my neck, and I realised that Jack had leaned in and was resting his arm along the back of the booth. I glanced at him to see he was staring daggers at the waiter, and my pulse hammered. Whoa, he looked angry. The waiter left quickly after taking in Jack's expression, and a quiet fell over the table.

Matilda gave me a playful grin. "Do you know what he just called you?"

I shook my head. "I don't know much Italian."

"He called you a beautiful girl. Methinks the waiter likes you, Lille."

I grew both tense and elated that Jack was pissed at the waiter flirting with me.

"I was chatting with a woman in the hotel spa the other day. She's from London, and she said she loves coming here because she gets so much attention from the men. They love the pale skin," Matilda went on, and I had a feeling she knew exactly what she was up to. She was trying to make Jack jealous, and it seemed to be working. I stole a peek at him again, my cheeks flushing, and I found he was staring at me intensely.

"So, tell me," said Jay, breaking my attention away from Jack. "How did you two kids meet?"

Jack gave him an annoyed look and remained silent, so I chose to answer, clearing my throat. "The circus was doing some shows in my hometown. I was working at my summer job in the local restaurant, and Jack used to come in a lot with Marina. She's the ringmaster." I could feel Jack watching me as I continued the story shyly. "I was always looking at him. I thought he was gorgeous. I dunno, I suppose you could say I had a bit of a crush."

Jack made a grunting sound that I wasn't quite sure how to interpret. Jay had been grinning at me while I spoke, but now his attention went to his brother. "Oh, yeah, and what did you think of lovely Lille when you first saw her, Jack?"

Jack didn't answer right away, but when he did, I felt myself grow weak at his low, fervent response. "I thought she was exquisite. And not for the likes of me."

Jay frowned, and I was blushing even harder now. God, I loved this man so much.

"Well, I don't think Lille agrees with that assessment, do you, darlin?" Jay asked, focusing back on me. I shook my head and felt my body lean slightly closer to Jack's. His fingertips brushed the back of my neck, and I sucked in a breath at the contact. The moment was broken when the waiter arrived back with our food. He didn't flirt with me this time, not after having Jack almost glower him to death before, and left as soon as he'd distributed the plates.

I lifted my spoon and began to eat. The stew was delicious, hot and salty. I had one hand resting on the edge of the booth and noticed that Jack's hand rested just a few inches away. Feeling bold, I moved my hand so it rested against his. I felt the heat of his skin all the way down to my toes. A few moments passed, but he didn't break the contact. Perhaps he craved it just as much as I did.

Throughout the meal, I stole glances at him. I knew Jay and Matilda could see, but I tried to ignore their indulgent smiles. At one point when I tried to look at Jack, I found he was already staring at me, his eyes trained on my mouth. I'd just eaten a spoonful of stew, and a little of the liquid had dribbled down my chin. Almost as though it was second nature, Jack lifted his thumb and wiped it away. I watched as he then brought his thumb to his mouth to suck it clean, and as soon as I saw him do it, I was wet and aching for him.

"Jack," I whispered, and moved my leg so our thighs touched.

"What is it, flower?" he asked, just as quietly.

"I'm sorry."

His lips turned down sadly. "I know you are. I know."

An agonising moment of quiet passed before Matilda spoke. "You know what I want to do tonight? I want to go dancing. We should all go to a club or something."

Jay chuckled. "Okay, Watson. Your wish is my command. Admit it, you just want to see me bust some sexy moves on the dance floor."

"Well, what's the point in having a husband who can dance if I'm not going to take advantage of it every now and again?"

Jay stared fondly down at his wife before looking to Jack. "What about you, bro? You like to bust a move, too?"

Jack looked uncomfortable for a second, so I answered for him. "Um, have you seen him on stage? Of course he likes to dance, but it's more like a tribal sort of thing." I slid my pinky around Jack's beneath the table, and he let me.

"It's actually called Poi dancing," Jack explained gruffly. "It's Maori, from New Zealand."

I rubbed my pinky along his, and a moment later he gripped my hand tight, giving it a squeeze. The emotions I was feeling in that moment were almost too much to bear.

"Oh, yeah, and where did you learn how to do that?" Jay probed.

Jack seemed embarrassed now. "I took classes."

Matilda leaned forward with interest. "In Dublin? Really? I didn't know you could learn that kind of thing back home."

Jack's brow crinkled slightly as he stuck his fork into his linguine. "It was combined with a belly dancing class." He paused, frowning, but then his lips twitched. "Don't laugh."

Despite Jack's instruction, Jay let out a big chuckle, and Matilda giggled. "That's nothing to be embarrassed about. I bet the ladies in the class were drooling all over themselves to have you there."

"Hey!" Jay protested, scowling impishly at his wife.

"What?" Matilda exclaimed. "Jack grew up well. Just like you did. Never let it be said that the McCabe/Fields brothers don't bulk up once they hit puberty."

"I can't believe you're the same girl I knew as a kid," said Jack with a smile. "I remember you used to give me chocolate chip cookies all the time. In my head, I called you Cookie Girl."

"In my head, I call her something else," Jay put in flirtatiously, and Matilda whacked him on the shoulder.

"You always have to lower the tone," she complained, but she was still grinning.

Jay flashed his teeth at her as he smiled. "You love it."

For a second I forgot the tension between Jack and me, and soaked in the fun-loving atmosphere that simply radiated off this couple. They were so enjoyable to be around, and I was sure it was their warmth that was lessening Jack's distance from me. I'd eaten way too much bread and olive oil, mostly out of nerves, so when it was time for dessert, I didn't have much room left. I turned to Jack, and he must have sensed my attention because his eyes came to mine.

"Do you want to share something? I don't have enough room left for a full dessert," I said, rubbing my hand over my tummy. Jack's gaze heated up and wandered to my stomach before rising to my chest. The dress I wore was a little bit low-cut and showed what I thought was a classy amount of cleavage.

"What do you want, flower?" he murmured quietly.

My attention flickered to the menu. "Um, the tiramisu looks good."

"Then order it, and we'll share."

I noticed Matilda giving me an encouraging smile, and I grew self-conscious. Still, I craved Jack's touch like a drug, and while the brothers chatted and we waited for dessert to arrive, I tentatively leaned my head on his shoulder. After an emotional two days I was tired, and I really just wished we could go somewhere and be alone. Talk things out. I heard him let out a long sigh, and before I knew it, his big arm came down around my shoulders and pulled me in tight.

"Awww!" said Matilda in delight the moment she saw. "You two make such a beautiful couple."

Jack gave his usual uncomfortable grunt, and I glanced away shyly.

"No, seriously," she went on. "You both look so striking together. Your colouring's so light, and Jack's is so dark."

I savoured the heat of Jack's body and hastened a glance at him from beneath my lashes. I wasn't expecting it when he leaned in, brought his mouth to my ear, and whispered, "She should see us when we fuck."

My eyes went wide, and I swear every hair on my body was standing on end. Jay was watching us with amusement, and Matilda looked like she was dying to know what Jack had said. I for one was glad that she hadn't. It would have been mortifying. I was grateful for the distraction when the dessert arrived. Jack handed me a spoon, our fingers grazing when I took it. He watched as I dug in. I could only manage three or four mouthfuls before my stomach started to complain, so I let him finish the rest.

After dinner Matilda used her phone to search for the nearest dance club. Apparently, when Jack told Marina about reuniting with his long-lost brother, she'd insisted he take some time off to be with him, so we didn't need to hurry back for the show. Since Turin had been such a successful stop for the circus, I'd made enough money painting faces to justify taking another night off, too. Besides, there was absolutely nothing right then that would make me leave Jack's side. He might have warmed up to

299

me over dinner, but I still wanted to apologise properly. Explain that I never had any ill intentions by sending Jay his letter.

The club we ended up in was loud and crowded. A couple of men gave me interested looks, but they quickly aimed that interest elsewhere when they saw Jack standing behind me. I hated to admit it, but I loved that he was being all possessive. It meant he still cared.

After we all shared a drink at the bar, Jay led Matilda to the dance floor, leaving Jack and me alone for the first time that night. We stood side by side, watching the gyrating bodies, and I didn't know what to say. It wasn't like he'd be able to hear me anyway, since the music was loud enough to wake the dead.

I felt his hot, humid breath on my neck when he leaned down and shouted over the music, "I'm going outside for a smoke."

"I'll come with you," I shouted back, and followed him out the side of the club and into an alleyway. A couple of people hung about, smoking and chatting in Italian. I stood close to the wall and watched as Jack pulled a pack of smokes from his pocket, then used a match to light one up. He took a drag, still holding the match in his hand as the smoke rose off it slowly and drifted into the air. His eyes came to me, and they held unmistakable heat. I knew we were both remembering the same thing, our first night together, making love out in the open. He'd used a hot match against my nipples, awakening a hunger inside me I didn't even know was there.

He seemed taken off guard when I closed the distance between us to stand before him. Our eyes met, and there was a question in his when I took the match from him and brought it to my chest. Dragging it over the rise of my

300

breasts, I gasped when its heat scorched my skin and heard Jack emit a strangled groan.

"What are you doing, Lille?"

"I miss you."

He dragged his hand through his hair. "I miss you, too."

"I'm so sorry for betraying your trust, Jack. You're the most important person in my life, and I'll do anything to win your forgiveness." I continued running the match over my skin, and my nipples were rock hard beneath my bra.

His voice was strained. "Will you...could you stop doing that? It's fucking distracting."

"I like distracting you," I murmured.

"You don't have to *try* to distract me, Lille. It already comes natural," he answered, his voice thick with warning. I dropped the match and let out a breath.

"You seem happy with Jay," I ventured.

Jack tilted his head, staring up at the sky as he spoke. "I am happy. I'm still trying to get my head around it all. It's kind of surreal. It's like there's this whole back story to our family that I never even knew about."

I nodded. "Yeah, Matilda and I talked last night. She told me all about it." I paused, trying to figure out what to say next. "I shouldn't have gone behind your back," I told him sadly. "I should have figured out a better way."

"You did what you thought was right. I'm not gonna lie, Lille. I'm still fucking angry that you stole the letter. You can't just go around meddling in people's lives like that, but I'll admit in this case, the end result was a good one. It wrecks me to know you took such a huge risk for me, and at the same time it makes me want to strangle someone, because shit, my words were private, and you read them."

I didn't disagree with a single thing he'd said. "I'm too curious. I really didn't read it with any kind of ulterior motives. I just wanted to know you so badly. I had such strong feelings for you even then, and I had a moment of weakness. But Jack, the pain in what you wrote wasn't something I could ignore. I cared about you too much to just let you go on suffering, so I put myself on the line. I thought that if I could reunite you with your family, then it would be worth it, even it meant you'd hate me after. Now I understand that the way I thought was silly, because I can't handle losing you. You're in my skin now, Jack. You're the love of my life, and I need you so much I can't breathe with it."

A solitary tear streamed down my face, and I cursed myself for crying. I was being an emotional fool, making a show of myself in a dirty alley outside a nightclub. But then Jack was in front of me, his hard body pressing into mine, caging me in warmth as he brought his hand to my cheek and wiped away the tear.

"Flower," he murmured, taking my chin in his hand, his fingers grazing my throat, "if you think I could let you go, then you seriously underestimate the kind of man I am."

His words made me crumble. I was gone. A mess. And when he brought his mouth to mine for an intense kiss full of unspoken words and promises, I almost lost the ability to hold myself upright. Jack's tongue slid inside my mouth and he let out a feral growl, backing me up into the wall almost painfully. His mouth captured mine, possessed every inch of my insides, causing tingles to radiate down my spine. I moaned and he swallowed it, gripping my neck in his tight grasp and pressing his hardness into my belly.

"I can't be gentle tonight, Lille," he said, his voice a carnal warning, and I whimpered.

"I don't want you to be."

"You need to be punished."

"Punish me, then."

Before I could think another thought, his hand was under the hem of my dress, smoothing up my thigh and seeking refuge inside my underwear. His long fingers opened me quickly, rubbing down my slit, finding my entrance, and plunging in without preamble. I gasped at how perfectly he filled me. There were people only feet away from us, but no street lights shone on our unlit corner. We were shrouded in the privacy of darkness.

I yelped in surprise when Jack's mouth came down on my neck, his sharp teeth grazing my skin before biting down hard. My entire body shook against him, my breaths coming out choppy and laboured.

"Jack," I breathed.

"I told you I couldn't be gentle, flower," he ground out, fingers pumping while his thumb found my clit. The pressure was delicious, perfect, and I knew it wasn't going to be long before I came.

"I want…to…ask you a question."

His tongue licked at the shell of my ear. "Then ask."

"Why do you call me flower?"

I didn't have to look to know he was smiling that glorious smile, the one that lit up his face from the inside out.

"Because when I touch you, you fucking *bloom*," he answered, and it was right on his final word that I came with a startling intensity. His fingers left me and rubbed along my folds. "I'll never get tired of the way you feel. This is mine," he grunted into my ear, but I had no answering words. All I could do was nod. When I finally found my voice, I let out a breathy, "Yours," and it felt like his entire body vibrated with approval. Just as he was setting my dress back to rights and I was nibbling at his neck, my face pressed into his hot skin, the door to the club opened, and someone stepped out.

A moment later I heard Jay call, "Jack, Lille, are you two out here?"

It only took a moment for him to spot us. I was still coming down from my orgasm, my body trembling against Jack's as he held me in his arms. My hands were fisted in his shirt.

"There you are," said Jay, a knowing lilt to his voice. I glanced at him for a moment to see him smirking to high heavens. Jack shook his head at his brother's cheery demeanour and said, "We'll be in in a minute."

Jay raised his hands in the air. "Hey, no rush. Matilda's in the bathroom, powdering her nose or whatever shit women do in bathrooms. She's been gone a while, so I was wondering if Lille could go check on her, but I see she's otherwise indisposed at the moment." I bristled with embarrassment, self-conscious that Jay could see the "I just came" flush to my cheeks. I drew in a deep breath and ran my hands down my dress.

"It's okay. I can go find her," I said, and slid out of the cage of Jack's body. I tried to put one foot in front of the other, which was difficult given my current state, but I just about managed to reach the door. Jay held it open, Jack heavy on my heels, and I stepped back inside to the throbbing beat of the music. Just before heading to the bathroom, I turned around to see Jay reach out and ruffle Jack's hair, like he was congratulating him. Jack half scowled, half grinned at his brother and gave him a little shove. It made my heart squeeze so see them acting like such siblings, and I hurried on to find Matilda. When I reached the bathroom, she was standing by the sinks, washing her hands.

"Lille," she said when she saw me. "Oh, you look like a woman who just got what she wanted. I take it you and Jack are back on track, then?"

I looked away sheepishly before replying, "Yeah, I think we are. I really should thank you for inviting me to dinner. I'll be honest, when I first realised it was a setup, I kind of wanted to strangle you for a second, but I know now that your heart was in the right place."

She seemed taken aback by my words and gave me a shy smile. "You're welcome. I'm happy to help."

A moment of quiet elapsed while Matilda reached inside her purse and retrieved some money to give to the bathroom attendant. I stood there, suddenly overcome with the need to embrace her. She must have noticed, because when she looked at me, she asked, "What?"

"This is going to sound weird, but can I give you a hug?"

She laughed. "Of course you can."

I went to her, wrapping my arms around her small frame. I guessed that after all we'd been through reuniting Jack and Jay, I felt a sense of kinship towards her.

"I suppose we're sort of sisters-in-law now," she said warmly.

"Well, if Jack and I ever marry, it won't be for a long time, but yeah, I suppose you could call us that."

Matilda grinned as she pulled away. "Hmm, I don't think you need a ring on your finger with Jack. The way he looks at you says it all. You're it for him."

"It's a little early to say that," I hastened, but she cut me off. The shine in her eyes told me she was tipsy, which explained the soppy sentiment that came out of her next.

"Oh, Lille, there's never too early when true love is involved."

Her words made me grin, because she'd definitely had a few. I let her lead me back out into the club. We didn't immediately find the brothers, but a song came on that Matilda liked, so I let her lead me onto the dance floor. We danced for a minute or two, the crush of the bodies surrounding us strangely liberating, when I felt familiar arms come around my middle.

"I can still smell you on my hand," Jack growled into my ear, his voice sending delicious spikes of awareness right to my core. Our bodies moved to the beat, and I looked to see Jay join Matilda, taking her into his arms and doing a cute little dancey hug.

"Wait 'til I get you home tonight — you're gonna fucking *ache* in the morning."

I twisted in his hold to face him, my breasts pushing into his hard chest as we continued to dance. I trembled, enjoying the friction between our bodies.

"I'm already aching for you," I said, going up on my tiptoes to shout into his ear.

His lips tipped up at the edges as he swept my hair over my shoulder and gripped the back of my neck. "What do you want me to do to you, flower?"

The loudness of the club, the heat, the sweat, and Jack's potent masculinity all combined to make me brave, more open with my desires. "I want your tongue between my legs," I said, and I felt rather than heard the rumble emanate from Jack's chest. "I want you to make love to me so hard I end up sore."

His other arm squeezed tighter around my waist, and when I met his eyes, they practically blazed with his desire for me. I could feel him hardening again, and it gave me a little thrill to know my words had done that to him, to know there were hundreds of people surrounding us. Jack used his grip on my neck to tilt my head back, and before I knew it, he was sinking his tongue deep inside my mouth, moving it in slow delicious thrusts that made me envision his cock inside me.

By the time we came up for air, the DJ was playing a completely different song, and Jay was tapping Jack on the shoulder.

"I think it's time we get out of there," he shouted as we followed him to the bar, where it was quieter. Jack held my hand in his. "How about we head out to the circus? I want to meet the people you live with."

Jack nodded, and a couple of minutes later we were huddled in a taxi. Jay sat in the front and began doing a card trick for the driver. Matilda scolded him for distracting the man, saying we'd all end up in a crash. I watched in fascination, the side of my body moulded to Jack's as Jay shuffled a deck of cards in a way I'd never seen before. At least not in real life.

It looked like the show had just ended when we arrived at the circus, because there were dozens of cars blocking the road as the audience left the tent and headed back into the city. We got out, the cool night air kissing my skin. Jack led the way to the gazebo, where most everyone would be hanging out after the show. I thought he seemed a little excited to introduce Jay as his brother. Before we got there, though, we stopped in our tracks as a terrified scream rang out somewhere close by.

"What was that?" Matilda asked, moving closer to her husband, a wary look on her face.

"It sounded like a scream," I said, skin prickling. This was eerily similar to the night Lola was attacked, and when

I met Jack's gaze, I knew he was thinking the exact same thing. Before any of us could say another word, we heard footsteps pounding hurriedly toward us, and I jumped in fright when Julie emerged around the side of a camper. She was wearing a silk robe that was torn at the shoulder, her stage outfit on underneath, and blood was trickling down from a cut on her eyebrow. Her eyes were wide and full of terror

It struck me as odd that my initial reaction was to go to her, help her, even after all she'd done to me. I let go of Jack's hand and stopped her by placing my hands on her shoulders.

"Julie, what happened?" I asked, frantic.

Her chest heaved in panic, but as she took us all in, she seemed to find her voice. "He came after me. He hurt me," she sobbed before breaking down into tears.

Jack stood in front of Julie and spoke firmly. "Listen to me, you need to tell us what happened."

"A man in a mask broke into my camper. He...he attacked me, tried to rape me, but I punched him and managed to get away."

Jay let out a low whistle, and I looked at him to see he had one eyebrow raised as he took in Julie's state of distress. He was staring at her very closely, but I couldn't tell what on earth he must have been thinking.

"I'm calling the police," said Matilda, her phone already out of her bag as she held it to her ear.

When I looked at Jack, it was almost as if we were having a silent conversation. We both knew what this meant. Julie's attacker sounded all too similar to Lola's, which had happened all the way back in Orléans. It was way too much of a coincidence. This was the same guy. And if it was the same guy, the chances were likely that this person was someone in the circus. We all helped lead Julie back to her camper, where, sure enough, the door was wide open and a few bits of furniture lay tossed aside from the scuffle.

A few minutes later her sisters arrived, full of concern, and I relayed to them what had happened. Matilda hung up the phone and told us that the police were on their way; we just had to wait for them to get there. Now that her sisters were with Julie, the rest of us weren't really needed anymore, so we began walking in the direction of Jack's camper. None of us were much in the mood for continuing with our night, though.

"So you're telling me this happened before," said Jay, now rolling a dice between his fingers as he walked beside us, Matilda on his left.

"Yes," I answered. "My friend Lola was attacked back in Orléans. And a couple of years ago, a dancer with the circus was raped and killed. All evidence seems to be indicating that the culprit works here."

"Hmm," Jay murmured, and rubbed at the stubble on his chin. "Curiouser and curiouser."

"What are you thinking?" Matilda asked, eyeing her husband with interest.

Instead of answering her, Jay stopped walking to stand in front of us. We all paused mid-stride, and Jay looked to Jack. "How many people live here? Forty? Fifty?"

Jack nodded. "About that, why?"

Jay waved aside his question to ask another of his own. "Do you think you could gather them all in the tent tomorrow, say around lunchtime?"

"I could try."

"It has to be everyone. And I mean, *everyone* — well, except for the kids," Jay went on, a wicked gleam in his eye and an expression that told me he was forming some kind of plan.

"Oh, God, what are you up to now? This better not be anything dodgy," said Matilda warily before addressing Jack and me. "He's always coming up with hare-brained schemes. He uses all his mentalist voodoo to trick people."

Jay tugged on her wrist and pulled her into him, staring down at her fondly. "Ah, dear Watson, I'm not trying to trick anyone this time." He paused for dramatic effect, eyeing each of us in turn. "I'm going to catch us a killer."

Nineteen
But the magician, alas, solved the riddle

As it happened, once Jack and I were finally alone in his camper, he wasn't rough with me at all. In fact, he was surprisingly tender. He poured hot wax on my skin, titillated me with hot matches and metal toys. He traced his hands over every inch of me and brought me to the cusp of euphoria before plunging me into the pleasurable depths of several mind-blowing orgasms.

The following morning we woke early, and after we ate breakfast, Jack went to find Marina to try to organise the meeting in the tent for Jay. I still had no idea what he was planning, but he had a reassuring sort of confidence that made me believe whatever he was going to try would work. It was a relief to think that in just a few hours we might have our culprit, and things around the circus could be safe once and for all.

I was on my way to the gazebo when I saw Bea wandering between the campers, wheeling along a battered old buggy with a baby doll inside. She looked tired, her hair was dirty, and it seemed like she hadn't changed her clothes in a while. She hadn't struck me as the best cared-for child, but I'd never seen her look this bad.

I was just about to approach and ask her how she was when her dad came marching out of their camper van, grabbed her roughly by the arm, and dragged her inside. It startled me, because Aiden had always struck me as a kind, though slightly *laissez faire* parent. He must have sensed me watching him, because our eyes met and his were hard.

"She's been misbehaving," he ground out in explanation, then went inside the camper, slamming the door shut behind him. I didn't feel right after witnessing that, but I knew it must be hard being a single dad, so I couldn't exactly judge. Still, he needed to take better care of Bea, at least make sure she was washed and had clean clothes. It made my heart hurt to think of her in her current state.

In an effort to lighten my mood, I went and had lunch with Lola and Luan in the gazebo. The two of them seemed to be slowly moving towards coupledom, which was nice to see. The entire circus was rife with talk of the meeting that was to take place after lunch, and once Lola, Luan, and I had finished eating, we all walked together to the Spiegeltent.

Inside people sat in various locations around the audience, chatting in earnest and speculating as to what was going on. I noticed King sitting in a corner on the floor, passed out and looking as dishevelled as always. It upset me a little. Somewhere deep down I thought maybe the painting would make him better somehow. Perhaps he was right after all, perhaps he was too far gone.

When I spotted Jack in the front row next to Matilda, my heart did a little leap. I got excited just at the sight of him and made my way towards the front.

"Hey," he greeted me, low and husky. I smiled at him, then gave Matilda a little wave, but before I could take the seat next to him, he pulled me down to sit on his lap. The action gave me tingles, and his gaze fixed on my bare collarbone, where there were some small red marks from the wax he'd dripped on me last night. His attention scorched far more than the wax, and I found myself trembling a little at the memory.

Then his thumb brushed over the markings, causing me to let out a tiny gasp. His chest rumbled with a muted growl, and I could tell Matilda was watching us, but she didn't say anything. I leaned up and had just enough time to lay a peck on Jack's lips before a hush fell over the gathering. Footsteps echoed around the tent as Jay stepped out onto the stage, all eyes focusing on him.

"Greetings," he said, scanning the space and flashing a big smile. He looked excited and full of energy. Electric. I wondered if this was what he was like during his performances and imagined watching him do a show would be quite the thrill ride. "Before I begin, could I ask you all to come and sit at the front in a circle? There should be enough room in the first two rows for everyone."

Slowly, those gathered began to come forward, and, just like Jay had requested, it seemed like everyone in the entire circus was present. I saw Marina carrying Pierre. I saw Winnie hand in hand with her husband Antonio. I saw Julie and her sisters. Even Pedro was present. All except for the kids. After a minute or two, we were seated. I remained on Jack's lap, staring at Jay as he continually moved his attention from one person to the next as though taking his time to study everyone individually. Then I saw him nodding as he began to count heads.

"Okay," he said, and glanced at Marina. "If my math skills are correct, we've got forty-six people, am I right?"

"That's correct," Marina answered.

"Great." He rubbed his hands together. "So, let's get down to business. My name is Jay Fields, and I'm a stage illusionist. I'm proficient in a number of arts, one of which includes cold reading and mentalism. Solving mysteries is something of a hobby of mine. Just think of me as a modern-day Sherlock Holmes, or better yet, consider me your *deus ex machina*, here to solve the unsolvable. At the very least, I'll endeavour to put a criminal behind bars. As you've all probably heard by now, there have been two separate incidents of violence and attempted rape against women in this circus in the past several weeks, as well as a murder two years ago. All evidence seems to suggest the crimes were carried out by the same person. The evidence also suggests that that person is in the room with us today."

Quiet elapsed, and a tension filled the space. Jack's arms tightened around me, and I wondered if he was thinking what I was thinking. That I could have fallen victim to this sicko if I had been in our room that night instead of Lola. Jay paused for a moment to let everyone absorb the information, and there were a couple of grumblings amongst the gathering. I heard Pedro swear and ask how Jay, an outsider, thought he could come in and begin pointing fingers at people. His argument made me wonder, and not for the first time, if he was the man we were looking for. His behaviour in the past certainly indicated a slight deviancy, but did that mean he had the ability to rape and kill? I wasn't quite sure. In the end Marina stood, her voice booming loud around the tent.

"Now, you all need to listen up and listen good. I agreed to have Mr Fields here today, and so long as you're innocent, you have nothing to worry about. So please, can you all shut up complaining and let the man get on with his job?"

Her reprimanding tone worked to hush the grumblings, and Jay sent her a look of gratitude before giving her a dashing little bow. "Thank you, Marina." She dipped her head to accept his thanks, and then Jay began to pace.

"Now, I'm going to go around the room and ask each one of you a set of three questions. These questions will consist of the following: What is your name? Where were you born? And what is the name of the street you grew up on? Of these three questions, I want you to give me two correct answers and one lie. You can lie on any one of the questions you wish, but do not, under any circumstances, tell me which one. Everybody got it?"

Once Jay's instructions were understood by all, he walked to the far right of the room and fired off his three questions. The first person to be asked was the stuntman, Raphael.

"What is your name?" said Jay.

"Raphael Suarez."

"Where were you born?"

"Brazil."

"What is the name of the street you grew up on?"

"Rua Santa Teresa."

I noticed that after each question was answered, Jay took a moment to stare at his interviewee. When he was done with Raphael, he moved on to the man sitting next to him. It was a long and tedious process, truth be told. Jack and I were sitting on the opposite end from where Jay had started, so it took about a half hour for him to reach us. He smiled at me warmly and asked me the questions. I decided to lie on the second one. I knew from my accent that my lie was probably obvious, but hey, just because I sounded Irish didn't mean I was born in Ireland.

"What's your name?"

"Lille Baker."

"Where were you born?"

"Argentina."

Jay give me a little grin before asking the final question. "And what is the name of the street you grew up on?"

"Fitzgerald Street."

"Thank you, darlin." The way he spoke to me gave me a warm feeling in my tummy, like he held an affection for me already, and he barely knew me. He only knew that I was in love with his brother, and that seemed to be good enough for him. He moved on to Jack next, and soon he was done asking everyone the same three questions. I had no idea what he was up to, but the glint in his eye told me he had a plan.

"Have I gotten everyone?" Jay asked, and there were a number of yeses from the gathering before a noise sounded from the back of the room. I twisted in Jack's lap to see King had knocked over a chair while trying to stand up. "Ah, not everyone, I see," said Jay as he hopped off the stage and strode towards King, who glowered at him and rubbed his temples like he was suffering from a headache.

"Hey, there," said Jay, eyeing King closely. Jack and I shared a look. We both knew that King was a wildcard, and there was a good chance he'd say something rude or insulting.

"What do you want?" King griped, and tried to move past him, but Jay did a suave little sidestep.

"I want to ask you some questions. Will you play ball?"

"Piss off."

Jay chuckled and took another step closer to King. I watched him as he tilted his head, taking a moment to study Marina's brother, and he seemed intrigued. "I bet you could tell me some stories," Jay observed almost absently.

"I need a smoke," King grumbled, and moved to walk by Jay again. He was clearly growing impatient.

"I'll tell you what. You come sit up the front, let me ask you some questions, and I'll buy all the cigs and booze you could wish for."

King eyed him suspiciously, then finally nodded his agreement. "You better not be lying."

"Cross my heart," said Jay, swiping his finger over the left side of his chest in an "X" shape before gesturing for King to go sit up at the front. King stumbled by him and took the seat on the other side of Matilda, who looked at him sadly when she saw how uncared for he was. Jay came to stand before him.

"I'm going to ask you three questions. I want you to answer two correctly and lie on one of them. Got it?"

"Yeah, yeah, two true, one false. I'm a drunk not an idiot."

"No, I imagine you're far from it," said Jay, his brows drawing together in what looked like concern. "So, the first question, what's your name?"

King coughed his pained cough and answered, "King. Oliver King."

"Where were you born?"

"London."

"And what is the name of the street you grew up on?"

King seemed pained as he considered his final answer. "Molesworth Street." I wasn't quite sure why, but I felt like his third answer was the lie.

"Thank you, sir," said Jay before turning to address the gathering again. "Okay, so this is where things start to speed up. Now I'm going to ask you all one question. I don't want you to lie here — I want you to tell the truth. The answer will be a simple yes or no. Once you've answered, I'll either tell you to move to the back of the tent or to stay where you are. I repeat, I do *not* want you to lie to me."

He began to the right again with Raphael, shooting off his question. "Did you attack Julie Young last night?"

Raphael seemed appalled by the very idea and answered immediately. "No."

317

"Thank you," said Jay. "You can go to the back of the tent."

Raphael rose and walked down the aisle before sitting in the very back row, folding his arms as he lowered himself into a seat. Jay moved on to the next person and then the next, asking everybody the same question in rapid-fire succession. Sometimes, if he wasn't happy with the answer, he asked twice. He even asked Julie herself. She furrowed her brow at him.

"How on earth can I attack myself?" she complained.

"Just answer the question, darlin."

"No, I didn't fucking attack myself," she deadpanned.

"Okay, good," said Jay, raising a hand. "Stay where you are for now."

In the end, both Jack and I were at the back of the tent with almost everyone else. He ran his hands soothingly up and down my arms, which worked to rid some of my restlessness. I wished Jay would speed things up and discover the culprit already. The only people left at the front were Julie, Pedro, King, Luan, Aiden, and Antonio. Jay asked all of them to stand in a circle around him. He paced a moment as they watched, and then began asking them all the same question again, though this time it was phrased slightly differently.

"Are you the attacker?" he asked Julie.

"No."

"Are you the attacker?" This time, Pedro.

"No."

"Are you the attacker?" Now it was Luan's turn.

"No."

Jay continued asking his question, and again he asked some of them twice, even three times. Each time every one of them answered no, and they all seemed to be growing irritated. Pedro swore in Portuguese, while Luan's cheeks grew red and Julie pulled a strop.

"This is a joke," she griped, and stared daggers at Jay. "Seriously, do you even know what you're doing?"

Jay put his finger to his lips to hush her, and quiet descended. He bowed his head for a moment, as though trying to think, then whipped it up and pointed to Antonio and Pedro. "You both can go join the others at the back." There was a light in his eyes now as he studied his final four suspects, and a chill came over me, because something told me Jay had finally decided who the guilty party was. Jack must have seen me shiver, because he pulled me close and wrapped both his arms around my shoulders. I sank into his hard, sturdy frame, seeking comfort as I listened to Jay speak.

"So, I should probably explain my method here. Otherwise, I can hardly go pointing fingers, now, can I? I asked everyone the same three questions, asking for two truths and one falsehood. This was to get your baselines. Most everybody has a tell when they lie. Therefore, if you were telling me two truths and one lie, the odd reaction out is the lie – the tell. You," he began, and pointed to Luan, "are typical. You look to the left when you lie. You're a very reliable liar. You look to the left *every* time. This transparency indicates that you're probably quite an honest person. However, you're also nervous under interrogation, which made you slightly more difficult to read when I asked the final two questions." Jay paused and took a breath, while I felt like I was holding mine. "Luckily for you, though, you aren't the one I'm looking for today. You can go to the back with the others." Luan seemed beside himself with relief as he ran a hand down his face and walked to the back. Lola immediately pulled him into her arms when he reached her and gave him a long hug.

This time Jay brought his attention to Julie. "Now you, my dear, are an interesting one. When you lie, you show almost no tell at all. But I have an eye for detail, and I did notice that you press your lips together ever so slightly when you're telling a fib. It's practically imperceptible, but what can I say? I have a talent for this."

"For crying out loud, will you just get to the point already," Julie complained, arms folded in a defensive posture.

"You're not the attacker," Jay answered her curtly. "Go to the back."

Julie shot Jay a sharp look that was all, *I told you so*, then strutted her way over to stand with the rest of us. I locked eyes with Matilda, and she gave me a tiny smile before whispering, "He's scary good at this, isn't he?"

I nodded, then only realised Marina was standing behind us when she added, "Your husband has a flair for the dramatic. I wonder if I could tempt him to come and join the circus."

Matilda smiled at her, shrugged, then returned her attention to the stage, as did I. King and Aiden were the only two men left standing, and a feeling of dread claimed my belly as I remembered Aiden's behaviour with Bea earlier this morning. He'd been rough and abrupt, and he clearly hadn't been taking proper care of his little girl. But did that make him a killer? Certainly not.

And then there was King. Such a mystery. Such an enigma. I'd heard so much about what a success he'd been once upon a time. Surely, to be so successful and then end up a homeless drunk meant something really bad must have happened to him. Or maybe he was the one who did the bad thing. Maybe he was the killer. I hated to admit that in an odd way I'd grown fond of King, and I didn't want it to be him. At same time, I didn't want it to be Aiden, either, because that would mean Bea would be left without a parent.

God, this was awful. Jay's attention rested on King for a moment before moving to Aiden, then went back to King.

"Your tell, Mr King, is that you don't have one. In fact, you really don't care at all if I know whether you're lying or telling the truth. Perhaps you've lied about far worse things than murder and rape in the past. But then, what's worse than that? No, I think you're an example of apathetic nihilism at its finest, and I would love to know the reason as to why. I'm still not even sure if you misled me at all on those first three questions. And this is where the rub lies, because if you don't have a tell, I can't determine whether or not you're lying."

Jay went silent, eyes flicking back and forth between the two men as he stopped pacing and stood in front of them, feet shoulder width apart and arms folded.

"Fortunately for you," Jay said while pointing a finger at King before swiping it to Aiden. "Aiden here has quite a spectacular tell. It's like a big, angry, throbbing vein that pulses in the forehead when a person is angry. Yes, when Aiden lies, he moves his jaw and his left eyebrow shoots right up to heaven. Quite frankly, it's glorious." Jay gestured wildly with his hands. "A mentalist's wet dream, because I barely have to look at you to know you're lying. You are as transparently deceptive as Luan is transparently honest. And when I asked if you attacked Julie, what happened?"

Aiden was breathing furiously, his eyes narrowed to slits as he adopted the posture of a man being branded with a guilty stamp. Emotion clutched at me, not because I cared about the man, but because I cared about Bea, and I had no idea what was going to happen to her now.

"You worked your jaw and raised your eyebrow," Jay finished.

Aiden stomped forward and pushed at Jay, almost knocking him over. "You've got it wrong! You don't know anything!"

"I know that you did it," said Jay confidently, dusting himself off. He didn't appear at all ruffled that Aiden had hit him. And when Aiden looked like he was about to flee, several stocky men who worked as labourers for the circus came forward and blocked his path. He had nowhere to run. "I also know," Jay began, pronouncing his words loudly and steadily so that everybody could hear, "that you didn't act alone." Now there were several shocked and surprised gasps from the crowd. I moved closer into the warmth of Jack's body, spooked. No one else in the world made me feel safe the way he did. And what did Jay mean, Aiden hadn't acted alone? It wasn't long before I found out.

"Well, at least you didn't *plan* the act alone. I don't mean to insult you, but you don't possess the intelligence, the flair, to cover up a killing, Aiden. Yes, you have the strength and indeed the fucked-up psychology to do it physically, but you don't have the shrewd mental acumen for a cover-up."

A hush came over the gathering, and a chill ran down my spine. I caught movement to my left and saw Julie hurrying through the crowd. In an instant, I recognised that she was trying to slip away before anyone saw. A moment later, Jay began walking towards us, calling out, "Oh, Miss Young, can I have a word?"

It was almost like a spotlight had landed on her, because she stopped dead in her tracks, and all forty-five pairs of eyes went to the beautiful red-headed gymnast. "What do you want?" she hissed, low and furious as she stared at the floor, refusing to meet Jay's gaze. Jay walked through the gathering, and people parted to let him by. A moment later, he was right in front of Julie. He reached out and caught her chin, tilting it up to make her look at him. She reeled away from his touch, her hatred clear as day in her bright blue eyes.

"When I told you that you're not the attacker, it was the truth. However, when I told you that you have a tell, I lied. In fact, you have two. You purse your lips when you're telling an outright lie, but you touch your index finger to your thumb when you're being deceptive. And when I asked you if you were the attacker, every time your body shouted your deceit. You were involved in Aiden's crime from the start."

"I wasn't," Julie hissed, but there was a waver in her voice, a solitary tear running down her face as she looked to those around her for support. She found none. Not even from her sisters, who looked positively broken at what they were hearing. "He's lying! You all have to believe me. We don't even know this guy. He could be anyone."

"Oh, please," Lola cut in as she moved through the crowd, hand in hand with Luan. "Jay Fields is fucking famous. We all know exactly who he is. He's won awards, for Chrissakes. Now, what I want to know is how the *hell* you're involved in all this." Anger slowly seeped into her voice as she pointed to Aiden. "That man almost raped me, Julie, and I want to know what exactly you had to do with it."

"I had absolutely nothing to do with it," Julie replied vehemently. "This thing about tells is all bullshit. The guy is trying to fuck with our heads. Aiden is the guilty one, plain and simple. Other than almost becoming one of his victims, this has nothing to do with me."

"You lying little tramp," Aiden fumed, lunging forward as three or four men held him in place. "She's been blackmailing me for years! Ever since she caught me burying Vera's body, she's been holding me hostage, forcing me to do her bidding or else she'd go to the police. I went to Lola's room that night because Julie told me to. Lola had slighted her in front of everyone, and Julie wanted payback. And since you've all been hating her ever since she attacked Lille, she made me rough her up so that you'd all see her as a victim and not the cold bitch that she really is."

"Shut the hell up, Aiden. Nobody believes you," Julie spat at him. Her face was red with fury, her hands balled into fists. Her sister Molly let out a pained cry before Mary took her into her arms. They were both shattered at what they were hearing and obviously had no clue what their sister was capable of. I couldn't say the same myself. Ever since the night I heard her say those cruel things to King in the gazebo, I knew her pretty face masked a rotten core. And then after she attacked me with her own two hands, I was pretty certain she was mad.

I'd been so wrapped up in watching everything unfold that I forgot Jack standing behind me. His hold on my shoulders had tightened further, almost to the point of pain. I twisted around and glanced up at him, taking in his agonised, contorted features. It was difficult for him to hear all this, I could tell. He'd been with Julie sexually with no clue of her true nature.

"Hey," I whispered. "Stop that. There was no way you could've known."

"I should have, though," he ground out. "I should have sensed something."

Julie had begun yelling and screaming like a crazy woman, proclaiming her innocence, but there didn't seem to be a single person present who believed her. She'd done too much to prove that she was capable of bad things, and now it was all coming back to haunt her. I'd like to say I felt vindicated, but I didn't. Yes, I was angry that she very well could have killed me when she hit me over the head that time, but mostly I just felt sad that any of this had happened in the first place.

A man and two women held in her in place as Marina pulled out her phone to call the police. Jack led me over to a chair to sit, rubbing my back soothingly even though he was the one who needed soothing. I just wanted to take him back to the camper and lie on his bed and hold him. Talk for hours. Make love. Try to forget the bad things both Aiden and Julie had done.

It wasn't long before the police arrived, and Italian police were quite impressive to see, all kitted out in their uniforms, weapons strapped to their bodies. Aiden and Julie were handcuffed and led away, and when Bea came looking for her dad, Winnie took her back to her camper for the night. Nobody knew what was going to happen to the little girl, and my heart hurt for her.

Slowly, the gathering started to disperse. There was an air of relief around the circus to know it was all over, but at the same time an air of melancholy. I stood with Matilda and Jack as Jay approached us. He didn't look smug or self-satisfied that he'd caught the culprits; he just seemed relaxed, happy that he'd been able to help. He approached

Matilda and planted a kiss on the top of her head before murmuring something in her ear. Then he turned and made his way to the corner of the tent where King was sitting and called, "Now, Mr King, just like the song, I believe I owe you a supply of cigarettes and alcohol."

King perked up at his words as Jay threw his arm around the man's shoulder, not once batting an eyelid at his dirty, unkempt appearance, and led him out of the tent.

***

It wasn't until the following day that we heard news of Aiden and Julie. Since all three crimes had been committed in different geographic locations, the Italian police were working in conjunction with both the French and British authorities. Lola had always been adamant she didn't want the police involved, but it was all out of her hands now. Besides, it looked like she'd be safe from her husband now that she had Luan by her side. Every time I saw them together it was clear that he was smitten.

Aiden's camper was searched top to bottom, but only one piece of evidence was found. There was an old blouse with blood on it tucked behind a ceiling panel, and Marina identified it as belonging to Vera. They still needed to test the blood and match the DNA, but all signs were pointing towards Aiden going to prison for a long time. It made me shiver right down to my toes to think of him keeping the blouse as some kind of trophy.

And then there was Julie. Aiden was clearly feeling spiteful and didn't want to go down alone, because he gave testimony that Julie had known about his crimes all along, had even incited some of them. It was suspected that there were more cases than those that took place in the circus, not least of which was the fact that Bea's mother had disappeared years ago and was never seen again. Lots of people were now beginning to think that she was another of Aiden's victims.

And then there was Bea, poor, sweet, lovely little Bea. Nobody was quite sure what was going to happen to her yet, but Winnie and Antonio had taken her under their wing for now. I even overheard the couple quietly discussing the possibility of adopting her. It warmed my heart and I hoped that they would, because they were good people and Bea deserved to have parents who wanted to look after her.

I was feeling pretty drained myself, and spent most of the morning in bed with Jack. So much had happened, and we talked a lot about Jay and Matilda, and how having them in our lives was going to change things for the better. Jay had already invited both of us to come and stay in Vegas for the month when the circus took a break at the end of the season. Needless to say, my excitement was hitting extreme levels at the very idea.

After lunch, Jack went to help the men take down the tent before we moved on the next day. I situated myself outside his camper, my easel set up and a painting in front of me that was almost complete. It was the picture of Jack on stage, and I was using a number of different shades of orange and yellow to get the flames that surrounded him to look just right. I planned on giving it to him soon as a present, since he'd asked if he could have it previously.

"You look...sweaty," Jack said, breaking me out of my trance. I'd been so concentrated on the painting that I hadn't noticed him approach. He stood in front of me, so he couldn't see the painting, which was good because I wanted it to be a surprise.

Self-consciously, I wiped the sweat from my brow with the back of my hand, at the same time feeling a tendril of arousal spike through me at his words. I happened to know that he quite liked me sweaty.

"Stay exactly where you are," I warned him. "Don't come any closer. I'm trying to finish my painting of you, and I want to give it to you as a present when it's done."

He raised a quizzical brow and brought a bottle of water to his mouth, knocking back a gulp. I might have been sweaty, but he was, too. In fact, the way his well-worn grey T-shirt stuck to his torso was a little mesmerising.

"Why does that mean I can't see it?"

"Because I want it to be a surprise."

The look in his eye right then told me he thought I was being nutty, but he rolled with it. "Okay. Well, I suppose I should give you a gift, too, if you're giving me one."

I grinned at this. "Yes, you should. And it should be something you've made yourself, the same as my painting."

He seemed stumped at this. "Like what?"

"That's not for me to decide. You need to think of something."

He went silent for a long moment. I stroked my paintbrush over the final patch of orange, and my heart filled. I was done. The painting was finished. I wanted it to dry first before I gave it to him, though. He was still watching me, and when he saw he had my attention, he crooked his finger at me.

"Come here," he said, voice low, eyes fixed on the sweat dripping down my neck. I hadn't checked the temperatures today, but I knew it felt a good deal hotter than usual. Why else would I be perspiring like mad? And since any kind of heat was such a big turn-on for Jack, I could practically sense his arousal like a physical thing.

Swallowing, I rose from my seat and walked to him. He caught my wrist in his hand and pulled me in close, then tilted my neck before capturing my mouth with his. I swear, I wanted to make a moulding of his tongue someday and set it on my mantel, because it was a thing of pure beauty. I loved how it licked at me, all silky and wet. I loved the taste of him. It was my favourite taste of all. His passion grew along with his breathing, and before I knew it, he was crowding me inside the camper, herding me like a predator intent on his prey.

He slammed the door shut. Then he twirled me around and pressed me chest first into the wall, his thick, hard cock grinding against my backside. His hands moved swiftly while his breaths filled my ears, and before I knew it, my skirt was shoved up, my knickers were down, and he was pulling himself out of his pants. Seconds later he was inside me, and I gasped in shock at how quickly and deeply he managed to fill me.

His mouth went to my neck, licking and sucking as his hips thrust in and out, hard and fast. I loved how rough he was, loved how he couldn't even wait long enough to get me into his bed, he had to take me right here in the lounge, standing up against the wall. Anybody could have walked by and seen us, but right then neither of us cared. In that moment, all we knew were our bodies, all we felt was our mutual pleasure.

He fisted my hair, yanking down on it and twisting my neck so I'd turn to him. He captured my mouth again, giving me his tongue a second time, the motion a mirror to his fucking. I felt invaded, possessed, and as we both raced toward orgasm, I broke the kiss to gasp a fervent declaration.

"I love you, Jack McCabe. I love you so much."

He smiled, and for a moment I was dazzled by his handsome expression, so full of affection, as he continued to hold my hair like a rein and move his hips in a steady rhythm. "I love you too, flower. Only you. Always."

When I collapsed against the wall, shivering as I came, Jack followed, and I felt him fill me until he was spent. He picked me up in his arms and carried to his bedroom, our bedroom, where I discovered the fun was not over yet. And man, did Jack McCabe like to play.

Hours later, I was vaguely aware of him leaving the bed and going into the lounge, but I was too exhausted to wake up. I napped for another hour, and when I woke, it was dark outside. I pulled on some clothes and left the room to find Jack sitting watching television and eating a bowl of noodles. I stepped outside, the night air a balm to the sweltering heat of the day, and collected the finished painting that I'd all but abandoned earlier in order to fulfil the needs of my hussy libido.

Jack gave me an indulgent, sexy smile when I carried it in and set it in front of him on the sofa. "I wasn't going to give this to you until tomorrow, but you outdid yourself and earned some bonus points," I told him sassily. "So here's your present."

Finished eating, he set the bowl aside and lifted the painting onto his lap. His eyes soaked it in, and I crossed my fingers, hoping that he liked it. Several agonising moments passed before he met my gaze, and a smile grew wide across his face. It was the biggest smile I'd ever seen on him; it lit up his features, made him seem so much lighter than the man I met all those weeks ago. The one who never trusted and never let anybody in.

"It's a masterpiece," he said finally. "I love how you see me. It makes me feel like I can be the man in the painting."

"You are the man in the painting, Jack."

He stood and carried the canvas to the kitchen table, set it down, and then pulled me over to the couch. He wrapped his arms tight around me and rested his head on my shoulder.

"I'm only that man because you made me so," he whispered, and I shivered. Emotion clutched at my throat, and I found it difficult to form words. He might have thought that I'd made him better, but it went both ways, because he'd made me better, too. He'd shown me that not everybody can be trusted, dulled some of the shine from my eyes, only to make my vision that much clearer. He'd also taught me that, though I can't trust everyone, I can trust him, and so long as it was within his power, he would never, ever let me down.

"I made you a gift, too, while you slept," he said, breaking me from my thoughts and surprising me. I hadn't actually expected him to make me anything. Reaching over to the window ledge, he picked up a folded piece of paper and slid it into my hands. I stared down at it.

"What's this?" I breathed, suddenly finding that my heart was beating double.

"It's our story," Jack answered. "I can't paint or create much of anything, and really, I'll never be a writer, but I love words, love learning all the ones I missed out on in the past. So I used my words and wrote you a story." He paused and laughed self-deprecatingly. "I even used the dictionary to make sure I got all the spellings right."

I wasn't sure what it was about that last bit, but the fact he'd wanted to get the spellings right made me even more emotional. He was going to turn me into a sobbing mess before the night was through.

Slowly, I unfolded the paper and read the words, my lungs burning, my heart aching with their raw, simple, honest beauty. I could see our entire journey laid out before me, his words creating the images in my mind, and I knew without a doubt that I was going to paint his words in a mural, keep them forever so I'd never forget a single one.

The Story of Jack and Lille

JACK AND LILLE MET ON A HILL
THEY CROSSED A SEA OF WATER
A KING FELL DOWN WHO WORE NO CROWN
AND LILLE'S HEART SURELY DID FALTER
A TATTOO LILLE GOT BUT JACK DID NOT
AND JACK'S BROTHER WAS IN THE PAPER

UNDER THE SUN JACK WATCHED LILLE
PAINT
UNDER THE STARS THEY CAME TOGETHER
LILLE LOST HER WAY
AN ATTACK LED THEM ASTRAY
IN SECRET LILLE STOLE JACK'S LETTER
WITH COURAGE JACK THREW HIS MASK
AWAY FOREVER

JULIE SHOWED LILLE HER TRUE COLOURS
A STORM FELL OVER THE LOVERS
A PICTURE LOST WAS THEN FOUND
A DISCOVERY MADE LILLE'S HEART POUND
AND TWO BLEEDING SOULS WERE REUNITED
MYSTERY CAME KNOCKING ONCE MORE
BUT THE MAGICIAN, ALAS, SOLVED THE
RIDDLE
HERE LIES THE STORY OF JACK AND LILLE
TWO HEARTS SO BIG YET SO LITTLE.

Epilogue

Las Vegas, Nevada

Four months later

I stared out my window and couldn't help smiling at the billboard. I could hardly believe Jay had even managed to get the thing up there on such short notice. The picture displayed the illusionist wearing a sleek black suit that Matilda had designed. The camera had managed to catch him mid card shuffle, and almost the entire deck was in the air as his hands waited outspread to catch them. Then, off to the side and shrouded in a sort of smoky mystery, was Jack's silhouette as he blew a flame from his mouth. Beneath the picture was a large bold font that read: **FIRE & LIGHT: Jay Fields & Jack McCabe together for a one-night-only special performance!!**

I wasn't sure why they were even bothering to advertise. As soon as Jay announced to his fans that he'd be doing a special show with his long-lost brother, who just so happened to be a dangerously sexy fire breather/ knife thrower, the tickets had sold like hot cakes.

The circus' month-long break had officially begun, and, as I'd hoped, both Jack and I were spending the time in Las Vegas with Jay and Matilda. Jay's contract was almost up, and when the circus started the new season, he was going to come and perform for a couple of months with us. Marina was over the moon to have him on board, especially since The Ladies of the Sky were now on a hiatus until they could find someone to replace Julie.

I had to admit that though I loved the circus and missed everybody dearly (well, except for Pedro), it was nice to experience a bit of luxury for a while. My heart had almost broken from adorability overload (yes, adorability is a word) when we first arrived at the swanky five-star hotel and Jack looked like he didn't know what to do with himself. For years he'd lived in a camper van, travelling from one location to the next, so, needless to say, the luxury had him more than a little perplexed. I was halfway through unpacking when I saw him standing in the corner of our suite, staring at the space like the cutest uncomfortable manly man I'd ever seen.

"What's wrong?" I asked as I sat down on an armchair, sinking into its heavenly softness.

Jack moved his mouth and glanced around before looking at me. "This place is just...I'm not used to this." His gaze wandered to the gigantic bed, eyeing it like he was facing a bear on the Rocky Mountains and trying to figure out how it would react to movement.

"The bed isn't going to bite you if you sit down on it, you know," I teased, soliciting a playful scowl from him.

"I know that."

"Well then, sit on it. Give it a go."

"I think I'll just go use the bathroom first," he said, evading the issue and walking around the bed.

"Oh, no you don't," I replied, standing and going over to grab his hand. "You, Jack McCabe, are going to face your fear of luxury beds, and the best way to do that is to have a mattress jumping party."

"Mattress jumping parties aren't a thing."

"I'm making them a thing." Yanking his arm, I pulled him over, slid off my shoes and stepped onto the bed. He looked at me like I was a mad woman when I began to jump up and down. "Come on," I said, urging him to join me.

"I'm not sure it can handle my weight."

"Pfft, of course it can. This thing probably cost thousands."

He let out a sigh and finally climbed on, discarding his shoes first. I took his hands in mine and stared him in the eye like this was dead serious business. "Okay, are you ready?"

His expression softened as he began to see the funny side. "As I'll ever be."

"Good. One, two, three, go!" I said and then began to jump up and down again, this time with Jack doing it alongside me. We laughed like two kids and dropped onto the mattress when we started to hear a creak. The bed might have cost thousands, but it could only endure so much. Jack rolled us so that he was on top of me, brushing my hair away from my face and cupping my cheeks in his hands.

A low, masculine laugh rumbled out of his chest as he muttered, "God, I fucking love you." The next thing I knew he was laying his mouth on me and giving me a deep, tongue laden kiss that melted my bones. It was a long time before either one of us came up for air.

"Right," I began breathlessly, my body fizzling with arousal. "I think a bath is next on the agenda."

One of Jack's eyebrows rose. "I won't argue with that. Stay where you are. I'll get it ready."

I lay there, admiring his spectacular bottom as he went inside the bathroom. A moment later I heard him turn on the water. It wasn't long before he returned, leading me inside and stripping off all of my clothes. Two candles had been lit and sat perched on the edge of the tub at either corner. Stepping in, I luxuriated in the heat of the water for a moment before Jack joined me, and thankfully the tub was big enough for the both of us. He sat at the opposite end and took my foot into his hands, massaging it before picking up the candle and dripping a little hot wax onto my ankle. A low moan escaped me and I couldn't help laughing softly.

"Oh, how quickly he takes to the luxury," I teased.

His dark eyes fixated on the wax marking my skin before rising to meet mine. "I only take to it because you're in it." His words were deep, carnal, and before I knew it I was being treated to the best bath I'd ever experienced.

***

Fast forward two and a half weeks and I was sitting in the front row of the theatre wearing a stunning black dress, my hair up in a fancy chignon. Matilda sat beside me, looking equally glamorous. The two of us had grown close quite quickly, and aside from Lola, I could probably count her as my best friend.

Jack and Jay's show was about to start and I was on pins and needles with excitement waiting to see what they had come up with. They'd both been very secretive as they planned it out, not wanting me or Matilda to see a thing until the night of the big show. The venue was completely packed out and Matilda squeezed my hand as the house lights went down and a song began to play. I recognised it as "Beautiful Pain" by Eminem and Sia.

The entire place was dark for a beat before a spotlight shone on one corner of the stage, illuminating Jay in his black suit. He stood right on the edge, looking down, as though perched on the precipice of a skyscraper. The lyrics took hold. There was something stark and completely striking about the visual. The moment Sia's voice began to sing about flames, real fire exploded in the background. It appeared to come out of nowhere, but then the lights shone on Jack and the audience erupted into cheers. He wore a sleeveless top and jeans as he twisted and turned his body, blowing a symphony of flames to the beat of the music. He barely looked human. In that moment he was transformed into an otherworldly being and I had goose bumps covering every inch of my skin.

Sia sang about finding a light and Jay came to life, his hands moving around his body. As he opened his palms, a blinding white light shone out. He continuously opened and closed them, the light erupting and disappearing with flashing intensity. Then he wasn't just controlling the light, he was throwing a beam of it clear across the stage where it seemingly bounced off the wall and flew right back into his hand. Noises of wonder and awe came from those around me. The next time he threw the light, though, he couldn't catch it, and he began to chase it. It constantly bounced around him, dancing beautifully, evading his reach.

I was stunned by the beauty of their act, a mix of performance art and illusion. The lyrics pulsed in my ears; I felt like my emotions were being clutched in someone's fist, because there was so much in the song that symbolised the brothers' history.

Standing in flames.

Worlds torn in half.

Burning away yesterday.

Greeting a new day.

Finding light after darkness.

My attention returned to Jack. He blew another flame, this one bigger than any of the others, but instead of dying out it turned to ash that slowly trickled to the floor. I had no idea how Jay had managed to orchestrate all this, but it was absolutely incredible to watch. I heard something in the lyrics about a thunderstorm right before the sound of thunder rang out and I swear I felt the room shake. I knew I wasn't imagining things when I looked around and saw everyone else was feeling it too.

Then, when a tornado was mentioned a deck of cards came flying out of Jay's back pocket, swirling through the air before scattering on the floor. The spotlight landed on Jack again as he tilted his head back, took in a deep breath, then blew out, and I swear to God, real live smoke emerged in misty grey tendrils. I saw his chest go still, his breathing cease, and the smoke paused in mid-air. Several people behind me gasped. A second later Jack resumed breathing and the smoke started to move again, drifting out of his mouth and slowly fading away. Next Jay walked towards Jack as he pulled a packet of matches from his pocket, removing one and flicking it to Jack. Jack threw his hand up and deftly caught the match in his closed fist. When he opened it a gigantic flame erupted, eliciting a huge round of applause.

The song was coming to an end when smoke began to rise from the ground up, shrouding the stage in mystery. Lifting a torch to his mouth, Jack blew one final flame, and out of the fire flew Jay's two white doves. I swear I was almost deafened by the applause that followed. Jay caught his birds in each hand and took a bow while Jack did the same. The audience broke into cheering, hooting and clapping, and then came the big finish. Jay gestured to the ceiling and we all looked up. My heart got caught in my throat when I saw the tiny little paper hot air balloons drifting down from up high.

One landed right in my lap and I marvelled at it before looking to Jack. He was staring directly at me, and in that moment I knew he'd put this part into the act just for me. I noticed something shiny inside the carriage of the balloon, and reached inside to find a small gold ring. Holding it in

340

my hand, I noted that it twisted in a loop, forming the infinity symbol. Jack held his hand over his heart, gazing down at me, and I knew he'd put the ring in there specifically so that I'd find it. I had a feeling I knew what it meant, too. Infinity symbolised forever, and by giving me the ring Jack was telling me that's what he wanted for us.

Swallowing my emotions, and believe me I was feeling a lot of them right then, I endeavoured to blink back the tears and slid the ring onto my finger. When Jack saw I was wearing it, his eyes blazed fiercely and I mouthed a thank you at him, the sound of my voice lost amid the cheers.

Time seemed to move in fast forward after that. The rest of the show played out, and before I knew it I was sitting backstage with Matilda, Jay and Jack enjoying some after show drinks. Jack kept my hand in his, smoothing his fingers over the ring, his eyes fixed on it like it gave him great pleasure to see me wearing it.

"You like it?" he murmured in my ear while Jay talked loudly about how well the show had gone.

"I don't just like it, I love it," I answered, turning my face and running my nose along the side of his jaw. "I'll wear it always." Jack's chest rumbled low with his approval.

"You know, I've really enjoyed performing here in Vegas but I have to admit, I can't fucking wait for a change of scenery. I have so many ideas for when we go on the road with the circus," said Jay, pulling our attention away from one another.

"You have more ideas than you know what to do with," Matilda said to him affectionately and he gave her a wink before knocking back a gulp of his beer.

"I'm also looking forward to spending more time with King. He's a real intriguing one," Jay went on and Jack nodded.

I personally couldn't disagree, and I was a little jealous that Jay had managed to get close to Marina's brother so quickly. It had taken weeks for him to warm up to me. Well, I guessed buying an alcoholic a load of booze would certainly endear you to him. Jay had all the best tactics. A few of the stage crew came to join us then, and we sat socialising for another hour or two. I smiled and made chit chat, but at the same time my mind remained on King.

I wondered what he would do for the next month. Would Marina let him stay with her, or would he be out on the streets, sleeping rough and drinking himself into a stupor? I worried that one of these days he was going to kill himself with it, and I didn't want him to die. Despite all appearances to the contrary, there was something about him that struck me as incredibly vital, and deep inside I felt like he still had so much more to give to the world, or at least to somebody. I wanted to help him, but I had no idea where to begin…

The next morning I sat in the lounge of our suite, mindlessly browsing the internet as I tried to figure out a plan. First of all, I needed to find out who he really was and where he came from. I knew he was Marina's half-brother and that he'd once lived a very different life, but that didn't really tell me anything of worth.

So I turned my attention back to my newly purchased secondhand laptop and started my quest where most modern-day investigations begin. Bringing up the page, I levelled my curser on the little white box and typed two words into Google.

Oliver King.

Welcome to the City, London's most prestigious square mile, where finance reigns and Oliver King is a rising prince.

I used to rule the world.

There might be wolves in Wall Street, but there are crocodiles in Canary Wharf. Some of us crave money. Some of us crave power.

I don't need money and I don't want power. I want to excel, to surpass the men who came before me. No cheating. No shortcuts. I want to know I did it all on my own merits.

The problem with achieving greatness, though, is that there's always someone lurking in the shadows, waiting to steal it as soon as you turn your back. And believe me, there's a lurker in my shadows, one who will destroy everything I hold dear.

Alexis is not just my employee, she's my very best friend. My shining star. She makes me laugh when I have nothing to laugh about. When I need a good dose of reality, she gives it to me, no hesitation.

Perhaps I fell for her the very moment she walked into the interview, with her outspoken charm and vivacious personality. She cast all the others in shadow, and I knew that I had to have her in my life.

I never thought I could have it all and lose it so catastrophically. Never thought I would rise so high only to fall so low. All of my riches disintegrated, leaving me with nothing but rags. I needed saving. I needed her. The question was, would she ever come and find me? And if she did, would there be anything left to save?

L.H. Cosway's next standalone romance, *King of Hearts,* will predominantly take place six years previous to the events of *Hearts of Fire*. It will be released in the summer of 2015.

Have you read Jay & Matilda's story yet? Check out L.H. Cosway's contemporary romance, *Six of Hearts*.

Step right up and meet Jay Fields: Illusionist. Mentalist. Trickster.

I think in triangles. You think in straight lines.

I show you a table and make you believe it's a chair.

Smoke and mirrors, sleight of hand, misdirection. I trick and deceive.

But most of all, I put on a good show.

The world thinks I killed a man, but I didn't. Bear with me. It's all a part of the plan.

Revenge is what I want. I want it for me and I want it for her.

I want it for all six of us.

She doesn't remember me, but she's the reason for everything. She'll be my prize at the end of all this – if I can hold onto my willpower, that is. Maybe I'll slip up a little, have a taste, just a small one.

So go ahead and pick a card. Come inside and see the show. Look at my hands, look so closely that you can't see what's happening while you're so focused on looking. I'll be destroying your world from right here in the spotlight.

You'll never see me coming until it's too late.

I've only got one heart, and after I've pulled off my grand deception I'll hand it right to her.

So, sit back, relax, and let my girl tell you our story. You're in for one hell of a ride.

Praise for *Six of Hearts*

"This book was sexy. Man was it hot! Cosway writes sexual tension so that it practically sizzles off the page." - A. Meredith Walters, *New York Times & USA Today Bestselling Author.*

"There is a way that certain authors write that just grips me by the throat because I can see the world, I can smell the sounds, I can hear the voices, and I can feel their hearts." - Marie Hall, *New York Times & USA Today Bestselling Author.*

"I loved the twist at the end. I loved how sexy it was. (DAMN IT WAS SEXY!!)" - Penny Reid, *Author of Neanderthal Seeks Human.*

"Six of Hearts is a book that will absorb you with its electric and all-consuming atmosphere." - Lucia, *Reading is my Breathing.*

"There is so much "swoonage" in these pages that romance readers will want to hold this book close and not let go." - Katie, *Babbling About Books.*

About the Author

L.H. Cosway has a BA in English Literature and Greek and Roman Civilisation and an MA in Postcolonial Literature. She lives in Dublin city. Her inspiration to write comes from music. Her favourite things in life include writing stories, vintage clothing, dark cabaret music, food, musical comedy, and of course, books.
She thinks that imperfect people are the most interesting kind. They tell the best stories.

Find L.H. Cosway online!

www.facebook.com/lhcosway
www.twitter.com/lhcosway
www.lhcoswayauthor.com

Also by L.H. Cosway

Contemporary Romance
Painted Faces
Killer Queen
The Nature of Cruelty
Still Life with Strings
Six of Hearts
The Hooker & the Hermit

Urban Fantasy
Tegan's Blood **(The Ultimate Power Series #1)**
Tegan's Return **(The Ultimate Power Series #2)**
Tegan's Magic **(The Ultimate Power Series #3)**
Tegan's Power **(The Ultimate Power Series #4)**
Crimson **(An Ultimate Power Series Novella)**